Christina's Courage

Plain Paths, Book 1

SUSAN LANTZ SIMPSON

To Rachel and Holly, thank you for your unwavering support during this writing journey.

Trust in the Lord with all your heart. Lean not on your own understanding. In all your ways acknowledge Him and He will direct your path. ~ Proverbs 3: 5–6

Your word is a lamp unto my feet and a light unto my path. ~ Psalm 119: 105

Glossary

The German dialect used by Amish and Old Order Mennonites is a spoken, rather than a written, language and varies from one community or location to another. The spellings are approximate.

Ach	Oh
Aenti	Aunt
Ausbund	Amish/Mennonite Hymnal
Boppli; bopplin	Baby, babies
Bruder	Brother
Bu; buwe	Boy, boys
Daed	Dad
Danki	Thank you
Dochder	Daughter
Englisch, Englischer	English or non-Plain
Fraa	Wife
Freind	Friend
Grossdawdi	Grandfather
Grossmammi	Grandmother
Gott	God
Gut	Good
Jah	Yes
Kaffi	Coffee
Kapp	Prayer cap/women's head covering
Kinner	Children
Lieb	Love
Maedel	Girl, young woman
Mamm	Mom
Mariye	Morning

Mudder	Mother
Narrisch	Crazy
Nee	No
Onkle	Uncle
Rumspringa	Period of "running around" before joining the church
Schweschder	Sister
Wilkom	Welcome
Wunderbaar	Wonderful

Chapter One

Christina Brubacher paused in counting the money from the cashbox when the bell over the front door of her shop jangled. A frown pulled at her brow. *Ach!* She'd meant to lock the door and flip the Closed sign. Now she'd lost count. She stuffed the bills back into the box and glanced up as the visitor poked her head inside the store.

"Stina, I thought you closed at six."

Of all the nicknames that a person could derive from "Christina," Annie Wenger came up with "Stina." When Christina had asked why, her best *freind* had shrugged and answered, "Why not?" Once Annie had latched onto something, getting her to change her mind was practically impossible, so Christina accepted the less-than-desirable nickname.

"I do close at six. I had a late customer and must have forgotten to lock the door on time." Ordinarily, Christina would have already counted the money during a lull in business so she'd be ready to head home shortly after closing. Lulls had been scarce today.

"Well, it's a *gut* thing it's only me, or you'd be even later getting out of here." Annie slipped all the way inside and closed the door behind her. She clicked the lock and turned the sign. "There."

"*Danki.*" Christina pulled the wad of money back out and began to count once again.

"Busy day?"

Christina nodded and began counting aloud. She'd never leave today if she had to keep starting over. As much as she loved The Green Thumb, the nursery and store her *Grossmammi* had left her, she generally was more than ready to head home at six o'clock.

Annie swished across the wood floor to peruse the newest items on the shelves. The Green Thumb also sold home-canned jams, jellies, pickles, and vegetables, as well as crafts, thereby providing an opportunity for some of the women in the Old Order Mennonite community to sell their wares on consignment.

"The produce shop was quite prosperous today too," Annie said.

Mid-July was the peak season for local farmers. Annie's *onkle*'s farm had been so productive that he'd erected a permanent building to sell his fruits and vegetables instead of operating out of a temporary stand. He'd even hired Annie to help out on a part-time basis.

Annie's shuffling about stopped abruptly. "I thought you kept the storage shed locked."

Christina scribbled in her ledger and dropped the money inside the deposit bag. She looked up and followed Annie's gaze out the back window. "I usually unlock it in the morning in case I need to get in there in a hurry when I'm busy, but I go out in the afternoon to lock it. I'm sure I locked it today." She glanced out the window. "How did that happen?" Christina sighed and hopped off the wooden stool, knocking the worn, quilted cushion to the floor. She stooped to retrieve it and tossed it back onto the seat. A new one was definitely in order. This poor old thing did little to offer padding for her slim backside.

"Are you going out there?"

"Of course, silly. That door won't lock itself." Christina strode toward the back of the building as fast as her short, thin legs could take her.

"Aren't you a bit leery about that mysterious open door?"

"You read too many suspense novels. I'll be right back."

"I'll *kumm* with you."

"I'll be fine. You can wait here." Christina hurried out the back door. This was one more thing to make her late leaving. *Mamm* would have supper all done without a shred of help from her. She'd give the shed a cursory glance to make sure everything was as it should be and then lock it up tight.

A shriek died in her throat. Everything was definitely *not* as it should be. "C-can I help you, sir?"

What was this *Englisch* man doing in her shed? Sitting in her shed, at that. He wasn't even rummaging through the contents. Why didn't he answer her?

"Sir?"

Christina shifted her weight, slight as it was, from one foot to the other. What should she do?

"Sir?" She ventured to take three baby steps forward and reached out a shaky hand. She scarcely made contact when the man toppled over, his unseeing eyes wide open. This time the shriek made its way out of her mouth followed by two more.

"Stina, what's wrong?"

Christina heard Annie run from the back door of the shop, but she couldn't drag her eyes away from the horrendous sight in front of her. Her heart beat in double time, and her stomach threatened to eject any morsel of food it might still contain from her earlier snack.

"Ahhh! What happened?"

Annie's scream penetrated Christina's fog and jerked her attention away from the shed. Annie's face blanched a whiter shade of its normal pale hue. The caramel-colored freckles scattered across her cheeks and nose provided the only color on her ghostly face. She plucked at a curly wisp of orange-red hair that had escaped from her bun and locked her eyes on Christina's.

"I-I don't know what happened. W-We have to call the p-police."

Annie, apparently recovered from her initial fright, bent forward as if she wanted to touch the man. She scooted closer and closer until Christina grabbed the girl's arm and tugged her back. "Y-you can't disturb the scene or c-contaminate the evidence."

"Who's been reading suspense novels?"

"I don't have much time for reading, but I've heard enough of your prattle over the years to have gleaned a little information. I know you can't go around touching things. *Ach*!" Christina gasped and squeezed Annie's arm until the girl yelped. "Oops! Sorry!"

"What's wrong?"

"I touched him—just barely—but it made him fall over. You don't think I'll get into trouble, do you? Will I be accused of causing whatever happened to him? He was just sitting there. When he didn't answer, I reached out. *Ach*, Annie! Am I going to..."

"Calm down, Stina. I don't think the police could possibly believe you killed this man and stuffed him in your shed. I mean, you weigh all of ninety pounds on a *gut* day. How could you manage such a feat?"

Christina shivered despite the lingering heat and humidity of the waning July day. For once, she didn't swat her *freind* for teasing her about her diminutive size. "I've never called the police before. Do we just dial 9-1-1?"

"How should I know? I guess we'll find out. Did you ever get a cell phone for your store?"

Christina shook her head, sending her *kapp* strings fluttering around her head. "I meant to, but it kept slipping my mind. I'll have to run to the Quick Stop. They're still open."

"They're always open. I'll go. You stay and finish up in the store."

Before she could reach the back door, Christina's knees wobbled. She had never fainted in her entire life, but she suddenly had the urge to slide to the ground.

"*Nee* you don't." Annie thrust her hands beneath Christina's arms and hoisted her up. "I'll help you."

Christina stumbled inside her shop and leaned against the wall. She dragged in a few ragged breaths. "I'm okay now."

"Aren't you glad you have a *freind* who is considerably taller and heavier than you are?"

"Oh, my! What would I ever do without you?"

"I'm not sure I like your attitude. I'll be right back." With that, Annie dashed back outside.

I have a feeling I won't be heading home any time soon. Christina shuffled to the front counter to make sure everything was secure. She checked that the money was still in the deposit bag. She had been too preoccupied to notice if anyone had slipped in the open back door while she was at the shed. She shivered again and rubbed her hands up and down her arms. This was certainly a day she would never forget.

~

Christina had finally calmed her galloping heart enough to breathe normally when Annie raced in the door, setting her poor heart back on a frenzied course. Annie heaved so hard that her breath came out in little wheezes.

"Are you all right?" Christina looked up from the money bag, but instead of her eyes connecting with Annie's brown ones, they stared directly into the crystal-clear blue ones belonging to Noah Zimmerman. Why was he here? He certainly didn't need to witness her interrogation or whatever the policemen's questions were called.

"Hi, Christina. I was at the Quick Stop when Annie used the phone. Are you all right?"

"Sure." *If you disregard the fact that I'm terrified beyond all belief after experiencing the biggest shock in my life and that I might very well be about to have a heart attack.*

"I'm relieved to hear that. I was worried."

He was worried? She had moved way beyond "worried" quite a while ago. Still, some little ripple of pleasure zipped up her spine over how Noah seemed concerned about her.

She had pined for him forever, but it seemed that he rarely deemed her worthy of consideration. Maybe that wasn't completely fair. It could be that Noah was a bit reserved or shy since he didn't seem to lavish attention on any of the girls in the community, unless he was awfully *gut* about keeping secrets.

Or it could be that he wasn't interested in younger girls. She was four years his junior. She had always tried to act so grown-up around him, but now he would witness her bawling like a *boppli* when the police grilled her. Grilled? Where did that word *kumm* from? She'd obviously absorbed more of Annie's descriptions of her beloved novels than she thought.

"The p-police are on t-the way." Annie seemed to have caught her breath enough to gasp out a few words.

"*Danki.*" Christina pulled her gaze away from Noah to search her *freind*'s now flushed face. She cocked her head ever so slightly in Noah's direction, hoping Annie would understand her unspoken question: what in the world is he doing here?

Annie gave an almost imperceptible shrug. "At least the store wasn't crowded. I don't think anyone overheard me, except Noah, so maybe there won't be a passel of gawkers."

"I hadn't thought of that." Christina flew to the window but staggered backward when her gaze fell on the shed where one large, worn sneaker peeked out the door. She was only barely cognizant of a shuffle behind her. Her next moment of awareness came when strong arms pulled her back against a broad chest. Her breath whooshed out.

"Steady, Christy." The deep voice spoke right into her ear.

Christy? Did Noah just call her that? Her *mudder* called her "Chris" every once in a blue moon when she was rushed and couldn't get the full name out or when she was flustered and did a roll call of all six of her *kinner* before spitting out the name of the one she wanted. Annie called her that despicable Stina. She couldn't recall ever being called Christy, but she rather liked the sound of it. Especially when it rolled off the tongue of Noah Zimmerman.

"*Kumm* sit down." He kept one arm wrapped around her waist as he half-dragged Christina to the stool.

The shock of seeing that minute part of the dead man's body and the surprise of Noah's solicitude brought unbidden tears to her eyes. She struggled to gain control over her emotions. Fainting and weeping would definitely not paint her as a self-assured, mature young woman. She could get through this ordeal. She *would* get through it.

"I-I'm okay." Did that croak really emerge from her mouth? How mortifying!

"I know you are. I'm only trying to be supportive."

"I appreciate that, Noah." There. Her voice sounded a bit more normal, at least to her own ears. A sudden flash of lights swirling around the room nearly made her gasp again. Her heart thudded loud enough for Noah to hear, for sure, and probably half of St. Mary's County as well.

"It's the cops." Annie sprinted to the window to watch their approach.

"Police, Annie, not cops." Christina shook her head. Loose wisps of nearly black hair danced around her face. She reached to tuck them back where they belonged, but her trembling fingers made the simple task difficult. How could her hands be as cold as if she'd plunged them into ice water on such a hot July day?

Christina had never had any dealings with the *Englisch* police. She'd lived her whole life in a peace-loving, close-knit community in the center of a mainly rural county. She'd read of crime that occurred in other areas of the county in the local newspaper, but she'd never personally encountered so much as a shoplifter.

Noah gently squeezed her arm, a gesture from which she tried to gather strength.

While she could be almost certain her expression registered her shock and trepidation, a quick glance at Annie's face told her the girl was gobbling up this adventure the way a starving man devoured a crust of bread. She was far too excited. Christina worried about possible irrelevant chatter that might fly from her *freind*'s mouth.

"Maybe you should go on home so your folks don't worry, Annie. You, too, Noah. I'll be fine." *Right!* "One of you can stop and let my parents know why I'm late."

"Are you kidding? I wouldn't miss this opportunity to witness an investigation firsthand for all the corn in *Onkle* Henry's field." Annie's eyes sparkled. Christina half expected her to whip out a pad of paper and a pencil so she could take notes.

"I won't leave you here alone." Noah gave her arm another little squeeze. "Besides, the police probably wouldn't allow either of us to go now before they determine if we have any useful information to offer."

Great! While she appreciated the company and ordinarily would have been thrilled to be within touching distance of Noah Zimmerman, now she would have him witness her fumbling, bumbling, and probable nervous breakdown.

What would the police ask her? What would they say? Heavy footsteps crunched on the gravel right outside the front door of The Green Thumb. Fear lodged like a boulder in Christina's throat, leaving precious little room for any air exchange. Her pounding heart threatened to leap through her skin. Life as she knew it had been completely and irrevocably altered.

Chapter Two

Christina shuffled across the cement floor on wooden legs to open the door for the policemen. Leaving Noah's side and the relative security that his presence offered had taken gargantuan effort. But this was *her* shop. *She* was the one who had discovered the body. *She* would be the person the police officers would need to question.

With a quick, slightly deeper breath than the shallow panting she'd been performing, Christina turned the lock and pulled open the door. Two officers in crisp, light blue shirts and dark blue trousers loomed in her doorway while several others headed for the shed and combed the vicinity. Either these two had just started their shift or else they had spent the day in an air-conditioned office since they looked so fresh and neat. She, on the other hand, knew her appearance resembled the wilting petunias in the hanging basket on the front porch at home. A plant woman, of all people, had neglected to water her own *mudder's* flowers! She couldn't fathom why such a trivial bit of information crept into her mind at the moment.

"Miss Brubacher?"

"*Jah*, I'm Christina Brubacher." She backpedaled to allow the two towering men to enter her shop. They weren't quite as tall or as broad-shouldered as Noah, but there were two of them, and they unnerved her. They stared at her as if she was some rare artifact on display at the nearby marine museum she had visited a few years ago.

She had enjoyed peeking into display cases full of sharks' teeth, shells, and bones. She had even sifted through the huge container of sand to find her very own sharks' teeth. She still had the two she had discovered in a quart-sized canning jar along with pretty rocks she had collected during her growing-up years. That museum trip had been a fun experience, totally unlike today's adventure.

Christina waited for the officers to speak. Had they already said something that she missed while her mind hiked down memory lane? Neither Annie nor Noah uttered a sound, so she assumed they were not waiting for her to respond to some comment.

The older officer cleared his throat and began the questioning. "Miss Brubacher, I'm Deputy Gaines, and this is Deputy Wilson. Are you the person that discovered the body?"

Christina gulped and would have shrunk back if she could have done so without plowing into Noah. "I, uh, *jah*." Her eyes wanted to stray to the window, but she kept them focused on the deputy. Actually, she focused more on his shiny badge than on his eyes.

"Can you tell me what happened?"

"I-I didn't mean to make him fall over. I mean, I touched him because he didn't answer me, and *ach*, I'm making a mess of this." Her nerves were jangled, her tongue was flapping before her brain could tell it what to say, and she had a tremendously strong urge to burst into tears. She had to get hold of herself. Noah's big hand patted her shoulder. Christina didn't dare turn to look at him for fear that any sign of compassion would be her complete undoing.

"Relax, ma'am. Take a deep breath." The younger deputy—Wilson, wasn't it?—spoke in a quiet, soothing voice.

Christina tried to obey, but her inhalation was more a quick gasp than a deep breath. *Relax. You only have to tell them what you know, which isn't a whole lot. Then they can be on their way and you will be free to go home and pretend this day never happened.* She nodded at the officers, indicating she was ready to continue.

"Now then, let's start with the events of the past hour or so. What were you doing around five forty-five?" Deputy Gaines resumed his questioning.

Christina deliberately forced her hunched shoulders to assume a more natural position. She could handle this. She was intelligent and observant. She could answer the questions. "At five forty-five, I was waiting on my last customer of the day. Mrs. Randolph is a regular. She asked for advice about her ailing hydrangea. It was almost six when I totaled up her purchases." Christina paused to gulp in a breath.

"When did you notice anything unusual about your shed?"

"I was the one who noticed the shed door was open." Annie tore herself away from the window and marched up to the deputies.

Christina resisted the temptation to roll her eyes. "This is my *freind,* Annie Wenger. She told me the shed door was open when she came in at six o'clock."

Deputy Wilson's pen made a soft, scratchy sound as he scribbled on a notepad.

"Okay. I'll ask you some questions in a moment. Let me finish with Miss Brubacher first."

He probably figures he'd better let me talk while I am somewhat coherent and not about to dissolve into tears. When Annie nodded and scooted back a bit, Christina felt slightly less claustrophobic. With Noah behind her, two deputies in front of her, and Annie shuffling in from the side, she had begun to feel like the room was folding inward on her.

"Okay, Miss Brubacher. After Miss Wenger told you the shed door was open, what did you do?"

"I rushed outside to check things out." Isn't that what anyone else would do? It certainly seemed logical to her.

"And what did you find?"

Here came the awful part. Christina squeezed her eyes shut for an instant and dragged in the deepest breath she could manage. She plunged into her recount of the gruesome discovery, precisely and accurately and without a single whimper.

~

Christina scooted closer to the battery-operated wall clock to make sure the second hand still circled the numbers. Could it really be only seven fifteen? Surely she'd spent a lifetime answering the questions that the deputies fired at her. But the clock ticked and the hand made its steady sweep. The lawmen had fewer questions for Annie since she hadn't made the discovery and only a couple of questions for Noah since he had arrived after Annie made the phone call.

"Are you ready to go?" Noah's deep voice broke into her mental rambling.

"*Jah.*" She'd been ready. In fact, she had wanted to flee right after her trek to the shed. She double-checked that everything in the shop was secure and ready for opening in the morning. Now she had to go home and face further interrogation by her family. She'd have to relive the whole ugly scenario yet again. This nightmare would never end!

The officers outside had finished searching for any possible evidence. At least, Christina assumed they were done. They certainly had not shared any information with her other than to tell her the lock had not been tampered with, which meant she must not have clicked it tightly. She had seen the big vehicle that arrived to transport the poor deceased man, but thankfully, she hadn't witnessed that whole procedure.

A shudder started at her head and ran to her toes. Could she go home, crawl into bed, pull the pillow over her head, and shut out the images that assaulted her? Would the memory of that man falling over when she touched him be forever burned into her brain? She looked at that hand and shook it as if that would erase the contact it had with the man. She wanted to wash her hand, her body, her memory.

Christina grabbed the quilted bag that she would stuff into the basket attached to the handlebars of her ancient one-speed bicycle. She waited for Annie and Noah to exit and stumbled outside behind them. She checked the door three times to make sure it was locked.

"The door is fine, Stina, unless you're trying to yank it off its hinges."

Christina dropped her hand before she could test the lock a fourth time. She wrinkled up her nose and made a little face at her *freind*. Then she remembered that Noah stood right there, watching. *That was certainly a mature thing to do, Christina.* Oh, well. He'd probably seen her at her very worst today as she struggled to keep tears at bay and to give some semblance of sensible answers to the deputies' questions.

When she hazarded a glance up into his handsome face, she nearly did a double take. Noah's smile didn't hold a speck of derision. It not only lifted the corners of his mouth, but it also spread up to his big, blue eyes, etching little crinkly lines at their corners. Concerned eyes, not mocking eyes. A genuine smile, not a phony one.

"You did great in there, Christina." Noah nodded toward the shop. "I was impressed. I don't know if I could have given such detailed answers under that stress. I'm sure you were a big help to the officers."

Immediately, much of the tension drained from Christina's body. Noah was impressed? She hadn't been a bumbling, blathering idiot? She wanted to dance a little jig—if dancing was allowed, which it wasn't. She smiled for the first time in hours. "*Danki*, Noah. And *danki* for waiting around."

Before Noah could utter a reply, Annie elbowed her way in between them. "*Jah.* Your big, strong presence was definitely a comfort." She batted her pale lashes at the tall man caught between the two young women. "I don't know how we would have managed without you."

Really? Was this her *freind*, Annie Wenger? The girl who loved reading mysteries and pulling pranks? Christina thought she knew Annie better than anyone else on the planet, but she certainly hadn't had any inkling that Annie was even remotely interested in Noah Zimmerman. When had that change *kumm* about?

Noah smiled at Annie. He glanced at Christina, who shrugged ever so slightly as if to say she didn't have a clue who this foreign creature was that had invaded her *freind*'s body. He looked back at Annie and seemed at a total loss for words. "I, uh, didn't do anything."

To Christina's surprise, Annie linked her arm with Noah's. His shock must have been even greater than Christina's, judging by the expression on his face. What had gotten into Annie?

"Your presence was enough all by itself. Wasn't it, Stina?"

Now she remembers I'm here! Did she also remember that once, in the dark of night, I told her I wished Noah Zimmerman noticed me, that I'd had a king-sized crush on him for years? Apparently not.

Christina stepped to the side. Maybe Noah came running over to the shop because he was concerned about Annie. Maybe he had never showed an interest in her because he cared for her *freind*. Whew! That felt like a blow to the back of the head with a two-by-four. "Uh-huh," was all she could mumble in reply to Annie's ridiculous gushing.

Well, Christina, swallow your disappointment, move aside, and let these two have a chance. You can wallow in your misery later. She darted around the side of the building.

"Christina, wait!"

The deep voice practically echoed through her head, but she didn't stop or even look over her shoulder. The tears were too close. She couldn't allow herself to fall apart in front of an audience.

"Christy, please wait!"

Okay. The "Christy" did it. She stopped in her tracks and turned around. Noah jogged to catch up with her. Annie gasped and panted behind him.

"I didn't want you to leave alone in case there was any other danger."

Christina's gaze roved the perimeter of the property. "The police didn't find anyone else here. It's still light out for a little longer. I think I'll be fine if you want to see Annie home." She grabbed her bike from its rack next to the building and pushed her bag into the basket.

"Why would I do that?"

"Why would you do what?" Annie wrapped an arm around her midsection as if that little trot she'd just made gave her a stitch in the side.

Honestly, the girl needed to get more exercise. She ought to work with me a few days!

Never one for patience, Annie didn't wait long for an answer before repeating her question. "I asked—"

"Never mind," Noah interrupted.

Didn't he want to see Annie home? A flicker of hope ignited in Christina's heart. She tried to douse it. There wasn't any use in setting herself up for heartache. She straddled the bike as gracefully as possible and plopped one black-shod foot on a pedal. "Do you want to ride with me, Annie?" *Or stand and gush over Noah for the rest of the night?*

Annie looked at Noah, batted her eyes twice, and lightly tapped her foot as if weighing her options. When neither Noah's nor Christina's voice filled the pregnant pause, she turned and reached for her own bike. "Sure, I'll ride with you."

"If you both give me two minutes, I'll run over to the Quick Stop to get my bike. Then I can make sure you *both* get home safely."

"We'll be fine. You don't have to trouble yourself—" The rest of Christina's reply was swallowed up by Annie's extra-syrupy voice.

"That is so sweet of you, Noah. We'll wait right here for you."

Christina whipped around to stare at the girl. What on earth had *kumm* over her? If she batted her eyes one more time, Christina might ask if she had suddenly developed some sort of tic. And where did that sugary voice *kumm* from? She had never heard Annie speak in that tone, even when she talked *boppli* talk to a litter of newborn kittens.

"Be right back." Noah sprinted away.

"What's gotten into you?" Christina asked as soon as Noah was out of hearing range. She tried not to scowl but could feel the scrunch in her forehead.

"What do you mean?" Annie poked that wavy strand of hair that she'd been playing with back under her *kapp*.

"The helpless, poor-little-me act?"

"Hmpf! I'm sure I don't know what you're talking about."

"I'm sure you do. When did you set your sights on Noah Zimmerman?"

"Isn't he dreamy?" Annie's sigh hung in the air like a cloud.

"Dreamy?"

"*Jah.*"

"I need to find you some different books to read. Maybe a history book or an etiquette book."

Annie slapped Christina's arm. "Don't be a fuddy-duddy."

"Me? How am I that?"

"You want to spoil my fun."

"It's fun to make goo-goo eyes at Noah and bat your eyes like you're trying to expel a bug that flew into them?" *Oops!* She hadn't meant to say that. Some thoughts are better kept inside. She certainly didn't want to hurt her *freind*'s feelings.

To Christina's surprise, Annie broke out into a fit of giggles. "Is it that obvious?"

"Is the grass green?"

"Then I guess Noah couldn't have missed my interest in him."

"He couldn't have missed it if he'd been blindfolded and wearing earplugs."

"Missed what?"

Great! He most likely heard her entire comment. How was it she didn't hear his approach?

"Nothing." Christina couldn't bring herself to look him in the eye. Though with a tiny sideways peek, she discovered he'd ridden across the grass between the two businesses, which would explain why his arrival had been silent. "I need to get home." Christina rocked the bike and pushed hard on the pedals for a quick takeoff.

"I'm so glad you're riding with us."

This time Christina did roll her eyes. Since she was in front of them, they wouldn't see whatever thoroughly disgusted expression crossed her face. The whir of bike tires speeding nearer on the blacktop road behind her caused her to glance over her shoulder. Noah had ridden close enough to touch, if she had any desire to do so. It wasn't that she would actually mind touching Noah, but if there was a likelihood that he and Annie cared for each other, she'd steer clear of him.

"Are you okay?"

Christina's foot slipped on the pedal, causing her bike to jerk. She managed to keep it from tipping over and embarrassing herself yet again. Why did the very sound of Noah's voice make her heart flip and flop and all reasoning leave her brain? "Sure." She cleared her throat so she could do more than croak. "Why not?"

"That had to have been a tremendous shock. I'd probably be more than a little shaky myself."

"Really?" That made her feel better since she hadn't been able to quash that case of nerves that plagued her.

"For sure."

"I just can't figure out how that man got in my shed or when he got there. I was in the shed early this morning and everything was as it should be."

"It is strange. The police should be able to pinpoint times."

Would they share that information with her, though? She had to find more clues. She needed answers.

"Hey, you two. Wait up!" Annie huffed and puffed between words.

So much for Christina's warm, fuzzy feeling over Noah's concern. She'd better send him back to ride beside Annie. She had hoped to brainstorm a few ideas with him since he seemed a clever fellow. That obviously would not be possible with Annie around to ooze sugar and flutter her eyes. Christina would simply have to launch some sort of investigation on her own.

Chapter Three

Christina bounced out of bed even earlier than usual. The old rooster hadn't needed to serve as her alarm this morning. She had expected to toss and turn all night or, at the very least, have snatches of sleep haunted by bodies toppling over on her. Instead, after only minimal restlessness, exhaustion had claimed her and she sank blissfully into the depths of slumber. Her only dream had been a pleasant one ruled by a tall, smiling, dark-haired man with sparkling, blue eyes.

Ach! Don't you remember? Annie likes him, and Annie generally has a way of getting what she wants.

Christina never figured out how her *freind* accomplished that feat. It had never bothered her before, but now Christina felt a little twinge of disappointment or frustration or possibly even jealousy. Suddenly, the bounce disappeared from her step. Christina crept from her room with a deep sigh. She comforted herself with the thought that perhaps people gave into Annie to quiet her incessant talking.

Mamm's worried gaze followed Christina around the kitchen as she arranged crisp bacon strips on a plate, poured mugs of *kaffi*, and set jars of homemade strawberry and peach preserves on the big oak table. Christina couldn't figure out how to reassure her *mudder* since she had some slight trepidation about going to work herself. But The Green Thumb was her business. The responsibilities and worries were hers, and even though she was only twenty, she shouldered them fine. At least, she always had before now.

Christina had worked alongside her *grossmammi* ever since she could toddle steadily. She'd absorbed everything the older woman had taught her about business and customer service. She'd inherited Grossmammi's gift with plants and could, as her *daed* teased, make a stick grow. It had seemed only natural for the older woman to leave the business to Christina when the time came.

"Everything will be fine." Christina patted her *mudder's* arm and even managed to coax a smile to her lips.

"Maybe your *daed* should go with you today."

"Daed has his own work to do. The feed mill is always busy. I'll be all right. I've always felt safe at the shop before. Yesterday was some peculiar once-in-a-lifetime happening."

"Let's hope so."

"What is causing the deep frown on my fraa's lovely face this morning?" Daed's voice boomed from the doorway.

If Daed was inside, that meant he and Christina's *bruders* had finished their morning chores. She scurried to put the remaining breakfast foods on the table.

"Ida?"

Even though Mamm spoke softly, Christina heard her words. "Ach, Norman, I'm worried about Christina being alone at The Green Thumb today. You know Deborah is away."

Deborah Martin, an older woman whose children were nearly grown, helped in the shop from time to time. Her family had traveled to Pennsylvania to welcome her *dochder's* new *boppli*, so she wouldn't be available to work with Christina for a while.

"The Lord Gott will take care of her, *fraa*."

"I know, but what if the police return for something? She'll need someone to mind the shop while she talks to them. I'd feel ever so much better if she wasn't there by herself."

Christina turned around in time to see her *daed* rub a hand across his forehead as he was wont to do when pondering a matter. "I suppose I could spare one of the *buwe* for at least part of the day."

Her bruders, twenty-two-year-old James, seventeen-year-old John, and fourteen-year-old David, would be needed in the feed mill or in the fields. This was a busy time of year on the farm. Besides, she didn't need a nanny. Christina would be perfectly fine. It was a work day like any other work day. Right?

She'd better say something before Mamm made her take her little *schweschders* along with her. She loved eleven-year-old Sallie and eight-year-old Grace, but they would be bickering and whining before the day's end. Christina couldn't handle either of those activities today.

"That's okay, Daed. I won't be alone all day. Several women are planning to stop by with items to sell. They will help me if any need arises. And Annie usually pops in when she's finished at her *onkle's* place." She didn't mention that her *freind* wasn't likely to be a whole lot of help since she would probably still be mooning over Noah Zimmerman.

~

Christina pedaled her bike to the rear of The Green Thumb. She didn't want to look toward the shed but couldn't keep her eyes from straying there. Whew! At least nothing appeared out of place today. The door was closed and the padlock was fastened. She'd leave that door locked from now on rather than unlocking it in the mornings in case she needed to rush in there for something.

She secured her bike and exhaled the breath she'd held captive. Everything seemed normal, even if she didn't feel so normal. Christina forced herself to calm down. The sun shone, the birds sang, the flowers bloomed, and the bees hummed in the clover. All was right with the world. Tension gradually seeped from her muscles as she slung her bag over her shoulder and hopped through the dewy grass toward the front of the shop.

"Ahhh!" Christina slapped one hand across her chest where her heart thundered out of control. Her bag slipped from her other shoulder and plopped on the wet ground. She didn't even notice that it fell. Her focus was on the man leaning against the front of her store. He hadn't been there when she rode by. From his dark broadfall pants, blue shirt, and straw hat, she assumed he was Plain. That should be some comfort, shouldn't it?

"Christina! I am so sorry. I didn't mean to startle you."

The man straightened to his full height, which must be over six feet, and pushed back his hat. The deep voice, the broad smile, and the sparkling eyes could only belong to the man who had traipsed through Christina's dreams last night.

"Wh-what are you doing here?" If her brain had kicked into gear before her mouth, she would have rephrased that question. Noah's presence was always a pleasure. She didn't mean to indicate otherwise.

He rushed forward and bent to retrieve her bag. "Are you all right?"

Christina suddenly realized she continued to pat her chest. Even though her heart still hammered against her hand, its staccato rhythm could now be attributed to the man looking down at her with genuinely concerned eyes. "I'm fine." She dropped her hand to her side. "I wasn't expecting someone to be standing at the door. I didn't see you when I rode up."

"I must have gotten here while you were putting your bike away." He held her bag out to her.

"Danki." Christina slipped her arm through the strap and hoisted the bag up onto her shoulder. "Did you leave something here yesterday?" She didn't think he had, but with all that transpired, anything was possible.

"Nee. I wanted to be here this morning in case you came alone."

Christina figured her face must have registered her surprise since he rushed to continue without giving her a chance to speak. Did her expression also mirror her delight at his concern? She'd better squelch that emotion right away.

"I mean, well, that was a pretty awful experience, and I was worried."

His last word came out as a whisper, but she heard it. A little thrill shot through every nerve in her body. "Really?" Honestly, Christina, is that all you can think of to say? He'll think you're a bumbling little girl for sure. Quick! Think of something halfway intelligent—and not some syrupy, gushing remark like Annie would utter. "That's very nice of you, Noah. I know you must be busy with your own work, so I appreciate your concern." There that sounded pretty mature.

"I'm not so busy that I can't check on a *freind*."

Freind? He considered her a *freind*? That was one step closer to... Enough! There went her crazy heart again, getting all flippity-floppity. And it was going to get crushed if she didn't keep it under control. "I appreciate that, Noah." Drat! Didn't she already say that? Well, she couldn't very well say it thrilled her to the marrow to think he might possibly care.

"Do you have your key handy? I'll open up and make sure everything is okay."

"You don't have to do that." As the words spilled from her mouth, she dug inside her bag for her keys. Secretly, she was relieved someone would walk into the shop with her.

"I know I don't have to, but I want to check things out."

"Oh." How many "ohs" and "ums" had she mumbled in the past few minutes? Her remarks didn't exactly make her look like the brightest star in the sky. She dropped her keys into Noah's outstretched hand and shuffled along behind him as closely as she dared. She wanted to peek inside the shop the minute the door opened too.

Christina rose to her tiptoes but still couldn't see over the man who stood a gut foot taller. Sometimes being so petite could be a problem, like when she needed to reach something on a high shelf or when she tried to find someone in a crowd or when she wanted to see something and a taller person blocked her view. She wiggled her way around Noah. This was her shop after all.

A tug on her arm stopped her in her tracks. "What are you doing?"

"Let me go first. Please."

Something about the way he said, "please," almost made her knees buckle. How *wunderbaar* it would be if he truly cared about her. But the tiny voice of reason leaped to the forefront of her mind to remind her he only considered her a *freind*. Nothing more. One of her *bruders* would have behaved in the same manner if he had accompanied her here, wouldn't he?

Since she was too short to see over him, Christina peeked through the little gap between Noah's arm and body. Her own arm still burned from his touch, even though the gesture had been brief. "Everything looks fine, ain't so?"

"It appears to be." Noah moved aside so Christina could survey the room. "I'm sure you would know better than I if anything was out of place, but everything looks neat and orderly just like it did when we left here."

She let her gaze travel over the whole room. "I don't see anything amiss."

"You are a gut business woman, Christy. I've heard that from lots of folks."

The nickname that only Noah used turned her brain into mush. "Danki."

"I'm going to peek into your closets and the store room. Then I'll check your greenhouses."

"I think everything will be fine. I don't want to make you late for your own work."

"I'm not worried about that. I want to make sure all is well here first or I won't be able to concentrate on any machinery repairs. I'll be quick while you prepare to open."

Christina nodded and headed to her old-fashioned cash register. Would he really think about her during his busy day? She could almost guarantee he would loom large in her own daydreams. She flipped the sign over to "open" on her way to the counter. The sooner she got her usual routine underway, the sooner her confidence would return. Then maybe she could dig around for any clues the police might have overlooked.

Christina didn't expect to find anything inside the store since she couldn't recall ever having seen the deceased man before, but maybe something would jump out at her in or around the storage shed. Or maybe in the greenhouses. The man must have approached the property from the rear. That was her best guess. But did he arrive here on his own steam? If he didn't, why would someone stash a body in her shed? A shiver snaked its way up her spine.

By the time Noah stepped through the door, Christina had the shop open for business. The scuffling sound his work boots made on the cement floor gave her a momentary fright. She hoped she wouldn't be so jittery all day.

"The shed was locked up tight, and the greenhouses are fine."

She hadn't expected otherwise, but Noah's announcement was a relief anyway. "Great. I appreciate your checking them out."

"Are you sure you'll be okay by yourself today?"

That warm, tingly feeling washed over her once again. "Like I told my parents, I expect several women to stop by later with items to sell. And this being peak season, I'll probably have a lot of customers too." She didn't mention the likelihood that Annie would drop by later. She'd prefer not to witness another interaction between Noah and Annie.

"Okay, but stay alert for anything unusual."

"I will for sure." She paused for a moment. "What do you think happened yesterday?"

Noah shrugged. "Do you have any ideas?"

"Well, I have serious doubts that the man died in my shed, but I haven't figured out how he was carried there without my seeing it." Christina tapped an index finger against her chin as she considered options.

"You were probably waiting on customers."

"That's what I figured since yesterday was a busy day."

"You know, the bishop would probably be fine with your having a cell phone here. Lots of businesses have them."

"I know. I've been meaning to check about getting one."

"Gut. I'll be off to work, then."

"Danki, Noah."

He smiled that wide smile that lit his entire face and made his eyes twinkle. Christina would surely drown in those eyes if she didn't force herself to look away.

"See you later, Christy."

Did he really mean that? Did he plan to stop back by the shop? Hope stirred in her heart. "Okay." She watched him stride to the door.

Noah stopped abruptly and returned to the counter. "I almost forgot. I found this in the greenhouse attached to your shop."

Chapter Four

Noah reached into his pocket and pulled out a shiny object. Christina couldn't determine what it was until he laid it on the counter. "I guess you dropped it when you were cutting twine or something. This time I really will leave."

Christina stared at the gold-colored penknife. Goose bumps prickled her arms despite the July heat. "W-wait, Noah!"

He turned back toward Christina and flashed another brilliant smile.

"T-this isn't mine. I-I don't use a penknife. I cut myself on one years ago and refused to use one ever since." She held up an index finger and pointed out the telltale trace of a scar. "I use scissors or pruning shears. I've never seen this before." She watched the smile melt from his face.

Once again, Noah returned to the counter. "Maybe a customer dropped it."

"Why didn't the police find this last night?"

"It was actually under a shelf. I probably would have missed it myself if the sun hadn't been shining at just the precise angle. Something shiny caught my eye, so I got down to investigate."

"Where in the greenhouse was this?"

"Near the back. Under the shelf with the little green pots of begonias, the ones with pink blooms."

"Oh." Christina's brain whirled dizzily. She would investigate further as soon as someone arrived who could watch the shop for a few minutes.

"Do you think the police would want this?"

"I don't know. Maybe. If they *kumm* back today, I'll show them." She placed the little knife under the counter, out of sight. She attempted a smile. "*Danki* for everything, Noah. I'm sorry I held you up."

"That's not a problem. See you later."

~

The morning flew by. Customers began streaming in almost as soon as Noah left. Christina waited on one person after another. She almost wished she'd brought Sallie along with her. Almost. Her little *schweschder* could be helpful, but she could also talk a person's ear off. Christina really needed to have some help on a regular basis during the busy season. *Mamm* worked in the shop from time to time, but she usually had too much to do at home, especially with the girls home from school for the summer and all the gardening and canning to do now.

Her busyness did not keep Christina's mind from straying to the little penknife or to the man who discovered it. Would he really drop back by later, or were those words simply uttered to be polite? Noah certainly seemed to be genuinely concerned about her, unless he loved a *gut* mystery and wanted to play sleuth. *Like me.* Christina wanted to get into that greenhouse and check around even though Noah probably already did that. But he wouldn't have noticed any subtle changes like she would.

Maybe there would be a lull after the lunchtime rush. Many *Englischers* stopped in during their lunch hour to purchase some of her home-baked treats. Christina almost always had an ample supply of whoopie pies, zucchini bread, muffins, and cookies. She tore a paper towel off the roll stashed under the counter to mop her damp brow and neck. There didn't seem to be a hint of a breeze blowing through the open doors or windows unless she'd been too busy to notice. Her eyes darted out the windows a lot more often than usual in her effort to be more vigilant.

"*Gut mariye*, Christina."

She nearly jumped out of her skin. So much for vigilance. While she stared out the side window, someone appeared at the front door without her ears detecting a sound. She needed to save her deep thoughts for later. "*Gut mariye*, Amelia." Was it truly still morning? It had definitely been a long one even if she had been busy. A quick glance at the big, battery-operated wall clock told her that it was indeed still morning. Eleven fifteen to be exact.

Amelia Stauffer bustled inside with a passel of *kinner* in her wake. Four little girls—three dressed in long, pale-green dresses with tiny white flowers and one in a slightly different styled royal-blue dress—squeezed inside all holding hands. A pink-cheeked nine-month-old baby cooed in Amelia's arms. A bulging tote bag hung from her shoulder.

"You've certainly got your hands full."

"*Jah*, I'm sorry I'm late getting here. It's been a bit hectic this morning. The girls' *daed* was a little late dropping them off. They hadn't eaten breakfast, so I needed to feed them. Of course, my own three then wanted to eat again. Little bottomless pits, that's what they are. I don't know how I'll keep enough food in the house when they're older." Amelia laughed and blew a wisp of pale-blonde hair out of her face.

"I don't know how you do it all. Here, let me take your bag." Christina lifted the heavy bag from Amelia's shoulder. The woman was maybe five or six years older and already a widow raising three youngsters alone. She regularly babysat for a modern Mennonite neighbor who had lost his wife right after the baby's birth. "What did you bring me today?"

Amelia gently pulled her *kapp* string from the *boppli*'s fingers. "You little monkey. You'll snatch it right off my head." She smiled and tickled the little girl. "I'm about overrun with zucchini, so I have loaves of zucchini bread and will definitely have more for you later in the week."

"*Gut*. Everyone loves your bread." Christina lifted neatly packaged loaves out of the tote bag. "You always put a list of ingredients on your food, and I like that. A lot of my customers want to know if something is made out of whole wheat flour or white flour or with sugar or honey. Your labels are ever so helpful."

"Well, I used to help prepare foods for my *grossmammi* who had a variety of health issues. I learned to bake in a more healthful way. I still do that most of the time." She laughed. "Of course, I also bake the regular old way with sugar, butter, and eggs because so many people like that."

Christina chuckled. "Treats sure go fast around here, regardless of how they're made." She nodded to the nearly empty shelf that held two whoopie pies and one package of brownies.

"Oh my! It looks like I got here at exactly the right time."

"That you did." Christina reached farther into the bag. "You have something else in here."

A sheepish expression crossed Amelia's pretty face. "Cookies. So much for the healthy baking. But they are made with whole wheat flour and fruit puree instead of oil."

Christina burst out laughing. How great it felt to laugh heartily and dispel some of the tension stored inside her body since yesterday. When Amelia's merry giggles joined in, Christina laughed harder until tears gathered in her eyes. "Oh, Amelia, if you could only have seen your expression. It was priceless." Christina swiped a hand across her eyes. "We all need some treats once in a while."

Amelia laid a small hand on Christina's arm. "I'm thinking you need something to lighten your load right about now, ain't so?"

Christina sobered instantly. "You heard?"

"I did."

It never ceased to amaze Christina how quickly news spread in her community, even without the assistance of telephones, computers, televisions, or whatever other devices *Englischers* used to communicate. They had none of those gadgets, except possibly a basic phone for emergencies or businesses, and yet everyone quickly knew what was going on with everyone else. Most of the time that was a *gut* thing. "You weren't afraid to *kumm* here today and bring the girls?"

"Absolutely not. You didn't do anything wrong. I've never been afraid to venture out before. I wouldn't let some random act of foul play cause me to hide in my house." Amelia glanced at the brood of little ones with her and chuckled. "If I'm not afraid to be totally alone with this crew, I must be pretty tough."

"You are indeed." Christina wasn't so sure how she would manage if she was a single *mudder* who took care of extra little ones to boot. "Let me enter your items in my book. I'm sure they will sell today. I have some money for you, too, from the last baking you did." She knew the money wasn't any great sum but figured every little bit would help Amelia and her family.

Christina's hand bumped the penknife and nearly sent it clattering to the floor when she reached for her ledger. Immediately, she pushed it away from the edge of the shelf. What she really wanted to do was check around where Noah said he found the knife. It was entirely possible that a customer had dropped the thing while looking at plants, but Christina had a hunch that wasn't the case.

The very thought of tall, dark-haired Noah Zimmerman made her heart do a quirky little dance. Would he really return today? She'd try not to get her hopes up. She'd better not have any hopes at all if she wanted to keep her best *freind*. Christina would ponder that whole issue later. Right now, she had two mysteries to solve: one involving the penknife and the other involving the body in the shed. Or were they parts of the same mystery?

Christina couldn't ask Amelia to tend the shop for a few minutes so she could search. The poor woman had her hands full as it was. As eager as she was to explore, Christina would have to bide her time.

~

He didn't quite understand why, but Noah experienced an uneasiness every time his mind wandered to Christina Brubacher alone in her store. Sure, she'd probably have a lot of customers so she wouldn't be totally on her own, but there was bound to be a lull every now and then. Noah had never particularly worried about her or anyone else before, but some strange protective instinct had kicked in yesterday.

Christina had seemed so small and fragile, though he knew she worked hard and was probably much stronger than she appeared. But he had seen the shock and fear in her silver eyes if only briefly. She was a tough one, though. He had to smile. Noah had once witnessed, from a distance of course, an exchange between Christina and a supplier who had delivered faulty merchandise. He seriously doubted that the man would ever again try to pull the wool over her eyes—or anyone else's for that matter. He chuckled and then cleared his throat to cover the sound in case anyone questioned him. That was doubtful, though, with all the assorted noises echoing in the machine shop.

It sure was a *gut* thing that he could repair engines and almost anything else in his sleep since his brain had decided to take a hike. His *mamm* used to say Noah must have been born with a screwdriver in his hand. He always liked figuring out how things worked and how to put them back together again if they broke. Some of his earliest memories involved taking toys apart, much to the chagrin of his siblings. But he always reassembled them. So this gasoline-powered engine on his workbench should not pose any problems whatsoever.

His thoughts, on the other hand, were creating a major ruckus. Noah couldn't recall another girl absorbing so much of his attention. Sure, he'd taken a few home after young folks' gatherings, but nothing serious ever developed. None of those girls ever invaded his brain. And now, this little slip of a girl, who barely stood as tall as his shoulder and who would blow away with a big puff of wind, occupied most of his waking moments for the past eighteen hours or so. His non-waking moments, too, if he wanted to be completely truthful.

How on earth had that man gotten to The Green Thumb? And how horrible for Christina to discover him in her shed. She must have been shocked and terrified. He hoped she wasn't scared today. Noah only observed a fleeting wariness in her expression this morning before she shored herself up to take care of business. He admired her determination and her spunk. Her nearly raven-colored hair and sparkling silver eyes were nothing to sneeze at either. He found himself uttering a silent prayer for her safety.

Noah truly didn't believe Christina was in any danger, but one could never be certain. He would take his lunchtime to check on her. Maybe they could brainstorm clues to solve this enigma. Apparently, the workings of machines and gadgets weren't the only things he liked figuring out!

~

"This is just in time for the folks who stop in on their lunch hour." Christina arranged the loaves of zucchini bread on the nearly empty shelf and placed the packages of cookies in a big basket. "These cookies look delicious. I might have to squirrel some away for my own lunch."

"I hope your customers like them." A worry line snaked across Amelia's forehead.

"I haven't had a single complaint about anything you've brought in before. In fact, I only get raves. I'm sure these will be snatched up and enjoyed as well."

"Hello, ladies and girls."

Christina glanced up from her display. "*Ach*, Marjorie. It's *gut* to see you." Marjorie Gehman, a forty-something woman whose *kinner* were mostly grown, bustled into the shop.

"I meant to get here earlier, but first one thing and then another kept me from getting out the door. When the barn cat deposited a nasty, headless mouse on my back step, I almost gave up altogether. What a mess! I hollered for Levi, who hadn't yet gotten outside to help his *daed*. I assigned him the task of cleaning off the step."

"Lucky *bu*." Christina imagined Marjorie's fifteen-year-old wasn't too pleased with his task, but he wouldn't dare refuse to do his *mudder's* bidding.

Marjorie sighed and poked a wavy strand of brown hair beneath her *kapp*. "This humid weather makes my hair do crazier things than usual. Oh, well. It can't be helped. I'm here now, and I've brought some treats." She barely paused for a breath. "Amelia, you've been baking too, and with all these little ones underfoot. You're still babysitting, I see." She tickled the *boppli* under her chin making the little girl draw back against Amelia with a giggle.

Christina, standing behind the older woman, rolled her eyes, which almost made Amelia burst out laughing. She loved Marjorie dearly, but it was definitely hard to get a word in, or even form a thought, with her around. "What did you bring today, Marjorie?"

"Nothing as yummy as these treats." She nodded at the breads and cookies before reaching into her bag. She pulled out individually wrapped slices of applesauce cake and an assortment of whoopie pies.

"Whoopie pies!" Amelia cried. "There can't be anything yummier than those."

"I don't know. Your cookies look pretty tasty to me. I might have to buy some."

"That's what I told her." Christina began arranging the new arrivals on the shelf. "I need to enter your items in the ledger."

"Why don't you let me finish putting these things out while you take care of your log books?"

Christina took Marjorie up on her offer. While she was happy to have help waiting on customers or ringing up the sales, Christina never let anyone else make a mark in her ledgers. She took care of all the record-keeping herself.

"I'd like to stay around, but I need to get the *kinner* home, fed yet again, and put down for naps. I've got a huge basket of mending to get to before these little ones completely run out of clothes to wear."

"You go right ahead, Amelia. I appreciate your bringing the bread and cookies in today."

"Are you okay here after, uh, yesterday? I hate to think of you alone."

"I'm fine. You have plenty to do without worrying about me."

Marjorie patted Amelia's arm. "I'll stay here with Christina for a while. I've got a little free time on my hands today."

"*Gut.*" Amelia seemed relieved.

Christina opened her arms wide to embrace the young woman and the *boppli* in her arms. "*Danki* for your concern and for dragging all these little ones out to bring your treats."

Amelia returned the hug with one arm and laughed. "I'm afraid this troop has to go with me wherever I go."

"That's quite all right. They are all *gut* girls and are *wilkom* any time."

Marjorie finished unloading her wares by the time Amelia hustled all the *kinner* out the door. "How can I help you, Christina?"

Would now be the right time to do a little investigative work?

Chapter Five

"Would you mind keeping an eye out up here while I check on something in the greenhouse?" Christina hoped her question sounded innocent enough to Marjorie and didn't belie her trepidations. She wasn't sure what she expected to find, but some little voice nudged her to have a look-see.

"Sure. You go right ahead."

"*Danki.* Holler if you need me."

"Will do."

Christina forced her feet to take their normal stride when they wanted to scurry out the door. She paused in the doorway of the greenhouse and dragged in a deep breath to calm her racing heart and jangled nerves. The scent of moist soil mingled with that of flowering plants. Some folks would have hurried right back out when assailed by the mixture of odors and the humid air. Not Christina. She'd always loved the earthy smells and moist atmosphere in the greenhouse.

She glanced over her shoulder to make sure that Marjorie hadn't followed her before slipping over to the begonias in the back. She carefully searched the flats of flowers and even looked among the blooms and leaves for any sign of... what? She didn't really have a clue what she was hunting for but trusted she would know when she found it. Whatever "it" was.

Christina's knee cracked loud enough to echo throughout the silent greenhouse when she crouched down on her haunches. *Ach! I must be getting old before my time.* She ran a hand under the shelf very lightly so she wouldn't disturb any possible evidence. *Listen to me! I sound like a character in one of Annie's books.* She tilted her head to peer beneath the shelf.

"Christina!"

Yikes! She jerked back so hard and so fast that she plopped down on her behind with her skirt hiked way above her knees. She yanked at the fabric and tried to right herself.

"Are you all right? What are you doing down there?"

She should have known she wouldn't be able to escape from Marjorie for long enough to complete her mission. "I-I had stooped down to check on something. You startled me, and I toppled over." She forced a little chuckle.

"My word! I am so sorry. Are you hurt?"

Christina scrambled to her feet. She brushed off her hands and then her dress. "I'm fine. Is something wrong out front?" She hurried toward the older woman who remained glued to her spot at the entrance. Why didn't she answer? Marjorie was never at a loss for words.

As soon as Christina drew alongside her, Marjorie hissed, "Psst! It's the police."

"Here? They're in my shop?"

"*Jah.* Two of them. They're wearing blue shirts, so I guess they are county rather than state police. They wanted to see you, so I told them I'd fetch you right away."

Didn't they finish with her last evening? Surely they didn't think she had anything to do with that poor man's mur—demise. "It's okay, Marjorie. I'll go talk to them." She patted the woman's arm. "Is anyone else here?"

"Not at the moment. I did sell two whoopie pies, one of Amelia's loaves of zucchini bread, and a hanging basket of petunias."

"You've been busy."

"Actually, it was two women who came in together."

"Oh. Okay."

"The one who didn't buy flowers said she would *kumm* back for some. She raved about how pretty they were. She liked the pink..."

Christina nodded. She didn't want to be rude, but she needed to hurry to the front of the store before the sight of a police cruiser scared off her business. She smiled. She needn't have worried about hurting Marjorie's feelings. The woman seemed not to have noticed Christina's hasty retreat. Her ramblings about the customers echoed through the greenhouse.

Thoughts circled through Christina's mind faster than the windmill spins on a blustery day. Would the police share any information with her? How did that man happen to be in her shed? How did he die? She hadn't seen any obvious injuries. Of course, she was not an expert by any means, but she certainly didn't see any wounds or blood. Could he have had a heart attack? But why would he sneak into her shed if he was ill? Wouldn't he seek help instead? Oh, it didn't make any sense. And the men waiting for her would probably not offer her even the tiniest detail. Should she tell them about the knife? It had been in the greenhouse, though. Surely it didn't have anything to do with the man in the shed.

Christina gave her head a tiny shake. Too many questions without answers. She tried to slow her breathing as she approached the front of the store. *I hope these men leave quickly. And I hope they don't have more questions that I can't answer.*

"Good morning, Miss Brubacher." Deputy Gaines spoke for himself and Deputy Wilson since the younger man merely nodded.

Was it still morning? Her mouth suddenly turned into a desert. She could barely utter a greeting.

"Could we please take a look in your shed again? I trust you haven't been in there today."

"*Nee.* It's still locked." She stepped behind the counter to remove the key from the cashbox where she had put it for safekeeping. "I'll open the door for you." Christina couldn't bring herself to simply hand over her key. Besides, maybe she could glean a bit of information if the two men discussed the case as they searched. She didn't give them a chance to take the key from her. She hustled to the back door and left the deputies to clomp along behind her.

Christina grabbed a quick deep breath and tried to ignore the butterflies flapping in her stomach. This was *her* shed. She couldn't always be afraid to open the door. Her fingers trembled slightly as she fit the key into the padlock. She peeked inside as she slowly opened the door and then stood back for the lawmen to enter. Everything appeared normal as far as she could tell. At least there weren't any bodies on the ground.

"Thank you." Deputy Gaines stepped closer to the open door. "I don't think we missed anything yesterday, but we wanted to double-check."

Christina nodded. Did she dare ask them if they knew who the man was or what happened to him, other than the fact that he died, of course? Maybe if she stayed out of sight but near the shed she'd overhear some snippet of conversation. *Ach!* She'd been listening to Annie's recaps of her beloved mystery novels for too long.

She scooted over so she was out of the men's view but still within earshot. If she squinted just right, she could peek through the crack of the door. Why did they have to practically close it? Christina's heart raced so fast that she feared she would faint. She should not be spying, but this was her property. Didn't she have a right to know what was going on? She needed to have a plausible excuse for standing here in case one of the deputies caught her eavesdropping. She should be ashamed of herself. She should feel guilty. Was it terribly wrong that she was neither?

Christina let her gaze shift to the store for a split second. She didn't see Marjorie peering out the window, which was a very *gut* thing. She truly didn't believe the older woman would reprimand her, but she was fairly certain Marjorie would pump her for information.

"Everything looks the same as yesterday." Christina's ears perked up at Deputy Gaines's announcement. "No obvious sign of foul play."

The younger man snickered. "You didn't think the Mennonite girl drugged him and left the evidence on the shelf, did you?"

Christina sucked in the gasp that tried to escape. They didn't think she did something to the man, did they? Drugs? She knew next to nothing about those, only what she read about them in the county newspaper. The men either shifted away from the door or spoke softer. She had to strain to hear more.

"I don't think the Mennonite girl had anything to do with this at all. Either our man decided this would be a private place to get high or someone deliberately gave him a tainted mixture and shoved him in here to die."

Christina shivered even with the sun beating down on her. Both of those scenarios gave her the willies.

"I wish my shed looked half this neat." Deputy Gaines chuckled at his own comment.

"Yeah. I know what you mean. Maybe we can hire her to organize our sheds."

"Right, Wilson, like she has spare time to straighten out your messy shed."

Christina tiptoed away from the shed, figuring she had better not tarry any longer. She hadn't devised a reason for her presence, so discovery could be disastrous. She probably wouldn't learn anything else anyway, and the deputies apparently didn't find any other clues inside her shed. She made a mental note to check that later, too, after finishing her greenhouse investigation. She picked her way through the grass, making a wide arc to avoid being in direct line with the shed door.

Gut. Three cars had parked in the gravel lot in front of the store. Marjorie would be occupied and maybe, just maybe, wouldn't question her. Christina checked on her outside displays before entering the shop. Two *Englisch* ladies browsed, and a third stepped up to the counter to unload her wicker shopping basket.

"I've got this, Marjorie." Christina quickly slipped behind the counter to tally her customer's purchases. She engaged in polite conversation, but her mind stayed at the shed. Had the man died of a drug overdose, then? Had those drugs been self-administered or forced on him? How awful! She sneaked a quick peek under the counter. The penknife was still there. Its presence in her greenhouse must have been totally innocent. Someone would probably walk in to inquire about it.

~

His idea about visiting Christina at midday did not pan out, but if he worked straight through lunchtime, he might finish up and head out early at the day's end. Ha! Who was he kidding? Noah often inhaled a sandwich while he worked and still didn't get out the door on time, let alone early. He would make a supreme effort today. He really wanted to check on Christina. He hoped she hadn't been scared or that the police hadn't questioned her again. It should have been obvious to them that she knew nothing about the crime and didn't have any information to offer them.

More importantly, Noah prayed for Christina's safety. Surely if someone else put that man in the shed, they would be long gone by now and wouldn't return to The Green Thumb to bother Christina. Any of the local *Englischers* would know that the Mennonites minded their own business and didn't get involved with legal matters if at all possible.

Unless the people weren't local. But in that case, how would they have known the shed even existed? It was all so perplexing.

Noah had to clean the gunk off the engine in front of him before he could even analyze the problem. Some people obviously didn't take *gut* care of their equipment. That was okay. He would have this thing purring like a kitten and shining like a new penny in a jiffy. If all went according to plan, that is.

"How's it going?"

The voice broke into his thoughts a short time later. Noah looked up from the engine that was now shining but not yet purring. "It's a bit more involved than I thought, but I'm almost done." His eyes briefly connected with the small brown eyes nearly hidden among the wrinkles on Henry Weaver's face. He had worked in Henry's machine shop ever since he finished school at age fourteen, and he had trailed his *daed* around, learning about gadgets and gizmos ever since he could toddle. Henry planned to sell him the business when he got around to retiring.

"You didn't eat again."

Noah patted his belly, which rumbled enough to rival a ferocious thunderstorm. "I got too involved in this project." His eyes slid from Henry's face to the battery-operated clock on the wall. Where had the afternoon gone? He wasn't going to be leaving early after all if he didn't hurry and finish with this engine.

"Why don't you take a little break and grab a bite to eat?"

"I want to get this thing done. Then, if it's okay with you, I'll scoot on out. I can wait a little longer to eat." Another rumble from his stomach said otherwise.

Henry chuckled. "Your belly doesn't seem very happy with that idea. Have you got a girl you're anxious to see?"

Noah's cheeks burned. "*Nee.* Nothing like that. I have something I need to check on, that's all."

"Are you sure it isn't *someone?*"

Noah looked down at the engine so his face wouldn't give him away. His *mudder* could always tell what he was thinking by gazing into his eyes. He didn't know if that was only a *mudder* thing or not, but he wasn't going to take any chances. "I'm sure."

"Go on with you, *bu*. I know you young folks don't discuss your courtships."

"I'm not courting anyone. That's for sure and for certain."

"Well, it's time you thought about doing that. What are you now, twenty-five or so?"

"Twenty-four. I've got plenty of time."

"I suppose, but don't wait too late to find a *fraa*. My Nancy and I have been together for forty-five years. Best thing I ever did was marry that woman."

Noah ventured a peek upward. The love that lit the older man's face sent a pang through his heart. He hoped he found that kind of love that endured for decades. He had been pondering that more and more lately. Maybe it was time to seriously consider courtship. The image of a certain tiny, raven-haired girl danced through his mind. *Ach!* Could his cheeks burn any hotter? "I'd better get this thing done."

"It will be here tomorrow if you want to skedaddle now."

"I hate leaving something halfway done, and I'm more than half finished with it. I'll try to complete it in the next thirty minutes." That should still give him time to pedal his bike to The Green Thumb before it closed for the day. He knew Christina kept the place open a little later during the summer since this was her busiest season.

"Suit yourself. Don't wait too late, son."

"I shouldn't be too much longer."

"I mean, to find a *fraa*." With that, Henry turned and loped off to his workbench, whistling as he did so.

Noah shook his head. How had talk about work ended up with an admonition to find a *fraa*? How had Henry tapped into his own thoughts? He had only recently considered settling down and only very recently discovered an interest in a girl he'd found had grown into a lovely young woman. He shook his head a bit harder. Best to leave these foreign thoughts for some other time and focus on something familiar, like fixing this engine.

Chapter Six

Deputy Gaines poked his head inside the shop to tell Christina they had finished in the shed and had secured the lock. She planned to dash out to see for herself as soon as she got the chance. It wasn't that she didn't trust the deputies. She didn't have any reason to mistrust them. She always checked everything at least several times before leaving the shop every day. Plus, she wanted to make sure nothing had been disturbed in her shed. Organization had been instilled in her by her *grossmammi* at a very young age. Her business would not run nearly as smoothly if she was an unorganized person. Annie called it obsessed, but Christina liked the word *organized* much better.

Marjorie headed home after the lunch hour quite disappointed that she had failed to gain any juicy tidbits of information from the deputies or Christina. "I guess I'll have to wait for an article in the newspaper."

"I guess so." Christina didn't share what she'd overheard earlier for two reasons. First, she did not want Marjorie to know she had been eavesdropping—a much nicer word than *snooping*. And second, she did not want Marjorie to spread tales that might not be true. The officers had not had any confirmation yet on the drug aspect as far as Christina could tell, so she didn't want to be the initiator of unfound rumors.

The afternoon wore on and still Christina had not been able to escape to the greenhouse or to the shed to inspect things. Even when a brief lull in customers occurred, she couldn't abandon the store to search. There wasn't any telling who could walk in while she was away from the counter. That point was driven home yesterday. She would certainly be wary for a while, maybe forever.

"Hi, Stina!"

Christina straightened up from the shelf she'd been bending over. She had been making notes of how many jars of each type of jam or jelly remained on the shelf. She might have to raid *Mamm*'s stash of apple butter and strawberry-rhubarb jam. For some reason, those two had been big sellers lately. "You're finished early today, ain't so?"

"A little. Uncle Henry said I'd done enough work for the day."

Translation: Annie had talked everyone nearly to death, and they all needed some peace and quiet. Christina loved her *freind* dearly, but the girl could talk the ears off a brass donkey.

"Did you have an exciting day?" Annie waltzed over to the stool behind the counter and plopped on it. She twirled that errant red curl that always escaped from her bun and sighed like she had run one of the *Englischer*'s marathons.

Knowing Annie as well as she did, Christina figured her *freind* sat as much as she could get away with in-between customers at her *onkle*'s produce business. Physical activity had never been Annie's passion. When they were scholars, Annie always offered to keep score during softball games, or she pretended to take her turn at kickball but ran to the back of the line when she thought no one was looking.

Christina's lips twitched as she tried to suppress a smile at the memory. Annie had never fooled her or probably anyone else for that matter. "I've had a busy day. I'm not sure that equals exciting."

"Weren't you afraid here today? Even a teensy bit?"

"Not really. I don't think I was the target of any wrongdoing. I think my shed happened to be a convenient hiding place. It won't be anymore, though. I intend to keep it locked at all times, even if that's a hardship when I need to run out there to grab something in a hurry."

Annie gave an exaggerated shudder and almost slid off the stool. "You're braver than I am, then. I'd have been looking over my shoulder all day long."

"You? The avid reader of suspense novels?"

"Hey, I like *reading* mysteries. I don't want to *participate* in them."

"I don't think I am part of a mystery. My shed was just used as the setting for one."

"Whichever it is, I wouldn't have wanted to be here alone all day."

"I did have customers, you know. Pretty steady too. Amelia came in to drop off things and so did Marjorie, who actually stayed a while."

"And talked up a storm, I'm thinking."

There's the pot calling the kettle black. Christina didn't dare voice that thought. "She was a big help. Anyway, I didn't have too much time on my own."

"Did the cops *kumm* back?"

"Cops? You really do read way too many novels, my *freind.*"

Annie shrugged. "Lots of people call the police 'cops'."

"Lots of *Englischers*, maybe."

"Whatever. Did the *deputies* visit again? Is that better?"

"I'm not sure you would call it a visit, but they did stop in."

Annie wiggled so far forward that the stool wobbled. Christina expected the girl and the stool to crash to the floor any second. "What did they have to say?"

"They didn't make me privy to any of their information."

"You didn't ask?"

"I couldn't very well do that, could I? I'm not on their staff." Heat crawled up her neck to lodge in her cheeks. She certainly didn't hesitate to eavesdrop, though, did she? She would keep that indiscretion to herself. Christina picked up a scrap of paper and fanned herself. "Whew! It's warm today."

"I'm perfectly fine."

"You've been sitting still near the open door." *And you aren't embarrassed by your shameful actions.* A sudden inspiration struck. Maybe she could trust Annie to mind the shop for a few minutes so she could finally check the greenhouse and shed. She tossed her makeshift fan into the metal trash can. She turned to tell Annie that she would be right back, but she didn't get the chance to do that.

Annie licked a finger and used it to smooth that unruly strand of hair back into place. She pulled herself to a prim and proper position and stared out the door. "Company is approaching."

"That's okay. I haven't shut down yet."

"I don't think this is a paying customer."

What other kinds were there? Christina followed Annie's gaze. "Oh, it's Noah." She didn't think he would really return, but evidently he was a man of his word. She almost reached up to smooth her own hair but refused to give in to that temptation. She couldn't control her silly heart, though. It danced around in her chest almost causing her to gasp for breath.

"I wonder how he knew I was here."

Annie had spoken softly, but Christina heard the words as if they had been broadcast from a megaphone like the firefighters sometimes used. Should she tell Annie that Noah had been at The Green Thumb this morning and that he had mentioned he would return to check in with her later?

"Hi, Noah. It's great to see you." Annie smiled and batted her eyes.

"Hi, Annie." He scarcely glanced in her direction as he took long strides to stand in front of Christina. "How did everything go today? You didn't have any problems after I left, did you?"

Ooh. Now he had let the cat out of the bag. His morning visit wasn't really a secret, but Christina couldn't be sure how Annie would react to the news. Maybe she didn't pick up on that remark.

"Oh, you were here earlier?"

So much for wishful thinking! Christina probably should have mentioned that fact earlier, but she truly hadn't thought of it until Annie announced Noah's approach. How could she smooth this over now? It wasn't like he was interested in either one of them, so Christina shouldn't be pestered by that little niggling of guilt. "Noah stopped by on his way to work this morning to, uh, make sure everything was okay here." That sounded innocent enough, didn't it?

"Oh. I see."

Did she? Christina didn't want her *freind* to be hurt. She didn't want her own heart stomped on either, so she'd better curtail its hyperactivity right away.

"So how was your day?" Noah studied Christina's face as if he genuinely cared about her well-being.

Don't be fooled by his broad smile and big, blue eyes. He is only being neighborly. You aren't anything special to Noah Zimmerman. He has never given any indication of that in the past, so don't expect anything to be different now. Too bad her heart didn't receive her head's message. It continued to flop around like a fish washed up on the shore of the Potomac River.

"My day was fine." It was easy to smile back at the tall man gazing at her so intently. It was easy to get lost in that smile and to drown in those eyes. Too easy.

"Did the deputies return?"

"I've been trying to wheedle information out of her too." Annie slid from the stool and sashayed over to stand right beside Noah. "I think I'd have an easier time snatching a bone from a starving dog." She giggled at her own comment.

"Like I told you before, they did return, but they certainly didn't reveal any clues that they might have discovered." And Christina was dying to know of any revelations. *Oops, not a great choice of words!* Could she leave Annie to gawk at Noah while she slipped away to do a little investigating of her own?

Noah sidestepped a few inches as if Annie had invaded his personal space. "I really didn't think they would divulge any details. I was more concerned that they would badger you or upset you."

"Aw, aren't you sweet." Annie batted her eyes again.

Christina choked back a chuckle. She had never seen her *freind* display such a show before and was both amused and worried at the same time. She couldn't believe how blatantly Annie displayed her interest, but she didn't want the girl to be hurt if Noah failed to reciprocate her feelings. As uncomfortable as he appeared at the moment, Christina doubted he had any interest in Annie.

Noah did not respond to Annie's comment, but his awkwardness was evident. "I know yesterday had to have been a shock. Since I was here yesterday, I—"

Christina had to dispel some of the tension that rose up in the room like a lion ready to spring on an unsuspecting doe. "Say, Noah, could you help me carry some things to the shed? That is, if Annie doesn't mind watching the store for a few minutes."

The other girl planted her fists on her hips and clucked her tongue. "I could have helped you, Stina."

"I know, but I have some heavy things to move."

"Sure, Christina. I can help you." Noah, obviously relieved to escape the present situation, hurried to offer his services.

Now I have to find something heavy for him to carry outside. Fast! Christina did a quick survey of the area. The pallets. She had several empty pallets since plant sales had been so *gut.* She usually left them in place, but since she needed a heavy job, today she would relocate them. She zipped over to the counter to snatch the shed key from the shelf beneath. In her haste, she knocked into the penknife, which clattered to the floor. She grabbed it and stowed it in a pocket. Maybe she should let Noah have another look at it and get his opinion about its possible owner.

"What can I move for you?"

"Some of the pallets back here." Christina strode to the back of her shop. "Be right back, Annie." She tried to ignore the girl's scowl and braced herself for the tongue-lashing that was bound to occur later.

Noah grunted as he hoisted two wooden pallets. Christina thought she heard him whisper, *"Danki,"* but she didn't attempt to clarify that. Most likely he was grateful to get out of such an uncomfortable situation. How could she have a little chat with Annie later without sounding mean or, worse yet, jealous? Christina plucked two large terra-cotta flowerpots off the shelf to carry to the shed. She needed this mission to at least *appear* authentic.

Christina turned the key in the padlock and tried to pull the door open without exhibiting any of the trepidation she experienced about entering the shed. At least Noah's presence was a help. The breath she hadn't realized she'd been holding whooshed out when she found her shed looking about like it usually did. At least no bodies tumbled out to greet her.

"Are you all right?"

"Jah." She set the pots on the first shelf right inside the shed before they slid from her sweating hands. She raised her eyes to meet Noah's questioning expression. "Could you lean the pallets against the back wall, please?"

"You really didn't need these brought out here, did you?"

Christina's face must surely be beet red. "Uh, well, uh…"

"You tried to spare me from Annie's flirtations, ain't so?"

"I did, but I'm sorry if I misunderstood. Maybe I should have left you in there with her to talk or whatever."

"*Nee, nee.* You read me exactly right."

"I don't know what's gotten into Annie. She doesn't normally behave in such a forward manner. She's actually a very nice girl. You would like her, I'm sure, if you got to know her."

"I believe you. You don't have to defend her. I already know her as well as I need to. I'm glad you rescued me." He gave Christina a lopsided grin before carrying the pallets to the back of the shed. "You, though, I wouldn't mind getting to know better."

The words had been mumbled when he turned his back, but Christina heard them as loud and clear as if he'd shouted them. Should she respond or ignore the comment? *Ignore it. What if you were mistaken? You'd be mortified.* Occasionally, the little voice in her head made sense.

Christina scrutinized every inch of the shed. She had been in too much shock yesterday to really give the place a thorough look-see. Everything had appeared normal to her then, as she told the deputies, but now after her nerves had settled—all except for the fluttering caused by being so close to Noah Zimmerman—she could be more precise.

"Are you looking for something in particular?" Noah leaned against a shelf and followed her with his eyes.

"Not really. I want to make sure everything is as it should be. I mean, it looked fine yesterday, but I might have missed something."

"Didn't the deputies *kumm* back in here today?"

"They did, so I also wanted to make sure they didn't move things around so that I wouldn't be able to find something I needed in a hurry." At least the men took that little stool. She would never have sat on it or even stepped on it again. She shivered involuntarily.

"Are you okay?"

Christina nodded, causing her *kapp* strings to dance around her face. Noah's blue eyes fixed on her, nearly causing another shiver. She couldn't recall another living soul ever making her feel the way she felt right now. Chill bumps ran up and down her arms, and hundreds of butterflies took flight in her stomach. These strange sensations were either due to the man standing less than a foot away from her or she was about to throw up. *Dear Lord, please don't let me do that!*

"Did you find anything amiss?"

Why did he study her so closely? Christina resisted the urge to run her hands up and down her arms to chase the little bumps away. As she swiped a hand down her dress to wipe off the sudden dampness, her fingers encountered a slight bulge in a pocket. She looked up into Noah's face, praying she wouldn't be mesmerized by those eyes and totally forget what was on her mind. "Can I ask you a question?"

Chapter Seven

"You just did."

"Huh? Oh." Christina burst out laughing despite her nervousness at his scrutiny. "I guess you're right." He had chuckled along with her, but his eyes had never left her face. His expression registered something different, but she couldn't decipher its meaning. "What's wrong?"

"You have a *wunderbaar* laugh, Christy. It's musical. It reminds me of the wind chimes that used to hang on my *grossmammi's* front porch. On a windless day, I would flick one of the pieces so I could be wrapped in that joyful sound. Your laugh gives me that same warm, happy feeling."

The use of his nickname for her and his heartfelt words nearly made her melt into a pool of contentment. Never before had anyone spoken to her in such a manner. She wouldn't have believed a person's laughter could evoke such intense emotion. At first, she thought he was teasing her, but she did not see so much as a trace of insincerity in his expression. His eyes bore into hers and held her captive. In them, she saw not only merriment but something far deeper. Concern? Caring? What unspoken emotions could he discover in her own eyes? She needed to break this spell.

Noah severed the connection before she could do so. He touched her arm for an instant, sending a bolt of lightning through her entire body. His own face registered shock when he drew his hand away. Did he experience something similar? "Y-you wanted to ask me something?"

She smiled. "*Jah*, besides that first question."

He chuckled. "I'm all ears."

Christina reached into her pocket to extract the decorative little penknife. "I didn't give this to the police. Do you think it's connected to the investigation in any way? Am I withholding evidence?"

"I found that knife in your greenhouse. You never saw that man in there, did you?"

"I never saw him anywhere before finding him in the shed."

"Then I don't see how the knife could be connected to him."

"That's what I thought at first."

"Did something happen to make you think differently?" He took the penknife from her hand and studied it. "I guess our fingerprints are all over it now, so they wouldn't be able to get any information from it anyway, even if it was related to the man's death." Noah turned the knife over and over as if studying it.

"I think the soil looks different in the flat of begonias where you found the knife. I've been trying to get in there to check all day but haven't been able to."

Noah continuously turned the knife every which way.

"What are you looking for?"

"On some of these fancy knives, *Englischers* sometimes have their initials engraved somewhere."

"I hadn't thought of that, but I haven't seen too many of these knives. Besides, I couldn't very well pull the thing out in front of customers or Marjorie."

"Or Annie."

Christina smacked her forehead. "Annie! I'd better get back inside the shop. It's a wonder she hasn't sent out a search party." She poked around one final time on the shelf nearest the door. "*Ach!* This isn't mine." She jerked her hand back as if it had been bitten by a viper.

"What is it?" Noah hurried to her side. He grabbed her hand, apparently thinking she had hurt it or else was holding some offensive object.

Christina couldn't help herself. She clutched his hand and held on for dear life. She nodded at that shelf. "That trowel isn't mine. It's old and big and bulky an-and not mine."

She dropped the hand that had momentarily served as her lifeline and inched forward a speck. She stood on tiptoe to examine the foreign object a bit more closely. There was some sort of dark stain on its edge. She leaned back as if she feared the thing would jump off the shelf and attack her, smacking into a solid wall behind her. Noah's free hand pressed into her shoulder, steadying her against his broad chest. She could feel his heart thumping in a staccato rhythm that matched her own.

"Are you sure it isn't an old one that you'd forgotten about?"

"Absolutely sure. There's something on it. I don't leave my tools dirty."

"It probably has ancient mud stains." Noah peered over Christina's head. "Oh, I see."

"Not mud, right?"

"I don't believe so." He reached over her to grab the trowel.

"Don't touch it!" Christina snatched his hand before it could make contact with the shelf or anything on it. "Oops, sorry." She tried to let go of him, but he threaded his fingers through hers. Now she really couldn't think straight.

"Hey, I don't mind holding your hand one little bit."

Heat rushed to her face. "I-I was trying to keep you from tampering with the evidence."

"Oh, and here I thought you just wanted to hold my hand." He gave her a smile that made little crinkly lines fan out around his dazzling eyes.

She wrinkled her nose at him and forbade her tongue from admitting how *wunderbaar* it really was to hold his hand. "I-I didn't want you to leave your fingerprints on that thing." Christina tried again to extract her hand from his, but he held tighter.

"Don't you think the police would have taken this if they thought it was related to the case?"

"I don't know. I suppose they saw it. They searched the shed twice. They probably thought it was mine. I mean, I have other tools in here, so that would be a natural assumption, ain't so?"

"That sounds pretty logical to me."

"But it isn't mine. And I don't have the slightest idea how it got into my shed or how that knife got into my greenhouse. Do you think the two things are connected with the crime?"

"The man hadn't been injured, had he?"

Christina shivered involuntarily at the memory of that poor man who had died in her shed or was hidden there after his death. Noah's gentle squeeze on her hand bolstered her courage and her resolve to figure out this whole bizarre incident. "He didn't have any injuries as far as I could tell. There wasn't any blood all over him to indicate that someone had attacked him."

"Then that trowel probably wasn't used on him. I'm not sure you could kill a person with it anyway, but who knows?"

"Why did someone put the thing in my shed?"

"Maybe they found it outside and assumed it belonged to you since you most likely use such tools."

"I guess that's possible. What's your theory on the penknife?" Christina studied Noah's face as he pondered her question. It was such a handsome face framed by dark brown hair. His clear, blue eyes reminded her of a picture she once saw of a mountain lake glittering in the sun. She could gaze into them all day. *Ach!* What was she thinking? She had to look over his shoulder to make her mind focus on something else.

"I'm not sure about that knife. It isn't like it would have rolled under that shelf if someone had dropped it."

"Did you find any initials on it?"

"*Nee.*" He pulled it from the pocket he'd thrust it into when he rushed over to the shelf after Christina's cry of distress. He examined the knife again and shook his head. "I don't see anything on it. What was it about the begonias? You started to say something earlier."

"That flat right above the place you said you found the knife looked different somehow, almost like the flowers had been disturbed. They were a little mashed and wobbly."

"Could it be because they'd grown taller and leaned a little because of the extra weight?"

"Possibly. Or someone could have picked up that flat to purchase it but then changed their mind, but I don't think so. Something in here," she tapped her chest with her free hand, "says something strange happened with the pink begonias even though my head tries to rationalize everything. I'm going to go check right now."

"There you are! I thought the earth had opened up and swallowed you two."

Christina yanked her hand free of Noah's and leaped away from him so fast she nearly lost her balance. She wobbled slightly but was relieved Noah had the *gut* sense not to reach out to steady her. She couldn't make herself look at Annie. "W-we were making sure nothing had been disturbed out here."

"Oh?"

"*Jah.* In case the deputies missed something," Noah added.

"Really? Don't you believe they are capable of performing their jobs?"

Christina finally lifted her gaze to meet her *freind*'s. Guilt washed over her when she encountered Annie's scowl even though she had done nothing wrong. Had she dropped Noah's hand before Annie poked her head inside the shed? The clasping of their hands had been an innocent gesture. Hadn't it? Of course, it had! It had been a quite natural response to her shock at finding that trowel. Never mind that he continued to clutch her hand as they talked. Was that pain she saw in Annie's eyes beneath the angry scowl?

"I'm sure the men knew how to do their jobs. I wanted to make sure everything out here was as it should be since I was too distraught yesterday to really focus on details."

Annie's red-orange eyebrows arched upward. "I suppose Noah was helping you do that since he's so familiar with the contents of your shed, huh?"

Ordinarily, Christina got a kick out of Annie's sarcasm. Today, it made her defensive. "I-I was asking his opinion on the investigation as I checked around." She felt like a scholar wrongly chastised by the teacher for cheating on a spelling test. She feared the more she tried to justify her actions, the bigger the hole she dug for herself. She would like to drop into a hole right about now and pull it in behind her.

"I'm sure he was a tremendous help." Annie's gaze shifted to Christina's hand that had recently been clutched in Noah's.

A little spark of anger tried to ignite. Christina shouldn't have to defend herself or justify her behavior. "I'd better check on my shop that was left untended." She hadn't meant for those words to slip out. She needed to douse that spark before it burst into flame.

"I'm not totally stupid, Christina. I locked the front door before walking out here and, uh, interrupting you two."

Uh-oh. When Annie called her by her full name instead of Stina, she was upset or angry—or both. Christina had better smooth things over fast. "I never said you were stupid. I'm sorry I snapped at you. Let me lock everything up so we can go home. And you weren't interrupting anything. I was a little upset by something that was out of place in here." She glanced up at Noah, silently seeking his opinion. Should she say more to her *freind?* Telling Annie something could be like telling the whole world.

"Don't tell me the cops missed something and you two put your little heads together and figured everything out."

Christina's mouth opened in surprise. She'd never heard Annie's sarcasm take a mean turn before. Now there wasn't any doubt in Christina's mind that Annie had glimpsed Noah holding her hand. How should she respond to that last comment? Her mind couldn't think beyond that barbed remark.

"Actually, Annie, Christina became a bit upset at a few things that were different out here. I guess the deputies had moved some things around. But you can imagine the horrible memories she must have from her discovery yesterday. I'm glad I was here when she stumbled in shock."

"*Ach!* Are you all right, Stina? I'm sorry. I didn't think how awful it would be for you to *kumm* out here. You should have let me check the shed out. But I guess I wouldn't know if anything was out of place, would I?"

Christina breathed a sigh of relief. Annie's concern sounded genuine. Maybe she was back to her usual chatty self. Christina would have to remember to thank Noah later for his quick thinking since her own brain couldn't fashion a thought in time for her to utter a reply. His words were true enough, but the lingering hand-holding probably had little to do with her stumbling.

"I'm okay, Annie. I can't let this place give me the creeps. I have to *kumm* out here every day."

"But maybe it was too soon. Why don't you sit inside for a few minutes before we head home?"

"I have to go inside, but I don't think I need to sit. Keeping busy often works wonders for a troubled mind." Not always, though. She'd raced about from one thing to another all day, but still her thoughts returned to Noah or to the poor man in the shed time and time throughout the entire day.

"I suppose that's true." Annie held out a hand as if she needed to help Christina out of the shed.

Christina forced a smile. She felt a gentle pressure on her back that sent a shock wave up her spine. Noah must have thought she needed help exiting the shed as well. Or was he trying to let her know he was there for her and, maybe, that he cared? *For goodness' sake, girl. Stop reading into a simple gesture. He probably wants you to hurry and get out of the way so he can go home.* She grabbed Annie's hand and squeezed it.

Annie squeezed back. "There. Take a deep breath of fresh air."

"I'm fine. Let me lock up the shed." When she turned to fasten the lock, she glanced up at Noah with a silent question in her eyes. What should she do about the trowel and the knife?

A slight nod told her that Noah understood her message. But how could he answer her in Annie's presence? True, the girl was chattering away about something, but she would probably hone in on any comments between the two of them. And how was she going to search in and around that flat of begonias with Annie peering over her shoulder? She'd been itching to do that all day. It looked like she would need to put that plan on hold a day longer. Wondering and worrying would most likely keep her tossing and turning all tonight.

"Are you ready to leave?" Annie stopped beside her bicycle.

"I need to do a couple of things, but don't let me hold you up. You can go ahead home."

"I won't leave without you! What sort of *freind* would leave you alone here after your experience?"

Christina was afraid the red-haired girl would say something like that. There wouldn't be any way to persuade Annie to leave, so she might as well not even try.

"I'll make sure you two get on the road safely before heading home myself."

"We'll be fine, Noah, but *danki*." Christina hoped he understood that she was thanking him for everything he'd done.

"Oh, it would be great if you stayed, Noah. You could keep me company while Stina finishes up whatever she has to do."

When Annie looked away, Noah rolled his eyes and smiled at Christina. Stealthily, he passed the little penknife to her, and she immediately pocketed it. Now what should she do with the thing?

Chapter Eight

If they hadn't followed her inside The Green Thumb, Christina would have done a quick search in the greenhouse. She wouldn't risk that, though, with Annie likely to spy on her. There wasn't any use involving her *freind* in something that could be dangerous in any way if she did discover some sort of evidence.

Silly girl! Now you sound like a character in one of Annie's novels. Who would hide anything among a bunch of begonias? And even if someone did, wouldn't that person have returned here today to retrieve whatever he left? "It would have to be awfully small."

"What, Stina?"

Oh great! She got caught talking to herself. "Uh, nothing. I'll only be a few minutes."

"Take your time."

Christina threw a glance over her shoulder in time to catch Annie fluttering her eyes again. The almost-sick expression on Noah's face made her choke back a giggle. "I'll hurry."

He nodded ever so slightly, but Christina caught the movement.

She scooted over to the counter to make sure her records for the day were completed and the cash drawer was secure. She wondered why Annie never before mentioned an interest in Noah. In their girlish, whispered confessions, Noah's name never rolled off Anne's tongue. Christina, on the other hand, had hinted at her secret crush several times. So why would her *freind* pursue a fellow *she* was interested in? Was it some sort of competition or challenge on Annie's part? *Nee.* Her best *freind* wasn't like that. She probably thought Christina had long since abandoned any fantasies about Noah Zimmerman.

"I'm ready," Christina announced after double-checking that the front door was locked. She felt only the tiniest bit rude that she interrupted the conversation between Noah and Annie. It had sounded pretty one-sided anyway. Sometimes a person just had to plunge right in when Annie was on a roll and simply throw manners to the wind.

"*Gut!*" Noah's relief practically wafted through the air. "I mean, uh, I'm sure you'll both be glad to get home."

"I'm not in any hurry. I've enjoyed talking with you so much that I hadn't noticed how much time has passed." Annie batted her eyes again.

Talking *to* him, not talking *with* him. Christina hadn't heard Noah so much as grunt a reply, and her ears surely would have pricked up at the resonance of his deep voice. "Well, I, for one, am ready to call it a day." She strode toward the back door. She heard the clomp of Noah's work shoes fairly close behind her and Annie's exaggerated sigh. Somehow, in a matter of two days, life had become so much more complicated.

~

How did one girl talk so much? Noah shook his head to clear his brain and stop the ringing in his ears. How did Christina endure the constant prattle? He supposed Annie was a nice girl, but he did not have any desire to find that out for himself. Whew! He pedaled faster to create more of a breeze.

Noah watched the girls until they were out of sight before turning on the road leading to his home. He would have gladly ridden the entire way with Christina, but he couldn't abide any more of Annie's chatter. And what was with that whole eye thing she had going on? She looked like she was trying to get a gnat out of her eye. If the flapping of her pale-lashed lids was supposed to entice him, the gesture fell short. The girl simply needed to be herself—a quieter self perhaps, but natural, like Christina.

Noah took one hand off the handlebar to flap at a horse-fly buzzing around his head. Maybe he should have used his buggy today. At least then he wouldn't have to fend off biting bugs. But he actually enjoyed riding his bike. And he enjoyed spending time with Christina Brubacher. Why hadn't he paid any attention to her before now?

She was probably about four years younger than he was, so that could be why he hadn't taken much notice of her. She would have been too young for him to have played with when they were scholars. When had she grown into such a lovely young woman?

Noah wiggled on the hard bike seat when a river of perspiration flowed down his back. Although his rapid cycling created a hint of a breeze, the effort caused his clothes to adhere to his skin like they had been glued there. Surely he and Christina had attended singings together. He had missed a few young folks' gatherings throughout the summer, but he usually attended. How had he missed her? She must have been right under his nose all along. What a dunce he was!

He could have talked to her, asked to take her home, gotten to know her better. Now he had Annie—who hadn't made any secret of her interest in him—to contend with. To make matters more difficult, Christina might want to keep her distance from him now so as not to hurt Annie's feelings. Yet, he had a hunch she wanted his help or support with this latest turn of events at her shop, and he would like to help her. Was Annie a constant afternoon visitor at The Green Thumb? Somehow Noah had to devise a way to see Christina without her gabby *freind* around. But how?

~

Christina sat up, punched her pillow twice to plump the feathers, and plopped down with a long, drawn-out sigh. She thought she would have sunk into an exhausted sleep right away after the stress and strain of the past couple of days. Not so. Her brain would not shut down so sleep could take over. Now she had more worries to add to her collection.

She had been wracking her brain to find a way to search her greenhouse and had been sorely tempted to sneak over there in the dead of night to investigate. The image of the man falling off the stool before her very eyes quickly squelched that idea. She would leave the house extra early in the morning but would have to devise a plausible excuse for doing so. Without a doubt, *Mamm* would ask why she was in such a hurry to get to work.

Visions of that poor man collided with images of that fancy penknife and the stained trowel. But the most over-powering picture in her mind was that of a tall, dark-haired, blue-eyed man. Whatever should Christina do about him? Her girlish crush had morphed into a nearly overpowering urge to spend more time with Noah Zimmerman, to get to know him better, to... what?

Her best *freind* had taken a sudden interest in the same man. Christina didn't think Noah returned that interest, but who was she to judge? She and Annie couldn't very well vie for the same fellow's attention. Someone would get hurt, for sure and for certain. She should stay far away from Noah, but the very thought of not seeing him or talking to him pierced her heart. In two days' time, she'd *kumm* to trust him. He'd become her confidant in the craziness at her shop.

Ach! She'd simply have to handle things on her own without Noah's help in order to keep the peace. And she absolutely had to get some sleep before that evil rooster crowed outside her window. She flipped over again and squeezed her eyes shut. If only she could squeeze out the troublesome thoughts.

~

Christina had told her *mudder* that she needed to get to The Green Thumb early to rearrange some things, which technically was legitimate if she stretched the truth a tad. *Mamm* had snagged Sallie and Grace to help in the kitchen before they could scamper off to play. Those two were certainly capable of drying and putting away the dishes. Christina had stood on a stool to help in the kitchen when she was even younger than Grace. Her little *schweschders* got away with shirking their chores a bit too often in Christina's opinion.

Usually, the early-morning bike ride invigorated her, even if the humid air wrapped around her like a wool blanket. Today, though, her legs strained to pump the pedals to propel her forward, and the mugginess weighed her down like she balanced a stack of heavy books on her head. Funny how a little sleep deprivation and a ton of worries could totally change a person's outlook.

Christina urged her legs to keep pedaling, just as she sometimes coaxed the horse to trot a little faster. Push! Push! Push! Once she checked out her greenhouse, she would feel better. Maybe. Her heart pounded harder the closer she got to her destination, and not from the exertion. She hoped she soon conquered her qualms about entering her shop. Christina loved her business and had never felt uncomfortable there before. Maybe she needed a little more than two days to get back to normal.

Her mood brightened considerably when she spied a familiar bicycle leaning against the side of The Green Thumb. The fatigue in her leg muscles miraculously disappeared, and she glided to the back door with ease. Noah looked her square in the eye and broke into that smile that lit his entire face. He hastened to meet her as she dismounted from her bike.

"*Gut mariye*, Christina. I just checked to make sure the shed was locked. Everything looks exactly as it did when we left yesterday."

"We." That little word had never sounded so sweet before. Christina's head knew the word was nothing special to Noah, but her heart soared at the very idea that the two of them were somehow linked. *You are supposed to be a grown woman who has outgrown foolish crushes. And you are supposed to keep your distance from this man so that Annie isn't hurt.* "*Danki.* Uh, what are you doing here? Oops, I wasn't trying to be rude. I mean, it's nice to see you. Oh, nothing is *kumming* out right."

He smiled again. "I understand. I'm sure you're used to having the place to yourself for a while before customers start pouring in. I sort of got the feeling yesterday that you wanted a little help or some moral support in your search. I know you wanted to investigate more thoroughly but couldn't do it yesterday. I'll help you dig, or I'll be the look-out and let you investigate or whatever you want."

"Don't you have to go to work?"

"I do, but it's still early." His gaze registered concern. At least that's what Christina wanted to believe. "Let me guess. You didn't get any sleep last night, ain't so?"

Christina reached up to rub her eyes. She must look a fright if he could guess that so easily.

Noah chuckled, gently pulled her hand away from her face, and gazed into her eyes. "You are as lovely as always. I merely assumed that you struggled with insomnia. I know I did."

"You did? Why?"

"Thinking about our discoveries and wondering how you were holding up."

"Y-you were concerned about me?"

He nodded. "Why does that surprise you?"

Christina stared up into Noah's eyes. Somewhere in the depths of her brain, a little voice commanded her to withdraw her hand from his. She shushed it. "I-I assumed you had plenty to do, and my troubles wouldn't be—"

"Don't say 'important.' You are important, and you experienced quite a shock."

Even more of a shock was that he considered her important! It must have been a slip of his tongue. "I-I'm important?" Was that squeaky, little voice hers? Heat climbed up her neck and flooded her cheeks.

"*Jah.*" Noah's word came out as a croak. He coughed, and his face flushed as deep a red as the homemade tomato sauce on the shelf inside The Green Thumb. "Do you want to poke around in the greenhouse before you open for business?"

"I do. That's why I came so early this morning."

"My hunch was correct, then."

Was the fellow a mind reader? "Is that why you're here?"

He looked at the ground and scuffed his toe in the dirt. The gesture reminded Christina of a little *bu* who had been caught with his hand in the cookie jar after his *mudder* told him to leave it alone. She swallowed a giggle and waited for his answer.

"I didn't want you to be alone. I mean, I thought you could use some help."

Christina's insides turned to mush. She was so touched by his words that a lump rose in her throat and tears threatened to flow. Even if Noah never cared for her in a romantic sort of way, or if all he wanted was to solve a mystery, she would forever treasure his kindness. "That's so thoughtful. I actually was a little leery of searching all by myself."

"We're partners, then, *jah*?"

As if his sweet words hadn't been enough, his bright smile nearly made her knees buckle. When he looped his arm through hers and led her toward the back door, a thrill shot through her body, leaving goose bumps in its wake. She would have an awfully hard time stepping aside if Noah decided to pursue a relationship with Annie.

Chapter Nine

One look at Christina's relieved expression told Noah that he'd made the right decision by showing up at The Green Thumb this morning. He could tell she tried hard to put on a brave face, but he read the apprehension in her big, silver eyes. He couldn't blame her one bit. It had to be unnerving even thinking of walking inside the place alone with the memory of a dead man in your storage shed. It was almost enough to give him goose bumps.

Did Christina have any inkling how much he admired her? It wasn't enough that she owned and ran her own successful business at such a young age, but she also met adversity head-on and tackled it. She had held herself together when she discovered that man, when the police questioned her, and when she had to face returning to her shop alone. She had even planned to play investigator all by herself. Well, he wouldn't let her do that.

Christina untwined her arm from his, leaving him feeling strangely bereft. How did his emotions intensify so quickly? One day, he scarcely noticed the girl, and the next, he couldn't get her out of his mind. She yanked a wad of keys from a pocket and fumbled with the lock on the back door.

Was she experiencing the same emotions he was? He took the keys from her trembling fingers and attacked the lock with only slightly steadier hands. His case of nerves could only be attributed to the lovely, raven-haired young woman beside him. Was hers caused by anxiety over what might lie ahead, or could she possibly be as affected by his nearness as much as he was by hers?

Noah blinked to encourage his eyes to adjust to the dimness inside the store. Although sunlight streamed in through the two windows, the room was not nearly as bright as outside. He closed the door behind them and turned the lock so they didn't have any surprise visitors. He handed Christina her keys. "Ready?"

"Let me put my bag away." She zoomed across the store to stow her bag on the shelf below the checkout counter and hurried back to where Noah waited. "Are you sure you don't have to be at work?"

"Not this early." He stifled a yawn.

"How long have you been waiting here?"

"I don't know. I guess about a half hour."

"What did you do? Leave home in the dark?"

Noah chuckled. "Not quite. I figured you would get here early today since we couldn't investigate last night with Annie watching every move. And I did pick up on your message that you'd rather not enlighten her with any information. Are you afraid she would take out an ad in the paper or something?"

Christina laughed. "I hope she's not that bad. Annie is a great person, but she does tend to talk a bit."

"A bit? Try nonstop."

"Be nice, Noah. She's not that bad."

"Really? My ears are still ringing." He tugged at one lobe for emphasis.

"All right. Annie talks a lot. I truly don't believe there is a malicious bone in her body. Not as far as I've seen, at least. I think her tongue runs away from her brain sometimes."

"That's one way to put it." He wasn't sure if the two body parts ever communicated.

"But she is nice, ain't so?"

Why was Christina trying to sell Annie to him? Did she honestly think he was interested in the red-haired girl? Maybe his feelings for Christina weren't as obvious as he thought. He wasn't sure if that was a *gut* thing or a bad thing. "I suppose she's nice enough. I really don't know her that well." And he didn't particularly want to know her any better, but he left that part unsaid.

"Let's go before any customers arrive."

Gut. She let the subject of Annie Wenger drop. Noah followed Christina into the greenhouse that could be entered right from the shop. She stopped in front of the shelf of pink begonias under which he had found that decorative penknife. "What did you notice different about the plants? I didn't pick up on anything."

"It's probably something only I would notice since I'm rather particular about my plants. The little individual containers aren't sitting level, and dirt has been spilled around the flat."

"Is that so unusual?"

Christina gave him a smile that made his heart flip-flop. "I'm sure it's logical that dirt would be everywhere in a greenhouse, but I try to keep things as neat as possible. When I turn the plants or water them, I make sure that they are sitting level, and I clean up any messes."

He nodded. Noah liked the fact that she was particular about her plants. She apparently showed them the same concern she showed to people. And she was organized. That was another positive trait. "Do you want to check every plant, every little pot?"

"I don't think I will need to." She pointed a slim finger at one section of begonias. "Only those two appear to have been disturbed."

"You don't think a customer simply picked up the pots and then plopped them back, leaving a mess?"

"That's always a possibility, but I don't think so. I always give the place a once-over before I leave, and I'm pretty *gut* at sensing when something isn't quite right. I didn't clean up last night because I wanted all evidence intact." Christina scooted closer to the flowers. She gently poked around in the dirt of one of the little pots.

Noah peered over her shoulder but didn't dare stick one of his big, clumsy fingers in a pot. He certainly didn't want to risk uprooting a plant or snapping a stem. That would be a sure way to put him on Christina's bad side—a place he definitely did not want to be.

~

Even though Noah stood close enough for his breath to tickle the back of her neck, Christina managed to keep her hands steady. Her plants grounded her—at least for the moment. She lovingly patted the soil back in place around the begonia in the first little container. She brushed the soil spilled on the shelf into her hand and sprinkled it into the pot. "Nothing there, as far as I can tell. Maybe my imagination has been working overtime. I'm sorry if I've led you on a wild goose chase."

"Hey, I *chose* to be here. You didn't ask me to *kumm*."

"If you want to be on your way to work, that's fine. I'll be okay."

"I'm in this for the long haul. Let's make sure the rest of the flowers don't harbor any surprises."

Christina inched over slightly to examine the next pot. Several little pink blossoms bent at unnatural angles. They would probably soon wither and turn brown. Poor *bopplin*. She might be considered a bit crazy, but she did think of her plants as her offspring. They had been entrusted to her care, and she did her best to keep them flourishing. She would return in a little while to snip off the broken blossoms. She didn't want to pinch them off with her fingers lest she do further harm to the plant.

Something wasn't right. Her nerves prickled. Her fingers shook. She flexed and extended them a couple of times to try to steady them.

"What's wrong?" Noah's voice, barely a whisper, let her know he picked up on her tension.

"I'm not sure, but something doesn't seem quite right."

"Do you want me to check this one?" He shuffled a little closer until he nearly touched her.

"I'm okay." She was as okay as she could be with her heart thumping at twice its normal speed. It must be due to the anxiety over what might be in this pot, not the fact that Noah stood so close that he was almost pressed against her back. *Concentrate on the task at hand, Christina. Don't even think that if you turned around you could lay your head against his chest.* Was his heart dancing as wildly as hers was doing at this very instant?

She forced her focus back on the little plant. She didn't want to uproot it. Carefully, Christina poked an index finger in the barely moist soil. Nothing. Her imagination must really have been running wild. She inched her finger around the pot, gently probing the soil. Just before she gave up, her finger encountered a foreign object. She had to dig a little deeper to extract whatever hid farther down in the dirt.

"What is it?"

Noah must be extra intuitive. She didn't think she had gasped or flinched, yet he knew she had made some sort of discovery. Amazing. It was almost as if they thought the same thoughts and experienced the same emotions. "I'm not sure, but there is something in here."

Christina used her left hand to stabilize the begonia while her right index finger continued to probe the soil. As gently as possible so as not to damage the delicate roots, she wiggled her finger back and forth until she brought the object to the surface. "It's a key." She pulled it from the pot and wiped off the dirt. "It's too small to go in a house lock or a car lock, ain't so?" She handed the little silver key to Noah.

While he studied the key, Christina tamped the soil back down around the begonia and snatched a scrap of hot-pink paper from among the leaves. Black squiggles that almost looked like letters had been scribbled on the paper. What was that doing there? Why would someone be so rude as to discard trash in a flowerpot? Disgusting! She crumpled the paper and stuffed it in a pocket to throw away later. Should she check other pots for foreign objects?

"I believe you're right about the key. Maybe it goes to one of those lockboxes or a jewelry box or something small."

"Why would someone hide a key in one of my plants? If someone bought that begonia, the key would be gone forever. Do you think the person who planted the key dropped the penknife?"

"That's entirely possible. It would be awfully coincidental to find two strange objects in the same location."

"I wonder when the person put the key there. It must have been the day before I found that poor man. I didn't notice that the plants looked different until after that." A tremor involuntarily traversed her entire body.

Noah placed the key in her empty hand and held onto it for a moment. "Your hand is ice cold, and it's already eighty degrees outside."

"Sometimes my hands do that when I get nervous about something."

"Are you nervous?"

"Well, sort of. Not about being here. It's the little memory flashes that set off my heebie-jeebies."

He squeezed her hand. "Do you want to dig in the other pots?"

"I don't think so. None of the others look like they were tampered with. Only the first two did." Christina reluctantly pulled her hand from Noah's and the little sense of warmth and security vanished. "What should I do with this key—and with the knife and trowel? Should I notify the police? Do you think these things are related to their case?"

"I don't know. I can't see how, though. You said that man had never been in your shop, so he couldn't have left the key and knife."

"I don't remember him ever being in here. I suppose it's entirely possible he could have *kumm* in when I was outside talking to a delivery truck driver."

"Did you get any deliveries day before yesterday?"

Christina tapped her chin and wrinkled her brow. "Let me think. It seems that when a person has had a shock, the brain gets a bit fuzzy."

"I would imagine that is normal. Take your time."

She snapped her fingers. "Shortly after noon, one of my suppliers delivered pots and canning jars. There are lots of women buying canning supplies here so they don't have to go all the way into town to the grocery store or the hardware store. But that was the day before I found that man."

"Who watched the shop while you were out with the driver?"

"*Mamm* had stopped by at lunchtime with Sallie and Grace."

"Your *mamm* would have noticed anything strange, wouldn't she?"

"Probably. Unless she'd gotten distracted by the girls, and believe me, that's easy to do. Those two are always into something."

Noah chuckled. "I know my own little *bruders* and *schweschders* can find all sorts of mischief to get them into trouble."

"Now that I think about it, the day before the man—it's funny how my life has become 'before the man' and 'after the man.'" She paused a moment to swipe at an unexpected tear.

"It won't always be that way, Christy."

Ach! There was that nickname again. She loved the sound of it on his lips. "I hope you're right." She tried clearing her throat to swallow the sudden lump that threatened to choke her. "Anyway, what I started to say was that on the day before the commotion, I didn't get to do my usual check before leaving the shop. I had a late customer, and Annie had been regaling me with the plot of the latest novel she'd been reading. By the time I rang up the customer, Annie had flipped the sign on the door and practically tugged me outside, still talking, mind you."

Noah burst out laughing. "I can certainly believe that. I think that girl could distract the bishop from his sermon. I don't know if I've ever met anyone who chatters so much. She drones on even more than Bishop Micah when he gets carried away. It will have to be a special fellow who gets up the nerve to court her."

Would he be that person? Christina should defend her *freind.* "Annie isn't all that bad."

"If you say so. I wonder how many people can get beyond her incessant talking to find that out."

"She doesn't always talk so much."

Noah cocked an eyebrow and gave Christina a doubtful look. "Really?"

"You have to give her a chance."

"Does she ever give anyone else a chance to get a word in edgewise, or are all of her conversations totally one-sided?"

"She listens too. Otherwise, it would be hard to be *freinden.*"

"I'll have to take your word for that."

Did that mean he hadn't any intention of pursuing a relationship with Annie? Christina's heart did a little happy dance. *You should be ashamed of yourself. You know that Annie has set her sights on Noah.* That nagging little voice cropped up from some dark corner of her mind only to be hushed by an incoming thought. *Why did Annie suddenly develop a king-sized crush when she knows of my interest in Noah?*

"Does she stop in here every day?"

"Not every day. Some days her *onkle* lets her leave his produce business early."

"I can't imagine why!" Noah's lips twitched as if he tried to hold back his laughter.

Christina giggled. "Be nice, Noah."

"Okay. Forget I said that. Does she show up here most days, then?"

"Not usually on Wednesday or Friday. Those seem to be her *onkle*'s busiest days, so she stays longer and then goes straight home."

"I'll have to remember that."

His words had been muffled, but Christina deciphered them just fine. Did that mean Noah thought about dropping by on the days Annie wouldn't be here? *Don't get your hopes up. He probably enjoys a* gut *mystery as much as Annie does. Get back to the business at hand.* She gave the begonias a final glance. "Do you think I should hang onto the penknife and key in case someone *kumms* looking for them?

"That would probably be fine. You don't know when they were left here, so they most likely aren't related to the police officers' case. Just put them in a safe place out of sight, and please stay alert." He reached for her hand and squeezed it.

"Alert?"

"Be vigilant. Don't be too trusting of strangers. I really don't think you are in any danger, but be wary anyway. Okay?"

Christina could only nod. She couldn't be sure why Noah was so concerned, but her heart took that as a positive sign.

"I wouldn't want anything to happen to you."

His soft voice and sincere expression were almost Christina's undoing. "I-I'll be careful."

"*Gut*. Now I need to get to work, and you need to open for business."

"And I need to ask *Mamm* about the day she stopped into The Green Thumb."

Chapter Ten

Christina waited on customer after customer all day. It was a *gut* thing the canning supplies had arrived when they did. Amish and *Englisch* women who wanted to avoid the trip into town, or who didn't want to stand in long checkout lines, stopped in for jars, lids, salt, vinegar, and other preserving necessities. Other people visited the store to select hanging baskets of petunias or geraniums for their front porches or other assorted flowers to spruce up their yards. Christina ran from the greenhouse to the shop and back again more times than she could count.

Despite her frantic pace, her mind still took little side trips away from The Green Thumb. She kept wanting to reassure herself that the penknife and key were safely hidden away but never had the chance to check on them. Should she contact the deputies who had left her their cards? How would those two items, or the trowel, have anything to do with the crime? She couldn't fathom a connection, but that was their job, not hers. When she wasn't wrestling with ways to piece the clues together, ice-blue eyes peered into her soul. She didn't know what to do about that little hint of a crush that had grown way out of bounds.

It was early afternoon when Christina finally sank onto the stool and retrieved the peanut-butter-and-strawberry-jam sandwich from her lunch cooler. She had begun to feel woozy and wobbly, so the break came just in the nick of time. The bowl of oatmeal she'd eaten early that morning had long since abandoned her. If oatmeal stuck to the ribs as the old folks said, her ribs had pried it loose long ago. She licked the jam that had oozed onto her thumb and then ran her tongue over her lips. How nice it was to sit for a moment.

"It's not there!"

Ach! She'd forgotten the young *Englisch* woman who had wanted to browse in the greenhouse. Christina jumped to her feet and watched in dismay as her sandwich slid to the floor. Well, she wouldn't be finishing that. And she'd only nibbled a couple of bites of it too! At least she had packed an apple and some chocolate chip cookies. If all else failed, she could tear into one of Amelia's whoopie pies.

"Can I help you find something?" She rubbed a paper napkin across her lips in case her tongue had missed a glob of jam.

"The pink begonias!"

The girl looked about ready to burst into tears. Over begonias! Christina knew she had sold begonias earlier. Pink ones. White ones. Red ones. Variegated ones. But she should have plenty left in the greenhouse. If by some chance there weren't any begonias there, she would check the bigger greenhouse behind the shop.

Christina snatched the ruined sandwich off the concrete floor and threw it into the metal trash can next to the counter. She hurried around to stand beside the *Englisch* girl who towered over her. "I'm sure there must be pink begonias in the greenhouse. I don't think I sold all of them today."

She glanced at the panic-stricken face and wondered at the girl's extreme reaction. The *Englischer's* huge emerald-green eyes clouded with tears. She swiped at them with the back of one hand, setting the long, dark curls framing her small, heart-shaped face into motion.

"Let me check for you." Christina scurried away without waiting for a reply. Was the girl always so sensitive, or was she simply being overdramatic for effect?

As Christina figured, an assortment of begonias remained, although there were bare spots on the shelves where flowers that had been purchased once sat. "Ma'am, there are pink begonias here. I can check my other greenhouse if you don't want any of these."

The girl shuffled to the greenhouse entrance and stared at Christina. "Did you move some pink begonias that were in here to your other greenhouse?"

"*Nee.* Uh, no. I always bring plants from that greenhouse in here whenever I run low."

"Oh no!" The girl turned a whiter shade of pale than she already was, slapped a hand across her mouth, and burst into tears. She ran from the shop before Christina could recover from her shock and make her way to the door.

"Wait! Please!" Christina rushed outside in time to see the strange lady peel away in a small, blue car, leaving a cloud of dust behind her. She watched until it disappeared from sight. "I've never seen anything so bizarre in all my life." She shook her head, unsure what to make of a woman so distraught over pink begonias when there were plenty of them available for her to choose from.

Christina watched for a moment longer to make sure the woman, who looked to be about her own age, didn't return or that other customers hadn't pulled into the parking lot. With the coast clear, at least for the moment, she could try to fish her apple from the lunch cooler. *Try not to drop anything this time, Christina.* With the way things had been going lately, she'd probably bite into a worm. Ew! That image was almost enough to make her toss the apple back into the cooler. Her rumbling stomach pooh-poohed that idea, though.

Taking a tentative bite of the Rome apple, Christina hurried into the greenhouse. Before swallowing, she studied the apple to make sure nothing wiggled. Okay. Everything appeared normal. At least with the apple. Something gnawed at the fringes of her memory. Something had been not quite right in the greenhouse. "Something besides that woman," she whispered to the plants.

Christina glanced in both directions as she made her way past the geraniums, dianthus, petunias, and vegetable plants. The peculiarity she sensed wasn't with any of those. At the back of the greenhouse, she stopped short. Something was definitely amiss with the begonias. Only the pink ones. Why were they all cockeyed and out of place? Had the woman been looking for a certain number of leaves or blooms? Maybe she was superstitious and had a lucky number or something. Some people had odd notions. Or could she have been looking for something else?

Quickly, Christina set the plants aright and jogged out to the front of the store to make sure no one had entered. Suddenly, the apple lost its appeal. She'd toss it outside later for the raccoons or deer that might venture out in the evening. She slid her hand under the counter and felt around for the little box she had found to house the knife and key. Surely it was still there. She hadn't seen anyone prowling around behind the counter. *You also didn't see anyone leave anything in the greenhouse either.*

Her heart pounded so hard that she wouldn't have been one bit surprised to see it leap from her chest and dance around on the counter. She scooted over a little and swept her hand back and forth. There! Her hand made contact with the box. Christina blew out the breath that she didn't realize she'd been holding until that very moment. She drew the box out and peeked inside. *Jah.* The penknife and key rested inside, safe and sound. At the slam of a car door, she thrust the box back into its hiding place and struggled to remove the pucker that tightened her brow before greeting her customer.

~

Like most Thursdays, Annie poked her head inside The Green Thumb at five o'clock. Christina still had an hour before she closed and wasn't at all sure she could endure her *freind's* chatter that long. The day had been trying and tiring, and while she loved the red-haired girl who was leaning on the checkout counter, her nerves were near the snapping point.

"How was your day?" Annie pried herself from her leaning post and shuffled around to plop on the stool behind the counter.

"Busy. And it isn't quite over yet." Christina suppressed a heavy sigh for fear Annie would demand an explanation.

"Too busy to eat, I see." Annie pointed to the trash can where the sandwich lay and picked up the apple with only one bite missing.

"I dropped the sandwich on the floor."

"I'd have wiped it off and eaten it."

"Yuck! You would not!"

"What's a few germs?"

Christina's hand flew to her belly. "I think I'm going to be sick."

Annie rolled her eyes. "Did you drop the apple too?"

"*Nee.* I guess I got distracted."

"I never get too distracted to eat, which is why I'm a lot bigger than you are."

"You are also a lot taller."

"So are you saying I carry my weight well?"

Christina laughed. "*Nee*, silly. I only meant that you should be heavier because you're taller. You are proportioned exactly right."

Annie smiled. "I suppose you've redeemed yourself." She held the apple out. "Are you going to eat this?"

"*Nee*, I'm going to throw it outside for any critter that wants it."

"You haven't eaten anything other than a bite of a sandwich and a nibble off an apple?"

"It appears that way."

Annie shook her head and clucked her tongue. "What am I going to do with you? What's the saying? All work and *nee* play makes for a dull person—or something like that?"

"I'm *supposed* to be working, not playing, so if that makes me dull, so be it."

"You aren't dull, but you are supposed to eat lunch, even if you are working."

Christina didn't mention that her stomach had been so tied in knots that food would never be able to work its way through. It would be best not to involve Annie in the strange occurrences at The Green Thumb, even though her *friend* would enjoy the mystery. Christina's mind had never turned to food in between customers. She'd stayed busy straightening the plants and rearranging baked goods to make room for new treats. Amelia and Marjorie both brought in fresh items on Friday for the weekend shoppers, so both would stop in sometime the next day.

"Are you okay, Stina?"

"Sure. Why?"

"You seem distracted."

"I'm just thinking. Tomorrow, I should get in more cookies and brownies or whatever the ladies bake, and I want to make sure I have room for them." *That was a lame excuse, Christina. Annie knows when you get stuff in. She knows you never fret over where to put things.* She could only hope Annie didn't dig deeper, as she was wont to do.

"Are you expecting more than usual?"

That hope just flew out the open door. "I don't think so, but you never know what sort of baking frenzy Amelia or Marjorie might get in."

"Marjorie, maybe. But I don't know how Amelia has time to do anything. Doesn't she have those *Englisch kinner* most days on top of her own three?"

"Mennonite. They are Mennonites. Amelia has them while their *daed* works. He's a widower, you know. I think Amelia understands what he's going through and wants to help."

"As long as she doesn't get too involved with him."

Christina didn't want to get into a lengthy discussion about Amelia, but at least the topic sidetracked Annie. Christina liked the young widow very much and believed that she used *gut* judgment. Having lost a spouse herself, Amelia could certainly offer support to those poor *mudderless* girls and their *daed*.

"Are you ready to go yet?"

Christina glanced at the big wall clock. "It's only five thirty."

"Do you honestly think you'll have a mad rush in the next half hour?"

"Even if I have only one customer, I need to be here for that person. That's what my sign says."

"You're so dedicated."

"I'm sure your *onkle* doesn't shut down early, ain't so?"

"Are you kidding? Onkle Henry wouldn't want to miss out on earning a single dime!"

"Annie! Shame on you!"

"I'm only being truthful."

"Your *onkle* has a big family to feed."

"Not any bigger than most. And don't look so shocked, Stina. You, as well as everyone else, know my *onkle*'s tendency to be, uh, stingy."

"He pays you for working there, doesn't he?"

"*Jah*, but he hands me my money most begrudgingly. I think he'd rather have only his own *kinner* work there. Then he wouldn't have to dole out one cent of his money to anyone."

"It was kind of him to hire you, then, ain't so?"

"He only hired me because my *daed* is his older *bruder*. At least I don't have to go there during the winter."

"You used to only complain once in a while. Now it's almost daily. I gather you like it there less and less."

"You could say that."

"What would you rather do?"

"Stay home, take care of my own *kinner*, and read books."

"If you were home taking care of little ones, I doubt you'd have much time to read books."

"I'd find time."

"You also have to find a husband before you can do any of that."

"*Jah*, there is that little flaw in my plan, but I'm working on correcting that."

Christina gave her a questioning look. "Do tell. You've been holding out on me."

Annie swung her legs so furiously that Christina feared the stool would topple over. Annie raised an index finger to her mouth and nibbled on a nail. "Sadly, there isn't anything to tell—yet. But I'm hoping..." Her voice trailed off as she stared out the window at some distant point.

Christina's heart thunked as it dropped to her toes. Was her *freind* talking about Noah? Was he the fellow she'd pinned her hopes on? Unless it happened to be her own wishful thinking clouding reality, Christina didn't believe that Noah had any romantic leanings toward Annie. In fact, he seemed to want to avoid her altogether. "Wh-what are you hoping?"

"Huh?" Annie swung her head around to look at Christina. Her *kapp* strings sailed around her head, and that errant red curl fluttered across her cheek.

"You said you were hoping but didn't finish your statement. Have you been sneaking away from singings without my noticing?" Usually, they left the gatherings at the same time, but that didn't mean Annie couldn't meet up with someone later.

"*Nee*. Not yet. I'm hoping a certain someone will ask to take me home—if he'd show up consistently."

Could her heart drop any lower than her toes? Now Christina was sure Annie referred to Noah. He didn't always attend singings and often left early when he did put in an appearance. Not with a girl, though, as far as she knew. Was there a way to discourage Annie without looking like a jealous rival? She wasn't that, was she? To be honest, she cared about Noah, but at the same time, she didn't want to see her *freind* hurt in any way. And she seemed to be heading for pain. "Maybe you should check out the fellows who do attend regularly. I've seen a few eyeing you from time to time."

"Really? Who?"

The crunch of automobile tires on gravel spared Christina from answering. "A customer. Someone made it just in time." She smoothed wisps of her own hair and barely resisted the urge to sigh in relief. Maybe Annie wouldn't want to wait and would head home while Christina waited on her customer. Maybe pigs would fly.

Chapter Eleven

Noah's whistle fizzled and hung in the air. The second bicycle next to The Green Thumb belonged to Annie Wenger. He was as sure of that as he was sure the sky was blue. *Ach!* He smacked his own forehead. Today was Thursday, not Friday. Christina had told him Annie generally stopped off at her shop every day except Wednesday and Friday.

He'd been so looking forward to seeing Christina again. Thoughts of her invaded his consciousness all day, interspersed with the problem-solving involved with his repair jobs. He'd never experienced such thought interruptions before. He searched his memory to be sure. *Nee.* He'd never been plagued by images of any girl in the past. Christy—as he liked to think of her—wasn't "any girl." A person with those big, silver eyes could never be considered ordinary. And she was so little that he wanted to wrap her in his arms to protect her from all possible harm.

Crazy! That's what he was. Maybe he had developed some strange malady. He took one hand off the handlebar and laid the back of it against his forehead. It felt cool. He didn't have a raging fever, so he must not be having hallucinations. Maybe he had some sort of inner ear problem that messed with his equilibrium and all his thought processes. He'd never heard of such a thing, but it was possible. Wasn't it?

Noah debated whether he should stop at The Green Thumb or keep pedaling toward home. He didn't really want to subject himself to more of Annie's unwanted attention. She was nice enough, he supposed, but she wasn't right for him. Could he find some tolerant fellow to nudge in her direction? *The man would have to have nerves of steel and the patience of a saint—or maybe simply be hard of hearing.* Noah almost chuckled aloud, but he knew he should be ashamed of himself for his unkind thoughts. A person couldn't help what popped into his head, though.

Noah pumped the pedals harder and faster when he heard voices at the shop's front door. But a car in the lot meant Christy wouldn't be leaving. The voice must belong to a customer on the way out, or maybe Annie decided to go on home. He fought not to get his hopes up. Just the same, he stopped near a copse of trees to observe the action. He needed to catch his breath after his heavy exertion anyway.

"I'll see you soon, Stina. I'd better take your advice and head home."

Noah would wait in the shade until he could be certain Annie truly left and didn't circle back for some reason. It looked like his patience had paid off. If he believed in luck, which he didn't, he would say this was his lucky day. Now he would be able to talk to the silver-eyed girl for at least a few minutes and then make sure she got safely on her way.

~

Christina rang up her customer's purchase and counted out the change. Mentally, she adjusted her day's sales since she had already tallied them. She had always been thankful she had a quick mind for figures. As soon as she bid the folks farewell, she flipped the sign on the door to "closed" and prepared to lock up for the evening.

"Wait! Christy, wait!"

A smile tugged at her lips. Only one person called her Christy. She paused with a hand on the door and looked around for the owner of that deep voice. Where was he that she could hear his voice but not see his face?

A moment later, she spotted him rounding the corner from the back of the building. Whatever was he doing back there?

"I was checking to make sure your shed was secure while you waited on your customer."

"I had already done that."

"So I discovered."

"How long have you been here?"

"Not long. I saw you had a straggler to wait on, so I decided to check out back."

"*Danki.* I'm about ready to call it a day. Do you want to *kumm* inside while I finish up?"

"Sure."

Christina heard the heavier footsteps behind her but kept facing forward. She'd never be able to keep him at arm's length for Annie's sake if she looked into those blue eyes. Fell into them would be more accurate.

"I'll lock the door behind me."

"Okay." She usually checked the door several times before leaving for the day. It was just some quirky little obsessive thing she did. She would have to trust Noah to do the job and not doubt the place was secure. After all, she did hear the click of the lock.

"Christina, I actually have a little confession to make."

She whirled around and almost collided with the tall, young man. She hadn't realized that he had stepped so close. She took several baby steps backward. "What kind of confession?" What could he possibly need to get off his mind that concerned her in any way?

He looked down at the floor that she'd recently swept. "Well, I was sort of here a little earlier than I said."

"Sort of? How can you be 'sort of' someplace? Either you're there or you're not."

"Right."

She felt the pucker in her brow. Whatever was he trying to say? She stared at his cheek rather than directly into those eyes as she waited for him to continue.

He looked up but avoided eye contact the same as she did. "I pedaled here as fast as I could when I got off work in the hope of catching you here. But I forgot today was Thursday until I got closer."

"Is there a problem with Thursday?"

"Not usually. But you told me Annie normally stopped in most days except for Wednesday and Friday. When I saw the bike by the building, it hit me that today was Thursday."

"You assumed the bike belonged to Annie."

"I was pretty sure. I saw it the other day."

"And you didn't want to confront her for some reason. Is that what you're trying to say?" Now she did gaze into his eyes.

"Guilty. I'm not trying to be mean or anything. I didn't feel like fending off her attention or watching her eyelids flutter."

Christina burst out laughing.

"You aren't mad at me?"

"Why would I be mad at you?"

"She's your *freind*, but I'm really not trying to offend her or you."

"Annie has always been my *best freind*, but I know she can sometimes be, uh, overbearing."

"Bordering on annoying."

"That too." Christina laughed again, and this time Noah joined in with a hearty chuckle.

"Annie likes you, you know." Christina clapped a hand across her mouth. She hadn't meant to allow that tidbit to slip out, but surely Noah had gathered that for himself. Just the same, Annie would never speak to her again if she knew Christina had voiced that thought. "Oops! Forget I said that."

Noah's lips twitched. "Said what?"

"I don't suppose that came as any great shock to you anyway given the peculiar way she's been acting."

"Not really."

"She has been behaving a bit out of character, even for her. Still, I shouldn't have said that."

"A mere slip of the tongue. But now that the *secret* is out, how do I discourage her without hurting her feelings?"

"You might have to be blunt. Sometimes Annie gets hung up on a notion and lets her imagination chase away her common sense."

"I don't want to be rude." His face suddenly brightened as if a sudden thought cheered him. "Maybe you could talk to her."

"That would not be a *gut* idea. I don't want to be in the middle." Her tongue almost betrayed her again. It almost revealed that Annie would accuse her of wanting Noah's attention for herself. To keep control of her thoughts and words, she had better occupy her mind with something else. Christina pulled out her record book and adjusted the day's sales total after that last customer.

"I can see that would put you in an awkward position. I suppose I'll have to think of a way to dissuade Annie myself."

"You mean if you accidentally show up where she is before you have a chance to backpedal?"

"*Jah.*"

Noah looked so ashamed that Christina couldn't help but laugh. "I'm sure you'll do your best not to be in that situation."

"I was successful today, but that doesn't mean I will always be able to escape. I probably should have a speech prepared in case I'm caught off guard. I mean, what if she didn't ride her bike? I wouldn't have any way of knowing she was here."

"Just be honest, Noah. That's always best." Christina put her book away and met his gaze. She hadn't had much experience with *buwe* since she'd never had one call on her or even ask to take her home after a singing. She always figured none of them wanted a girl who had a business to run. At least, she didn't think it was because her appearance frightened them. After all, little *kinner* never ran away from her shrieking in terror. Maybe she was simply incredibly boring, so the fellows didn't bother with her.

"Hey, where did you go?"

"What?"

"I was agreeing that honesty was the best, but you disappeared somewhere."

"Oh. Sorry." She certainly couldn't relate that little jaunt her brain took, but she needed to offer him some explanation. "I had the most unusual customer today. I'm still trying to figure it all out."

"Can you tell me about it?"

"Sure. I'd be glad to get another opinion, but I really need to start home now."

"I'll ride with you. You can tell me on the way."

Christina glanced at the front door. She wanted to run over and check the lock for herself, but she didn't want Noah to believe she didn't trust him.

"Go ahead."

"Go ahead what?"

"Check the door. I know you want to."

"Is mind reading one of your talents?"

"Not really, but I can tell you're used to doing everything yourself in your own way. And I'm almost certain you will toss and turn all night if you don't check that lock the way you do every evening."

Christina giggled. "I didn't know I was so transparent."

"You're a business person and a *gut* one. All successful store owners have an agenda they adhere to."

"What you really mean is we all have quirks."

Noah laughed. "You won't hurt my feelings by checking the door. Go satisfy your need to ensure that it's locked, and then we'll be on our way."

Christina had to do it. Noah had her pegged correctly. She scurried to the door and examined the lock. "It isn't that I don't trust you," she threw over her shoulder.

"I know."

She heard the amusement in his voice, so she knew she had not angered him.

"Is everything all right?"

"Fine."

They exited the back door, and Christina only checked that lock twice instead of her usual four times. She cast a worried glance toward the shed.

"I promise that it's locked, but if you'll rest easier by examining it again for yourself, by all means, go right ahead."

"That's all right."

"Are you sure?"

"Absolutely. Let's go."

Noah offered a smile that would melt a heavy frost on a subzero February morning. Christina's heart nearly dissolved. Her knees turned to jelly. She hoped she could convince her muscles to power the bicycle. She plopped her bag in the bike basket, situated herself on the seat, and glanced over her shoulder to make sure Noah was ready.

They pedaled briskly on the main road where commuters zoomed by them in a hurry to get home or to wherever their destination might be. Once they turned onto a side road lined with Mennonite farms and *Englisch* homes, they slowed their pace a bit. Christina's racing heart began to settle as she breathed without panting and gasping.

"Tell me about your strange visitor." Since traffic was scarce on this road, Noah pushed forward to ride beside Christina.

"It was the strangest thing. This young *Englisch* woman got upset to the point of tears over begonias."

"Let me guess. Were they pink begonias?"

"They were. I had sold begonias earlier in the day and offered to bring her some from the big greenhouse if she didn't like what she saw, but she ran out before I could even make a move. Do you think she was looking for the key or the knife or both?"

"That's very likely since she was so upset."

"I suppose there's nothing I can do unless she visits again. I don't know her name or anything about her. I only know she drove a small, blue car."

"*Jah*, your hands are tied at this point." Noah slowed his pace and fell in behind Christina as a car approached. As soon as it passed, he sped up to ride beside her again. "You don't think the woman was dangerous, do you?"

"She didn't threaten me or show me a weapon or anything."

"Sometimes people aren't mentally stable and that can make them do bad things."

"I didn't get the sense that the woman was a threat in any way. I didn't break out in goose bumps. My hair didn't stand on end. I didn't feel scared. Actually, I felt sorry for her. She seemed so distraught."

"Promise me that you'll be careful if she returns."

Christina shifted her gaze to look straight at Noah. The concern etched on his face almost made her swerve and crash into him. She couldn't recall ever seeing such an expression on anyone's face before, except perhaps her *mudder*.

He reached over and grabbed the handlebar of her bike to steady her. "I hope I didn't scare you. I'm not trying to do that. I don't want you to be hurt in any way, that's all."

"Oh."

Noah patted her arm before returning his hand to his own handlebar. "Will you be at the shop alone tomorrow?"

"Amelia and Marjorie usually stop in on Fridays to bring me fresh-baked items for the weekend. They generally stay around for a little while, especially Marjorie since she doesn't have any *kinner* with her."

"*Gut.* That makes me feel better."

Was that apprehension in his voice? Could Noah Zimmerman truly care about her, or was he simply a nice fellow who liked mysteries?

chairs at the same instant to sop up the mess and console the sniffling girl.

What seemed eons later, everyone trooped from the table, leaving Christina and her *mudder* to clean the kitchen. A mountain of plates, cups, and bowls waited to be washed, and the still-sticky table needed to be scrubbed more thoroughly. Weariness had already seeped into Christina's bones, but the day was not done yet. She snatched the dishcloth from the hook, squirted liquid soap into the big stainless-steel sink, and ran the water. Tiny bubbles floated in the air around her head. Her sigh made them scatter.

"Long day?" Ida picked up the thick dish towel and dried the plates Christina stacked in the drainer.

"Busy." Christina plunked a glass in the drainer and then turned to look at her *mudder*. "Do you remember a man entering the shop the last time you were there?"

"A man? That's pretty vague. Is there someone in particular you're thinking of?"

"I-I don't know him. It's..."

"Not an Amish man."

"*Nee.*"

Ida dropped the towel and nearly dropped the glass.

Christina reached out to catch it before it crashed to the floor and left a sudsy trail across the counter as she did so.

"Do you mean the man who was found in the shed?" Ida's voice had dropped to a whisper.

"I was wondering if he had *kumm* into the shop the day before. Maybe when I was outside with the delivery man."

"If I remember correctly, several customers milled about during the time you were outside, but I couldn't tell you who they were or what they looked like. Your *schweschders* nearly destroyed your jam-and-jelly shelf, so I got distracted. I had told them to dust, but that was like turning loose two bulls in a china shop."

"Oh."

"Why do you want to know?"

"I was trying to figure out if that man had been in the store before, if there was a reason he happened to be at my place."

"That's something you need to let the police determine. You answered their questions. That's all you need to do."

"*Jah*, but I've been thinking..."

"Well, stop! You don't need to think about that horrible day at all. Put it out of your mind." Ida clamped a hand on Christina's forearm. "I know that must have been awful for you, but you have to try to forget it and leave crime-solving to the police."

Christina nodded. She obviously wouldn't glean any more information from her *mudder*. And she'd only upset *Mamm* further if she described the strange customer who had visited earlier today. She knew she shouldn't get involved in any way. The *Englisch* had their own methods for investigating. What could a young Mennonite woman possibly uncover that seasoned lawmen could not? Still, the puzzle pieces nagged at her, begging her to assemble them into a complete picture.

~

Christina tried to sneak a peek out the window every so often so she'd have a little advance warning if a small, blue car drove into the parking lot of The Green Thumb. Since her view was somewhat limited, she feared she would be in for a surprise despite her vigilance.

Her next visitor turned out to be someone totally different from the person she had anticipated. The clomp of heavy footsteps drew her attention from counting out her customer's change. A large shadow darkened the doorway. Deputy Gaines stepped aside and held the screen door for the woman carrying a huge azalea. Christina gulped. Was the man here to question her again?

"Good morning, Miss Brubacher."

"Hello." She hated that her voice wobbled just a little. Christina shouldn't be nervous or afraid. She hadn't done anything wrong. *Please don't let him make me rehash everything again. I don't want to keep reliving that nightmare.*

"I wanted to tell you the investigation has been wrapped up. We didn't find evidence of foul play. That means we don't believe a crime was committed."

Christina wanted to tell the man that she understood the meaning of "foul play." She had heard the term before. She read the local newspaper. Just because she was Plain, that didn't mean she lacked intelligence. She said nothing but simply nodded.

"I don't think you will have anything to worry about or fear."

Except a strange woman in a blue car. "That's *gut* to know." She couldn't let the deputy leave without trying to satisfy her curiosity at least a little. "Did that man die of natural causes? In my shed?"

"I will tell you since the investigation is over. It's in today's paper anyway. It was a drug overdose."

"In my shed? Why would he have gone in there?" The deputies hadn't found drugs in her shed, had they? Was someone stashing them there and using her building to take them? Would she be accused of helping them or of hiding something?

"He apparently used the drugs elsewhere. He was probably confused and stumbled in there. We didn't find evidence of drugs in your shed, and there was no evidence that he had been injured."

Christina swallowed her sigh of relief. At least her shed was in the clear. Where did that trowel with the dark stain *kumm* from? She supposed it could have been some kind of mud or clay stain, but it didn't look like any dirt she'd ever gotten on her tools before. "The poor man must have been very troubled."

"You never know with drug addicts. This guy wasn't one of the regulars we haul in. In fact, everyone thought he was an upstanding, straight-arrow kind of person. I mean..."

"I understand."

"You can't always tell what lurks beneath someone's surface."

"I suppose not."

"Anyway, I wanted you to know everything is over so you can breathe easier."

"*Danki.* I mean, thank you."

The big man rapped his knuckles on the counter. "You have a good day, Miss Brubacher, and don't hesitate to call us if you need us."

Christina nodded. "I appreciate your stopping by to give me the news. Have a *gut* day."

"Say, can I grab a couple of those whoopie pies? They're the best things ever." He reached into a hip pocket for his wallet.

"Certainly. They're on the house."

"Thanks. My compliments to the baker."

Christina smiled. "I'll be sure to tell her."

Her smile fled as soon as the deputy cleared the doorway. Something didn't seem to fit. Why would a man everyone believed to be a fine person suddenly die of a drug overdose? How did the key, the knife, and the dark-haired young woman fit in? She had to obtain a copy of today's paper to read the article.

~

"Hello! Christina?"

Only Marjorie or Annie would yell for her as soon as they stepped inside the shop. The little bell attached to the top of the screen door hadn't even finished jingling. Christina hurried through the greenhouse, brushing dirt from her hands and dress as she made her way toward the front of the shop.

"There you are."

"Hello, Marjorie. I was pruning a few plants."

"Someone could have walked right in and carried the whole place off and you wouldn't have known it." The older woman clucked her tongue.

"I can hear the bell when the door opens."

"You didn't hear me."

"I most certainly did. You just didn't give me time to get out here before you started hollering."

"Oh. I guess I did call out as soon as I got inside."

"Make that before you even got completely inside. I heard your voice before the door clicked closed."

"Okay. Okay. I can't help it if I'm a mother hen. Did the police car I met on the road leave from here?"

"What makes you think that?"

"Jumpy nerves, I guess."

"Actually, Deputy Gaines did stop by to tell me that the investigation was over and that I should be perfectly safe here."

"Did he now? Well, what did they find out?"

"He said there was an article in today's newspaper."

Marjorie plunked one bag down on the counter and let another one slide to the floor. "It just so happens I snatched the paper from the box on my way here." She rummaged through the larger bag on the floor. "Here, let's read the article." She spread the paper out on the counter. "It's right here on the first page."

Christina cringed at the headline. *Drug Overdose Victim Discovered in Mennonite Establishment.* She did not welcome that kind of attention being drawn to herself or her business. Would people stay away out of fear or disgust, or would they flock here out of curiosity? Neither would be *gut*. Since she wasn't tall enough to read over Marjorie's shoulder, she peered through the crook of her *freind's* arm.

"I wonder what makes a decent person take drugs?" Marjorie wagged her head. "Unless he wasn't such a *gut* person after all."

"The article says folks all thought highly of him."

"True, but they only interviewed his *freinden*. They certainly wouldn't say anything bad about him."

"Maybe, but I have a feeling in here that he was a *gut* person." Christina tapped her chest.

Marjorie patted Christina's cheek. "You always like to believe the best about people."

"Shouldn't we all do that?"

"Probably. You're such a sweet person, though. I doubt you would know evil if it tapped you on the shoulder."

"Are you saying I'm too naïve or too gullible or too immature?"

"Never. A young woman who runs a successful business like this could not be any of those things. But you are very trusting and very optimistic. Those are fine characteristics to have. Much better than being old, grumpy, and pessimistic, like me."

Christina laughed. "You are never grumpy, are rarely pessimistic, and are forever young."

"See what I mean? You never think ill of anyone."

"What did you bring today?" The conversation had grown too heavy. Christina strove for a lighter topic.

"I have all sorts of treats for your customers this weekend." Marjorie plunged her hands into the big bag and drew out loaves of applesauce bread, individual plastic baggies full of snickerdoodles, and lots of whoopie pies.

"These all look scrumptious."

"Let's hope they taste as *gut* as they look."

"I'm sure they will." Christina carried as many items as she could to her bakery shelves. Marjorie followed with her smaller bag. "Do you have more in there?"

"These are brownies and cookies from Amelia. I stopped to pick them up so she didn't have to drag all those *kinner* out."

"You are a very sweet person too."

Marjorie cackled. "I haven't been called sweet in about a hundred years."

The women chatted and laughed as they arranged the items on the shelves. Christina patted the last bag of cookies. "I think I'm well stocked for a busy Saturday."

~

Noah rocked on his stool and bit into a thick ham sandwich as he spread the newspaper on the counter in front of him. The stool tilted, almost throwing him to the hard, cement floor, and his teeth clamped down on his tongue as his eyes focused on the headlines. He gagged, coughed, and swigged water from the plastic bottle. He was pretty sure he swallowed a hunk of his tongue too. Had Christina seen the paper?

He dropped the sandwich onto the wax paper it had been wrapped in and hunched over to read more closely. Christina would be mortified to see mention of her business right there on the front page. Who could miss that bold headline and the picture beneath it? At least the photographer knew better than to snap a photograph of Christina. Noah hadn't spied anyone with a camera any of the times he'd been at The Green Thumb, but *Englischers* had all sorts of cameras these days. They could even take pictures with their phones. Maybe this picture had been taken after work hours since there weren't any people milling about.

Noah scanned the article and then went back to reread it more slowly. How odd. That a respected twenty-four-year-old man would so shock everyone by overdosing on drugs. And at Christina's place too! Why, the fellow was his own age. Didn't he have responsibilities, a job, a *fraa*, or anything to live for? Noah fingered his sandwich but left it on the paper. Lunch had suddenly lost its appeal.

The case had certainly been wrapped up fast. If the man had died from drugs and not been murdered, that would at least mean that Christina was safe at her shop. She shouldn't have anyone snooping around or threatening her. But what about the rest of the mystery? Who did that penknife belong to, and how did that key get planted in the begonia pot? If that trowel didn't belong to Christina—and Noah was certain she knew her own tools—then whose was it, and why was it in her shed?

The exact same questions must be running through Christina's mind. Knowing her, she'd be working hard at trying to fit the puzzle pieces together in between customers. He would certainly have a hard time concentrating this afternoon, so she would undoubtedly be struggling to do so. He needed to finish the time-consuming project he'd been working on and pedal like crazy to get to her shop before she closed. Maybe they could brainstorm together for at least a few minutes. Noah tossed his sandwich into his lunch box and flipped open the paper. There must be happy news somewhere!

Chapter Thirteen

The shop had been extremely busy for a Friday. Christina was grateful that Marjorie had stayed for a while after bringing in her items to sell. She even offered to get something from the shed for Christina. Even though Christina hadn't voiced her apprehension, Marjorie must have sensed her trepidation about entering the shed. Maybe her body had stiffened or an expression of stark fear had crossed her face. Whatever it was, Marjorie honed in on it immediately. Christina refused Marjorie's kind offer, though. She had to go back into the shed alone sometime, so it might as well have been then while someone was within hollering distance in case she panicked.

Thankfully, the jaunt to the shed had gone well. Christina retrieved what she needed and deliberately avoided looking in the direction of that foreign trowel. Not knowing what to do with it meant that it would stay right where it was.

Customers continued to flow through the shop even after Marjorie left. Christina flitted from one area to another, waiting on customers at the counter, helping others select a plant, and giving advice to folks who were trying to doctor ailing flowers. Staying busy was a very *gut* thing. Not only did it keep her mind occupied, but it assured adequate income to hold her over during the winter months.

Poinsettia sales at Christmas and lilies at Easter were great, but the months in-between could be lean. Christina's dried flower and herb business still flourished during those slower times, but those items weren't nearly as popular as the flowers and plants folks wanted in the spring and summer to spruce up their yards and gardens.

A quick swig from her water bottle after ringing up the customer who had been milling about for a while was just what her parched throat had been begging for. She swallowed quickly and stashed her bottle when the sound of tires on gravel heralded the arrival of another customer. If this person bought cookies or breads too, she might have to bake when she got home. Marjorie's and Amelia's treats had sold quickly. And here she thought they would last through Saturday.

Christina looked up to find a petite, dark-haired woman standing in the doorway. Now she wished she had let Marjorie stay longer instead of sending her home to get her own work done. How could her throat suddenly be desert dry after guzzling water a mere minute ago? She tried to brace herself for the woman's hysterics if history repeated itself.

The woman's eyes darted around the entire perimeter of the store. Was she looking for someone or something? The lovely green eyes she finally turned on Christina looked sadder than sad. Christina cleared her throat, but her voice still came out raspy. "C-can I help you with something?"

The girl crossed to the counter. Slightly taller than Christina, she only had to look down a tiny bit to stare into Christina's eyes. "I want to apologize for my behavior yesterday."

Taken aback, Christina struggled to find words. "I-it's quite all right."

"No. I'm sure it was frightening or at least unsettling. I bet you don't have crazy people running around in your store very often. Maybe never." She forced a little laugh that was devoid of any merriment.

Again, Christina hesitated. She didn't want to say something that might set the woman off again. She looked perfectly calm at the moment, but she could be mentally unbalanced and change in an instant. Christina coaxed her lips into a tremulous smile but still did not know how to respond. The silence, though brief, was almost painful. Christina had to say something before her nerves snapped. She forced her fingers to release the edge of her apron that she had unknowingly been clutching. "You seemed very upset."

"That's putting it mildly!" The girl smiled a dazzling smile.

She was quite pretty with her dainty, heart-shaped face framed by long, dark curls that practically begged to be touched. What must it be like to have a headful of spiral curls hanging loose around your shoulders?

Christina had pinned her hair beneath a *kapp* for as long as she could remember, the same as every other Plain female. The only individuality that ladies in her community had was the color dress they chose to wear that day and whether it would be a solid color fabric or one with a small print. Christina actually liked things that way. One person was not any better than another. All were equal. "Is there something I can help you with?"

"Oh, I hope so."

Christina started to scoot around the counter to help the young woman. Would she want to see pink begonias again? "I have more..."

"It's not about flowers, though you do have some beautiful ones here."

Christina's mouth dropped open. What on earth could she possibly help this stranger with if it wasn't plants? She stared and waited for an explanation. The beautiful emerald eyes filled with tears, and Christina feared another outburst was forthcoming.

"M-my name is Jill Sheridan." She stopped speaking and sniffed. She fished around in her jeans pocket and produced a tissue to swipe at her eyes and nose.

Christina continued to stare. Was the name supposed to ring a bell? She was certain she'd never met this lady prior to her frenzied search for pink begonias.

"M-my brother, Blake Sheridan, was the man you found in your shed."

Christina's knees threatened to buckle and her hands trembled so violently that she had to clasp them together. Her lungs seemed incapable of expanding. She would likely suffocate right on the spot. "I-I'm so sorry for your loss," she managed to squeak out. As inadequate as they were, the words came from Christina's heart. She couldn't imagine losing one of her *bruders* or *schweschders*. It was too awful a thing to ponder.

"Thank you." Jill dipped her head down. The long curls surrounded her face like a thick curtain.

Christina shuffled around to stand closer to the bereaved girl. She tentatively placed a hand on one of Jill's arms and hoped she wasn't being too forward. "How can I help you?"

"Can you show me where you found him?"

Christina sucked in a gasp. She had great difficulty going into that shed, so how was this girl going to handle it? "I, uh, don't think..." Thoughts would not turn into words.

"I'm sorry, Christina. I know this all must be very hard for you too."

"You know my name?"

"It was in that awful newspaper article."

"That's right." Christina had tried to erase that from her memory. If the article had been difficult for her to read, it must have been ten times harder for Jill. If the purpose of her previous visit to The Green Thumb had been to see where her *bruder* had been found, why did she wander the greenhouse and become hysterical over pink begonias? Christina nearly jumped out of her black athletic shoes at the girl's next words.

"My brother was not a drug addict!" Tears trickled down pale cheeks. Jill almost angrily flicked them away with the back of one hand. She must have realized that she had frightened Christina with her outburst. Her expression softened as she took one of Christina's hands. "I'm sorry. I didn't mean to raise my voice. I really am a quiet person—usually." She sniffed. "That newspaper article made my brother sound like a no-good drug addict."

"I'm sure he was a fine person." Christina didn't have a clue how to respond to Jill's words. She wanted to offer comfort or help but didn't quite know how to do that. All she could think to do was to listen and act as a sounding board if that's what the poor girl needed. She knew she would be upset if one of her siblings was wrongly accused of something.

"He was. Blake was the best big brother a person could have. He always stuck up for me. He encouraged my dreams and listened to me. He was there for me when no one else was."

Just like James was for Christina. "He sounds like a *wunderbaar bruder.*"

"He truly was. He would never use drugs. He was an addiction counselor, for Pete's sake, and he was a youth leader at church. Those teenagers looked up to him. I can't stand for them to believe he had been lying to them or was a hypocrite. Now he will be remembered as an addict who was mixed up with bad people, not as the caring, God-fearing man he was." Several more tears trickled down Jill's cheeks.

"I'm sure the people who knew him won't believe bad things about him." Christina hadn't any idea how *Englischers* thought, but for some reason she believed that Jill spoke the truth. She didn't get the impression that Jill simply shared a biased opinion.

"Will you help me clear my brother's name?"

"Me?" Christina pulled her hand away as if it had been bitten by a viper and jumped back several inches. "How could I possibly help?" What did she think a Mennonite girl would know about helping an *Englischer* with legal problems? The police made their report and closed the case. How could she help change things? Plain folks did not get involved in such matters.

"I think Blake might have left some clue here."

"Here? I'd never seen your *bruder* before that day." How could she discourage this bereft girl and get her out of The Green Thumb?

"Isn't it possible he could have come in when you were busy with other customers or out at your greenhouse or something?"

It didn't help matters that Christina had wondered that very same thing herself. "I-I suppose so."

"He could have left something here?"

"Why here of all places? What exactly are you looking for?"

Suddenly, the girl wilted before Christina's eyes. "I don't know, but I have a distinct feeling he was trying to tell me something. Maybe he knew something and was being threatened. Or maybe he was worried about my safety. I don't know." She wiped her nose and eyes again. "Our parents are gone. We only had each other."

Christina couldn't begin to imagine life without her parents or family. How would she feel if she only had James and he was suddenly taken from her? *I'd feel exactly like Jill.*

"What kind of clue led you to start searching here?"

Jill dug in her pocket and pulled out a slip of bright pink paper.

Christina gasped and reached for the counter to steady herself.

"You've seen something like this before!" Excitement overtook the despair on the girl's pale, little face, and the emerald eyes shimmered with hope mixed in with the tears.

"I-I don't know for sure."

Jill tugged on Christina's arm. "Please, you have to tell me why you reacted as you did." She laid the paper on the counter so that black squiggly lines were visible.

"Oh my!"

"What is it? Please talk to me. You have seen something like this before, haven't you?"

Christina could only nod. Still grasping the counter, she scooted over to reach the shelf. Should she show Jill everything she had stashed there? Her fingers brushed the scrap of paper all the way at the back. She eased it out. This could be simply a coincidence. A zillion people must have notepads with hot-pink paper. She smoothed it out on the counter with the black lines face up. Jill moved her paper next to it. The squiggles matched exactly.

"I was right to come here!" Jill flicked away another runaway tear. "Your paper looks exactly like this one I found in my mailbox."

"What do those lines mean? Do they have something to do with my business?" Was something illegal going on here that would get her into trouble and eventually close her shop? Christina couldn't bear that. She had never done anything to break a law. She ran an honest business and worked hard to be fair and courteous to all of her customers. She had never had a single complaint.

Jill pointed at the black marks. "These are actually letters."

Christina leaned down to see better. She shook her head. She couldn't distinguish anything legible. "What kind of letters?"

With one slender finger, Jill traced the first scrawl. "This is a *p* and this is a *b*. It's just in a fancy calligraphy script."

Christina squinted. "I see it now!" She couldn't believe she sounded as excited as if she'd discovered the cure for the common cold. And the marks on Jill's paper looked the same as the ones on the scrap of paper she had found.

Jill slid her finger over to the next pair of joined squiggles. "This is a *g* and this is a *t*. Do you see them?"

"*Jah*. I mean, yes. I do now. What do the letters stand for?"

"My brother knows—uh, knew—that I've always loved pink begonias. I have pots of them lining the entire balcony of my apartment. If I had a yard, I'd plant them everywhere. I don't know why I'm so fond of them. Maybe it's something from my childhood. Anyway, the *p* and *b* are for pink begonias. At least that's what I think."

"I like begonias too," Christina mumbled as she continued to stare at the pink papers. Suddenly, she clapped a hand over her mouth to keep from crying out. Although she had never fainted in her life, for the second time this week lightheadedness nearly rendered her unconscious. She whispered through her fingers, "Do the *g* and the *t* mean Green Thumb?"

Chapter Fourteen

"I believe so."

Christina dropped her hand to her side. "Why? What is going on? Why involve me and my shop?" She wanted to stomp her foot in frustration or cry out of fear that she would be accused of some wrongdoing.

"Probably because of the pink begonias."

"You could buy those at any *Englisch* nursery. Even the hardware store and discount stores sell flowers. Why here?"

"Maybe my brother felt safe here."

"Safe from what?"

"I'm not sure, but I think Blake hid a clue here or something. I think someone was after him and murdered him."

Christina shuddered and sucked in a sharp gasp. She moved her hand back to the counter to ground herself in the spinning room. "W-why would someone murder your *bruder* if he wasn't using drugs or doing anything wrong?" Was she hopelessly naïve or just plain dim-witted? She didn't see a connection between that poor man and her shop.

"Maybe he had information that could get someone else in trouble. It could be that he knew the person who was selling drugs or something. I knew he had been concerned about something, but he wouldn't share it with me."

"Why would he write two identical notes?"

"I'm just guessing, but he probably thought if I figured out the first note and came here to find the second one, I would know he really left some kind of clue here."

"What kind of clue would he hide here?" A key, perhaps?

"I'm not sure. But I am pretty sure it has to do with pink begonias. I mean, look at the notes."

"If you interpreted them correctly, that is. *Pb* could stand for peanut butter. What if he wanted you to pick up peanut butter? The *gt* could be grocery today. You know, pick up peanut butter at the grocery today. Isn't that possible?"

"Highly unlikely. Blake has always hated peanut butter. He didn't even like peanut butter cookies or peanut butter fudge or peanut butter and chocolate candy."

"Oh." Christina's hopes deflated like a pinpricked balloon. "When you were here yesterday, did you search through the pots of begonias?"

"I did. I'm sorry if I made a mess. I wasn't seeing or thinking very clearly. I'd be happy to clean up after myself."

"I've already taken care of that."

"Where did you find that piece of paper? I certainly didn't see it anywhere."

"I found it before you came here. It was in a different pot of pink begonias that I sold."

Jill's shoulders slumped. "Now I'll never know what else might have been in that pot. If Blake had been trying to get a message to me, I've lost the opportunity to retrieve it." Tears streamed from her huge, green eyes. "Oh, Blake, I'm so sorry. I tried."

The girl's lower lip trembled until she clamped it hard between her teeth. Christina feared she would have to mop up blood any second. She knew Jill was trying not to weep aloud. Her whole body shook with the effort. Christina laid a hand on the distraught girl's arm. "All might not be lost."

"T-thanks for t-trying to c-comfort me." She tried to smile through her tears but had little success.

"*Nee*, I mean it. Things might not be so hopeless, but I'm not sure."

Jill raised troubled, but questioning, eyes and fixed them on Christina's face. "How so?"

"Wait a minute." Christina scooted over to the shelf and once again reached all the way back until her fingers touched two small objects. She enclosed them in her hand and pulled them out. She would show them to Jill one at a time and gauge her reaction. With her free hand, she plucked the key from her fist and laid it on the counter. "This is what I dug out of a pink begonia pot."

Jill gasped and reached out a shaky hand. "How did you possibly know to dig around in that particular pot?"

"A *freind* found something on the floor in the attached greenhouse. When I went to check things out, I noticed that the plants on the end of the row had been disturbed."

"You must be awfully observant."

"I try to take *gut* care of my plants. Only two pots looked a bit messy. The first one checked out fine. The second one had some crushed leaves and blossoms, and dirt had been spilled around the pot. The plant also sported that pink slip of paper. When I carefully dug around the plant, I discovered the key."

Jill turned the key over and over in her hand as if looking for some identifying feature.

"Do you know what the key goes to? It looks too small to fit a house or car lock."

"I'm not sure, but it could go to a security box."

"Did your *bruder* have one of those?"

"He did. We both had boxes for important papers, like birth certificates, car titles, and things like that. This key looks very much like the key to my box."

"Why would someone hide it in a plant in my shop, and who could have done that other than your *bruder*? Would he have given the key to someone else?" Now Christina felt like a sleuth in one of Annie's beloved suspense novels. But this was not fiction. She was in the thick of this mystery whether she wanted to be or not. That gave her the right to ask questions, didn't it?

"Blake would not have given anyone access to his documents, not willingly anyway. I'm the only one who knew where he kept the key, the same as he is the only one who knows—knew—where I keep my key. He must have hidden the key here himself. Are you sure you've never seen him in here?"

Was the woman questioning her honesty? And here she'd begun to feel a connection with her and had started to care about her! That's what she got for being too trusting. She bristled like a cat stalking a mouse. Christina drew herself up to her full five-foot-nothing stature. "I can assure you that I spoke the truth when I told you and the deputies that I had never seen your *bruder* prior to that day."

Jill immediately reached out to tap Christina's arm. "I am so sorry. I didn't mean to sound like I was accusing you of withholding information. I believe everything you've said. It's just that sometimes we all forget something until an event or a comment triggers our memory. That's all I meant. Please don't be angry with me."

Christina's agitation melted. "I'm not angry. I didn't want you to think that I lied or that I'm incompetent."

"I would never think either thing. Somehow, I feel a bond with you. It's kind of weird, but I sense a sort of kinship. I guess I'm crazy."

Uncanny that this *Englisch* girl's words could mirror Christina's own thoughts. She smiled and patted Jill's hand. "That's nice of you to say."

"I'm so glad you dug in the flowerpot before you sold it. By the way, what was it your friend found that led you to search the begonias?"

Christina opened her hand. "This." The decorative little penknife rested smack in the center of her palm.

This time, Jill reached for the counter for support. Her face progressed from ashen to ghostly pale. Christina feared the girl would keel over any second. "You should sit."

Jill shook her head, sending the long, dark curls flying. She opened her mouth to speak, but no sound issued forth.

"Do you recognize this?"

Jill nodded so hard that Christina expected to hear her neck snap. Jill plucked the knife from Christina's hand. She turned it over and over as she had done with the key. She didn't even attempt to brush away the tears that leaked from her eyes. "Daddy." The single word was nothing more than a whisper. Jill sniffed and cleared her throat. "This was my father's knife. Blake always carried it with him. He had to have been here. I don't suppose you have security cameras installed here, do you?"

"I'm afraid not."

"Was there a time this week when you weren't here and someone else minded the store for you?"

"I was here every day. On Tuesday, I was outside with a delivery man, but only briefly. My *mudder* and little *schweschders* were here, though. *Mamm* admitted she got distracted by the girls and could have missed someone roaming in the shop. That's the only time I can think of me not being in here."

"That must be when Blake came in."

"*If* he came in."

"Oh, it's all so confusing. Someone must have followed him here and later brought him back here after..."

"I know what you mean." This must be so difficult for Jill. Christina didn't know how the poor girl could think a single logical thought.

"You'll help me, won't you, Christina?"

"Help you with what?"

"Clear my brother's name. I have to prove that he was not a drug dealer."

"Me?" Christina couldn't get involved in this case any further than she already was. "I-I can't."

"How would you react if it was your brother? You'd want him to be remembered as a good person, right?"

Christina couldn't have felt worse if she'd been kicked in the belly by a cantankerous old cow. How could she refuse to help? Yet, how could she get more entangled in this nightmare? "Plain people don't get involved in legal matters."

"But you help people, don't you? You want to do what is right, I'm sure."

"True, but my parents and the bishop would never want me to participate in an investigation other than to truthfully answer the policemen's questions."

"But what does your heart say?"

Ugh! Why did she have to ask that question? Her heart and her brain were engaged in a battle at the moment. Her brain made her tongue say the words she had just spoken and was quite satisfied with itself. Her heart jumped up and down in her chest, throwing a nasty tantrum. It cried out for justice. It knew Christina would do anything for one of her siblings. It pounded so hard that it angered her stomach, which threatened to expel any of its undigested contents.

Christina didn't have to raise her eyes to know that Jill stared at her. She hoped her facial expression remained passive and didn't reveal the turmoil going on inside of her. She needed to be firm and stick by the answer she had already given.

"Christina?"

Did she imagine the whisper? She certainly did not imagine the tug on her hand. *Don't look up!* Her brain issued the command, but her eyes did not obey. Hesitantly, she lifted her gaze to meet the glimmer of hope in Jill's sad eyes. *Now you've done it! You looked. You might not turn into a pillar of salt like Lot's wife in the Bible, but you've doomed yourself just the same.*

"Will you help me?"

Christina barely nodded. "How?" Jill threw her arms around her in a tight embrace, nearly throwing Christina off-balance.

"Oh, thank you, thank you. I know the two of us can figure this out."

Christina wanted to say that Jill grossly overestimated her abilities. What experience did Christina have with legal matters and criminal investigations? Annie might be a better partner, but Christina needed to protect her loved ones. They did not need to be involved in anything that could prove to be dangerous. She, on the other hand, was already in this mess up to her eyeballs. "I'm not sure how to help. I have very limited experience, you know. I do my work, go to church, spend time with my family and *freinden*, and not much more."

"But you aren't limited in intelligence. You're a thinker. I can tell you have a quick mind. I heard you with customers when I wandered through the greenhouse."

Christina doubted any snippets of conversation penetrated the other girl's sorrow and agitation that day, but who was she to judge? She never considered herself dim-witted, but she never thought much about her capabilities. She knew she was quick with numbers and caught on to new concepts and skills quickly, but she didn't pride herself on any of that. Pride was wrong. The Mennonites strove to avoid feelings of pride, hence their conformity to dress, hairstyle, and just about everything else. Christina pulled her mind from its wandering to focus on Jill's words.

"We have to figure out for sure that it was Blake who came in here and planted the key in the begonia pot."

"How? I already told you I don't have surveillance cameras here." Where did that word *kumm* from? It certainly was not a part of her everyday vocabulary. She must have stored it in her memory from one of Annie's stories about her books. It popped right out of her mouth like she used it all the time. Maybe she'd stored some other helpful information from Annie's books too. She must have paid more attention than she thought.

Jill dug into a pocket and produced a wallet. She flipped through cards in little plastic sleeves and slowed when she reached photographs. Christina watched silently as the other young woman almost reverently extracted a picture and held it out. "Here. This is Blake. You can show this to your mother and see if it jogs her memory."

Christina glanced at the handsome young man with dark hair and green eyes identical to his *schweschder's*. "I could if we were *Englisch*." She gently pushed away Jill's hand.

"Huh?"

"We don't have our pictures taken. We don't carry photographs of loved ones around with us. We remember them here." Christina tapped her head and her heart. "Though sometimes I wish I had a picture of my *grossmammi*, uh, grandmother. I'm afraid I'll forget what she looked like." Christina shook her head as if to erase the image of Grossmammi's bright smile and crinkly eyes. "So you see, I couldn't very well walk into my house carrying a picture of Blake. That would stir up all sorts of problems. Besides, they would all want to know how I happened to have the picture, and well, I would be forbidden from helping you."

"Oh." Jill returned her beloved picture to her wallet but not before Christina caught the crestfallen expression on her face. An instant later, the girl snapped her fingers and raised her head. Christina could practically see an idea churning inside her head. "Unfortunately, Blake's picture was in the newspaper for the whole world to see him as a criminal. I have a copy, more than one, actually. You could show that to your mother."

Christina hated to burst Jill's bubble of hope, but she couldn't fathom how that would work either. "I don't know."

"It's worth a try."

"You don't know my little *schweschders*. If Mamm got distracted by them, I'm pretty sure she didn't observe anything else around her. She said they almost broke jars on my shelves, so I know *Mamm* focused on avoiding a disaster." Besides, what plausible reason could she concoct for clipping out the newspaper article? Her people did not seek out or want such publicity as The Green Thumb received in that story.

"Please try, Christina. Pretty please? If she says she doesn't recall a thing about Blake, we'll look for another avenue to explore. But my gut feeling is that Blake buried that key in the begonia pot and hoped I'd figure out his cryptic message and search here." Jill opened a zippered section of her wallet and extracted a folded newspaper clipping. "This picture isn't as clear as my photo, but it's pretty good." She laid the paper on the counter and pressed out the wrinkles.

"It looks like your picture, but it isn't in color."

"They don't print a lot of things in color. I guess it's too costly for the newspaper." Jill took one hand from the clipping and clasped Christina's hand. "Please take this and see if your mother remembers any little thing that could indicate Blake was here. I'm sure he was. No one else knew my fondness for pink begonias. No one else would leave me a note matching the one you found here." She squeezed Christina's hand. "I have to know for sure and I need to figure out what really happened to him. Please?"

The final whispered word tugged at Christina's heart. Her own reply was barely audible. "I'll try." *Forgive me, Lord Gott, if this is wrong.*

Chapter Fifteen

How could helping someone be wrong? "The Lord *Gott* wants us to help others, ain't so?" Christina spoke to the plants in her greenhouse, but unfortunately, they could not offer her any advice. Even though that premise sounded *gut* to her, she didn't think it would fly with her parents or the ministers or the bishop. She shivered despite the heat and humidity. She'd never been called before the ministers before or had the bishop visit to warn her of some infraction. Christina had always abided by the rules and never gave her parents cause for worry. This venture she'd promised to help with could put an end to her spotless reputation. Not "could" but "would." She would definitely be in trouble once this cat was out of the bag. She heaved a mighty sigh. Too bad the begonias that got her into this mess couldn't get her out of it.

"You sound like you're bearing the weight of the world on your shoulders."

"Ahh!" Christina's hand flew to her chest where her heart thundered. She whirled around to face the owner of the deep voice. "You nearly scared the life out of me." She really needed to be more attentive. What if whoever sat poor Blake

Sheridan in her shed was the person who had sneaked in on her?

"I'm sorry."

"Oh my, is it quitting time already?"

Noah nodded. "Either you've been awfully busy or else you've been totally preoccupied."

Christina forced a little laugh that sounded phony even to her own ears. "A little of both, I guess."

"What can I do to help you close up?"

"I appreciate the offer, but you've worked all day. You don't need to worry about me. I can close."

"I do worry about you. I mean, I know you can take care of yourself and your business just fine, but I am concerned for your well-being."

"Everything is great here. I don't feel like I'm in any danger." Well, perhaps she did have a twinge of apprehension occasionally, but she would keep that to herself. She certainly didn't want to cause anyone to feel they needed to babysit her.

Christina hurried to the front of the store to close and lock the heavy wooden door. She flipped the sign in the window so it read "closed." She scooted behind the counter to count the money and update her ledger. She did these same things every single day.

"Is there anything I can do outside?"

"I don't want to hold you up, Noah. You must be tired and hungry, and I'm sure you must have chores to do at home."

"You aren't holding me up at all. The chores will still be there when I get home, unless my *bruders* do them. Is your big greenhouse secured for the night?"

"I haven't closed it up yet, but the shed is locked."

"I'll take care of the greenhouse while you count money."

"If you're sure you don't mind."

"Not at all."

Ugh! She lost count and started over again. Scatter-brained, that's what she was. What was wrong with her to-day? She usually didn't get flustered so easily. If she didn't calm herself, her *mudder* would surely notice. Christina sighed and began recounting for at least the fourth time.

"Are you okay?"

Christina jumped again. *Get hold of yourself!* "Sure, why?"

"I don't know. You seem a little edgy."

If Noah noticed, *Mamm* definitely would pick up on even the most subtle quirk in her behavior. She shrugged. "Sorry. I don't mean to appear that way."

"Did someone or something upset you today?"

That had to be the biggest understatement ever! She was actually more befuddled than upset. Should she mention Jill's visit to Noah? What would he say if he knew she had agreed to help the *Englisch* girl? "Not really."

"That didn't sound very convincing. The police didn't return with more questions, did they?"

"*Nee.* I think they consider the case closed." She curled the edges of the dollar bills with her fidgety fingers.

"Something tells me you don't share their opinion."

Christina shrugged. She looked down at the money she'd been crinkling and willed her hands to be still. "It's not my place to decide such things." She gasped when Noah cupped her chin, forcing her to meet his gaze.

"What aren't you telling me?"

"W-who said I wasn't telling you something?" She tried to look away, but her eyes stayed fastened on his the same way a nail clung to a magnet.

"I can tell. Was that girl here again pawing through the begonias?"

Christina smiled. "She was not digging up flowers." Noah dropped his hand, and her chin instantly felt cold.

"But she was here?"

"*Jah.*" How did he manage to extract information from her so easily?

"Was she upset again or acting crazy?"

"She was quite calm, all things considered. She actually apologized for her previous behavior. She, uh, asked for my help." Now why had she blurted that out?

"How can you help her?"

Christina concentrated on entering the day's total in her ledger. She stacked the money and slipped it into the zippered bag. Since her tongue had run away with itself, she would now have to explain the situation and pray that Noah would at least understand even if he didn't agree with her decision. She snagged as deep a breath as she could and plunged into her story.

"Am I wrong to agree to help her? In the Bible, the Samaritan helped a stranger." Christina feared the answer to her question. She discovered that Noah's opinion was important to her. She didn't want him to think ill of her, but she had to follow her heart. And her heart told her Jill's hunch was valid.

"It's never wrong to help people."

Noah patted the hand that wasn't fiddling with the zipper on the money bag. Warmth shot up Christina's arm and spread throughout her entire body. Her pulse sped up a couple of notches. She dreaded asking but suspected Noah had more to say on the subject. "But?"

"But?" Confusion laced his voice.

"It sounded like a 'but something' was about to drop off your tongue."

Noah chuckled. "You can read me well."

Almost as well as you read me. Uncanny. "Well?"

"I was going to say I don't want you to get hurt. It could be a dangerous venture you've agreed to, and I'm sure it would be frowned upon by the bishop, to put it mildly."

"If he finds out. I wasn't planning to shout it out from the rooftop."

He laughed again. "I see."

"Do you think that's wrong?"

"You have a *gut* heart, Christy. You want to help people. You certainly can't be faulted for that."

That same little thrill rippled through her at the use of his special nickname. "Jill obviously loved her *bruder*. I know I would want to clear my *bruder's* name. Oh, it's all so confusing. What would you have done, Noah?"

In his moment of hesitation, Christina observed a variety of emotions cross his handsome face. Which one would his words match? She held her breath afraid to hear his answer.

Noah ran a hand across his face, massaged the wrinkle between his dark brows, and heaved a sigh of resignation. "I would have done the exact same thing. I would not want people to believe my *bruder* was a bad person."

Christina blew out the breath she had been holding. "Really? Would you tell the bishop or your parents or anyone else?"

He shook his head. "Only you."

"Pardon me?"

He cleared his throat and spoke a little louder. "I'd only tell you. We think alike. You would understand."

He must feel the same connection between them that she did. How strange! Christina wasn't sure what that meant, but she knew she was definitely relieved that she had shared her burden with someone.

"How will you approach your *mudder* with that picture from the paper?"

Christina had been wondering the very same thing. "I'm not sure. I've been rehearsing ideas, but nothing sounds right. Do you have any suggestions?"

Noah's brow wrinkled again. "I wish I knew what to tell you. I guess this is one time where the old saying 'honesty is the best policy' won't work."

"It's not that I'm planning to be dishonest. I'm simply not revealing my intentions. Is that a lie?"

"I don't think so. You aren't trying to deceive them."

"Exactly. And if it did become necessary, I'd bare my soul. It would get me in deep trouble, but I wouldn't blatantly lie."

"I believe you. Are you ready to head out now?"

"I suppose I might as well get this over with."

"Let me run out and double-check that everything is secure outside. Be right back."

"You don't have to..." Christina swallowed the rest of her comment since Noah had already dashed out the back door. Why was he being so solicitous? If he truly cared about her, that would be *wunderbaar*. For her but not for Annie. Dear Annie. She'd be as mad as a hornet whose nest had been doused with gasoline if she knew Noah was at The Green Thumb again today. She shouldn't be since Noah had not given her a reason to believe he was interested in her. But Annie did not always think rationally. And Christina could not be the person to convince the girl that her pursuit of Noah needed to be abandoned.

At the shuffle of footsteps at the back door, Christina checked that all was as it should be in the store. She peeked into her bag to ensure the newspaper clipping was still there before slinging the bag over her shoulder. She hurried to the door and called out to Noah. "I'm as ready as I'll ever be."

Christina checked the front door twice to make sure it was locked. "You don't have to ride home with me, Noah. I'm sure you have many other things to do. I'll be fine."

"I don't have anything to do better than riding with you. Do you mind?"

Mind? She was delighted. Thrilled. Ecstatic. But she had to remain as calm and as aloof as possible. She managed a slight shrug. "I don't mind." Not even a teensy bit.

"*Gut.*" Noah straddled his bike and waited for her to do likewise.

Christina tucked her bag in the basket attached to her handlebars and pushed off. They pedaled across the parking lot toward the paved road without speaking. Only the crunch of rubber tires on loose gravel and the chirp of a few blackbirds filled the comfortable silence between them. Until they reached the blacktop.

"Hey! Wait up!"

Christina should not be filled with dread at the approach of her *freind*, but that was exactly the emotion she experienced. She sneaked a peak at Noah and almost giggled at his woebegone expression. She turned and forced as much enthusiasm as possible into her voice. "Hi, Annie."

"You're late leaving, ain't so?"

"Maybe. A little."

"What a surprise to see Noah with you."

Did she emphasize the word *with*? Or was that Christina's imagination? She didn't have any justification for the guilt that suddenly washed over her. It wasn't like she was stealing Annie's beau.

Annie turned her fluttering eyes and her exaggerated charm on Noah. "It sure is nice to see you again." Flutter. Flutter.

"Uh... hi, Annie."

Christina wanted to ease Noah's discomfort but couldn't figure out how to do that. If only she could tell Annie to stop gushing. If the girl could see herself, she would probably be mortified by her own behavior.

"Were you helping Christina with something?" Annie threw a scowl in Christina's direction but reapplied her smile when turning back to Noah.

"I guess you could say that." He shot Christina a helpless look.

Although she would have enjoyed his company in normal circumstances, Christina had to try to help Noah. He squirmed like a worm on a hook. "*Danki*, Noah. I do appreciate your help. Annie will ride home with me, so you don't need to go out of your way to do that."

His gratitude was obvious. "Are you sure?"

"Absolutely."

"All right, then. I'll see you soon."

"Real soon, I hope." Annie batted her eyes again.

Since she was slightly behind Annie, Christina lifted her shoulders ever so slightly and mouthed, "I'll talk to her."

Noah nodded and sped away faster than lightning.

"Why did you send him away?" Annie's charm vanished only to be replaced by surliness.

"I thought he probably had chores to do at home."

"Was he planning to ride home with you before I came along and spoiled things for you?"

"We merely left at the same time."

"What was he helping you with?"

This was a side of her *freind* that Christina was unfamiliar with, a side she didn't particularly care for. "He, uh, helped me make sure everything was secure."

"Huh! Like you haven't done that all by yourself every single day since you started running the shop."

Christina swerved a tiny bit closer to the other girl.

"Hey! What are you doing? Trying to run me off the road?"

"Of course not, silly. Why would I do that?"

"To get me out of the way so you could have Noah all to yourself."

Christina made a split decision to ignore that comment. "I wanted to check your eyes for you, to make sure you don't have something in them."

"My eyes are fine. Why on earth would you think otherwise?"

Christina did her best to ignore Annie's acidic tone. She forced herself to speak calmly in as soothing a manner as she could manage considering the tension crackling in the air between them. "You kept blinking them, so I thought you might have gotten something in them."

"I wasn't blinking."

"You certainly were. A lot. Are they burning or hurting you? Maybe you have allergies. The pollen count has been pretty high."

"I've never been allergic to anything in my life."

"Some people develop allergies later, I've heard." Christina leaned a bit closer, took her eyes off the road for a second, and studied the red-haired girl's eyes.

"Leave me alone, Christina. I'm fine."

Uh-oh. She used the full name. She must be furious with me.

Before Christina knew what happened, her bike wobbled and skidded on loose gravel along the shoulder of the road. She couldn't react fast enough to avoid a catastrophe. A split second later, the bike toppled over, pinning her beneath it. Peering up from her unladylike sprawl, with metal handlebars digging into her ribs, she spied Annie zooming off toward her house.

She pushed me! I can't believe my best freind *pushed me down and didn't even check to see if I was hurt!*

Chapter Sixteen

Christina couldn't determine if she was more miffed or hurt. How could the person she considered her best *freind* have treated her so shabbily? She shook her head and blew a loose wisp of hair off of her face. Grunting, she pushed herself to a sitting position with throbbing, sticky hands. Why were they so sticky? She decided to look at them before wiping them on her dirt-streaked dress.

Blood. A zillion little pebble scrapes left trails of blood trickling across her palms. Christina examined her hands more closely to make sure there wasn't any debris embedded in the wounds. Satisfied the scrapes didn't contain foreign materials, she grabbed the bike and used it to help her to a standing position. She stared down the empty road. Annie was long gone. She really hadn't expected the girl to return.

The side of her leg ached too, but she certainly couldn't check that out here where anyone who might pass by could see her. She retrieved her bag that had shot out of the bike basket like a missile and poked it back inside.

"*Ach*, now I'll have to walk!" Right as she had been about to straddle the bike to pedal the last two miles home, she caught sight of the flat rear tire. Since she didn't have a pump with her, she and the bike would have to hobble home, nursing their respective wounds. She'd be extra late now and probably wouldn't be able to talk to *Mamm* alone until after supper. Two miles had never seemed so long.

"What happened to you?"

Leave it to eleven-year-old Sallie to notice her bedraggled appearance before Christina had a chance to get cleaned up. Not only did she notice, but she also blabbed loud enough to alert anyone within a ten-mile radius as well. Could a person ever do anything around here in private? Christina had knelt in the straw on the barn floor to pump up the bike tire, so with the combination of dirt, grease, and straw covering her she probably looked the scarecrow out in the cornfield.

"What happened?" Sallie repeated her question slightly louder as if her big *schweschder* had suddenly grown hard of hearing.

"I had a little problem."

"Little? It looks like you got into a fight with the horse, and the horse won."

"Funny. Mennonites don't fight."

"Couldn't prove that by you! Did you fall?"

"I had a slight mishap."

"Looks like a major one to me."

"Did you help *Mamm* with supper?"

The younger girl whirled around and skipped off toward the house.

"Sallie Brubacher, did you help *Mamm*?"

"I did."

A tug on her soiled dress made Christina look down. She wrapped an arm around her youngest *schweschder* and smiled. "I didn't even hear you walk over here, Gracie. You must have been hiding somewhere."

"I was behind the bushes looking at the new kittens. The *mudder* cat was feeding them."

"You didn't touch them, did you? We don't want the *mudder* to carry the kittens off somewhere. New *mamms* tend to be very protective."

"I didn't touch them."

"*Gut* girl."

"And I helped *Mamm* before I came outside."

"Doubly *gut*." Christina gave the eight-year-old another gentle squeeze. "Was *Mamm* upset that I wasn't here?"

Grace shrugged. "I think she was more worried than mad. Who could get mad at you?"

"You're a sweet girl. I'd better get cleaned up and explain to *Mamm* why I'm late."

Grace latched onto Christina's hand and trotted along beside her. Christina hoped the little girl was right and that *Mamm* wasn't angry over her tardiness. Her *mudder* knew Christina couldn't always get away from the store in a timely manner, but this was later than usual. "I have to clean up a bit before I walk into the kitchen, Gracie. You could run and tell *Mamm* I'm home and will be right there to help."

"Okay. Then I'll *kumm* back and wait for you. Are you going to change your dress?"

Christina dropped her *schweschder's* hand and brushed at her dress.

"That didn't help much."

Christina looked down. "You're right. I guess I will have to change, but I'll be quick about it." It looked like she would have to do a bit of mending later. She dashed up the stairs and into the bathroom. She only had time to scrub her face and hands so she could change her dress and neaten her hair and *kapp* before hurrying downstairs.

She almost fell over Grace when she darted out of her room. "*Ach*, Gracie. I didn't know you were there."

"I told you I would wait for you."

"True, but I didn't expect you to be camped outside my door."

Grace gave her oldest *schweschder* a puzzled look. "I don't have a tent, silly. I wasn't camping."

Christina smiled. She forgot how literally young ones took everything. "It's just an expression."

"Oh."

"Is something wrong? You don't usually track my every move."

"I wait for you sometimes." The little lower lip protruded.

"You do. And I'm always happy to see you." Christina took the girl's hand and squeezed it. "Do you have some special reason to wait for me today?"

"I made a mess when *Mamm* was making jelly. I was only trying to help, but the jar slipped. Sallie laughed and called me a *boppli*. I'm *not* a *boppli!*"

Christina saw the tears shimmering in Grace's brown eyes. She needed to think fast and make sure she said the right thing. "Of course, you aren't. Everybody has accidents sometimes."

"Like you on your bike?"

"Exactly." She wouldn't mention the fact that her mishap couldn't actually be classified as an accident. She had been pushed. She hadn't simply toppled off her bike for no reason.

"You didn't get hurt, did you?"

"How sweet of you to ask." Christina couldn't fault Sallie for ignoring the possibility of injuries. She was at that flighty in-between age, not quite a little girl but not yet a teenager either. On the other hand, it did annoy her that Annie did not return to check on her. "I have some scrapes on my hands and legs, but I didn't bang my head on the pavement, so that's a *gut* thing."

"I'm glad you didn't get hurt bad."

"Badly," Christina murmured and was instantly sorry she corrected the little girl. Poor thing had already had a rough day. "So what did you help *Mamm* fix for supper?"

"She trusted me to put the biscuits on the baking pan after she cut them out and to set the table."

"Why wouldn't she trust you? You're a great helper. I'm sure *Mamm* knew you didn't deliberately make a mess at jelly time. Did you know I once saw bubbling jelly spurt out of the pan and splat on *Mamm*'s face? Right on her nose too."

Grace giggled. "It didn't do that today."

"Silly things happen to all of us."

"*Mamm* didn't get upset with me. It was only Sallie who was mean." Her lip quivered. Being called a *boppli* must have been a great insult to an eight-year-old.

"Sometimes *schweschders* and *bruders* tease each other and don't act very nice. I don't think they intend to be mean, but sometimes it *kumms* across that way."

"You're never mean."

Annie might hold an entirely different opinion on that matter, though, and might not be very forgiving if she knew Noah had been dropping by The Green Thumb. But it wasn't like she invited Noah to stop in after work. Truth be told, Christina was rather surprised by his repeated appearances. She would be ecstatic if her secret crush finally seemed to notice her as long as Annie wasn't hurt. She tugged on Grace's hand. "Let's see if *Mamm* needs any more help."

⁓

Was it her imagination or did supper truly drag on interminably? James and John bantered back and forth incessantly. Usually, Christina found them amusing. This evening, she wanted them to hush and eat. And David ate like he hadn't seen food in a year and wouldn't see it again for another one. Where did he put everything? She knew he was a growing fourteen-year-old, but he would be as round as the silo out beside the big red barn if he continued to eat like a famine was expected.

"Are you going to eat that?"

Christina followed David's finger that pointed to her nearly full plate. "Eat what?"

"That biscuit or anything else on your plate." He reached for the untouched bread.

"Do you have a tapeworm or something?" Christina pulled her plate away from his clutches. "Leave my food alone."

"Well, you haven't eaten anything, and I've already finished two platefuls."

"I can't help it that you're a bottomless pit. Why don't you give your teeth and throat a break? They've been working hard."

"I'll give you ten minutes to eat that food, and then it's up for grabs."

"You'd better leave her alone, *bruder*. A *gut*, strong wind could blow her away as it is. We'll have to put rocks in her pockets this winter." James elbowed David and laughed.

John guffawed and coughed. He slurped iced tea before sputtering, "If she gets any smaller, she'll be invisible."

Christina wrinkled her nose at her *bruders*. "You are all so funny." She turned to her youngest *schweschder* sitting beside her. "You see, Grace, *bruders* and *schweschders* say silly things to each other and tease mercilessly."

The little girl nodded. "I think you're fine just the way you are."

"That's because she's almost your size." John pointed first at one girl and then at the other. James and David roared.

"I'm already taller than Christina." Sallie apparently felt compelled to get in on the act.

Daed cleared his throat and all laughter subsided. "I think we all need to finish our supper and get on with the evening."

Bless you, Daed. Christina tried hard not to be offended, but sometimes it was difficult being the brunt of her siblings' teasing, so she knew exactly how Grace felt. She knew they really cared about her, but sometimes they went a little overboard. After Daed's intervention, everyone finished the meal in relative silence. That suited Christina fine. If they all concentrated on eating, they could leave the table faster. She even managed to force down a few forkfuls of green beans and coleslaw.

Christina didn't get to work in the kitchen with only *Mamm* after the rest of the family drifted away. Apparently, Grace feared more teasing. She sat at the big oak table with paper and crayons. But maybe if Christina spoke softly enough, her little *schweschder* wouldn't hear the conversation.

The newspaper clipping in her pocket practically burned through the cotton material of her dress. She hadn't yet nailed down her speech, and the words she had rehearsed in her head flew right out of her brain. She would have to wing it. She took a deep breath and reached into her pocket. She offered a silent plea for help. Was it wrong to beg for help with something her parents and church would disapprove of? She didn't know.

"*Mamm*?"

"Hmm?"

Christina dropped the yellow-checked dish towel on the counter. "Do you remember the day before I, uh..." She cut her eyes over to the table to make sure Grace still busily colored. "The day before I found that man?"

"Of course, I remember."

"You said you never saw him enter The Green Thumb."

"That's right." Ida stopped scrubbing the pot she'd been scouring and turned to look at Christina.

"Do you think he could have been wandering around inside the greenhouse and you didn't see him *kumm* in because you were busy with the girls?"

"Anything is possible, I suppose. I told you I had been distracted by a near catastrophe."

"Right."

"Why are you concerned? Has something else happened? Did the police return for some reason?"

"*Nee*, they haven't." Could she get away with only answering *Mamm*'s last question?

"Then what's going on?"

"Nothing is going on." Much. "I'm trying to settle things in my head." That was true enough.

"I'm sure that was an awful day for you, dear, but you have to let it go."

"I know, but I still have questions." Did she ever! Christina pulled the article from its hiding place and tried to smooth out the wrinkles. "This is the man. His picture was in the paper." She held the clipping closer to her *mudder's* face. "Does he seem at all familiar to you?"

"I saw him." The soft, high-pitched voice did not belong to *Mamm*.

Chapter Seventeen

Christina and Ida gasped in unison. Both looked down at Grace who tugged on her *schweschder's* dress. When had the little girl left the table and joined them at the sink? Christina opened her mouth to speak, but not even a whisper would emerge.

"I saw him, Christina. I really did."

Christina held the picture for Grace to get a better view. "Look closely, Gracie."

"*Jah*. He's the one."

"The one what?" Ida voiced the question before Christina's brain could command her tongue to speak.

"The one who was at The Green Thumb the day we were there. I saw him looking at the plants. That's why I almost knocked over all those jars of jam and jelly. I was watching him."

Christina's knees wobbled. Maybe she should sit down before she sprawled on the floor. "Are you sure, Gracie? Sometimes our mind plays tricks on us."

"I'm sure. He looked like a nice man. He smiled at me and did this." Grace stuck her thumb up. "What did that mean?"

"It's sort of a sign for 'okay'."

"Oh. And I remember he had a spot on his cheek."

"A what?" Ida's forehead scrunched into a frown.

"A brown spot." Grace pointed to a barely visible spot at the lower edge of the man's right cheek.

"You saw that?" Christina couldn't believe how observant the little girl was. She and *Mamm* never saw the man. Yet, an eight-year-old noticed a mole on his cheek. "How on earth did you see that from the jelly shelf where you were standing?"

Grace's face flushed a lovely light-rose color. "I-I tried to juggle two peaches like James does. I dropped one and it rolled into the greenhouse. That's when the man smiled and did that sign with his thumb. I kept watching him while I dusted that shelf. If Sallie hadn't bumped my arm, I probably wouldn't have knocked over the jars."

"Grace Brubacher, you know better than to play with the produce in the store." Ida shook a finger at her youngest.

"I'm sorry. I checked. The peach didn't get bruised or anything."

Christina needed to steer the conversation back to the man. "Gracie, do you know what the man was looking at in the greenhouse?" Did her question sound as innocent as she tried to make it? Ordinarily, she might hesitate to take the word of such a young person, but if Grace noticed something so small as a tiny mole on the man's face, her account must be pretty accurate.

Since Ida had gone back to scrubbing the pot she had abandoned earlier, Christina figured her *mudder* had lost interest in the conversation.

"He wandered around a little, but he mostly stayed by the plants in the back."

"Oh? Which ones?" Christina sounded anything but casual even to her own ears. She would definitely not make a very *gut* spy or detective.

"You know, the ones with the little pink flowers. I forgot the name of them."

"The begonias?"

"*Jah. Jah.* The begonias. That's the ones. They're pretty. The man seemed to like them too."

So he *was* there. He must have been the person who tucked that slip of paper and the key inside the flowerpot. He must have hoped his *schweschder* would put the clues together just as she'd said. He apparently had a lot of faith in Jill's sleuthing abilities and must have counted on the pink begonias not selling well. If Christina had waited one more day to investigate, some unsuspecting customer would have taken home more than a pretty plant. The Lord *Gott* did work in mysterious ways.

"Do you want to see my picture?" Grace hopped from one foot to another. Evidently, all thoughts of the begonia man had been relegated to the back of her mind.

"Sure, as soon as I finish helping *Mamm* with the dishes."

"Okay." The little girl bounced back to the table to resume coloring.

Christina retrieved the dish towel and extracted a handful of silverware from the dish drainer.

"Did you get all the information you needed?"

"Huh?" Christina's heart skipped a beat and then thumped so hard it nearly stole her breath.

"You were on a fishing expedition, ain't so?"

Had she been that transparent? And here she was all set to congratulate herself on her craftiness. "I-I was curious, that's all. I've been trying to understand why the man ended up at my shop of all places." Those words were certainly true enough, even if they masked the entire truth.

"Are you sure that's all it is?"

"What else would it be?" Christina was skating on thin ice now. She needed to find some other topic to discuss immediately. There wasn't time to be subtle about the switch either.

"*Mamm, Mamm,* look!"

Leave it to Sallie to cause a distraction. She certainly didn't like to see her younger *schweschder* upset, but her dramatics definitely derailed *Mamm's* train of thought.

Soapsuds flew when their *mudder* jerked her hands out of the water. "What is it, Sallie?"

Grace jumped up from the table again, obviously anxious to be part of the action.

"Go away!" Sallie flung over her shoulder.

"Be nice, *dochder.* Even if something is wrong with you, you can still be nice to others. Now what has you all riled up?"

"Look!"

"What do you want me to see?"

"Just look at this!" Sallie shrieked and waved her hand practically under *Mamm's* nose. Not a smart thing to do. Christina would never so challenge their *mudder.* That would have gotten her a severe scolding at the very least.

Ida grabbed the flapping hand and jerked it away from her face. "I am neither deaf or blind. You do not need to yell or to flap your hand in my face. Now, calm yourself and tell me what I'm supposed to see wrong with your hand."

"This huge splinter. It really hurts."

Christina squinted as if that would improve her vision. From where she stood about a foot away from the distraught girl, the "huge" splinter looked like a speck of dirt. She resisted the urge to roll her eyes and tried to assume an appropriately serious attitude, which was pretty hard to do when she spied *Mamm's* lips twitching.

"Oh my!" *Mamm* clucked her tongue. "Find a sharp knife, Christina. We might have to amputate."

"Aaahh!" Sallie pulled with all her might but couldn't free her hand from *Mamm's* grasp.

The terror on Sallie's face and the horror on Grace's sent Christina into a fit of laughter. A moment later, *Mamm* joined in.

"What's so funny about chopping off someone's hand?" Sallie tugged again in vain.

"Hold still, *dochder*. You know I wouldn't hurt you. I'm only teasing. I can't help you, though, if you don't stop squirming."

"You aren't going to cut it off?"

"Of course she isn't, you silly goose." Christina patted the girl's shoulder. "Haven't you ever had a splinter before?"

"I-I don't know." The fear had vanished from Sallie's face, but she still sniffed back tears.

"I'll have to get tweezers." *Mamm* ran her hand over the affected palm. "I think I can get it without a needle as long as it doesn't break off."

Sallie cringed. "A needle? You'll have to sew it?"

Christina bit her tongue to keep from laughing. She didn't dare explain that sometimes splinters needed to be dug out. Apparently, *Mamm* thought better about mentioning that detail as well.

Ida shuffled sideways to grab tweezers out of a drawer dragging Sallie along with her. Christina figured she must be afraid the poor girl would bolt if she loosened her grip. "Let's move closer to the light." The pair sidestepped their way over to the propane lantern.

"I'll finish washing dishes, *Mamm*. Gracie, do you want to dry them?"

"Will she holler?" Grace whispered as she followed Christina to the sink.

"Probably, but that's Sallie. She tends to get carried away. She'll be fine." Christina handed the dish towel to Grace and plunged her hands into the still-hot water. She sincerely hoped Sallie's tragedy chased all thoughts of their previous conversation out of *Mamm*'s mind.

~

Alone in her room after finishing the dishes, oohing and ah-hing over Grace's artwork, and trying rather unsuccessfully to focus on Daed's Bible reading, Christina attempted to sort her jumbled thoughts.

Blake Sheridan, for some unknown reason, chose The Green Thumb to stealthily communicate with his *schweschder*. He had to have actually planned to use her shop since he came prepared with a note and the key. Why didn't he simply go to Jill's apartment and hand her the key and tell her his plans? Wouldn't that have made more sense and been easier? Wouldn't it have been safer? If someone had purchased that plant before she and Noah made their discovery, the key would be long gone. What did that key go to anyway?

Was someone after Blake as Jill believed? Or had he been involved in something bad? Maybe he didn't go to Jill's apartment because he didn't want to endanger her. *So he endangered me instead!* Poor man. If he had been anything like his *schweschder*, he was probably a nice person. Of course, she didn't know Jill well, but she had an unfamiliar stirring in her midsection and a whisper in her heart that told her the pretty, dark-haired young woman was trustworthy. If only she could talk to Noah...

Noah? How interesting that he was her first choice of a confidant. Previously, Annie would have been the first person she confided in, but she might very well have alienated her *freind* forever. Besides, it would not be at all wise to throw Annie into the middle of the strange goings-on at The Green Thumb and thereby put her in harm's way. Noah was in this with her up to his eyeballs already, whether he wanted to be or not. He must want to be involved, though, or else he loved a *gut* mystery. Why else would he keep appearing at her shop?

~

Noah rubbed a hand across his stubbly chin. He hoped Christina got home all right. If Annie hadn't shown up at the wrong time, he would have made sure Christina reached her destination safely. Fending off Annie's silly flirtations had become tedious, not to mention embarrassing, and the tension among the three of them had risen to an almost unbearable level. Noah believed he would make things better by leaving the girls on their own and removing his contribution to the uncomfortable atmosphere surrounding them. Surely they had not encountered any problems or suffered any mishaps along the way.

He had not seen any evidence to support his concern that some evil person might pursue Christina, but a strange fear niggled at the back of his brain. His senses remained on high alert despite his repeated attempts to calm them. And when had he become so taken with Christina Brubacher? Noah shook his head. He couldn't pinpoint an exact date or event that heralded a change in his feelings, but something had definitely caused thoughts of her to take up residence at the forefront of his mind.

Noah didn't think Christy, as he called her in his thoughts and occasionally out loud to her face, minded his impromptu visits. Judging by her smile and the little sparkle in her silver eyes, he surmised that she rather enjoyed the moments they spent in each other's presence. He certainly had. He hoped she didn't feel smothered by his protectiveness. Noah didn't want to alarm her, but neither did he want to leave her alone to fend for herself. She was such a tiny thing. She wouldn't deter a stalker in the least.

Stalker? His imagination was working overtime these days. Christina didn't have a stalker. He would try to make sure she never did. Why did her shop have to be the scene of the crime, as the *Englisch* say? At least he had been at the Quick Stop the day Annie had burst in to report the man in the shed. That announcement stoked his spark of interest in Christina into full flame.

Why had he never approached her after a singing or at any other activity? Fortunately, some other fellow didn't step up and do exactly that. He did have a chance with her, didn't he? Maybe he would have to be less subtle about his feelings. But he didn't want to scare her off. He got the impression she wavered between showing interest in him and sparing her *freind* from any pain. But he had definitely never given Annie any indication that he had the slightest desire for a relationship with her. A casual acquaintance worked just fine for him.

Where had that sudden gushiness Annie exhibited *kumm* from? He had never seen such a bid for attention before, and even Christina seemed surprised. Noah would have to be very careful that he did not encourage her in any way. At the same time, he had to make sure Christina did not slip through his fingers. *Ach!* Could life become more difficult?

Chapter Eighteen

She couldn't believe how a simple spill from her bike could wreak such havoc on her body. Christina groaned as she dragged herself out of bed. Her scraped hands had throbbed all night like they had little heartbeats of their own. She hadn't been able to roll onto her right side without grunting with pain. She'd have to check how much the bruising had progressed. Purple and black splotches had just begun to appear when she got ready for bed last night. At least she hadn't suffered any fractures or sprains. Scrapes, cuts, and bruises were bad enough.

Christina had suffered far worse injuries as a little girl trying to keep up with James and John. Once, she even tried to climb the big oak tree after them. That did not have a happy ending. She hadn't realized she needed to grab a thick, sturdy limb instead of a skinny branch.

The knot on the back of her head had been large enough for *Mamm* to summon an *Englisch* driver to take her to the doctor.

The sooner she got moving this morning, the sooner she could work out the kinks. At least, Christina hoped so. If she could get herself out the door early enough, she should be able to avoid running into Annie. She didn't feel up to dealing with another unpleasant encounter.

Sadness overcame her as she wound her waist-length hair into its customary bun. She and Annie had been *freinden* forever. She had never felt the need to avoid Annie before. But now she didn't know how to act around her or what to say to her. Should she pretend that nothing had happened, that Annie hadn't caused her to get hurt? Should she simply talk about the weather and leave any serious topic of conversation, like the bike incident or Noah Zimmerman, alone? She wished she could ask *Mamm* for advice, but she wasn't yet ready to divulge her secrets.

And that was another thing! Christina did not enjoy keeping secrets. It was too close to lying, and she had always been an honest person. The only person she could speak freely to at the moment was Noah, and she had mixed emotions about that. On the one hand, it was fun spending time with Noah. She had dreamed of doing exactly that on many occasions, though not under the strange circumstances they had found themselves a part of. On the other hand, she feared alienating her *freind* forever. She didn't understand Annie's behavior of late and did not like having to tiptoe around on eggshells to avoid hurting her. *Ach!* If she wanted to leave early for work, she'd better stop ruminating and haul her aching body downstairs to help with breakfast.

Christina didn't gallop down the stairs as she normally did. She took one step at a time and clung to the handrail, even though the contact irritated her scraped hand. *Ignore the aches. You have too much to do.* The little pep talk helped marginally. She tried to put a zip in her step and to conjure up some sort of smile before facing her *mudder* in the kitchen.

"You're limping."

"I am?" *Mamm* had hardly glanced in her direction. How could she detect a limp? Christina hadn't noticed she walked with an awkward gait.

"You are, and you look like you're in pain."

So much for zip and a smile. Christina hoped she would be as perceptive if she ever became a *mudder*. "I'm fine." She hurried to pour orange juice into the waiting glasses.

This time, *Mamm* turned from the cast iron skillet full of bubbling eggs and stared at Christina. A plate of crisp, fried bacon sat on the nearby counter. *Mamm* must have gotten up earlier than usual too. "You don't look so fine. Even though you're trying to sound cheerful and put on a brave front, I can tell you're hurting. Maybe you should get your injuries checked out."

"I only have bruises and scrapes, and I'm a bit stiff, but I'm sure the kinks will work out once I get busy." She wasn't sure of any such thing. And she didn't know if the kinks in her relationship with Annie would ever smooth out.

"Do you have help today?"

"Amelia is going to bring some bread and treats by. She'll stay for a while."

"With the *kinner*? That might be more of a hindrance than a help."

"Since it's Saturday, she will only have her own."

"That's still three little ones. Maybe I could send Sallie along to entertain them."

Grace would probably be better with Amelia's girls. Sallie had been too unpredictable lately. She was at that age where she alternated between acting like a little girl and acting like an adult. One minute, she was happy and helpful. The next minute, she turned moody or downright surly. At least Gracie remained even-tempered. A person knew what to expect with Grace. Not so with Sallie. "We'll be fine, *Mamm*. Amelia might even leave her girls with a family member. Occasionally, she does that." Most of the time she didn't, but Christina didn't mention that.

"All right. If you change your mind, I can spare Sallie today."

"Spare me for what?" The subject of the kitchen conversation shuffled into the room almost too late to help with anything.

Ida turned back to the eggs. "I'd thought about sending you to help Christina at The Green Thumb, but she said she wouldn't need you."

"Whew!" Sallie unwrinkled her nose and stopped frowning. "That's a relief."

Christina figured she probably experienced greater relief than Sallie. Obviously, this was one of her *schweschder's* surly days. It would definitely be best if she stayed home with *Mamm*. Best for Christina, that is, but she pitied *Mamm* and Gracie. "If Sallie and Gracie help you in the kitchen, is it all right if I take my breakfast with me? I want to get to the shop earlier this morning."

"Oh? Are you having a sale or something?"

"I got in those new flowerpots and a few other items. I might need to rearrange things before Amelia gets there, especially if she brings very many treats to sell."

"I don't know how that girl finds extra time for all the baking she does."

Christina smiled. Amelia was a twenty-eight-year-old widow with three small *kinner*, but *Mamm* still thought of her as a girl. "I think she really enjoys baking the way some women enjoy sewing or knitting."

"I suppose. Is Annie going to work early today too?"

Since Christina and Annie usually biked together in the mornings, it would only be natural for Ida to make that assumption. "I'm not sure, but she probably doesn't need to arrive any earlier than usual. Her *onkle* takes care of any displaying or arranging of items for his business." If she didn't stop talking and get out the door, she'd likely run smack into her possibly former best *freind*. She'd really rather not start her morning with a continuation of yesterday's issues.

Christina threw a couple of blueberry muffins in her cooler on top of the ham sandwich she'd made last night for today's lunch. She tossed in an extra apple and made sure a water bottle was tucked inside before adding a cold pack and fastening the cooler. "See you in time to help with supper, *Mamm*."

"Can't you wait two more minutes for the eggs and toast to get done? Then you can make a breakfast sandwich to take with you."

"The muffins will be fine." Every second she delayed compromised her plan to avoid Annie. She knew she would have to face the other girl sooner or later, but she preferred to make that encounter later. Annie needed time to cool off and to consider her actions. And Christina needed time to figure out what to say.

The day promised to be another hot, sticky, typical Southern Maryland summer day. The humidity weighed down on her like a giant hand from the sky pressing on her head. Christina pedaled at a moderate pace so she wouldn't arrive at The Green Thumb soaked with perspiration and smelling like she'd just finished mucking the horse stalls. She cast a wary eye in all directions from time to time, half afraid she'd spy Annie on her way to her *onkle*'s place.

How odd to want to avoid the girl. How did their relationship sink to such a low level? Only a few days ago, they had talked and laughed and shared dreams like always. Now she feared a chance meeting with the person she had trusted with all of her secrets. Most of her secrets, anyway.

Christina heaved a sigh of relief when The Green Thumb came into view. Almost there. Almost in the clear. She sped up a bit and turned into the parking lot. She coasted around to the back of the shop to leave her bike out of the way and to enter through the back door. She didn't plan to open for business yet, but she wanted to get inside quickly to make sure everything was ready for the day.

She probably didn't need to rearrange a single thing before Amelia arrived with her baked goods, but Christina shifted a few flowerpots and jars of jam around so the explanation she gave *Mamm* wouldn't be a lie. After a few minutes in her beloved store, her tension finally eased. A rumble from her stomach reminded her she had not yet eaten breakfast. She'd better consume her muffins before she flipped the sign and opened the front door. Saturday mornings tended to be very busy, so this might be the only opportunity she got to wolf down some sustenance.

Christina had licked the last muffin crumb from her index finger when she heard a car door slam in the parking lot out front. Someone had arrived awfully early. According to the clock on the far wall, she still had twenty minutes before opening time. She'd let the customer in early, though. If she stayed busy, she would have less time to think about Annie or about Jill and her *bruder*, or about Noah Zimmerman. Funny how that last name brought a smile to her lips. She really needed to curb that reaction until she figured out his feelings and her feelings and everything else.

"Christina! Are you in there?"

She jumped from the stool and wiped her hands on a scrap of paper towel. Her heart roared in her ears. She hadn't expected *this* visitor so soon. Maybe she shouldn't have arrived early after all. Christina's hands felt clammy and cold despite the fact that she had just wiped them off and despite the nearly eighty-degree morning. She needed to face the person on the other side of the door, though, even if she hadn't decided what to say. A little part of her wanted to hightail it out the back door and hide in the woods beyond.

"Christina? Please?"

Chapter Nineteen

She couldn't delay the inevitable any longer. She tamped down a mixture of fear, sadness, and helplessness before dragging in a deep breath. The pounding at the door practically shook the building. "Just a minute!" Christina forced her reluctant feet to move. She turned the lock and jerked the door open. "For a little person, you sure have a powerful knock. I thought the roof would cave in."

"I'm sorry, Christina. I just need to speak to you. I was hoping you would be here early. I wanted to talk to you before your customers arrived."

Christina tugged the curly-haired girl, who was only slightly taller and heavier than herself, inside the still-shadowy store. She closed and relocked the door. It would be better if they were not interrupted.

"Did you find out anything? Did your mother remember seeing Blake here?"

"*Nee.* I mean, no. She did not. But my little *schweschder* did."

"How old is your sister? Old enough to be reliable?" Jill waved her hands about, obviously flustered. "I don't mean I think your sister would lie or anything. I mean..."

Christina held up a hand to stop the other young woman's nervous prattle. "Grace is eight. And before you say that she's too young to know anything, let me tell you about my youngest *schweschder*. Grace is very observant. She is honest through and through. She described your *bruder* down to a tiny mole on his cheek. I hadn't even noticed it and had to squint at the picture to see it. But Grace didn't miss it."

"Okay, so tell me what she saw."

Christina relayed the story as Grace had told it the previous evening. She saw tears fill Jill's emerald eyes and watched her stoically blink them away. "I'm sorry to cause you more pain, Jill. I know you grieve your loss."

"I do, and I will for some time, I fear, but I need to know the truth. Every little piece of information is important. We just have to figure out how to assemble all the little pieces into a complete picture to clear Blake's name."

"We?" Christina stepped back. Hadn't she done her part already? She risked raising her *mudder's* suspicions, and she might not be out of the woods yet once *Mamm* had a chance to process everything. Christina sincerely hoped canning and jam-making would crowd out any other thoughts *Mamm* might have.

"You're in this with me, aren't you?"

"What more can I do? I got the information you asked for. As much as I could anyway. I don't see how else I can help you."

"You're the only other person who knows all these details unless you've told someone else."

"Just one other person."

"Who?"

"Noah Zimmerman. He is actually the person who found the penknife. He was with me when I dug through the begonias and found the key. It seemed only right to clue him in since he was already unknowingly involved."

Jill sighed. "I suppose you're right."

"Noah is very trustworthy. I didn't want to risk telling anyone else for fear they could be in danger, but Noah was part of this from the beginning."

"I'm so sorry you had to be involved, Christina. You haven't received any kind of threat, have you?"

"*Nee.* Do you think I will?"

"I hope not, but I don't know."

"Have you been threatened?"

"Not yet, but anything could happen. I keep glancing over my shoulder. I try to sleep with one eye open. I jump at every little sound and am seriously considering adopting a dog from the animal shelter. A big dog."

Christina giggled but then clapped a hand over her mouth. She bit down on the tender flesh of her palm to curb the mirth bubbling up from inside. "I'm sorry."

"What's so funny?"

"Forgive me. The situation is far from funny. It's just that in my mind I saw a big dog pulling you along instead of the other way around. You aren't very big, you know." She choked down another chuckle.

Jill smiled and flung a dark curl over her shoulder. "I might not be a giant, but I am pretty tough."

Christina raised her eyebrows. She couldn't imagine the delicate-looking girl as being tough, but who was she to question?

"You look like you don't believe me. I guess I'll have to adopt a St. Bernard and bring him in to show you."

"You might ride him in here, but I doubt you'll walk him in on a leash."

Jill laughed. "Thanks, Christina. I needed a laugh. There has been way too much tension."

"I'm sure you've been under a great deal of stress." Christina hated to ask the question nagging at her. She wanted to know the answer, but at the same time didn't want to know. "What is your plan now that you're sure your *bruder* was here?"

"I've been wracking my brain trying to figure this out. I mean, I was reasonably sure Blake had been here because of the matching notes and other things. And I don't know that very many people are aware of my penchant for pink begonias. I'm assuming that's why he chose your place. He must have been hoping I would associate the pink paper and pink begonias with The Green Thumb."

"It's a *gut* thing you figured that out pretty quickly."

"It was a hunch, but maybe my mind works the same way Blake's does, uh, did." Sadness overshadowed her like a curtain draping a window.

"Have you figured out what the key belongs to?"

"It must be a security box key."

"Can you go to the bank and check since you are his *schweschder*?"

"I think he kept the box at home."

"Oh." Christina stole a glance at the clock. She needed to open for business in three minutes. "I assume you haven't checked yet, then."

"I-I can't make myself go in his place alone. I have a key to Blake's townhouse, but, uh, would you come with me?"

"Me?" Her shrill shriek stung her own ears. Christina couldn't understand why Jill didn't cover her ears to muffle that sound.

"Please, Christina? I need your help."

"I've already done what I could." She shook her head so hard that her *kapp* strings flew about her face. She'd already taken a huge risk by questioning her *mudder* and carrying around the newspaper photo.

"You're the only one who knows everything. And I trust you."

"I'm sure you have plenty of *freinden* you could take with you."

"Actually, I don't."

Christina stared in disbelief. This beautiful, kind young woman didn't have a passel of *freinden* who would eagerly help her? Wasn't there a special young man who would jump at the chance to protect her if need be?

"You're looking at me like a second head sprouted from my neck. What's wrong?"

"I find it hard to believe you don't have a throng of folks who would be happy to help you."

"I grew up here but only recently moved back. I didn't keep up with old friends. Most of them have moved anyway. And I tend to keep to myself, so I haven't really made friends since I returned."

Christina pitied the girl who didn't have loved ones. How lonely her life must be. But she couldn't let sympathy pull her deeper into the mystery she was already way too involved in. "Oh" was all she could think to say. She cast another glance at the old clock on the wall. She really needed to unlock the door now.

"I know you need to get to work, but please say you'll come with me. I could pick you up after work."

And what excuse would she give *Mamm*? "I have things to do after work. I need to get home to help with supper and chores."

"What about tomorrow?"

"Tomorrow is Sunday." Christina edged toward the door.

"I know you don't have church every Sunday. Is tomorrow one of your off days? I could pick you up here so I wouldn't have to suddenly appear at your house."

"Jill, I can't simply wander away without any explanation. We usually do things as a family."

"You could bring—what was his name—Noah? Maybe you could say you were going for a ride with him."

Christina gasped. "That would be dishonest. I couldn't do that."

"If he came along, it wouldn't be dishonest."

"Then people would get the wrong idea. They would think we were courting." Heat seared her cheeks.

Jill laughed. "From your reaction, I gather you wouldn't exactly mind that, but it isn't something you would want to advertise."

"We wouldn't court even if I did want that—and I'm not saying that I do." This was becoming such a tangled-up mess! If Annie hadn't made such an outward display of her interest in Noah, and she had remembered Christina's whispered dreams, things might be different. But as it was right now, she had to try to keep her distance from him.

"He's at least a friend, isn't he?"

"Of course."

"All right, then. Friends do things together all the time."

Maybe in Jill's world that was true. In Christina's world, a fellow and a girl didn't traipse off somewhere together and claim they were merely *freinden*. "Not like that." She had reached the door and flipped the sign to "open." Before she could turn the lock, Jill raced over and clamped a hand on her arm. "I need to open up now, Jill."

"I know, but please Christina, please come with me. Please help me."

A customer pulling into the parking lot saved Christina from giving in to the pleading. *Mamm* always said she was soft-hearted. Now she knew her *mudder* was right. Her heart broke for Jill. She could easily put herself in Jill's place and feel her pain. Christina would be beside herself if something awful happened to one of her siblings. She wanted to help Jill, but how could she? This whole situation was way beyond her abilities. A gentle squeeze on her arm brought her attention back to the girl she hadn't yet answered.

"Can I come back later, please?"

Christina wanted to shake her head. Instead, she nodded and whispered, "Okay." She would kick herself later, but those tear-filled emerald eyes would haunt her for the rest of the day if she didn't do something to try to alleviate the intense sadness.

"Thank you, Christina. I really appreciate your help."

Help? She didn't recall saying she would help, but apparently that was Jill's assumption. She would have to find a way to correct that notion by this evening. Christina wiped the concern from her face and smiled at her customers as Jill slid out past them.

~

"I don't know how you do it, Amelia." Christina stared at the heavy bag the other woman plunked down on the counter a short time later. "All those *kinner* underfoot, and you baked. Well, let me see..." Christina reached into the bag and carefully pulled out items, laying them aside. "Oatmeal raisin cookies, fudge brownies, applesauce bread, whoopie pies—how in the world did you get all these yummy treats baked?"

"Mr. Miller got off work early yesterday and picked up his two little ones around midday."

"But you still had your own girls."

"They played or watched me. And then I gave them a little dough to play with. Everything worked out well."

"I'm amazed. And grateful. Yesterday, I sold most of the baked food I thought would last all weekend."

"I can put them on the shelf while you do other things if you like."

"*Danki*. Where are your girls today? They aren't in the buggy, are they?"

"Of course not. Their *aenti* was feeling lonely and wanted some company today. She might get more than she bargained for." Amelia laughed.

"She'll have fun. You have *gut* girls."

"Hmmm. The girls will have fun, but I'm not so sure about their *aenti*."

Christina laughed. She was glad Amelia had arrived early. If only she had been a tiny bit earlier, she could have spared Christina that awkward conversation with Jill. Christina had been so preoccupied with thoughts of her confrontation with Annie that she hadn't been prepared for Jill's early appearance. Being so taken by surprise must have rendered her more vulnerable to Jill's pleading and tears.

"Did you hear me, Christina?"

"Oops. Sorry, Amelia. My mind had wandered off. What did you say?"

"I asked if the display looked all right because I can rearrange things however you like."

"It looks just fine. You have a flair for making things look nice." A loud rumble from her stomach punctuated her sentence.

"Maybe you should try a whoopie pie or a brownie."

"I might have to. My stomach must not have been satisfied with the muffin I fed it."

"If that's all you gave it, then I'm not surprised. Didn't you take time for breakfast this morning?"

Christina shook her head. "I wanted to get in a little earlier than usual." *And avoid running into Annie.*

"Oh. If you want to take a minute to eat something, I can mind the store."

"Don't you want to do errands or things at home while you don't have the girls to interrupt you?"

"I don't have anything I need to do at the moment. I want to help out here. I do my housework while the *kinner* play. I mend or do other chores while they nap. I have a routine that generally works well." Amelia paused to laugh. "Of course, nothing is totally predictable with five little girls around."

Christina shook her head. "I don't know how you can even think straight. Will you continue to watch the *Englisch* girls indefinitely?"

"Actually, they are Mennonite, but not Old Order."

Christina smacked her forehead. "I knew that! What's wrong with me? I see them with you often and know that they dress very much like us, but I guess because I also see them in the car with their *daed*, I tend to think of them as *Englisch*."

"They are very sweet girls. I feel so sorry for them. Baby Jessie will not have any memories of her *mudder*, and at four, Gabby's memories will be few. I'll watch them as long as their *daed* wants me to."

"Such a shame that they lost their *mamm* so young. It's great that they have you in their lives, Amelia."

"I do whatever I can to show them they are loved. I hope I say and do the right things."

"I'm sure you do. It must be a big relief for their *daed* to entrust his *kinner* to you."

"I enjoy them, and my own girls think of them as *schweschders*."

"That's *wunderbaar*." Christina squeezed the other woman's arm. It was great that Amelia had worked through her own sorrow and could now reach out to help someone else.

An influx of customers kept both women busy until noon. Christina never had a moment to grab her other muffin or even a bag of Amelia's cookies. Her stomach had begun to protest loudly. She would have to mollify it soon. "I know you will need to pick up your girls soon, Amelia, so please feel free to leave whenever you need to. I certainly appreciate your help today. It has been a very busy morning."

"It has indeed." Amelia blew at a wisp of pale-blonde hair that had loosened itself from her bun and plastered itself to her cheek. "Why don't you grab something to eat while I'm still here?"

"I don't want to hold you up. Besides, I'm used to grabbing a bite to eat here and there."

"That can't be very pleasant for your body. My girls are fine with their *aenti* for a bit longer. We don't need you passing out from lack of food."

Christina laughed. "That hasn't happened yet, so I doubt it will today. But if it makes you happy, I'll go eat my apple while there's a lull in customers."

"An apple? Only an apple?"

"You worry too much, my *freind*." Christina scurried off to take a few bites of her fruit. *I sure wish Amelia could stay here all day in case Jill returns. Surely Jill wouldn't press me to go with her if someone else was here.*

Chapter Twenty

As the afternoon wore on, Christina's nervousness mounted. She truly felt sorry for Jill and wanted to help, but how could she get involved? Her parents, the bishop—everyone she knew would frown on her playing detective. And that was putting it mildly. Yet, wasn't it her Christian duty to help others if she possibly could? What a pickle she'd gotten into.

Every time she heard a car pull into the parking lot, or a shadow crossed the threshold, Christina's breath caught somewhere between her lungs and her nose. Since it was now almost time to close for the day, she feared the newcomer would be Jill. She still hadn't figured out what to say to the girl. If she could make it for only another thirty minutes, she would lock the door, flip the sign, and pretend she wasn't here if someone knocked before she could escape.

When she finally rang up the last customer of the day, Christina breathed a bit easier. She did exactly as she had planned and even tiptoed away from the locked door, taking great care to avoid passing in front of a window. The sandwich she hadn't eaten earlier called to her, but she ignored it. She wanted to hurry and tally up the day's sales, do a minimal straightening up, and sneak out the back door. She'd plan to arrive early on Monday morning to sweep any debris that might have littered the floor since Amelia's earlier sweeping.

Christina's heart flip-flopped when knuckles rapped sharply on the front door. If she kept perfectly still, maybe the person would assume she had already left for the day and would go away. *Ach!* Her bicycle. She should have dragged it inside. Maybe whoever was out there wouldn't wander around back and spy it. She held her breath and listened. Did the sudden silence mean that the person had given up? She could only hope so.

~

She must have closed up a little early today, but there wasn't a note attached to the door saying so. Only the Closed sign hung in the window. Strange. He had finished work ahead of schedule, so he thought for sure he would catch Christina before she left.

He couldn't see anyone through the window. Everything looked orderly, but then again, she always kept the place just so. Even with a horde of customers milling about, the shop appeared neat and clean. Noah scrunched down and craned his neck, but he still couldn't visualize the counter where Christina usually sat to perform the day's accounting.

Noah raised a fist and rapped on the door again. Not a single sound reached his ears. He couldn't detect any voice or any scurrying of feet toward the door. He knocked a little louder. Nothing. He might as well give up and head home.

To his surprise, Noah felt overcome with disappointment. He hadn't realized how much he had looked forward to seeing Christina. She could brighten the dreariest day simply by smiling. Gazing into her big, sparkling silver eyes always made his heart dance a strange little jig. And if he touched her hand or arm, a lightning bolt shot through his body. Did she feel that? It certainly was a new experience for him, something he tried to prevent. But a person couldn't stop his feelings, could he?

Noah's next thought thunderstruck him. He didn't really want to switch off those strange emotions. Unfamiliar as they were, he welcomed them. He hoped and prayed Christina felt the very same way. Every now and then, he observed that little spark in her eyes that lit her entire face and led him to believe that she did indeed share his feelings. That was enough to send his hopes soaring. He wanted so much to see her today. Maybe she was still here. She could have gone out to the big greenhouse behind the store.

He jogged around the building. Her bike leaned against the back of it. Noah scanned the area. Both the greenhouse and the shed were securely locked. Christina must be inside, but why didn't she answer the door? Had she fallen or had some other accident? Had someone crept into the store and hurt her? Visions of the man in the shed paraded through his mind. His heart raced and pounded like thunder. He'd break the door down if he had to. She had to be okay. Noah hustled to the back door.

~

"Christina!"

The voice came from the back door, but it was a deep voice. Noah?

"Christy, are you all right?"

Her brain finally sent the message to tell her feet to move. Unsure why she did so, she tiptoed toward the back door and still took care to avoid the window. With one hand on the doorknob, she paused. "Noah?" Even though she had heard his voice in her dreams and was almost completely sure Noah Zimmerman stood on the other side of the door, she decided to use caution.

"*Jah.* It's Noah. What's wrong?"

She fumbled with the lock but finally managed to pull the door open a crack. A pair of blue eyes full of concern stared at her. She opened the door wide enough for the tall, broad-shouldered man to squeeze through and then firmly closed and locked the door behind him.

"What's wrong?"

"Nothing."

"Why is your face the same color as the milk I poured on my cornflakes this morning?"

She pressed a hand to her cheek. "I didn't know that it was."

"Why did you close and lock the door practically before I got all the way inside?"

Christina shrugged. "Because I'm closed now."

"Do you have a lot of customers trying to enter through the back door?"

"Not usually, but you never know if someone will wander around back thinking the greenhouse is open or hoping to get a look at the crime scene."

"Did someone scare you today or threaten you?"

"*Nee.*" Christina was scared all right, but not of anyone who threatened to harm her. She was afraid to face Jill because she knew she would not be able to refuse to help that distraught young woman.

"You aren't telling me something."

She couldn't look Noah in the eye. She tried to brush past him and did her best to make her voice light. "I'm almost ready to leave." A large hand clamped around her arm, halting her forward progress.

"Why do I get the feeling something isn't quite right?"

"I-I wouldn't know." How could he be so in tune with her moods?

"Please talk to me. Don't you trust me?"

"Of course, I do." *I simply can't think straight with your hand on my arm.*

"Then tell me what's troubling you."

"I didn't say anything was troubling me." But they needed to hurry and get out of the shop before trouble knocked on the front door.

"You don't have to say the words. I can tell."

"Really?" His hand squeezed her arm, but reassuringly not uncomfortably.

"Who has upset you?"

Christina sighed. She wasn't going to get out of here with Noah latched onto her arm, so she might as well tell him. Maybe she could persuade him to leave if she promised to explain everything as they cycled. "I'm not really upset. I'm, uh... oh, I don't know what I am!"

"Nervous?"

"Why do you say that?"

With his free hand, Noah gently pried open her fingers to release the edge of her apron balled up in her fist. "You don't usually attack your clothing."

Christina smiled. With Noah holding onto both of her arms now, she was forced to stand face-to-face, practically nose-to-nose. Now that made her nervous! Her heart drummed loud enough to echo around the room. "Can I tell you while we ride?"

"You really are anxious to leave. I hope nothing happened here to frighten you."

She shook her head and slid free of his grasp. "Let me grab my bag." She hustled to the counter, stowed her record book away, and yanked her bag off the shelf. The crackly sound of tires crunching on gravel and a flash of blue outside the window made Christina want to weep. "*Ach!* We almost made it!"

"Who is it, Christy?" Noah strode across the room in an instant. Once again, he took her hand and squeezed it.

"Jill," she croaked. Speaking as quickly as possible, she filled him in on her morning encounter with the *Englisch* girl. "How can I not help her, Noah? She is beside herself with grief and is determined to clear her *bruder* of any wrongdoing. I have to do whatever I can for her."

"We, not you. We're in this together."

Christina didn't want to drag Noah further into her problems, but his willingness to support her gave her immense relief. "I don't want to get you in trouble because of me. You can slip right out the back door and pretend you never heard of all this mess."

Noah chuckled. "I couldn't do that. I *wouldn't* do that. I've been in this with you from the beginning. I won't desert you now."

"But you don't have to be involved."

"I chose to be. I found the knife. I was here when you unearthed that key. You've filled me in on all the details you know. I'm here for the duration. Besides, maybe three heads can figure this out faster."

"You're sure?"

"Absolutely."

"Don't blame me if the bishop threatens you with the *bann*."

"I wouldn't dream of doing such a thing."

Noah's lopsided grin sent Christina's heart tripping over itself. How could one little smile bolster her spirits and her confidence? She shuffled toward the front door. With one hand poised over the lock, she glanced over her shoulder. "Last chance to run."

"I'm not going anywhere. Let your visitor inside."

Christina sighed and clicked the lock. *What am I getting myself into now?*

"Oh, Christina! I'm so glad you're still here. I was afraid I'd missed you." Jill scurried inside and blinked as her eyes adjusted to the dimmer light. "I'm sorry. You have company."

"This is Noah Zimmerman. I told you about him."

"Right. I remember. Nice to meet you." Before Noah could utter a greeting, Jill rushed on. "Can you come with me to Blake's townhouse, Christina? I really don't want to go alone."

Christina cut her eyes to Noah and then back to the dark-haired young woman with the pleading expression covering her face. "I-I can't go with you right now. I'm expected at home. I'm late leaving as it is."

Jill's shoulders slumped. "I understand. Would our plan for tomorrow work?"

"What plan? I don't recall making a plan." Christina glanced at Noah and shrugged.

"You know, we talked about going for a ride tomorrow. We could meet here—all of us—and head over to Blake's place."

"*You* talked about that idea. I did not agree to that. I told you that I couldn't simply sneak away from my house. And what if someone saw me, uh, us get in the car with you? How would we explain that?"

"We'll think of some explanation."

"Like what?"

"I could be taking you shopping."

"We don't do business on Sundays."

Jill twirled a long, spiral curl. "You don't go to movies or plays either, right?"

Christina wagged her head. "So you see, there really isn't any plausible excuse."

"But you work all day the other six days and have to rush home afterward. Sunday is the only day we can go."

"I'm sorry, Jill. I don't know what else we can do."

"I do."

Both young women snapped their attention to Noah. Christina couldn't believe he could possibly have thought of a suitable reason for two Old Order Mennonites to climb into a car with an *Englischer* on a Sunday. She could only squeak out one word. "What?"

Chapter Twenty-One

Christina's heartbeat roared in her ears. Surely the other two heard its pounding. What sort of plan rattled around in Noah's brain? Completely dumbfounded, she could only stare at him. From the corner of her eye, she could see that Jill's reaction mimicked her own.

Noah cleared his throat. "Did you hear that Bishop Micah's younger *schweschder*, Eleanore, had been admitted to the hospital?"

Christina nodded. "I heard that. She had complications with her diabetes, I think." What did the bishop's *schweschder* have to do with their dilemma? Christina hoped she didn't look as stupid as she felt.

"We can always say we went to visit her."

"Not unless we really do that. Lying would only compound our problem." Surely Noah wasn't suggesting that they fabricate a story. She would never have expected such a thing from him.

"Of course, we'll really visit. You can take her a pretty plant since we can't take her any sweet treats."

Christina mulled the idea over in her mind for a few seconds. It had potential, but...

"How do we explain the two of us being there together?" Her cheeks grew warm and probably glowed a bright red.

"That would be perfect," Jill broke in before Noah could answer. Hope shone in her face. "My brother's place isn't far from the hospital. What time do you want to go?"

Christina held up a hand. "Wait a minute. We have to think about this." She hated to burst Jill's bubble, but she needed to figure out how this whole plan would work. She turned to Noah. "Have you thought of an answer to my question?"

"I'm working on it."

Christina paced. Sometimes she thought better when she participated in some physical activity. In the confines of The Green Thumb, pacing would have to suffice. She felt two pairs of eyes following her movement, but she struggled to tune those out. She needed to formulate a plan fast so she could get home before her *mudder* sent her *bruders* out to search for her. She tried and discarded several ideas. "Well, Eleanore and I are *freinden* even though she's a few years older. It wouldn't be a huge stretch of the imagination to believe I would want to visit her. And I do sometimes take flowers or plants to people who are ailing. That part might work out fine." She stopped right in front of Noah. "But how do we explain your accompanying me there?"

"Um, how about you ran into me and I decided to go with you?"

Christina wrinkled up her nose and shook her head. "That probably wouldn't work. How would I just happen to run into you?"

Noah cracked a huge smile and snapped his fingers. "I've got it!"

"Let's hear your brilliant idea." His smile was contagious. Christina couldn't keep her lips from curving upward. How did he have such an effect on her?

"My *mudder* loves to do those word searches and has tons of those little books filled with the puzzles. I think she gets one whenever she goes in the grocery store."

Christina tapped a foot on the cement floor. "And?"

"I can ask if she wants to send one to Eleanore. You know, something to do to fill the long, boring hours in a lonely hospital room. If she says she wants to do that, I'll tell her I can give it to someone who plans to visit Eleanore. That would be you. Brilliant, *jah?*"

"What if she doesn't have a spare book to send?"

Noah chuckled. "That would be like you not having a plant in the greenhouse. I could then say I tagged along to take the book and any message *Mamm* might want to send."

Jill clapped her hands. "It sounds like a plan. Is it all right with you, Christina? Do you think this will work?"

"It's hard to tell. It's rather flimsy, but it's the only idea we have at the moment. I really do need to get home now."

"Where should I pick you up? Is here a good place?"

Christina shrugged. She'd have even more explaining to do if Jill pulled up to the Brubacher house to fetch her. She turned a questioning glance on Noah.

"Or we could meet next door at the Quick Stop," Jill offered.

Christina shook her head. "*Nee*, a Mennonite would not be at a store on Sunday. We'd better meet here." She didn't like that idea either, but ideas and time were both in short supply at the moment. "We can't stand out front, though, like we're waiting for a bus. Let's agree on a time. Noah and I can stay in the back and keep a watch out for you. At least that way we won't be on public display." She hazarded a peek at Noah, who nodded in agreement.

"Sounds fine." Jill's voice took on a more hopeful tone. "Thank you both so much."

Christina's mind spun so fast that she feared she would become dizzy and drop to the floor. How was she going to slip away from the house tomorrow without raising suspicion? She supposed she could say that she was taking a walk, which she would. She could say she was meeting a *freind*, which she was. And she could find herself in a fine mess too! *Ach!* She would probably spend a sleepless night tonight trying to figure everything out.

~

Christina had managed to spend the morning in what she hoped was a normal manner. At least none of her family members questioned any kind of bizarre behavior. She sopped up the mess when Grace knocked over her entire bowl of cereal, sending fat raisins afloat in a river of milk. She even kept her hands from trembling when she poured her little *schweschder* another bowl of cereal, although she trembled violently inside.

Focusing on morning devotions had proved a bit more challenging. Her weary brain constantly wandered away to try out and discard possible conversations about her afternoon plans. Nothing she considered seemed appropriate. She would simply have to hope something occurred to her when the time came for her to leave.

Christina sneaked covert glances at the battery-operated clock as she played a board game with Sallie and Grace. Their squabbling over whose turn it was brought her waning attention back to the girls. Before long, it would be time to set out cold salads and make sandwiches for the noon meal. The lazy Sunday morning passed much more quickly than usual off-Sunday mornings.

After the meal, James said he planned to visit a *freind*. Christina caught his sheepish grin and surmised that person was a girl. John and David planned to play horseshoes. *Mamm* and *Daed* and the little girls prepared to visit relatives.

"Do you want to go with us, Christina?" *Mamm* asked as she set leftover pickled beets and dill pickles back inside the gas-powered refrigerator.

"Uh, *nee*, I think I'll take a walk." There. That was all she could think to say. *Please don't ask questions. Please don't ask questions.* She forced her hands to loosen their grip on the hunks of fabric they clutched. That would certainly be a dead giveaway that something was amiss.

"It's rather warm. You might want to take a bottle of water with you."

That was it? No questioning or probing? Christina tried to let her pent-up breath out slowly and quietly rather than in a long, loud sigh. "Great idea." She shuffled to the refrigerator to extract a bottle and forced her feet to walk normally to the back door. That turned out to be easier than she had anticipated. Now she needed to get to The Green Thumb without being observed.

Christina sauntered along at a leisurely pace until she cleared the property and would be less likely to be observed from the yard or house. Then she doubled her speed. She stuck to shaded areas as much as possible since she didn't want to arrive at the hospital smelling like a goat. She watched her footing lest she trip over a root and sprawl flat on her face. She didn't want to arrive covered in dirt and blood either. Besides, one spill this week was quite enough.

As she drew closer to The Green Thumb, her heart rate kicked up a notch, and not from the exertion. Every sense heightened. Tension knotted her shoulders. She had to cross the road and a little clearing in order to reach the store. She would be exposed to anyone and everyone who happened along. *Please let all the folks already be wherever they are going today and not out on the road at this very minute.*

Christina paused before stepping out of her shadowy haven. She held perfectly still and didn't even suck in a breath just so she could detect any noise or movement. When she didn't hear any clip-clopping of horses' hooves or any screeching buggy wheels, she ventured out. She considered running all the way to the back greenhouse but quickly discarded that idea. If someone came along and spied her sprinting through the field and parking lot, she wouldn't be able to offer him or her a plausible excuse for such behavior.

She decided a brisk, determined walk would be her best choice. Her attempt at nonchalance was most likely a failure, but at least she didn't encounter anyone who would question her actions. *Only a few more feet. Don't run. Stay calm.* Christina's mind issued the orders over and over until she reached the greenhouse, which was well out of view from the road or parking lot. Only the squirrels and deer in the woods could see her now.

"Christina?" The sound was more of a hiss than a word.

"Aaahh!" Either squirrels had learned to speak or someone lurked out of sight in the woods. Twigs snapped. Should she run? She raised a hand to her mouth and bit down on her knuckles to keep from screaming.

A tall form emerged from the woods brushing debris from his pants.

"Noah! You nearly scared the life out of me." She patted her chest.

"I'm sorry, Christy. I've been here a while and didn't want to be spotted lurking around a closed business, so I stepped into the woods. It was cooler there too."

"I thought I would be early, but you beat me." She dropped her hand since her heart had slowed to a trot from its gallop. "I guess my nerves are on edge."

"Mine are a little taut too. I got the puzzle book. *Mamm* was happy to send it to Eleanore."

"*Gut.* I need to grab a plant from the greenhouse." She extracted her keys from a pocket and jiggled them until she could pluck the correct one from the tangle. She hesitated only a fraction of a second as the memory of entering her shed that fateful evening pushed to the forefront of her mind. She gulped down rising panic, took a deep breath, and forced that memory to the depths of her brain where it belonged.

"Do you need some help?"

Did he sense her apprehension? "I think I can get everything." She had to be strong, to take charge. After all, this was *her* place.

With that little pep talk under her belt, Christina shored up her courage and marched inside her greenhouse. She knew exactly the type of plant she wanted. It had to be hardy and easy to care for. It needed to have cheerful blooms. A geranium would be perfect. Eleanore could keep it as a house plant or she could add it to an outside flower bed. A geranium would do fine in either situation.

Christina inspected her rows of geraniums, searching for the perfect size and color. She lifted a medium-sized pot containing a bushy, green plant with pink and white blossoms. Perfect. She carried the specimen to a workbench, where she cut a length of white ribbon. She tied a bow around the pot to spruce it up a bit. Satisfied with her end product, she hurried outside. It should be time for Jill to arrive. The sooner they got this whole business over with, the better.

She pulled the greenhouse door closed behind her and turned to lock it.

"I'll get the door since your hands are full." Noah hopped over to her side and took the keys from her. "The plant looks nice."

"I hope Eleanore will like it. Jill hasn't arrived yet?"

"I haven't seen any cars pass by."

"Any buggies?"

"Not a single one."

"That's a relief." Christina stood perfectly still for a moment, straining to hear if a vehicle approached. "Do you think she changed her mind?"

"I doubt it. We both arrived early, so it probably isn't quite our meeting time yet."

"You must be right." She began pacing, taking care to stay behind the building and out of sight of any passersby. "Are we doing the right thing?"

Noah swiped a hand across his face before answering. "I don't like the sneaking around part, but I think helping Jill is the right thing. Are you having second thoughts?"

"Not about helping. I know I'd want my *bruder's* name cleared if I was in Jill's place. Like you, I don't like sneaking around and pretending. Even though visiting Eleanore is a *gut* thing, I don't like using her as an excuse."

"I know. Maybe this will be the only time we need to do this."

"I sure hope Jill finds what she needs today for all our sakes." Christina paced a few more steps. It was too bad she didn't own a watch. Where was Jill? As if on cue, a car turned into the gravel parking lot out front.

"I'll make sure it's her," Noah offered. "It could be someone turning around." He crept to the edge of the building and peeked around the edge.

Christina nodded. At least it was the sound of an automobile's wheels and not a buggy's wheels. She didn't want to have to invent any more stories to explain why she and Noah were hiding behind the store. Though she hadn't technically told any lies, guilt still assailed her.

"It's her!" Noah turned back and offered a reassuring smile. "Are you ready?"

Did she have a choice at this point?

Chapter Twenty-Two

Christina jumped in surprise when Noah wrapped a large hand around her upper arm and hustled her to the waiting blue car. Evidently he was as concerned about being spotted by a member of their community as she was. He yanked open the back door and stood in such a way as to block her from view. What a considerate fellow!

She slid across the seat as quickly as she could without upsetting her plant. The last thing Christina wanted was to sprinkle dirt all over Jill's car. Noah had to practically fold his long body in half to crawl into the back seat of the small car. He trapped the edge of Christina's dress beneath a thigh, hindering her ability to get out of his way. His head thunked against hers, and she clutched the plant tighter to keep it from flying out of her hands.

"*Ach!* I'm sorry, Christina."

She tugged at her dress. "If you lift your leg, I can free my dress and move over to give you more room."

"Sorry." He wiggled enough to release the fabric.

"Someone can sit up front with me. I won't bite. I promise." Jill smiled at them in the rearview mirror.

Noah grunted as he shifted to fit his legs between the seats. "We're fine."

Christina's shoulder bumped the window. She angled herself to face the center of the car so her face would not be visible to anyone who might be able to see inside. Once Noah got settled, she noticed that he did the exact same thing.

Jill shifted the car into gear and eased out of the parking lot. "I suppose we should visit your friend at the hospital first, right?"

"*Jah*, if that's all right with you," Christina replied. "I'm afraid the plant will wither in the hot car if we stop at your *bruder's* place first."

"Sounds good to me." Jill adjusted a couple of knobs on the dashboard. "I cranked the air up, but you two let me know if you get too cold."

"It feels great to me." Noah had removed his black hat and balanced it on his knees.

"How about you, Christina?" Jill threw over her shoulder.

"I'm fine. It's a real treat to have air conditioning on such a hot day and not to have to rely solely on whatever whisper of a breeze might blow."

"I don't know how you stand it without air conditioning. How do you sleep at night when it's so hot?" Jill glanced in the rearview mirror at her passengers.

"You get used to it. It's really all we've ever known. We only have air conditioning if we go to the grocery store or to a doctor's office or something. We keep the windows open and stay too busy to think about it—most of the time." Christina laughed. "That's not to say we don't appreciate a ride in an air-conditioned vehicle from time to time."

Jill shook her head as if she couldn't possibly imagine such a hardship. "I've lived a soft life, I guess. I like my comforts."

"Not a soft life. An *Englisch* life," Christina said. "If I grew up the way you did, I'd most likely feel the same way."

It took no time at all to reach St. Mary's Hospital by car. A horse and buggy took considerably longer to travel the seven miles from Charity to Lewistown, even at a fast trot.

"I'll pull up to the entrance and let you out. Take your time visiting. I'll watch for you and drive back up here to pick you up." Jill braked under the portico at the hospital's main entrance.

"You'll suffocate waiting in your car. You can *kumm* in with us." Christina might be more used to the heat than the *Englisch* girl, but she sure wouldn't want to be fastened up in a boiling car.

"No. I'd feel awkward since I don't know the patient."

"You could wait in the lobby," Noah suggested. "At least then you wouldn't melt."

Jill laughed. "I'll tell you what. I'll park and see how hot I get. If the car becomes too unbearable, you'll find me sitting in the lobby when you walk out."

"Okay." Christina scanned the area before exiting the car. Noah did the same thing as he plopped his hat back on his head. She really didn't expect any of their *freinden* or neighbors to be milling about, but she couldn't be completely sure that someone else hadn't taken a notion to visit Eleanore. The fact that she and Noah were at the hospital together might raise a few eyebrows, but the greater problem would be explaining their connection with Jill.

Before Christina could get herself and the geranium completely out of the car, Noah had shot around to open the door and reached in to assist her. "We won't be too long," she called to Jill before Noah hustled her through the hissing automatic glass doors. She nudged Noah. "I don't know Eleanore's room number, so we'll have to ask."

Noah nodded and continued to propel her across the gleaming laminate floor to the big reception desk where two white-haired ladies sat. If he kept up this galloping pace, she would be completely breathless before they even reached Eleanore's room. In his determination to get them out of sight, he must have forgotten that his legs were nearly twice as long as hers. Christina practically had to skip to keep up with him.

Once they had slapped sticky visitor passes on their chests and obtained the proper room number, Noah hurried them down the hallway that one of the ladies pointed out to them. "Do you think you could jog instead of sprint?" Christina panted between each word. Her heart had already been racing due to nerves. Now it pounded even harder.

"I'm sorry, Christy. I forget everyone doesn't have such long legs."

"I'm all right. Just a little out of breath."

Noah deliberately took tiny steps until they reached the nurses' station of the medical unit.

"We don't have to stay long," Christina whispered. "I'll follow your lead."

~

They visited as long as they dared, fearing Bishop Micah or some other member of the community would pop in at any moment. Christina promised to visit Eleanore when she got home in a day or so. "I think she was glad to see us. I'm happy she liked the geranium." Christina kept her voice soft as they retraced their steps to the lobby. For some reason, she felt the need to whisper in the hospital, just like in the library.

"She's going to tell, you know."

"Tell what?"

"That we were here together."

"Well, we told her your *mudder* sent you along with the puzzle book. You don't think she believed it was a spur-of-the-moment decision for us to ride together?"

"Eleanore *might* believe that, but I don't know about everyone else along the grapevine. Don't get me wrong, it doesn't bother me in the least for folks to know we were together, but I don't want you to be embarrassed or ashamed."

"I'm certainly not embarrassed or ashamed to be seen with you, but I don't want to give people the wrong impression." Suddenly, Christina gasped and stopped mid-stride.

"What's wrong?"

She shook her head and reached out to touch the wall for support. The air conditioning that had felt so nice earlier now raised a crop of goose bumps along both arms.

"Christina? You're so pale. What's wrong?"

"Annie."

"Annie?" Noah whipped his head around in each direction.

"She isn't here. It's just that she's already mad at me, and now she'll never forgive me. I think I've alienated my *freind* forever." Tears blurred Christina's vision and her nose burned.

"What does Annie have to do with anything? And why is she mad at you? I would think that would be the other way around."

"Why would I be mad at her?"

"She hasn't been behaving too well as far as I can tell."

You don't know the half of it! You didn't see her cause me to fall off my bike. But Annie was hurt. Did that justify causing someone else to be injured?

"I'm sorry. I didn't mean to criticize your *freind*."

Noah must have thought her lack of response to his statement meant that she was upset with him. "Y-you're right. She has been acting different." Did he know that he was the reason for that?

"So why did you have that look of horror when you realized Annie would know we came to the hospital together?"

Were men really not able to pick up on the obvious clues women threw at them? Were their brains wired so differently? How should she answer the question? "Well, haven't you noticed, I mean, maybe you don't know Annie well, but... *ach*! Can't you tell she's interested in you?" Nothing like blurting out exactly the wrong thing. The color that sprang into Noah's cheeks rivaled the pink blooms on the geranium she had just left with Eleanore.

"I, uh, never encouraged her in any way. To tell the truth, I've tried to steer clear of her. Honest."

"I believe you. And I know once Annie gets an idea fixed in her head, wild horses can't drag it out."

"It seemed kind of sudden. Her interest, that is."

"*Jah.*"

"She never gave any indication whatsoever until this past week, unless I was too dense to notice."

"I didn't pick up any clues either until she kind of..."

"Started with the wiggly eyes and sugary smiles."

Christina burst out laughing and then clapped a hand over her mouth to stifle the sound. At least they were out of the patient area now so a stern nurse wouldn't dart out to shush her.

"You won't tell her I said that, will you?"

Christina made a zipping motion across her lips. Probably after today's adventure got passed along the grapevine, Annie wouldn't even glance in her direction, much less talk to her. She sighed. She was going to miss her best *freind* even if she could sometimes be annoying.

"What was the deep sigh for?"

"After today, I will most likely have lost my *freind* forever."

"Why?"

Christina's cheeks burned as she mumbled, "Because she'll think I stole you from her."

"You can't steal something that never belonged to a person. And trust me, I never belonged to Annie Wenger, not by any stretch of the imagination."

"Annie probably won't see it that way."

"She needs to face reality, and sooner will be better than later."

Christina shrugged. "We'd better go out and tell Jill we're ready to complete the remainder of today's mission."

They resumed their march to the hospital lobby in silence. Noah's tap on her shoulder sent a shock wave reverberating throughout Christina's body. "What do you suppose we'll find at Jill's *bruder's* place?"

"It's hard to tell." Christina sighed again. Noah squeezed her hand, creating another shock wave.

~

Jill jumped to her feet as soon as Christina and Noah stepped into the lobby. "You were right," she said. "I lasted in the car for about ten minutes before I thought I'd suffocate."

"I hope we didn't keep you waiting too long." Christina glanced around at the stark walls punctuated by occasional framed pictures of some local setting, but she didn't spy a clock anywhere. She didn't think they had visited with Eleanore an exorbitant amount of time but wasn't sure.

"Oh, no. Not at all. You were quick actually."

"*Gut.*" Now if they could be quick at Blake's home, Christina would be grateful. How relieved she would be to climb out of Jill's car back at The Green Thumb.

"Do you want to wait here while I get the car?"

Christina glanced at Noah. "We can walk out with you."

Noah nodded. "Sure. Let's walk fast, though."

"You got it." Jill led the way to the exit. "I'm not parked too far out. Since it's Sunday, there were a lot more parking spots."

Once again, they piled into the little, blue car. Christina's nerves made her hands feel like they had been plunged in ice water. What would they find at the home of the poor man who was snatched from this world so suddenly? Would they find anything at all that would lead them to the truth or that would at least ease Jill's mind? She picked at her nails until Noah dropped one of his hands over her fidgeting fingers. Christina nodded and gave him a lopsided smile. She read his thoughts of reassurance and appreciated them.

Jill's attempt at small talk fell flat. Christina couldn't even imagine what must be racing through the girl's mind. "We're almost there." Jill clicked on the turn signal and waited for two cars to pass before crossing the road.

Christina bit her lip. Would they be able to get in and out of the place unnoticed and find whatever they needed quickly? Maybe after this first time visiting her *bruder*'s place, Jill would feel comfortable enough to make any return trips on her own. Christina could certainly understand the other woman's apprehension, though. It must be terribly unsettling and incredibly sad to enter a loved one's home knowing that person would never be there again.

Whatever happened to Blake Sheridan should not have happened. Christina knew that for sure. Deep down inside, she believed Blake had been a *gut* person who wanted to help people. True, she had never met the man that she was aware of, but she had a serious hunch that he was not a drug user or a criminal.

She didn't think it was her imagination that the car slowed to nearly crawling. Peeking over the seat, Christina could see that Jill gripped the steering wheel so hard that her fingers appeared bloodless. Her apprehension seemed to have progressed to terror. How could she and Noah make this easier for her? Should they try to engage her in some sort of small talk to fill the tense silence?

They drove past several large single-family homes before turning onto another street where clumps of three-story homes were connected together. These must be town-houses. How odd it must be to practically live on top of another family. The monstrous single-family homes had been close enough to toss a ball from one into the window of the next one. But these homes were joined. Christina didn't think she would like that at all.

Jill slowed the car even more and turned into the driveway of the end unit of the last clump of buildings on the street. "This is it."

Chapter Twenty-Three

As in "this is the house" or "this is our moment of discovery" or "this is more than I can handle"? Maybe Jill meant all three things. Christina cast a wary glance at Noah. As if he read the discomfiture in her own mind, he reached across the seat to squeeze her hand. Reassurance, comfort, and strength flowed from his fingers into hers and shot up her arm. How did he do that?

Jill switched off the engine and pushed open her door. She snatched the keys out of the ignition, silencing that infernal dinging noise. She didn't hop out of the car as Christina had seen her do on several other occasions. Instead, she grasped the door to pull herself out like a much older person might do. When she looked back inside the car, Christina read the fear in her lovely, green eyes.

Christina and Noah threw open the back doors at the same time and hurried to Jill's side. Christina patted the other girl's arm. "Are you sure you want to do this now?"

"I-I have to."

"When was the last time you were here?"

"Two days before, uh, before Blake, uh…"

Christina reached for Jill's hand and squeezed. The little hand was ice cold on such a hot, summer day. "I understand." She hoped she could transfer a bit of heat to that hand as they shuffled side by side toward the door. Maybe she could convey strength and comfort, just as Noah had done for her moments earlier.

Jill paused at the top step as if gathering her courage. She drew in a shaky breath. Her hand shook so uncontrollably that she couldn't insert the key into the lock. She sniffed, took another deep breath, and tried the key again.

Noah stepped around Christina and gently pulled the key from Jill's hand. "Why don't you let me open the door and go in first?"

Jill nodded and sighed as if relieved to have this small obstacle removed.

Christina wrapped a hand around Jill's upper arm. The poor girl looked like she could faint at any moment, and Christina didn't want her to tumble down the concrete steps. She wondered if Jill's dark hair made her face appear so white or if the girl had truly grown that pale. "It will be okay," she whispered. *Please, Lord Gott, let it be okay.*

Noah had the door open in a matter of seconds. He held up one hand toward the women, which Christina interpreted as "wait." Her own heartbeat roared in her ears. Her face had probably turned the same shade of pasty white as Jill's.

"The place might be a mess. I-I'm sure the police have been through everything. I-I gave them the extra key I had. Blake had given me an extra one in case we both lost the ones on our key ring. He has—had—a key to my place too."

"That was a *gut* idea." Christina wasn't sure a reply had actually been necessary. She had a hunch Jill's chatter was due to nerves and didn't really require a response, but it seemed rude not to acknowledge her words. Noah stepped inside but hadn't called out for them to enter. Was everything all right in there?

"Let's go!" Jill broke from Christina's grasp and pushed the door wide open. Her gasp when she crossed the threshold made Christina hurry in behind her. "Oh my goodness!" Jill wobbled until Christina again latched onto her arm.

An end table had been overturned and a lamp lay on the floor beside it. The lightbulb had shattered into a million minute fragments. Chair cushions perched at odd angles, and a crocheted tan, green, and white afghan dangled half off the sofa. Even the few local lighthouse prints in frames on the beige walls were cockeyed. Had there been a small earthquake that set things awry? Surely the police wouldn't have left such a mess, would they? That didn't seem quite right, but what did Christina know about police procedures?

She glanced across the living room to the kitchen. Cabinet doors yawned wide open. Drawers were ajar, and one small one had been dumped out. Pens, pencils, paper clips, and notepads had been strewn across the countertop. Christina turned to watch as Noah emerged from a bedroom. She raised her eyebrows in an unspoken question. His almost imperceptible nod told her that room had been ransacked as well. Who made this mess? What had they been searching for?

"Blake didn't do this." Jill turned around and around, eyes flitting from one area to another. "H-he was very neat, very organized." She stopped spinning and reached to flick away a tear. "The police wouldn't do this either. Someone was looking for something."

An icy finger of fear traced down Christina's spine. Had that person done this before dragging Blake out of the house, or had he returned afterward? She assumed that Blake had not willingly gone to her shed or taken whatever drugs had been found in his body. The twisted, scatter rugs on the laminate floor indicated a struggle had occurred. Of course, she was not any sort of expert on crimes, but that was what it looked like to her. Maybe whoever had pillaged the townhouse kicked the rugs out of place in their haste, but Christina's gut told her that had not been the case.

She trailed along behind Jill through the living room and steeled herself for whatever they might discover in the bedroom. She prayed Jill did the same thing. What on earth had someone been searching for?

This room turned out to be a bigger mess than the living room. Dresser drawers had been dumped out or pulled open and rummaged through. Sweatshirts, tee shirts, and blue jeans littered the floor. Even the quilt and sheets had been pulled from the bed and left in a heap on the floor.

"What could they have been searching for?" Christina couldn't resist asking the question any longer.

"I don't know. It isn't like Blake had a lot of money or valuables. I'm sure his paychecks were deposited into his checking account, so he wouldn't have had a lot of cash lying around."

"Where would that security box be?" Noah's gaze swept the ravaged room. "Would that have been in this room? Maybe that's what the person was after."

"That seems logical. I sure hope they didn't find it."

How could they not have found it? Christina thought the intruders made a pretty thorough search of the place, gauging by the mess they left behind. It didn't appear that any area was left untouched. Hadn't Jill picked up on that, or did she not want to admit it? "It certainly seems like whoever was here prowled through everything."

"I know." Jill heaved a huge, exasperated sigh. "But I'm crossing my fingers they didn't discover Blake's hiding place."

"Hiding place?" Christina tried not to let her skepticism show, but she couldn't identify a single portion of the room that had not been turned upside down.

"Hang on a second." Jill dashed from the room.

Christina lifted her eyes to meet Noah's big, blue ones. He lifted his shoulders and opened his mouth to speak when

Jill lumbered through the doorway half dragging and half lifting a kitchen chair. Noah jumped across debris and relieved her of her burden. "I could have gotten this for you. Where do you want it?"

Jill hesitated as she gasped for breath. "The closet."

From the looks of the open closet, that area had been torn apart like the rest of the room. If Blake had hidden a box among clothes or shoes, Christina imagined the thieves had found it and carted it away. What would Blake have stored in it anyway? What valuables did *Englischers* keep under lock and key?

Noah deposited the chair right inside the closet. "I assume the hiding place is up high since you dragged in the chair. Would you like me to climb up and search? Just point out the direction."

The contents on the closet shelves had been shuffled about or thrown on the floor. Anything that had once been hidden would have been exposed, wouldn't it? Christina watched open-mouthed as Jill scooted the chair to a particular spot. She looked up at the nearly empty shelf but saw nothing resembling a sturdy security box, only a couple of baseball caps and an umbrella. Even the smallest security box Christina had seen in the hardware store could not be hidden beneath those.

Jill scrambled onto the chair, stood on tiptoe, and stretched her arms toward the ceiling.

"I could get something for you so you don't have to climb." Noah's expression showed the concern Christina felt.

"I'm okay. I won't fall."

Just the same, Christina wormed her way into the closet to hold the chair steady. It was a *gut* thing the closet was one of those big, walk-in varieties since they had all crammed inside. "Be careful." She felt like she was watching one of her little *schweschders* climb a tree while she waited to catch whoever fell. "Noah is taller than both of us, you know. This job would be easier for him."

"But he doesn't know what to do. It's easier for me to do it than to explain it."

Was there some secret compartment in the ceiling? Christina strained to view every inch above Jill's head but couldn't detect any kind of seam that indicated the presence of a trap door. Had Blake possessed something so valuable that he had to squirrel it away, or had he had some inkling that someone was after him and he had to hide some sort of evidence? Her mouth dropped open as she watched Jill tug at a light fixture. "Wait! Let me turn off the switch." Christina didn't know a whole lot about electricity, but she did know people could receive a shock when they messed with outlets, wires, and fixtures.

Jill laughed. "It's okay. Watch!" She pulled hard enough to topple the chair if Christina hadn't been gripping it. She handed down the square-shaped fixture. "See? It's a fake."

Christina peered inside the hollow container lined with some sort of paper. Now she was totally baffled.

"It picks up light from the other fixture, but it's actually just a piece of glass with reflective tape inside."

Christina looked at the ceiling. Instead of a lightbulb, she saw the outline of a square. Had that been made by the phony fixture or... All thoughts left her head. She gasped when Jill pressed on one edge of the square, causing a little door to spring open. "What was he so afraid would be found?" Had the man truly been involved in drugs or some other illegal activity? Was Jill privy to her *bruder*'s shenanigans and had tricked her and Noah into accompanying her? Were they going to be in trouble or in danger now? She should have never trusted this innocent-looking young woman.

Jill grunted as she slid a box toward the opening in the ceiling. "As far as I know," she paused to pant, "he only had important papers, like bank account information and mementos from our parents in the box."

Noah brushed past Christina, setting every little nerve ending atwitter at even that brief touch. He reached up to effortlessly remove the box from its hiding place.

"Why would he go to so much trouble to hide papers and keepsakes? Why did he have a secret place carved into his closet ceiling? Had he expected someone to be after him?" Christina hated playing the part of inquisitor, but she had to know what they were up against.

Jill jumped from the chair and brushed dust from her hands. "I don't know that he *expected* someone to come after him. I think in his work as an addiction counselor he sometimes came across unsavory characters who would do anything to get money for their next fix."

"Fix?"

"Their next supply of drugs."

"Oh."

"How about if I set this box on the bed?' Noah threw a wary glance in Jill's direction. "It isn't' very heavy. I'm not sure if that is a *gut* thing or a bad thing."

"Maybe you're just used to carrying much heavier things so the box seems light." Jill trotted to the bed behind Noah, hope shining in her emerald eyes. She pulled the little key that had been buried in the begonia pot from her pants pocket and wiggled it into the lock. After a bit of jiggling, the lock released. Jill lifted the box's lid and groaned. "It's empty. What did Blake do with everything?"

"Did he have any other secret hiding places?" Noah scanned the room.

"N-not that I know of."

Christina could see that Jill was on the verge of tears or maybe even a complete breakdown. She scooted closer to lay a hand on the young woman's arm. She peered into the box. "Why would Blake hide an empty box?" She felt around the contours of the box. "Do you know if there is some sort of secret compartment in this box?"

"I-I don't know."

Christina kept pressing around until a side piece of the box popped off in her hand. Jill gasped. "Your *bruder* certainly liked things with nooks and crannies."

"Apparently. My box definitely doesn't have anything like this."

Christina's fingers were small enough to fit into the little slot she'd uncovered. "There's something here."

"Well, it certainly can't be all his vital information or our parents' wedding rings and things."

Christina's fingernails scraped against the side of the box as she wiggled her fingers to free the paper that she could feel but not extract.

"Can you get it out?" Jill practically whispered as if afraid the room sported unseen ears that would learn whatever secrets might be revealed.

"It feels like a piece of paper. I think I can get it." Christina grasped the edge of the paper between her index and middle fingers and tugged it out. Blake must have spent a lot of time inserting the paper in this tiny space. Why? And where were the other things Jill had so hoped to find? "I've got it." Christina withdrew her hand and held out the rolled-up piece of paper to the sniffling girl beside her.

Jill hesitated a fraction of a second before accepting the paper. Her face grew even paler. She sank onto the bed, scanned the note, and burst into tears.

"What is it, Jill?" Christina dropped onto the bed beside her. Even Noah shuffled closer.

Jill shook her head and waved the crinkled paper. "Read it."

"Are you sure?" Christina hated to intrude on someone's privacy. Jill might later regret that she shared the contents of the note with anyone.

"I'm sure."

Christina smoothed out the wrinkles as best as she could and read. A sudden chill swept throughout her body. It was if she was reading correspondence from the grave.

Dear Jill,

If you are reading this, then I am no longer walking this earth. Don't mourn for me. I will be resting in my Savior's arms. As you can see from this empty box, I have moved all the contents except for this note, which I am glad you found. I feared something bad would happen, and apparently it did. I have placed everything in a secure location. I just can't tell you specifically where in case you aren't the one who finds this note. I'll give you clues, though. You're a smart girl, so I know if you think about it you will figure out exactly where to look. I love you, sis.

Blake

Tears clouded Christina's vision. Next to her, Jill's body trembled with her silent sobs. Christina pulled the slightly larger girl into her arms and let her cry. "We'll figure this out, Jill. Noah and I will help you." She glanced at the man standing a few inches away for confirmation. His nod reassured her. "When you're ready, we'll work on this puzzle." Now she had totally committed not only herself but also Noah to this cause. She prayed they wouldn't be sorry.

Chapter Twenty-Four

"I-I'm so sorry." Jill pulled back from Christina's shoulder. "I'm n-not usually such a crybaby." She tossed a dark curl over her shoulder. "Oh! I got your dress all wet."

"It's all right. I don't think you are a crybaby. You have been through a lot. Anyone would be sad. And the dress will dry."

Jill nodded and sniffed. "Thank you both for coming here with me." Her eyes roved the room. "I have a mess to clean up. This whole place has been trashed." She drew in a shaky breath. "And now I have to add solving another riddle to my list of things to do." She retrieved the note from the bed where Christina had dropped it. "Why did he have to be so mysterious? How will I ever figure this out?"

Christina peered over the other woman's shoulder and read the words aloud. Maybe Noah could offer some suggestions. "Mary, not so ordinary, where does your garden grow? Near silver bells and oyster shells and pretty tykes all in a row."

She felt a pucker pull at her forehead. What was Blake trying to tell his *schweschder?* She raised her gaze to meet Noah's. His expression mirrored her own confusion. Jill looked equally perplexed. "It sounds like a sing-song. Do you have any idea what this means?"

"Not me," Noah declared.

"None at all." Jill twirled a springy curl around her finger. "I recognize that it's similar to a nursery rhyme. You know, 'Mary, Mary, quite contrary. How does your garden grow?'"

"*Jah*. I've heard that before. It was in a library book *Mamm* checked out when my *schweschders* were younger, but Blake changed some of the words."

"He did. That's what we have to figure out."

"I need to find a piece of paper to write this down so I can think about it." In all the mess lying about, Christina couldn't believe a scrap of paper and a pencil were nowhere in sight.

"I think I saw pens on the kitchen counter. Maybe there was a pad of paper too." Noah slipped from the room to search for the items.

Jill tapped her head. "I can't seem to think straight. I can't understand what Blake was trying to tell me. Why in the world did he make this so complicated? How did he think I could possibly figure everything out? Oooh! It's so frustrating."

"Give it some time, Jill. You've had a lot of shocking news to sort through."

"I don't know how much time I have. I don't know if someone is following me to find out whatever information Blake had. I don't know if that's what he hid away or if it was only personal papers and keepsakes. What if he knew something about a crime or wrongdoing and someone would do anything to keep that from coming to light?"

Christina involuntarily shivered. She had wondered the same thing. Any thought of distancing herself from this whole situation fled. She couldn't abandon Jill now.

She and Jill jumped and gasped in unison when a shadow blocked the sunlight that streamed into the window only seconds before. Jill slid to the floor pulling Christina off the rumpled bed with her. Christina hit the floor with a thud, cracking an elbow on the nightstand on her way down. At least the carpet somewhat cushioned her fall.

"What...?" Christina rubbed her throbbing elbow before trying to push herself up into a more ladylike position.

"Shhh! Stay down!" Jill grabbed Christina's shoulder and yanked her back down. "Somebody's out there."

Christina whispered as Jill had done. "Maybe Noah went outside."

"He went into the kitchen. I didn't hear him open a door."

"Maybe a neighbor walked by." Christina wasn't accustomed to having close neighbors whose shadows would fall upon her house simply by walking past. But in a community like this, where the houses were even connected together, a person must see and hear neighbors all the time.

Jill shook her head. Dark curls flew around her head. She peeked around the edge of the bed in the direction of the window. Her green eyes had grown as large as dinner plates and registered her fear. "They're still out there. The shadow hasn't completely moved away."

"You locked the door, ain't so?"

"I did. I hope that was good enough. Where did I leave my phone?" Jill patted her pockets but came up empty-handed. "I need to call the police."

"Maybe we should have called them when we first got here to report this mess." Christina had no basis for her hunch, but she was reasonably sure the law officers did not wreak the havoc displayed in Blake's townhouse. "Noah?" Christina tried to call loud enough for Noah to hear in the next room but not so loud as to be heard by whoever lurked outside the window.

"Shhh!"

"I don't want him to open the door thinking it's a neighbor or something."

"Good point."

Christina didn't know where sudden sleuthing skills came from. Could they be innate? Perhaps she had paid more attention to Annie's book reviews than she thought. She ignored her bruised elbow and crawled closer to the door. "Psst! Noah!"

"*Jah.*"

"Shhh!" Both women hissed in unison.

Heavy footsteps foretold Noah's approach. Apparently, he didn't have any idea they were being stalked. Christina wondered if this was the way a mouse felt when it was aware that a cat waited outside its hole. "Get down, Noah. Crawl!" She spoke as loudly as she dared. *Please just let him do it and not ask questions.*

A moment later, Noah crawled around the corner. The fact that he listened and reacted immediately brought Christina some small measure of relief. "Someone is outside the window," she explained before he could ask.

"A neighbor?"

"I don't think so. Whoever it is has been standing there for a while." Christina slithered back to where Jill crouched beside the bed. Noah followed.

"Do you want me to go outside and check what's going on?" Noah handed Christina the small pad of paper and ink pen he'd found.

"*Nee!*"

"No!"

"It could be that someone is only passing by or is looking for something. I can go see."

"They're looking for something, all right. Me!" Jill tucked a curl behind her ear, but it bounced back out.

"Us!" Christina mumbled. She had the distinct impression that whoever searched for Jill would also be searching for her. He, or they, most likely knew she had conspired with the *Englisch* girl. They probably also knew that she and Noah were here in the house with Jill at this very moment. Christina bit down hard on a knuckle to keep from crying out.

How could she have involved Noah in this whole dangerous mess?

A crash outside made them all nearly jump out of their skin. Noah struggled to push to his feet, but Christina grabbed his hand and held on tightly. "What do you think you're going to do?"

"I'm going to find out what's happening."

"You're going to get yourself hurt—or worse."

"I can't merely crouch down here and wait. If I can distract them, I might be able to buy some time for Jill to call the police."

"You can't go out there, Noah. You wouldn't be able to defend yourself. That's not our way."

"I don't plan to get into any fight, Christy. If I talk to them, it might give enough time for the police to arrive."

"I-I don't have my phone." Jill trembled so violently that the words had to squeeze through her lips.

"Where is it?" Noah pulled against Christina's death grip on his hand but couldn't free himself.

"I th-think it's in the living room. M-my purse m-must be there."

"Let me check."

A second crash had them huddling together.

"Did the window break?" Christina didn't detect the sound of shattering glass, but the person outside must be throwing something at the window. It wouldn't take many more blows like that last one to crack the pane.

Before another attempt could be made, angry barking and growling filled the air. A gruff shout and scuffling noises meant either the dog—a large one judging from the deep, loud bark—attacked his prey or he chased it off.

Christina sighed and eased up on her grip, giving Noah the opportunity to free his hand. Keeping hunkered down, he waddled to the window and raised up only far enough to lift the edge of the curtain to peek outside.

"What is it? What do you see?" Christina raised up a bit higher. Jill still sat flat on the floor with her hands covering her face. Christina wasn't sure if the girl was crying or praying or both.

"Two men are running, and a German shepherd is chasing them."

"*Gut* dog!" Christina pulled one of Jill's hands. "Get your phone and call so the police can find out what's going on."

Jill nodded and sniffed. "I'm definitely going to get a dog. The biggest one I can find. I'm going to visit the shelter tomorrow." She pushed to her feet and sprinted from the room.

~

Thirty minutes later, the police wrapped up their questioning, gathered whatever evidence they deemed pertinent, and left.

"Why didn't you show them the note with the mysterious riddle?" Christina thought she knew Jill's reason but wanted to make sure the girl hadn't simply forgotten to mention it. After all, Christina's brain had been spinning with all the strange events of late, so Jill's must be totally malfunctioning.

"They wouldn't take it seriously if I did let them see it. And they would keep it as some sort of evidence, probably evidence against Blake to prove he was under the influence of drugs or something. This is the last thing he wrote to me. I want to keep it."

"I understand."

"Christina, did either you or Noah get the impression the police weren't taking me seriously?"

"I kind of thought they were listening politely but not terribly concerned for your safety," Christina replied.

"Exactly!" Jill made her voice deeper to imitate one of the officers. "Maybe you should stay away from here, Ms.

Sheridan. We'll place a watch on the place to see if any other, uh, associates of your brother show up." Jill rolled her eyes. "Honestly! What he meant was 'in case any drug dealers show up.' They are so convinced my brother was involved in drugs that they don't want to dig any deeper. Look around this place." Jill chuckled mirthlessly. "Well, if you can filter out the mess, does this look like the abode of a drug addict?"

Christina surveyed the room. Framed nature pictures with Bible verses lined the walls. A well-worn Bible lay open on the floor next to the nightstand. The crumpled pages sported highlighted passages and scribbling in the margins. A pillow on the bed, miraculously untouched, had been embroidered with the words "God is love," circled by flowers and butterflies. "This looks like the room of a man who took his faith seriously."

"He did." Jill nodded at the pillow Christina had been studying. "I made that for him when he finished his counselor training."

"It's beautiful."

"I used to enjoy cross-stitch and embroidery. Blake had a few of my wall hangings in the living room. I didn't notice if they were still there. I can't imagine any thugs wanting religious pictures, though."

"Well, if they took them, they were truly in need of the messages." Noah had been standing near the doorway and kept his thoughts to himself until now. "I'll be right back. I'll see if those hangings are still there."

"You said you used to stitch. Don't you do it anymore? You do very nice work."

"I haven't done any since shortly before I moved here. I was so busy packing and unpacking and getting situated in a new place. Now I don't seem to have the desire to do anything creative."

"It might help you to relax. I always find that crocheting or knitting helps me calm down when I am upset or agitated or when I am trying to make a decision."

Jill smiled. "I can't imagine you agitated. You appear to be a very calm, together type of person."

"I'm not sure what you mean by 'together.' I'm usually calm, but there are times when things happen that make me anxious."

"That's normal. By 'together,' I mean that you always have your wits about you. You're smart. You're efficient. You're good at figuring things out."

Heat flooded Christina's cheeks. Plain folks rarely complimented or praised one another. Pride was to be avoided at all costs. But Christina would have to admit she felt the teensiest bit proud when her plants sold so well or when people sought her advice about caring for them. She sometimes believed her afghans or quilts turned out pretty, but she always kept that opinion to herself.

Jill laughed. "I didn't mean to embarrass you, Christina. I'm simply stating the facts as I see them."

Christina was spared of concocting a response since Noah chose that instant to return. "I don't know for sure since this is my first time here, but it doesn't appear that anything has been removed from the wall. There aren't any telltale marks or faded areas. I even saw a few framed photographs on a small table."

Jill sighed. "Those would be pictures of happier times. Blake always kept photos of our whole family, back when we were a complete family."

"Don't you have pictures too?" Christina hoped her question didn't upset the girl.

"I do. Somewhere. Most likely they are still buried in a box to unpack, all except for the few tucked underneath clothes in a dresser drawer. It always made me sad to look at them." She sniffed and blinked several times. "Maybe you're right about the stitching, Christina. I need to do something to help me forget about my troubles for at least a little while."

Christina's heart ached for the *Englisch* girl who must have experienced great loneliness and pain. She had the urge to throw her arms around Jill and tell her that everything would be all right. But would those words be a lie?

Chapter Twenty-Five

Christina alternately bit her lips and picked at her fingernails as they drove toward home. How would she explain her lengthy absence? She would have to tell her family she visited Eleanore with Noah since Eleanore was bound to let people know. But how did she explain the trip to the hospital in the first place? She had told *Mamm* she was going for a walk. Did she say that she happened to run into Noah and that they decided to share a ride to the hospital? *Nee*, that didn't make sense. She should have thought this whole thing through more carefully. Christina wasn't really an impulsive person, and here she had just jumped from the frying pan into the fire without considering the burns she would receive.

Would her parents be ready to send out neighbors to search the woods for her? Her walks didn't usually last so long. Maybe they would think she stopped in to see Annie. *Ach!* Her best *freind* would never forgive her for going off someplace with Noah. She might as well figure that she'd lost Annie as a *freind* forever. "Ugh!"

"What's wrong?"

The concern in Noah's eyes made her heart flop about like a wiggly fish washed up on the sand. "Sorry. I didn't mean to sigh aloud."

"Why the sigh?"

"What are you planning to tell your family about today?" Christina knocked on her forehead. "Oh, never mind. Your *mudder* already knows you were going to the hospital. She gave you the book. My *mamm* thinks I was going for a walk. It's been the longest walk I've ever taken. I just hope my *daed* and *bruders* aren't out beating the bushes for me." She slumped in the seat and leaned her head against the window.

"I'm sorry if I got you into trouble." Jill's eyes connected with Christina's in the rearview mirror. "But I really appreciate your coming with me today. Both of you. I don't know what I would have done if I'd been at Blake's townhouse alone."

"I'm glad you weren't alone, Jill. That would have been way too scary and dangerous."

"I'm more confused than ever now, though." Jill tapped her fingers on the steering wheel.

Christina fingered the paper in her pocket. She had scribbled down Blake's riddle. Now she needed time to think about it. "We'll figure it out." She spoke with more confidence than she felt. What did she know about crime-solving?

"I hope so. At least I was able to rescue those pictures before anything happened to them."

"You aren't going to go back there, are you?" Christina involuntarily shivered at the thought.

"I'll have to clear things out of there by the end of the month before the rent is due. At least he didn't own the place, so I don't have to worry about making payments or putting it up for sale. I'd never be able to afford the payments on my paycheck. I can barely cover my own rent and necessities. I can't say that I'm looking forward to going back inside that townhouse, though."

"We'll help you." Noah shot Christina a questioning glance.

She jerked upright at his offer. Christina wanted to help but certainly didn't want him to feel he had to commit to further involvement. "Sure, we'll help you, Jill." She peeked at Noah and mouthed, "Are you sure?" His nod and smile confirmed his commitment. How they would manage to help, though, Christina hadn't a clue.

Her brain spun at a dizzying speed as she considered first one explanation for today's jaunt and then another. Christina wouldn't lie, but she couldn't reveal information that could put her family at risk. She picked at her nails again until Noah's big hand covered hers.

"Let's work together," he whispered. "We'll find the right thing to tell your parents."

Home was getting closer and closer. "We had better work fast."

~

Christina aimed for a carefree, casual appearance as she sauntered up the long, gravel driveway from the paved road where Jill had let her out about a quarter of a mile away. She had a feeling, though, that to any observer her gait would appear stilted and anything but confident. She tried in vain to ease the tightness in her forehead. She hoped that she could at least get her words out smoothly. She rehearsed her speech over and over in her mind. What was the chance that she could slip into the house unnoticed?

"I was beginning to worry." Ida pushed to her feet from the front porch swing.

"I-I'm sorry, Mamm." Christina had been so preoccupied with her internal dialogue that she failed to notice her *mudder* in the shadowy corner of the porch. It was a *gut* thing that Jill didn't drive any closer to let her out. She might as well launch into her explanation and get it over with. "I, um, ran into Noah Zimmerman. His *mamm* wanted him to take a puzzle book to the hospital for Eleanore since she couldn't go herself. He felt a little hesitant about going alone and asked if I'd ride along with him. I thought Eleanore could probably use some company, so I tagged along." Did that sound normal? She tried so hard to speak slowly but knew her words tumbled out on top of each other.

"How did you get there?"

"An *Englisch* girl that I met at The Green Thumb happened along and took us. She had some things to do, which is the reason I'm late getting back."

They hadn't accidentally encountered Jill, but that was a mere technicality, wasn't it? *Please let Mamm accept my flimsy reasons and not have any more questions.*

Ida dropped back onto the wooden swing and set it in motion. "I'm sure Eleanore was glad to have visitors. How is she getting along?"

Christina nearly cried with relief. Was she off the hook? "She said she was feeling better now that her blood sugar was more under control. She might be released from the hospital tomorrow."

"I wonder if she's been following her diet like she's supposed to. That girl has always had a huge sweet tooth." Ida chuckled. "As a little one, she used to sneak cookie after cookie from the plates at gatherings. It must be very hard for her to make such changes."

"Probably. Hasn't she been diabetic for a while?"

"I think so. You know, though, some people are eager to do what they are supposed to at first but then get a little lax and backslide."

"*Jah*, I was young, but I still remember how Grossdawdi hated giving up salty foods when he got high blood pressure."

Ida smiled. "My *daed* sure loved the salt shaker, thick slices of bacon, fat dill pickles, and handfuls of potato chips. He always tried to sneak them past *Mamm*."

"I'm sure Grossmammi didn't buy those foods for him. Most likely, she watched him like a hawk to make sure he ate what he was supposed to eat."

"She did, but whenever he stopped at a convenience store or stole off to the Quick Stop, he bought a bag of the saltiest chips he could find."

Christina laughed. She could picture her little, gray-haired *grossmammi* shaking a finger at and scolding her husband.

"Maybe we'll all have to keep a watchful eye on Eleanore to help her stay on the straight and narrow."

"*Gut* idea, *Mamm*. Is there anything you need me to do?"

"Not right now. It's too early to set out supper foods."

"Okay. I think I'll go knit for a while." Christina made her feet shuffle along when they really wanted to race away before *Mamm* thought of any new questions to ask. She tiptoed up the stairs, careful to avoid the squeaky one, and softly closed her door behind her in case her little *schweschders* were in their room. They would surely want Christina to play with them or color with them, and she needed some alone time to think. She grabbed her knitting bag, threw it onto the bed, and flopped down beside it.

Guilt pressed heavily upon her. Christina had never needed to concoct a story to tell her *mudder* before. Even though the words she just uttered out on the porch were true enough, they certainly did not tell the complete story. She reached up to rub little circles on her temples where a headache threatened. How was she going to get herself—and Noah—out of the mess they had inadvertently become part of? What did Blake's silly riddle mean?

Christina sighed. She pushed up to her elbows and surveyed her familiar room as if the walls held an answer for her. Her blue, purple, and green dresses hung on pegs as always. Her comb and brush sat atop her polished dresser as always. The cedar chest *Daed* had given her on her sixteenth birthday occupied the space at the foot of her bed as always. Nothing had changed. Except her.

Now Christina was a person with secrets. She had started glancing behind her to make sure that whoever murdered Blake Sheridan wasn't following her. She worried that her family or Noah might be in danger all because she happened to be involved in a crime purely by chance. She jumped at any loud, unfamiliar noise and scrutinized every car that drove past her, even though she didn't have any idea who she was looking for. She wanted her old, quiet, predictable life back. Was that too much to ask for?

Christina jerked upright and yanked her knitting needles and dark blue yarn out of the bag when she heard footsteps ascending the stairs. She'd said she was going to knit, so she'd better be doing exactly that. She cocked her head as if that would help her decipher the sound better. The footsteps were too heavy to belong to Sallie or Grace and not quite house-shaking enough to belong to James, John, or David. Could it be *Mamm*? Christina inserted a needle into the stitch and wrapped the yarn around it. She tried to appear as if she was concentrating and not fretting.

The footsteps halted right outside her door. Christina gnawed on her lower lip. If it was *Mamm*, why didn't she enter the room? One of her siblings would have been hollering her name long before now. With her taut nerves approaching the snapping point, Christina dropped her knitting into her lap. Maybe she should simply call out to whoever stood in the hallway.

Before she could do anything, the door was flung open so roughly that it banged against the doorstop on the wall. Christina gasped and nearly slid off the bed. She only saw the wall through the open door. Where was the person? Was someone playing a trick on her? She didn't think her nerves or heart could handle one more shock. She had always considered herself a tough person who could handle almost any situation, but the past few days had seriously shaken her confidence and courage.

Why didn't the person say something or walk through the door? The girls would be giggling if they were the perpetrators. Her *bruders* would never have had the patience to remain hidden or silent for very long. All right. Enough was enough. She would simply march over to the door and confront the prankster. It was time for her to be take-charge Christina again.

Chapter Twenty-Six

Before she could get both feet on the floor or call out, she caught a glimpse of orange-red hair. It couldn't possibly be who she thought it was lurking outside her door. "Hello?"

The visitor shuffled a bit to stand right in the center of the open door. She only stared. She didn't utter a sound.

"Annie?" Why didn't she speak or enter the room? Had she dropped by to apologize but didn't know how to begin? "You can *kumm* in, Annie. You aren't interrupting me. I'm only knitting."

"Humpf!"

"What was that for?" Christina held up her yarn and needles. "See?"

"But you haven't been knitting very long, ain't so?" Annie crossed the threshold and slammed the door behind her.

Christina nearly jumped to the ceiling. Her nerves must be more jangled than she thought. "What is that supposed to mean?" Why was Annie angry to find her knitting? Something bothered the girl, and it had nothing to do with stitching at all.

"I mean you must have run right inside the house and up to your room to knit."

Christina felt her brow pucker. She couldn't make any sense out of Annie's comments. "I was talking to *Mamm* and then came upstairs, so I haven't been knitting for too long." She shook her head, but the action didn't help her sort out her *freind's* words. "Annie, I don't understand why you are asking me these things or why you are so upset. You act like I've done something wrong."

Annie scooted closer to the bed. Her usually pale cheeks held red splotches. Her eyes shot daggers straight into Christina's heart. "I saw you!" She ground the words out between clenched teeth.

"You saw me when? I'm not following you." Christina patted the bed for Annie to sit beside her as she'd done countless times over the years. Annie ignored the gesture. Her eyebrows drew together in a fierce scowl that almost frightened Christina.

"I saw you get out of that car a *very short* time ago."

Christina's heart skipped a beat. What else had Annie seen? Or maybe she should worry about who else Annie had seen. "You're right. I did get out of a car. I had been to the hospital to visit Eleanore."

"Since when did you and Eleanore become such chums?"

This conversation was definitely not going well. "I don't know that we're close, but we are *freinden*. She's been in the hospital for a few days. I figured a visit would cheer her up."

"Is that what Noah Zimmerman figured too?"

"Noah?"

Annie marched over and planted herself smack in front of Christina. She balled her hands into fists which she plunked on her hips. Her nostrils flared, and her breath came in little gasps between her words. "I. Saw. Him. In. The. Car."

"Oh."

"Oh? That's all you can say?"

"Noah's *mudder* sent a puzzle book to Eleanore to help her pass the time. Noah and I shared a ride."

"And you coincidentally ran into each other and a mysterious *Englisch* driver. I think you can do better than that."

"I'm not making this up, Annie. Besides, I don't understand why you are so upset. You and Noah are not stepping out or anything."

"How could we if you're always in the way, always interfering somehow?"

"How do you know he wants to step out with you?" Christina spoke as gently as she could. She didn't want to inflict pain, but she did want her *freind* to think clearly about this whole twisted situation.

"Why wouldn't he? Do you think I'm not *gut* enough for him?"

"Don't be silly, Annie. You're my *freind.*" They used to be *freinden* anyway.

"You didn't answer the question." Annie's black sneaker tapped on the wood floor. Otherwise, she hadn't altered the belligerent stance that she had assumed a few moments earlier.

"I'm sure you and whatever fellow is right for you would have a fine relationship. I want you to be happy." Did she handle that appropriately? Annie's next remark indicated she had not.

"So, are you saying that Noah isn't right for me? What makes you the expert?"

"I don't claim to be any expert at all." Again, she patted the bed next to her. "Sit down, Annie, and talk to me." The girl's glare had become quite unnerving.

"I don't want to sit beside you."

"You came here to visit me."

"Not really visit. More like confront."

"I don't understand what's going on. All those times I confided in you about my interest in Noah, you never said a word about your own hopes. Why not?"

Annie shrugged. "Maybe I wasn't interested in him then."

"Why the sudden interest now?"

She shrugged again. "People are allowed to change their minds, aren't they?"

"Sure, but…"

"But you want to keep Noah away from me. You deliberately scheme to keep us apart."

Christina's mouth dropped open. How could Annie think such a thing? And she never said a word about the whole bicycle incident. Christina tried to sort out her thoughts so she didn't blurt out the first thing that popped into her mind.

"Don't you have anything to say for yourself?"

"I don't know what to say, Annie. You know me, and you know that I am not a conniving person." She paused to drag in a steadying breath and forced a gentleness into her voice that she truly did not feel at the moment. "Don't you think Noah would approach you if—"

"If you didn't always stick your nose in?"

"Annie! How can you say such a thing? I don't have any control over anyone, least of all Noah Zimmerman. If he wanted to pursue you, he certainly could." Christina gasped. She prayed that her words didn't sound as harsh to Annie as they sounded in her own ears.

"Well, I happen to think that if you left him alone and gave him some space, he would certainly show his interest in me."

Evidently, Christina's words had fallen on deaf ears. "You are entitled to your own thoughts." *Regardless of how irrational they might be.* Christina didn't have any idea what to say next. Apparently, they were at a standstill.

"Hmpf! At least you could apologize."

"For what?"

"For messing up my chances with Noah."

"If anyone needs to apologize, it's you. You pushed me so that I fell off my bike, and you never even checked to see if I was hurt!" Christina struggled to maintain some semblance of self-control.

"You're crazy. I didn't do any such thing."

"You most certainly did! How can you not remember? We were riding home. Noah left to go his way and we continued on until you got upset. And you pushed me!"

"Well, you deserved it."

The words had been mumbled, but Christina didn't have any trouble deciphering them. Tears sprang into her eyes, and her heart ached. What had happened to her *freind?* Had she ever known Annie at all? "I can't believe you said that." Christina blinked hard and sniffed. She would not cry. "I don't understand what is going on with you, Annie. You aren't acting like the girl I've known forever. Have you only pretended to be my *freind* all these years for some crazy reason?"

"Are you calling me crazy now?"

"Of course not. Aren't you listening to me at all? I'm trying to understand what is going on here, but I can't make sense of it all. In a matter of days, you changed from the sweet girl I've always known into an angry, mean person making all sorts of false accusations. What happened?"

"As if you didn't know! I've only said it a thousand times. You must be the dense one."

Christina stared at her fidgeting hands as she choked back a sob. Life had become much too difficult lately. Blake's rhyme swirled around in her head demanding her attention. She had promised Jill she would try to figure out possible meanings. Now her brain had been bombarded with Annie's barbs. The pounding that had begun behind her eyes threatened to explode into a full-blown headache. She wished that Annie would leave and let her try to sort things out.

"Well, don't you have anything to say?"

Christina raised her eyes to find Annie still glaring at her. "I'm afraid I am completely at a loss for words. You don't want to be reasonable. Everything I say simply makes you angrier."

"I am not being unreasonable." Annie stomped hard.

Christina glanced at the floor, expecting to find a hole. She was glad her own feet were well out of the way or they surely would have been crushed. *As crushed as my spirits. How can Annie be so mean? She doesn't even think she was wrong to cause my fall from the bike.* "You can scowl at me all you like, but I have nothing else to say."

With a final "hmpf!" Annie spun about and clomped across the room and down the steps. A deep voice hollered, "Whoa!" so Christina could only think that the girl must have nearly mowed someone down. She wished Annie had closed the door behind her so everyone would leave her alone. She needed to think.

"What's wrong with her?" James poked his head inside Christina's room. "She almost knocked me down the steps and never said, 'Hello, excuse me, get out of my way, or anything else.'"

Christina sighed. "I don't know what's going on with her. She isn't acting like herself at all."

James chuckled. "I don't know if that's a *gut* thing or a bad thing."

Christina frowned at her older *bruder* but didn't reply.

"At least before we knew we would have nonstop talking. This person that almost killed me without uttering a word is totally foreign. She looked as mad as an old, wet hen."

"That's for sure."

"You don't know why?"

"It's hard to say." Christina really didn't want to get into the whole strange story right now. She craved peace and quiet. Once James moved on to his room, she would have quiet, but she wouldn't know peace as long as that riddle played in her head and Annie's angry accusations echoed in her brain.

"I thought you two were best *freinden.*"

"I thought so too. I guess you and I were both wrong."

"Something awful must have happened."

Ugh! She did not want to talk about it, even though James had often been her confidant in the past. She merely shrugged.

"If you want to talk, I'm available."

"*Danki.*"

"It should be a lot quieter around here without Annie's constant prattle. See, Christina, there's a bright side to everything." James whistled as he continued down the hall to his own room.

Christina smiled. James was a *gut* big *bruder*—most of the time.

~

She untangled the yarn from the mess she had made of it when Annie arrived and jabbed the needle through a loop. If she could lose herself in some mindless activity for at least a little while, maybe the fog would lift from her brain. She needed to focus on something ordinary, something pleasurable, for a few minutes before she even attempted to consider the riddle or Annie's animosity.

When Christina purled instead of knitted and knitted where she should have purled, she dropped the project in frustration. She had better lay it aside before she made a mess so big that she wouldn't be able to correct it. She rubbed her forehead to smooth the furrow. If only the throbbing in her head would ease. She flopped back on the bed and squeezed her eyes shut to block out the light. She forced herself to take slow, deep breaths.

"Christina, will you play with us?"

She rubbed her eyes. She must have dozed off. She hadn't even heard her little *schweschders* gallop up the steps, and they almost always ran when they could have walked, and they were rarely quiet. She raised up on her elbows and squinted at them.

"Were you asleep?" Grace asked. "I haven't taken naps for years."

"I know. You have become such a big girl. I had a headache and must have fallen asleep while I rested."

"Well, get up and play with us."

"Ugh! My brain is foggy. I don't like falling asleep in the daytime. You two were fine playing by yourselves."

"*Jah*, but we were playing *boppli* games. I need something more challenging." Sallie tipped her head toward Grace and rolled her eyes. In return, she received an elbow jab from Grace.

"Because you are so grown-up, right?" Christina fought to keep from smiling. She remembered being at that in-between age.

"Exactly."

This time, Grace rolled her eyes. Christina couldn't help but laugh at her *schweschders*. Since she couldn't concentrate on knitting, she might as well play a game with them. She pushed herself to a sitting position. "All right. I'll play a game with you. A short one, though. I have some things to do."

Chapter Twenty-Seven

One game led to another and another until suppertime. Christina didn't get a moment to herself until she closed her bedroom door to prepare for sleep. *Sleep? Who am I kidding? All those thoughts I've been avoiding are going to pounce on me as soon as I lie down.* At least she had climbed the stairs a little earlier than usual, claiming that she had a headache—which was not a false statement. The pain had dulled only briefly while she played with her *schweschders*, but now it roared back to life.

Christina knelt beside her bed to say her nightly prayers and dropped her head into her hands. "Please give me wisdom, Lord *Gott*," she whispered. "Tell me how to help Jill figure out what her *bruder* was trying to tell her. Help me decipher this riddle. And please help me know what to do about Annie."

Weary, she crawled into the bed. She yanked the cotton sheet up to her neck despite the warmth of the room and the lack of a steady breeze blowing in the window. Somehow, the cool sheet brought her the comfort she desperately needed right now. Christina begged her muscles to relax. The crickets outside her window had begun their nightly song even though the sky hadn't completely darkened. If only they would lull her to sleep.

Annie's mumbled "You deserved it" reverberated through her brain. Did her *freind* actually believe that? Is that how she justified her actions? Christina had great difficulty believing anyone could think it was all right to hurt someone else. Could she and Annie ever salvage their relationship? Christina would forgive, of course. That was their way. But could she ever trust Annie again? The wounds were still too raw. Christina needed to shelve thoughts of Annie until she could distance herself from those ugly words.

She turned onto her side, punched her pillow, and tried to settle her mind and body. All efforts proved to be in vain. *Mary, Mary, quite contrary.* The rhyme sang in her head. That wasn't what Blake's note said, though. She rolled to the edge of the bed and fumbled in the nightstand drawer for a flashlight. She clicked it on and snatched the crumpled piece of paper off the top of the stand. If she wasn't going to sleep, she might as well ponder the riddle.

Think, Christina, think. She read the first line. Blake used the name "Mary," not the word "merry," so he apparently was not referring to happiness. Did he mean someone named Mary? She knew a zillion Marys, but she doubted Blake had been acquainted with any of them since they were all Mennonite women or girls. And Christina hadn't any way of knowing how many people Blake had known with that name.

Could he have been talking about a place? They did live in St. Mary's County—in Maryland. But what did the "not so ordinary" mean? Since Christina was now wide awake with little hope that sleep would overtake her, she propped her pillow against the headboard and sat up against it. She might as well be comfortable if she wanted her brain to focus on something besides the pins and needles in her arm from balancing her weight on her elbow.

If it was an unordinary Mary, it must not be a familiar person or place to either Blake or Jill. *Hmmm.* Christina couldn't think of a single thing. What about the next line? The actual nursery rhyme read, "How does your garden grow," but Blake wrote, "where does your garden grow." Most people grew vegetable or flower gardens pretty close to their houses, especially the *Englisch* folks who didn't generally have as much land to space things out. So whoever Mary was, she grew a garden. That did not narrow possibilities down at all.

"Near silver bells and oyster shells." Not much help there. St. Mary's County was surrounded by water—the Potomac River, the Patuxent River, the Chesapeake Bay, and a slew of other rivers and bays. Oyster shells were everywhere. Where were there silver bells? What kinds of place would have bells?

Christina slid down a bit in the bed. Weariness had crept in. She read the last line of the riddle and switched off the flashlight. She would surely use up the batteries if she fell asleep with it on. Besides, she could remember that last line. "With pretty tykes all in a row." What were tykes? Didn't *Englischers* sometimes call *kinner* tykes? Bells and shells and *kinner.* What in the world had Blake been trying to tell his *schweschder?* How was Christina ever going to help her? She should never have made such a promise.

Little ones marched in a row through Christina's dreams. Their feet crunched on oyster shells while silver bells rang a merry tune. Next, a young girl chased a flock of sheep through the waving gladiolas in a flower garden while a single lamb followed a different girl into the schoolhouse.

When the rooster crowed, Christina jerked awake and groaned as she attempted to move her head. She must have fallen asleep with her head half on and half off the pillow. She would probably have a stiff neck all day. That would definitely make the day more challenging—as if she needed any additional stress. She forced herself to a sitting position and rubbed the sleep from her eyes. Too bad she couldn't rub the worries from her mind as easily.

What was that crazy dream all about? It was a nursery rhyme jumble with "Little Bo Peep," "Mary Had a Little Lamb," and Blake's riddle all swirled together. At the rooster's second crow, Christina jumped from the bed. Maybe the silly dream would fade from her memory as she got busy with the day's routine. She didn't usually remember her dreams, so there was a fair chance that this one would vanish as well. She could only hope so. She hurried to dress so she could help with breakfast.

"You're awfully quiet this morning, *dochder*," Ida remarked a few minutes later as she cracked eggs into a large, ceramic mixing bowl. "Didn't you sleep well?"

Terrible! I was plagued by a hodgepodge of nursery rhymes. Mamm would think she had lost her mind if she voiced that thought. Instead, she shrugged. "I must have slept crooked. I have a stiff neck this morning."

"So that's why you're turning your whole body instead of just your head. You look funny." Sallie giggled as she plunked silverware on the scarred, oak table.

"Does it hurt very bad?" Grace tapped her big *schweschder's* arm.

Christina hugged the sensitive little girl. "It's uncomfortable, Gracie, but I'll live. It should be better by the end of the day."

"I hope so. I'll say a prayer for you."

"*Danki*, I'd appreciate that. You're such a sweet girl." *And I need all the prayers I can get!*

"Do you want me to send Sallie to help you today? I was going to have her help me make jam, but I can spare her if you need her."

From the corner of her eye, Christina caught Sallie's head bobbing up and down as if signaling she would rather go to work with Christina than stay home. Apparently, making jam was not on her list of favorite things to do, but Christina couldn't risk having her at the store. There wasn't any use in getting another innocent person involved in the mysterious happenings that could prove dangerous. She'd already dragged Noah into this mess. "*Nee*, I'll be fine, *Mamm*. I'm sure the stiffness will go away once I get busy." Truth be told, she wasn't sure of anything anymore except that she should keep her *schweschder* away from The Green Thumb, despite her pout.

Christina hoped she hadn't hurt Sallie's feelings. The talkative little girl could be *gut* company and she would probably be at least minimum help if she didn't have Grace along to pick at. Either girl would be fine alone, but putting them together could definitely spell trouble. Maybe one day Christina would be able to explain to Sallie why she refused to let her tag along this time.

She nibbled at a strip of bacon and gulped down a small cup of orange juice before gathering up her lunch cooler and heading out. She successfully avoided *Mamm*'s raised eyebrows and escaped before she could question Christina about her lack of appetite. Food would definitely not settle very well this morning. After riding her bike in the fresh air to the store, her stomach might be more willing to accept food. She already regretted that one bite of bacon.

Christina kept her senses on high alert as she pedaled the few miles to The Green Thumb. The robins sang and the crows cawed, but Christina did not detect any human sounds other than the noise of the two cars that passed her. She had scooted way over on the shoulder of the road but still held her breath until the vehicles zoomed by. She wasn't ordinarily so skittish while riding her bike. Funny how drastically things could change in a matter of days.

She threw a glance over her shoulder from time to time to make sure another bicyclist wasn't advancing on her. She didn't have any desire to eat gravel again today. Her scraped arm and leg still smarted. She didn't believe Annie would pull such a stunt again, but now Christina wondered if she ever knew the girl at all. How could a person be *freinden* with someone for years and not know that she had a mean streak a mile wide? Did Annie's jealousy over Noah's attention cause that ugly trait to surface in Annie's otherwise sweet nature? Christina shook her head. As hard as she tried, she couldn't understand the girl's actions.

The Green Thumb came into view around the next curve. *Gut.* She needed to get busy. Occupying her body and mind with her plants and customers should thwart any fears and doubts lurking in her brain. At least for a little while.

Christina slowed down as her bike tires hit the gravel to avoid sliding. She continued around to the back of the store where she would prop her bike against the building in the sliver of shade afforded by the roof's overhang. At least that helped keep the seat and handlebars from becoming too hot to touch. She snatched the cooler from the basket and dug her key out of her bag.

Every morning when she arrived, she thanked the Lord *Gott* for her successful store and for her *grossmammi*, who taught her everything she knew about plants. Leaving the business to Christina had been a *wunderbaar* gesture. Thankfully, none of the *aentis* or *onkles* had any desire to raise and sell plants. Not a one of them minded that, young as she was, Christina took on the whole burden of the business. That's what they called it. To Christina, though, The Green Thumb was a blessing, a dream *kumm* true.

Her gaze wandered to the big greenhouse and the shed. She sighed with relief that the padlocks were fastened and everything looked exactly as she had left it on Saturday. She could begin her day, her week, in peace. If she knew how to whistle, she would have trilled out a tune, but her mouth never wanted to cooperate. James used to get the biggest kick out of her efforts. He tried to teach her how to purse her lips just so and how to blow through them, but she always ended up making a whooshing sound and spitting all over both of them. She smiled at the memory.

Christina settled for humming a song from the Ausbund as she approached the back door with key in hand. Her focus had been on the lock above the doorknob until the flutter of paper caught her attention. A sheet of notebook paper had been taped about a foot above the doorknob. She swallowed the last note of the song and clapped her hand to her galloping heart. She didn't even feel the key dig into her chest. "Mind your own business!" The lopsided words scrawled in black marker reached out and grabbed her.

Breathe, Christina. It's only some silly, childish prank. She wished that was all it was, but her brain knew better. Someone must know she agreed to help Jill. Did that person see her get into the car with Noah and Jill yesterday? Was he watching her every move? Christina shivered despite the heat and humidity that promised another scorching day.

She reached up to yank the paper down but paused with her hand in midair. Should she touch it? There might be fingerprints on it or some other useful evidence. She shook her head. She wouldn't call the police. What was she thinking of? She snatched the paper down. Out of sight, out of mind? Probably not.

Christina inserted the key into the lock but quickly scanned her surroundings before turning it. There weren't any signs that someone had tried to pry the door open. Everything appeared normal. She shouldn't discover any surprises inside.

"Christy! Are you okay?"

She whirled around to watch the approach of the only person who ever called her Christy. How was Noah Zimmerman always around when she needed him? Coincidence? More like a miracle.

Noah jumped off his bike and let it drop to the ground. He sprinted to the back door, where Christina stood as if frozen. "What's wrong?"

He stood close enough for Christina to get a whiff of soap and aftershave. Pleasant, spicy scents. She wanted to lean against him for support, but she would not give in to that temptation. She was brave. She was strong. She was scared out of her wits!

"What is that?" Noah nodded toward the paper in her hand.

"I-it was taped to the door. I-I just pulled it off." She held the scrawled message out to him.

"Maybe we should notify the police."

"You know we don't get involved in legal proceedings."

"But this could be related to the crime."

"The police don't think there was a crime, remember? They think Jill's *bruder* took his own life, maybe not intentionally, but they believe he took the drugs himself."

"*Gut* point."

Noah slid the key from her loose grasp. "Let me go inside first."

"Do you think I'm being watched?"

Chapter Twenty-Eight

Christina stole a glance over her shoulder, expecting to find eyes staring at her through the trees.

Noah turned the ancient doorknob and pushed the heavy, wooden door open. He flung back a hand in a "keep back" motion. "Give me a minute."

Christina mentally counted the seconds, shifting from foot to foot. She hated feeling so nervous standing in the open doorway of her own business. This would never do. She had to be able to hurry to the shed or greenhouse at a moment's notice if a customer needed something or if she had to replenish her supply of one of her plants. She couldn't be afraid to stick her head out the door. *Be brave, Christina. Don't give in to fear or to the lunatic that wrote that cryptic message.* She dragged in a deep breath, pushed the door all the way open, and marched inside.

"I thought you were going to give me a minute," Noah called over his shoulder as he headed into the smaller, attached greenhouse.

"I can't be scared to enter my own place. I have work to do."

"Better to be scared than hurt—or worse."

Christina got the impression that Noah hadn't meant to mumble those words aloud and that the cough afterward was an attempt to cover up the comment.

"Everything looks okay inside as far as I can tell. I'll wait here while you check to see if anything is out of place."

"There weren't any signs of a forced entry, so I'm sure everything will be exactly as I left it on Saturday."

Noah's brows shot upward. "Forced entry?"

Christina giggled. "Thanks to Annie's constant reviews of the suspense novels she reads, I guess all sorts of terms seeped into my subconscious mind." She grabbed the dog-eared piece of paper off the counter where Noah left it and stuffed it under her bag on a low shelf.

"What are you going to do with that?"

"I'll show it to Jill the next time I see her. She might have received a similar note."

"I don't know, Christy. I get a bad taste in my mouth when I think of leaving you here alone."

His concern warmed her heart, but she didn't want Noah to worry about her. She forced a bright smile, or what she hoped would pass for one. "I'll be fine. *Danki* for your help, but I don't want you to be late for work."

"Henry will understand."

"*Ach!* You haven't told him about any of this, have you?"

"*Nee*, I haven't told a soul."

"*Gut.* We don't need to involve anyone else. I feel guilty enough getting you involved."

"You didn't twist my arm or beat me with a stick to get me involved. I got my own self involved. I *chose* to help."

Christina giggled at the image of her forcing a man—who was more than a foot taller than she was and a whole lot heavier—to do anything against his will. "Maybe you did, but I still don't like thinking you could be in danger."

"It's *you* we need to be concerned about at the moment. I'll be with Henry and a dozen customers throughout the day, so I won't be alone."

"I'm sure I'll have my usual influx of customers, so I won't be by myself all day." At least not for long periods, she hoped. "Besides, Marjorie almost always stops in on Mondays."

"Does she only drop things off?"

Christina smiled. "Have you ever known Marjorie Gehman to breeze in and out of someplace?"

"Now that you mention it, *nee*. She and Annie are a lot alike in that respect, ain't so?"

"They are." Sadness elbowed its way into her thoughts.

"Why the downcast expression?"

Christina shrugged and struggled to smile.

"Are you two still having problems?"

"That's putting it mildly."

"I'm sorry to hear that."

"It's not your fault." *It is because of you, but it is not your fault.* Christina did not have any desire to discuss the latest installment in the Annie saga with anyone, least of all Noah. She cleared her throat. "I appreciate your being here today, Noah. Somehow you always show up at the right time."

"Intuition, I guess. Just don't suspect me as the perpetrator. See, I've learned a few terms lately too."

Christina laughed. "We've learned whether we wanted to or not. And you certainly are not on my list of suspects. Actually, I don't have a list at all." She started to touch his arm but thought better of it. "I don't want to interfere with your job. You go ahead to work. I'll be fine."

"Are you sure?"

"Absolutely." More or less.

~

Christina's heart skipped a beat every time a customer entered the store, but each one meant that she had less time to be alone. She kept her hands busy, but her mind kept returning to the riddle. Images of gardens and bells and oyster shells chased one another around and around in her brain.

"Hey!"

Christina jumped so violently that she banged her head on the shelf above the one she had been straightening. Her gasp hinged on a scream.

"My, my. You are awfully distracted today—and jumpy."

Christina thumped her chest as if that could make her heart rate slow down to a normal speed. "*Ach*, Marjorie! You startled me." If Marjorie could sneak up on her, then anyone could have. She needed to pay closer attention. She couldn't let herself get so lost in thought that someone would have the opportunity to do her harm.

"You must have been doing some heavy thinking if you didn't hear me call to you when I first came through the door."

Christina shrugged. *If you only knew!* "It's great to see you this morning. Can you stay around for a while?" She hoped she didn't sound too desperate or frightened.

"I sure can. It looks like you've been busy."

"Business has been steady this morning."

"I hope each person that walked in didn't give you such a fright."

Christina forced a little chuckle. "*Nee*, they didn't."

"Are you all right? You look a little pale."

"I'm fine. What did you bring today?" She needed to change the subject before Marjorie pried information out of her that she really did not want to share.

"Early this morning, I baked lemon pound cake that I've wrapped in individual slices and, of course, whoopie pies."

"*Gut.* Those always go fast. I'm sure the cake will too. A lot of folks prefer to buy a slice or two instead of a whole cake, so cutting it was a great idea."

"I'll put them in the usual spot."

Christina couldn't prevent the gasp that escaped at the slam of a car door. The open front door and windows allowed her to hear every sound—when she wasn't lost in thought—but she would have heard that door with the building closed up and cotton balls stuffed in her ears.

"Easy, girl. It's only a car door."

"True, but it sounded like they demolished the car with that slam."

Marjorie laughed and kept right on unloading her baked items.

Christina barely greeted the new arrival before a large van arrived and a half dozen small *kinner* hopped out the sliding side door. She would stay plenty busy now. Little hands often got into things they shouldn't.

Marjorie stayed at the store until mid-afternoon, which gave Christina a chance to eat at least a few bites of her noon meal. The older woman's chatter eased the tension so Christina could gradually relax her stiff neck and shoulders.

"I hear you visited Eleanore," Marjorie mumbled around the bite of apple she mauled with her back teeth.

News couldn't possibly travel faster if they used telephones. "I did. I think she was glad for the company."

"I'm sure you cheered her." Marjorie swallowed. Before she took another bite, she wiggled her eyebrows and lowered her voice as if the plants and jars on the shelves possessed listening ears and tattling tongues. "I hear you didn't go alone either."

Christina wished she could control the warmth that crept up her neck and across her cheeks. She fidgeted with her order notebook on the counter. "Did you also hear that I happened to run into Noah, who had planned to deliver a book to Eleanore for his *mudder*?"

"I did. *Happened* to run into him, did you?"

Christina let the remark slide by. "Eleanore said she hoped to be released today or tomorrow. *Mamm* said we needed to figure out how to help her stick to her diet."

Immediately, Marjorie began rattling off suggestions. Christina smiled. Another tricky topic successfully avoided.

Eleanore remained the subject of Marjorie's prattling up until the time she left The Green Thumb. Christina nearly collapsed in relief after she bid the woman farewell. She loved Marjorie and was grateful for her help and her contributions to the shop, but the older woman truly had a gift for gab. She didn't have a malicious bone in her body, but she often had great difficulty keeping a conversation confidential.

As if her wagging tongue wasn't bad enough, Marjorie also had a gift of siphoning information out of people whether they wanted to reveal anything or not. Christina knew that Marjorie would eventually wheedle the details of the hospital visit out of her. Thank goodness she hadn't had the chance to try. Christina certainly did not want to be fodder for the gossip mill.

She hadn't quite finished congratulating herself for avoiding Marjorie's interrogation when she heard tires crunch in the gravel parking lot. Music boomed so loud that she figured the car must be bouncing in time with that awful bass beat. Usually, her customers approached the property in a bit more subtle manner.

Christina peeked out the window to try to identify the occupants of the noisy car but was unable to do so. They were not regular customers, for sure and for certain. In fact, she had never seen them before. Two young men about her own age swaggered across the parking lot toward the entrance. Strange. Usually, young men did not visit her shop alone. They usually accompanied a *fraa* or a *mudder*. Christina scurried behind the counter so it wouldn't look like she had been watching them.

Now she wished Marjorie had stayed around a bit longer. What was that old adage? Something about always wanting what you don't have. She resisted the urge to nibble on a fingernail. She had broken the nail-biting habit when she was eight. Funny how that temptation suddenly arose.

After a brief pause, Christina replied to the muffled greeting. At first, she thought the young men were talking to each other but then realized the garbled words were directed at her. "May I help you with something?" She still clung to the hope that they had been sent to her shop by their *mudders* and that she could quickly supply their need and send them on their way.

They shuffled past her without answering her question. Christina shrugged and pretended to be busy with paperwork. Something didn't seem quite right, though. She covertly watched their every move and tried to memorize details about their appearance. Something told her she should remember everything she could about these two fellows. Their dusty boots scuffed along the concrete floor as they swaggered toward the greenhouse. What did they want?

Chapter Twenty-Nine

Please, Lord, let another customer walk through the door. Safety in numbers. Isn't that what people said? She mentally repeated their descriptions to store the information in her brain.

One man, the taller one, had dark hair in need of a trim and shampoo, and he had small, dark eyes. The slightly shorter man had a scruffier appearance. His hair, a sandy color, could also use a *gut* washing. A light-colored, raggedy fuzz covered his cheeks and chin but couldn't hide the many acne scars and pockmarks. Both were skinny enough to slip through a crack in the door at the same time.

Christina needed to follow them into the greenhouse to see what they were up to. That's what she would do with any other suspicious-looking customer. *Breathe! Act normal!* They probably only needed help finding the perfect plant for someone. *Keep telling yourself that, girl.*

She stuffed the sheaf of papers on the shelf below the counter and forced her feet to transport her around the corner. She gulped in a deep breath. *This is your place. You are in charge.* Christina marched to the greenhouse entrance and peeked inside. The men were rifling through her plants. They would surely destroy the delicate blossoms and stems of the flowers she had nurtured and cared for like *bopplin*. They couldn't do that!

She rushed through the doorway. "You have to be gentle with plants. They can't take such rough handling. What can I help you find?" Her voice wobbled a bit, more from anger than fear. She glared at the gangly fellows and tapped a foot on the cement floor. Couldn't they give her some sort of answer? A grunt? A headshake? This whole encounter was more than disturbing. It was totally ridiculous. "Were you looking for a particular flower or a certain color?"

"This all you got?" The dark-haired man grunted, making his words nearly indecipherable.

"Did you not see what you wanted?"

The pimply-faced fellow snorted. "You might say that." He, too, grunted when his companion gave him a sharp elbow jab to the ribs. "Bet she took it," he mumbled out the side of his mouth.

Were they looking for Blake's key? Would they have known about that? How could they unless they had been watching Blake's every move? Christina had never seen Blake inside her shop, so why would these men *kumm* here?

"Let's go!" The bigger man shoved his buddy toward the door.

Christina jumped back out of the way since the pair acted as if they would plow over her. The smaller man looked right at her for a fraction of a second before his companion jabbed him again and muttered, "Keep your head down, you idiot."

"She's already seen us, man."

"She wouldn't have if you'd kept your head down in the first place."

Did they think she couldn't hear or understand their words? Christina slipped behind the counter where she felt marginally safer. Her knees weakened with relief at the slam of a car door and the sound of women's voices. *Danki, Lord, for rescuing me.*

"Go!" The bigger fellow barked the order but didn't give the other man time to react before pushing him out the front door and nearly knocking down an elderly lady on the threshold.

The woman gasped and grabbed the door for support. "Well, I never! Young people these days have absolutely no manners."

"I'm so sorry." Christina rushed around to offer assistance. "Are you all right?"

"It's not your fault at all, young lady. I'm fine. Let me look at all the lovely flowers. I've heard you have the best ones. Come on, Lorraine." She motioned to the younger woman behind her, who rolled her eyes before dutifully following.

~

Finally, the hands on the big, battery-operated clock hanging on the wall behind the counter reached five o'clock. One more hour to go. Those men had not returned, but Christina had cringed every time she heard a vehicle approach. She rolled her head from side to side to work out the kinks in her neck and shoulders.

Her muscles immediately tensed back up when, yet again, tires crunched on the gravel of the parking lot. She should have closed and locked the door five minutes ago. But her sign said she was open until six, so it would not be *gut* business to close up early. She would only do that in a dire emergency. *Please don't let this be a dire emergency.*

"Hey, Christina!"

Christina sank onto the stool and exhaled the breath she had been holding. "*Ach*, Jill. It's you." Her heart still pounded.

"In the flesh. What's wrong? You're as pale as a sheet and trembling."

"I, uh, nothing."

"Don't give me that. I haven't known you long, but I can certainly tell when something is wrong. Spill."

"Spill?"

"Yes. Tell me why you're upset or frightened. What has you so on edge?"

On edge. That was an excellent description. For days now, she'd been perched on the edge of a precipice expecting to be hurled over into some fathomless abyss at any second. Somehow, Jill's soft hand on her forearm loosened her tongue. Christina relayed the escapade with the two strange young men.

"They couldn't have been involved in your *bruder's* death, could they? I mean, if they had committed a crime, they wouldn't dare to show their faces, right? Wouldn't they have worn masks or hoods or something so I wouldn't be able to identify them like in Annie's books?"

"I doubt they are the brightest crayons in the box if you know what I mean." Jill patted Christina's arm. "Oh, Christina, I am so sorry for bringing trouble to your doorstep."

"You didn't. Trouble was already here before you arrived."

"Well then, my brother brought trouble. I truly don't believe he meant to cause harm to you or anyone else."

"I haven't been harmed."

"Y—uh—that's good."

Christina knew Jill had almost said, "yet," which certainly did nothing to calm her nerves. "You think they meant to harm me, ain't so? You believe they will return."

"It's hard to say. They must know Blake left something here. They must have been tracking his movements. And maybe mine now too."

"And mine?" Christina knew the answer to her question without Jill's slight nod.

"I'm so sorry." Jill scampered to peer out the window.

"I would have heard a car drive up. I've jumped to the roof every time I heard one today."

"But you might not hear someone *walking* toward the building, especially if they were taking care to be quiet."

Christina shivered. That was not something she wanted to think about. How would she ever feel safe in her own shop again? This must be some crazy nightmare that she'd wake up from soon.

"Are you always here alone?"

"Often, except when one of my bakers drops by or when customers are here or when a delivery is made."

"Maybe you should come to the shelter with me to adopt a big, ferocious dog of your own."

Christina burst out laughing despite the seriousness of the situation. "How would I explain that?"

"You could say that due to break-ins in the area, you thought getting a dog would be a good idea."

"There haven't been break-ins as far as I know."

"Surely your folks and ministers, or whoever is in charge, would understand your qualms after what happened here. Your people allow pets, don't they?"

"Some folks have pets, but I usually ride my bike here. I couldn't expect a dog to trot along behind me, and I certainly couldn't stuff him inside my basket."

Jill laughed. "You've got a point. Maybe he could live here."

Christina shook her head. "That probably would not work. Dogs like to be with their owners. I couldn't stand the thought of the poor thing left here all alone. What if he knocked over his water and had nothing to drink? What if he whined all night?"

"You're a softie."

"What does that mean?"

"You're caring. You have a tender heart. That's a good thing. And you must be an animal lover. I am too."

"I do like animals. I've grown up with all sorts of animals around—chickens, horses, a pig or two—but I've never had a pet of my own."

"Really? I've had cats and dogs, goldfish from the county fair, and even a box turtle. Maybe it's time for you to get a pet."

"I doubt it." But Christina decided she would think about that idea later. She lowered her voice even though she and Jill were alone in the store. "What did you find out about the key?"

"I still don't know what it goes to. I checked at the bank where Blake had savings and checking accounts. He didn't have a safety deposit box there. I checked at the other local bank too, and he didn't have a box there either."

"It must have something to do with that riddle." Christina tapped her fingers on the counter. "I've been trying to figure it out."

"Me too, but I never was very good with riddles and puzzles. My brain doesn't think that way it seems. Have you come up with anything?"

"I'm still working on it."

"I can't imagine why Blake was so secretive. Unless he had information that could incriminate someone in some way."

"Like those two men?"

"Maybe. Who knows?" Jill heaved a heavy sigh. "This should be the job of the police, not the victim's sister, but they are still content with their nice, tidy conclusion that my brother was just another overdose victim. I know better!" Her voice rose before breaking off in a near sob.

Both young women gasped when a shadow fell across the rays of sun streaked across the floor. Christina clapped a hand to her mouth to stifle a scream.

"We should have been more vigilant," Jill whispered.

Jill started to tiptoe toward the door, but Christina snagged her arm to pull her back. "Don't you want to know what we are about to face?"

Christina shook her head hard. She'd much rather close her eyes and pretend she was home or on the moon or anywhere but in The Green Thumb.

Heavy footsteps clomped to the front door. Those fellows earlier in the day had been wearing heavy work boots. But Christina only heard one set of footsteps this time. Did the bigger man return alone? He seemed to be in charge.

Jill's brave façade disappeared. She zoomed around the counter and jerked Christina down to a squatting position right as the door squeaked open.

Christina sucked in a breath and held it. Her brain scarcely registered the pain in her fingers from Jill's tight grip.

"Christina?"

Weak with relief, she toppled from her crouched position, pulling Jill down on her rear too. She raised her eyes to find Noah staring over the counter with his lips twitching in a near smile. She and Jill must make a very comical sight.

"Is there a reason you two are down there?"

"We thought you were someone else." Christina scrambled to her feet in as ladylike a manner as she could manage. If the heat in her cheeks was any indication, her face must surely be glowing. She reached out a hand to help Jill to her feet.

"Do you always hide from your customers?"

"Almost never."

"Who were you expecting to walk through the door?" Noah looked from one young woman to the other.

"I wasn't exactly expecting someone." She didn't want to confess that she *feared* it was someone she never wanted to see again."

"Do you care to explain?"

Christina checked the clock. One minute until six. Close enough. She scooted past Jill and hurried to lock the front door. Noah's eyes bored a hole through her back. If she told him about the two men, would she be putting him in more danger than she had already done? Guilt already ate a hole through her heart and soul. Jill remained silent, obviously letting Christina handle Noah's questions.

"You didn't answer me, Christy."

Why did he have to use the nickname? It always turned her knees to jelly and her brain to mush. She had to stop letting him affect her this way. She grabbed a deep breath for fortification and allowed her eyes to travel up and up to meet Noah's questioning, crystal-blue ones. Before she could change her mind, she blurted out the entire story.

"I don't like this." Noah shook his head for emphasis. "I don't think it is very safe for you to be here alone."

Jill finally found her voice. "I told her she should come to the shelter with me to adopt a big dog."

Christina laughed. "You go right ahead, Jill, but I believe I will hold off on that." She turned back to Noah. "I told her how that probably wouldn't work for me."

Jill wagged a scolding finger. "You never know. It could turn out great. Sometimes dogs become people's best friends."

Well, I am in the market for one of those! "I don't think so, Jill."

"At least get the largest dog dish you can find and write the name "Killer" or "Brute" on it so people think you have a humongous dog."

Noah chuckled along with the women. "You know, Christy, it might be a solution."

"Setting out a dog dish?" She couldn't imagine such a ploy would work.

"*Nee*, adopting a dog."

"You're both *narrisch*."

"What's that?" Jill tugged on Christina's arm. "What did you call me?"

"Crazy. I said you were both crazy."

"What's crazy is those two thugs moseying through your shop. I wish I had a picture of them, but it isn't like I knew any of Blake's clients. Someone else might be able to identify them, though."

"I'm sorry I don't have pictures or even a camera."

"I know. You gave excellent descriptions, though."

Noah glanced around the shop. "Do you suppose those fellows knew about the key and were searching for it?"

Jill sighed. "That's what we were wondering. If only we knew what that key went to."

Christina patted the *Englisch* girl's arm. "I'm working on that."

Chapter Thirty

"You don't have to go all the way home with me, Noah. I don't want to take up anymore of your time." Although she enjoyed his company more than she liked to admit, Christina did not want him to feel responsible for her. After Jill drove away from The Green Thumb, Noah announced that he would accompany Christina on her evening trek. When he had ridden with her previously, he always turned off when they reached the road leading to his house. Today, he kept pace with her without giving any indication that he planned to leave her.

"You aren't taking my time or keeping me from anything. I want to make sure you get home safely."

"There are usually enough cars traveling this road or there are people in their yards so it would be hard for anyone to bother me without being seen. I'm sure I will be fine." The only problem she had ever encountered on this road had been instigated by Annie.

"Let's not take any chances."

Secretly, Christina's heart did an extra pitter-patter at Noah's concern. *He's a nice fellow, Christina. He would be concerned about anyone.* Now if only her heart would listen to her brain. She smiled in spite of her brain's caution until a fleeting image of Annie's angry face sobered her. She hoped they did not run into her *freind*—her former *freind*—during this last mile of the trip. Christina would never be able to explain why Noah accompanied her home. She didn't know how she would explain his presence to her family, either, if anyone should notice their arrival.

"*Danki* for riding home with me." Christina braked at the end of the long dirt driveway leading to her family's home.

"Maybe I should escort you to and from work at least for the next few days."

"That would be way too much trouble, but I do appreciate your offer." She would enjoy spending more time with him, though.

"Honest, it wouldn't be any trouble at all. We both go to work early."

"True, but..."

"Unless you'd rather not be seen with me."

"*Ach!* It's not that at all!" Quite the opposite, actually.

Noah gave her a lopsided grin. "*Gut.* I was afraid I smelled bad or something."

Christina giggled. "Of course you don't."

He reached out to touch her arm but drew his hand back as if afraid he shouldn't do so. "What did Jill think of that paper you found taped to your door this morning?"

"I completely forgot to tell her about that."

"That's okay. She probably wouldn't be able to shed any light on the matter anyway."

"Probably not, and it would be one more burden for her to carry around. Her load is very heavy as it is. I know she feels guilty for getting me involved in this mess, even though it isn't her fault. Just like I feel guilty for involving you."

"You can stop that right now. I jumped into the middle of this with my eyes open."

"But I'm not sure you realized how dangerous this could become. I certainly wasn't thinking along those lines. I figured I would help Jill sort things out and be done with the whole business."

"I had a hunch that things could get more intense. I couldn't let you go through that alone."

What was he implying? Dare she risk drowning in his eyes if she glanced up?

"When I ran over that evening from the Quick Stop, you looked so lost, so vulnerable. I knew I would do whatever I could to help you."

"I hope I don't always look that way!"

"*Nee.* You always look confident and in control, but that was not a normal day at all."

"For sure. But you could have gone your way after the police took your statement. There wasn't any reason to stay involved."

"There certainly was. You! You were the reason I couldn't leave."

"I know I probably looked a mess, but I could have handled things fine—probably."

"I'm sure you could have, but I couldn't stand the thought of your facing whatever else might happen all by yourself. I wanted to help you, and I still do, even if it is only to listen to your concerns."

"I appreciate that, Noah."

"I'm sorry I wasn't at The Green Thumb earlier today when those men came in."

"They were probably harmless. My imagination has been running away with itself lately."

"That's understandable. I wish I could stay at the shop with you all day, you know, in case you need something."

Christina smiled. The rosy glow in his cheeks made him look like a little *bu.* "That's nice of you, but you have your own job. Please don't worry about me. I'll be fine." *I hope.*

"Isn't there someone who could stay at the store with you so you won't be alone? School is out, so maybe one of your *schweschders* could go to work with you."

Christina wrinkled her nose. "*Mamm* tried to send the girls with me, but to tell the truth, I think my work day would go easier by myself rather than adding refereeing those two to my schedule."

"How about one of them at a time? Even if they aren't able to assist you very much, they could at least run for help if you needed it."

"I don't know, Noah. I really don't want to involve them in any of this mess."

"I can understand that. It's just something to think about."

Christina nodded, but she wouldn't have to think much. She didn't want to expose Sallie and Grace to any harm.

"Maybe Jill's idea about a dog would be a solution. I can check around. Someone always has a litter they are trying to find homes for."

"I'm even more sure that wouldn't work, Noah."

"You never know. Think about it."

All she did lately was think about the problems she'd inherited in the blink of an eye and wonder how she could solve them.

~

Thank goodness his feet could pedal on their own volition because Noah's brain had totally wandered off. Did Christina have any idea how lovely she was? Did she know she was a fun, interesting person to be around? Did she pick up on his interest in her?

Here he was twenty-four years old and could not voice his feelings clearly. He thought he conveyed his interest, but he didn't want to *kumm* on too strong and scare her off. Maybe she had a fellow she was interested in, but Noah didn't think so. Or perhaps she didn't consider him a possible beau since he'd never asked to take her home after any of the occasional singings he had attended.

For the life of him, he didn't understand why he had never approached Christina at the conclusion of one of the young folks' gatherings. He had watched her from afar and had feared she would head out the door with some other fellow, but he had never made a move in her direction. Why? And when had his casual interest developed into something much stronger? Now he experienced an overwhelming desire to protect the young woman. A day did not seem complete if he had not at least glimpsed her in the distance.

"Face it, Noah. You've been a complete idiot. And if you don't change your approach, you're going to lose this amazing girl to someone who can make his feelings known."

"Hey, Noah! Are you talking to yourself or do you have someone in your pocket?" A giggle followed the question.

Noah jumped and jerked the handlebars, nearly sending the bicycle into a skid on the loose pebbles dotting the pavement. He had been so deep in thought that he hadn't heard the whir of spinning bike tires behind him. After gaining control of the bike, he glanced over his shoulder, even though he knew who owned that voice. The rider sped up to pedal right beside him. "Hello, Annie. You know, it might not be wise to ride side by side. Sometimes the cars appear out of nowhere."

"I'll keep a watch. You're going the wrong way, ain't so?"

"*Nee.* I'm headed home."

"But you don't work in the direction you came from."

Her tone was accusing, demanding, but Noah decided he wouldn't fall into her trap. "You're going the wrong way too. You're traveling away from your home instead of toward it."

She shrugged. "I got off work early and went home. I, uh, decided to go back out."

"It's nearly suppertime, ain't so?"

"I suppose. My *mudder* already had everything under control and didn't need my help." She batted her eyes. "So where are you going?"

"Home. Just like I said before."

"Did you go someplace else after work?"

She really was overstepping her bounds as far as Noah was concerned. She didn't have any right to interrogate him. He tried not to let the girl irk him. He glanced over in time to catch the fluttering eyes again. "Did you get something in your eye?"

"*Nee.* Why?"

"You keep blinking. I thought a piece of dirt or a bug got in your eye. If not, maybe you should get the doctor to check your eyes. It can't be safe to be out here on the road if you have to keep closing your eyes."

"Hmpf! A lot you know!"

She had muttered mostly under her breath, but Noah caught the words and had to work hard to keep from chuckling. He wasn't trying to be mean, but the girl needed to know how ridiculous she looked. "I only wanted to make sure you could see all right."

"My eyes are fine!" Annie spit the words out like watermelon seeds but then immediately softened her tone. "I appreciate your concern."

Noah wasn't at all sure how appreciative she was, but he nodded in acknowledgment of her words. How could he get her to go her own way and let him continue home in peace?

"Were you visiting someone after work?"

Ugh! His attempt at diversion failed. "Not really." Technically, that was the truth. He had not been visiting Christina. He had accompanied her home. He would try again to turn this whole conversation around. "How about you? Are you on your way to visit someone?"

"You might say that. Were—"

"Car!" The quickly approaching car meant Annie would have to file in behind him. Noah pedaled faster so he would reach his turnoff before Annie had the chance to further question him. He heard her grunt in an effort to keep up. "See you, Annie!" he called over his shoulder as he swerved onto his road. He kept his pace steady and pretended he didn't hear her call out.

"Wait! Noah, I wasn't finished."

Noah kept pedaling. Was he being rude? Probably, but that couldn't be helped at the moment. Annie seemed determined to know his whereabouts, and he hadn't any intention of enlightening her.

~

Christina crawled into her bed, scrunched her eyes closed, and begged sleep to claim her. How could a person be so utterly exhausted yet unable to rest, much less sleep? She'd tried every relaxation tip she'd ever heard of, but nothing worked. If she tiptoed downstairs for a mug of warm milk—which did not appeal to her in the least—someone in a household of eight people was bound to see or hear her and bombard her with questions.

She rolled onto her side and drew her legs up into a fetal position, hoping that might soother her to sleep. It used to work when she was a little girl. Maybe she should try sucking her thumb again too. Christina groaned and flopped over onto her back. She opened her eyes to stare into the blackness. She counted sheep. Boring, but apparently not boring enough to induce slumber. She closed her eyes gently this time. Maybe scrunching increased tension.

Blue eyes bore into her brain. Crystal-clear, sparkling eyes. Eyes full of concern and, possibly, caring. Eyes that crinkled around the edges in amusement. Eyes that made her knees buckle and her heart skip beats when they gazed into her own.

Aghh! Enough, Christina! You'd better go back to the sheep or try reciting the alphabet forward and backward or anything else. Think of anything other than Noah Zimmerman and his magnificent eyes.

Silver bells, oyster shells, and little tykes in a row... Yikes! This line of thought was even less conducive to sleep.

Images whirled in Christina's brain like a top spinning out of control on a wood floor. She might as well forget about sleep. Again.

Bells would usually be found at a church. She had already mentally reviewed all the churches she was familiar with. Of course, there were many others in the county that she had never seen, but she had a hunch that Blake referred to some nearby place. Christina couldn't think of a single store that had a silver bell. Many had some kind of gizmo attached to the door to let employees know that a customer had arrived, but she wouldn't consider those "silver bells."

Bells and shells. Where would a person find bells and shells? Somewhere near a river or bay, but that did not narrow her choices down much since the county sported so many bodies of water. And what did *kinner* have to do with the whole mess? It was all so confusing and frustrating.

Urgency nagged at Christina. Somehow, she knew that if she didn't hurry and solve this riddle, something terrible would happen to Jill or maybe even to Noah and herself. She had to prevent that. Something tickled the back of her mind, but she couldn't bring it forefront.

Christina shivered and yanked the cotton sheet up to her chin despite the hot July evening. Fear was an unaccustomed emotion. Barring the past few days, she couldn't remember when she'd been scared of something. David's prank of thrusting a big, hairy spider in her face hadn't sent her screaming. Spiders weren't her favorite of the Lord *Gott*'s creatures, but she didn't fear them. The last severe thunderstorm had been threatening and loud, but she had not cowered under the bed. *Nee*, she had always taken things in stride. But this whole murder mystery was an entirely different matter. She sighed. *One sheep. Two sheep.*

Christina's legs moved about as easily as two concrete pillars as she pedaled down the dirt driveway. Her basket had not been overloaded. It contained only her quilted carry-all bag and her lunch cooler, so it couldn't be hampering her progress. She could only hope the pedaling would become easier when she reached the paved road. "It can't be any worse."

"You talk to yourself too, I see."

Christina yelped and clutched the handlebars. She managed to correct her swerve before the bicycle toppled over. "Y-you scared me half to death."

"That's practically the same thing the other person I caught talking to himself said. You must think alike. How interesting!"

"Hi, Annie." Christina maneuvered her bike to stay at arm's length from the other girl. She didn't want to be pushed over again and arrive at work covered in blood. The menacing expression on Annie's face led Christina to believe that just such a thing might happen. Had Annie been baiting her with that comment? Christina was too tired to rise to the challenge. She remained silent.

"I'm sure you know who I'm talking about, ain't so?"

Christina blew out a sigh. "I don't know who or what you're talking about, and frankly, I'm too exhausted to try to figure it out."

"Were you out late last night? Or maybe someone visited you until the wee hours of the morning?"

"Neither." Christina concentrated on steering in a straight path outside of Annie's reach.

"Hmpf! A likely story."

"Look, Annie, I don't know what your problem is, but I have a lot on my mind and haven't been sleeping well. I don't want to be blamed for your anger or pain. I don't know what imaginary infraction you believe I've committed, but I'll say I'm sorry anyway."

"Imaginary? I am not imagining things. I see things perfectly clear."

"I'm glad, Annie. Now, I really have to get to the shop." Christina forced her leaden legs to pedal faster, leaving a fuming Annie behind. Would she ever have her sweet-natured *freind* back? The prospects did not look favorable.

Chapter Thirty-One

Christina triple-checked the back door to make sure it was locked as soon as she got inside The Green Thumb. She had glanced at the shed and greenhouse when she hopped off her bike to ensure they were exactly as she left them. She hastily surveyed the shop as she made her way to the front counter to stow her belongings. Nothing looked out of place. She did not see any new cryptic messages anywhere. Now that all that was settled in her mind, Christina could concentrate on work.

Christina hummed as she prepared to open the store. The familiar songs from the Ausbund always soothed her. She pulled open the front door and flipped the sign in the window to let passersby know she was ready for business. She had missed seeing Noah this morning. She hadn't realized how much she looked forward to talking to him.

She shook her head. *Stop being silly. You don't have any claim on Noah. He was only being polite and helpful as he would be with anyone.* While Christina's brain might make this rationalization, her heart could not accept it. That crush she had on Noah Zimmerman for quite some time had blossomed into... what? She didn't know for sure, but whatever it was, it was more powerful than a crush. She needed to subdue that if she wanted to guard her heart from pain.

Noah was a *gut* four years older than she was. Undoubtedly, he would look for a girl closer to his own age. But Christina had never seen him with any girls. She had never heard any of the girls whispering about him. Maybe he had figured out a way to court someone without the whole community getting wind of it. Not likely. News traveled fast, even in their slower-paced world.

Christina told herself she should be thankful that she didn't run into Noah this morning since Annie had caught up to her and made such snide remarks. The situation would have been far worse if Annie had discovered Christina and Noah riding together.

Whatever should she do about Annie? Had the girl gone off the deep end? Christina had never seen this side of her *freind* before. She didn't quite know how to deal with the "mean Annie" and couldn't fathom a way to patch their tattered relationship. She had prayed but had not received an answer. "All in *gut* time. *Gott*'s time," *Mamm* would say.

The morning sped by. Many of her customers liked to buy their plants and supplies early in the morning so they could complete their outside work before the heat of the day made merely breathing a chore. This summer had been a hot one as far as Southern Maryland summers went, and they were only halfway through the season. Christina raised her water bottle, took a swig, and tucked it back inside her cooler.

Footsteps approaching the front door sent her heart galloping. The earlier flow of customers had left her too busy to worry about potential problems, but this afternoon lull allowed her imagination to run wild.

"Hi, Christina."

"*Ach*, Jill. How are you?" The *Englisch* girl exuded a deep sadness that made Christina's heart ache for her.

"Blake's funeral was this morning."

"I'm so sorry." Christina reached across the counter to squeeze Jill's thin arm.

"At least it's over. I hate funerals."

Christina nodded. She didn't imagine anyone liked them, but they did provide time to say farewell to a loved one. At all the funerals Christina had ever attended, families and *freinden* had been there to support the grief-stricken folks. Who had been there for Jill? Did anyone offer a helping hand?

Jill's sigh had to have been one of the most mournful sounds Christina had ever heard. She watched the *Englisch* girl gather her dark curls in her hands and hold them off of her neck. "Whew! It certainly is hot today, isn't it?" She fanned herself with her free hand.

"It has been a hot summer."

"That's for sure. Do you have a rubber band?"

"I might. I'll have to scrounge around a bit. Someone once told me that rubber bands aren't *gut* for your hair."

"I've heard that too, but right now I'm so hot that I don't really care if my hair breaks off."

"You have such pretty curls. I would hate to see them mangled. Hey! I can snip off a piece of ribbon, and you can tie your hair with that. How does that sound?"

"It sounds like you're a genius. A piece of ribbon should work fine."

"I'll be right back."

When Christina returned, she found Jill perusing the baked items for sale. "Here's your ribbon. Why don't you pick out a snack? No charge." The poor girl's heart-shaped face looked smaller than ever, and the emerald eyes looked almost too large for her face. Had she been eating at all?

Jill reached for the ribbon and maneuvered it beneath the mass of curls. "Thanks. The treats all look yummy, but I haven't had much of an appetite lately."

"It shows."

"Huh?"

Had she offended the girl? "I didn't mean anything bad. You look lovely as always but a bit thinner."

"Maybe. Food hasn't been a priority lately."

"Well, try one of Marjorie's whoopie pies. She makes delicious treats."

Jill picked up a chocolate one and fished around in her pocket until she produced a dollar bill and some change.

Christina held up her hand in protest. "*Nee*, you don't have to pay. It's a free treat. Consider it a gift to a *freind*."

"No, I want to be a paying customer." She thrust the money into Christina's hand.

Christina shook her head and scooted over to deposit the money in her cashbox.

"Can I hang out here this afternoon? I promise I won't bother you. I'll even run outside and hide when customers come in."

Christina giggled. "You do not have to hide from my customers."

"I don't want to embarrass you or anything."

"Why do you think you would do that?"

"Well, I'm not exactly dressed like you. I might stick out like a sore thumb."

Christina clucked her tongue. "A great many of my customers are *Englisch*. And they *kumm* in here wearing shorts and shirts that leave little to the imagination or they might be wearing dresses or shirts and ties if they are stopping in after work. Most of my customers this morning were *Englisch*, so you should definitely not feel out of place."

"If you say so." Jill finally unwrapped the whoopie pie and took a bite. "So I can stay? I really don't want to go home right now." She nibbled at the treat again. "This is very good by the way."

"I'll pass your compliment on to Marjorie. And of course, you can stay, for as long as you like." Christina wasn't entirely sure letting Jill "hang out," as she called it, at The Green Thumb was a great idea, especially if anyone had been following her, but how could she turn the girl away? Jill needed a *freind* right now, and Christina could at least offer to be one.

"Thanks."

Christina wanted to ask how the funeral went but wasn't sure she should broach that subject. She knew practically nothing about *Englischer's* customs. She had seen parades of cars with headlights switched on following a hearse to the cemetery in town, and she knew flowers were a part of the service or whatever they called it, but that was the extent of her knowledge. She couldn't be sure if it would help Jill to talk about the day or if it would make her sadder.

She peeked at the young woman who, at the moment, looked like a little girl as she licked chocolate from her lips.

"You know, those guys who came in here could have been at the funeral," Jill murmured after swallowing her bite of whoopie pie.

Christina gasped. "Surely not."

"A lot of the people Blake counseled attended the service. There were several young men who fit the description you gave, but I guess most of the guys in that group had the same basic appearance."

"Why would a person responsible for ending his life show up at the funeral?"

"To throw off suspicion would be my guess."

"Oh. That makes sense. If they had stayed away, they would have been pointing fingers at themselves or at least would have caused folks to wonder."

"Bingo!"

"I'm sorry that I couldn't have given a better description."

"Your description was fine. It's just that all the guys from the counseling center fit it. I wish I could figure out what Blake was trying to tell me." She paused to stare out the window. "You have customers coming. Do you want me to go outside?"

"Of course not. If you saw a car drive up, they must be *Englisch*, ain't so?"

"Some Mennonites drive cars, don't they?"

"Sure, but not members of my community. We're Old Order Mennonites. We don't drive cars or use electricity in our homes or—"

"Like the Amish?"

"*Jah.*"

"But there are more modern Mennonites around here too, right? I've seen ladies dressed like you step out of dark-colored minivans and cars."

"You're right."

Jill stole another glance out the window. "These people are *Englischers* as you call us. I'll mill about like a regular customer."

Christina nodded before greeting the couple who walked through the doorway. She watched Jill head for the attached greenhouse.

More customers arrived. Christina stayed busy explaining plant care, helping people make appropriate selections, and ringing up sales. Jill continued to wander about, reminding Christina of a little girl who had lost her way. In between customers, her mind puzzled over the modified nursery rhyme stuck in her brain.

What or who was the unordinary Mary? Such a common name. Did this Mary grow a garden? All the Marys she knew certainly did. Not all *Englischers* did, though. Many of them lived in houses so close together that they could lean out their windows to shake hands. Was there a Mary who lived near the water and grew a garden? Could the row of *kinner* be marching through the garden? *Ach!* It was so frustrating. And something still nagged at the edge of her mind. Why couldn't she grasp it?

A car door signaling the arrival of another customer dragged Christina out of her reverie. She would have to let all these strange thoughts stew a little longer while she performed her job.

Business did not slow down until a half hour before closing. Christina had not had more than five minutes between customers, not nearly long enough to ponder her troubling thoughts. Jill had resorted to perching on the stool behind the counter and observing the goings-on like an owl on a tree branch surveying the forest.

"I don't know how you do it." Jill shook her head, setting the springy, dark curls that had escaped from the ribbon into motion.

"Do what?"

"Wait on all these people, patiently answer their questions, and keep your cheery attitude. Your feet must be killing you."

"*Nee*. I'm used to moving all day. And these are great!" Christina kicked out a foot and pointed to her black athletic shoe.

"Okay. That explains the feet part, but how about the bright attitude after a long, busy day?"

Christina shrugged. "I suppose we can all choose to be happy or grumpy. I prefer happy, and I try to treat people the way I want to be treated."

"You could teach customer service skills to a lot of business people I know."

Christina frowned. "What do you mean?"

"I've gone into a lot of stores and businesses where the employees were not very polite. They seemed to have a chip on their shoulders and waited on customers begrudgingly."

"That seems strange. If you don't treat your customers well, they won't return. If you don't have customers, you won't have a business."

"You're absolutely right, but I'm afraid a lot of people don't share your sentiments. Well, maybe the owners do, but I'm not sure about some of the employees."

Christina scurried about straightening shelves. "It sounds like those folks don't really want their jobs."

Jill jumped off the stool. "I can help you put things in order."

"You don't have to do that."

"I want to help. My goodness, you've been kind enough to let me sit on your stool for hours."

"You don't need to compensate for that."

"I *want* to help." Jill shuffled to the next row to restore order.

Christina paused with a jar of strawberry-rhubarb jam in her hand. "I think I've got it!"

Chapter Thirty-Two

Jill yelped. The flowerpot she'd been repositioning tumbled to the floor. "You scared me to death." She dropped to her hands and knees to retrieve the pot. "It's a good thing this wasn't a terra-cotta pot."

"I'm sorry I frightened you. I think I have an idea."

"I hope it's a good idea since my heart went into spasms and I lost ten years off my life."

Christina laughed. "I hope I'm on the right track."

Jill replaced the flowerpot and brushed off her hands. "Let's hear it."

"I can't stop thinking about your *bruder's* riddle."

"That makes two of us, but I haven't come close to solving it. What did you think of?"

"I don't know if my idea even makes sense."

"Any idea is better than no idea, which is where I am." Jill backed away from the shelf. "I don't want to knock anything else to the floor if I get excited or if you yell again."

"I didn't yell."

"Spoke loudly. How's that?"

"All right." Christina glanced toward the door to make sure there weren't any late customers or eavesdroppers. She lowered her voice in case someone appeared out of the blue.

"Can we close and lock the door?"

Christina turned to check the clock. "Fifteen more minutes."

"Precise, aren't you?"

"I try to be."

"I can't wait fifteen minutes. Go ahead and tell me your idea."

"Okay. First, I thought Mary was a person, but that is a pretty common name, at least in my community."

"It isn't as common as it used to be for us, but there are quite a few Marys running around."

"Then I thought Mary meant a place, not a person."

Jill's forehead puckered. "That would be equally hard to pinpoint. Practically everything around here is St. Mary's or Maryland or some variation of the two."

"You're right. I puzzled over the bell and shells for a long time, trying to remember all the churches that I'd seen with bells. Of course, you would know more of those than I would. I couldn't think of any churches close to the water to account for the oyster shells, but there could be other places in the county that I am not aware of." Christina paused to gulp in air.

"I'd have to think about other areas, but Blake lived here, so..."

"So I started thinking of other places that might have bells. Suddenly, it came to me. Doesn't that little private school near the wharf, St. Mary's Academy or something like that, have a bell like a church bell? There would definitely be oyster shells near the school, and *kinner*, or tykes, might walk in rows or lines. I don't know about the garden part, though."

"You're a genius!" Jill squealed and ran to throw her arms around Christina. "That has to be it."

"I always knew you were smart!"

Both women jumped and gasped in unison.

"I'm sorry. I thought you heard me at the door." Noah looked down at his scuffed work shoes. "I'm not exactly light on my feet in these."

Christina giggled. As tall and as muscular as he was, she doubted Noah could be terribly light on his feet, even if he was barefoot.

"So much for our vigilance." Jill shook her head. "We didn't even hear a sound from outside."

"Well, to tell you the truth, I rode my bike through the grass and not the gravel, so you probably wouldn't have heard my approach even if you weren't engrossed in your conversation."

"Why were you being so sneaky, Noah Zimmerman?" Christina tapped her foot and fixed the big man with a mock stern look.

"I wasn't exactly sneaking."

"What would you call it, then?" Christina struggled not to smile.

"I, uh, wanted to make sure you didn't have another, uh, visitor." He shifted from foot to foot and gave Christina a knowing look.

"I see." She knew precisely what he meant. Noah did not want to deal with Annie again. Christina wanted to avoid such a confrontation herself.

"She did have a visitor. Me." Jill frowned until realization dawned. "Oh. There was someone in particular you wanted to avoid."

"Shhh!" Christina and Noah hissed at the same time. Both glanced toward the door.

Jill laughed. "You two are hysterical."

Noah tugged on Christina's arm. "Do you want to tell me what earned you the 'genius' label?"

Jill jerked on Christina's other arm. She prepared to tell them to make a wish before they ripped her in two, but Jill spoke first. "She is absolutely brilliant. She figured out my brother's riddle."

"We don't know that for sure and for certain, Jill, so don't pin all your hopes on that."

"I feel it in my bones that you are right, but we need to check it out."

We? Jill expects me to check it out? How am I supposed to manage that? Christina didn't have an answer to her own question, but she knew she absolutely had to find out for herself if her hunch was correct. She was way too involved to back out now. Christina had begun this journey with Jill, so she would see it through. Some little mystery-solving segment in her brain that she had never been aware of had been awakened. She had always enjoyed solving puzzles, and this one was the biggest, most challenging one she had ever encountered. She had to know if she had assembled all the clues correctly.

Christina struggled not to absorb Jill's excitement as she explained the possible solution to Noah. She wished she could get Jill to calm down in case the solution she'd proposed was completely wrong.

"What do you think?" Jill practically jumped up and down while waiting for Noah's response.

He rubbed a hand across his jaw. "It makes sense. I suppose it's worth checking into, but what will you do when you get to the school?"

"We can take a look around, see if something jumps out at us to tie in with the riddle. You two will come with me, won't you? It's almost six. We can go as soon as you lock up."

"We have chores to do at home." Christina shook her head as she spoke. "I'm expected to help with supper too." A quick glance at Jill's crestfallen face told her the girl was on the verge of tears. She peeked at Noah, who nodded in agreement with her.

"Wait!" Jill brightened instantly. "It stays light until nearly nine o'clock. I could pick you up after your supper."

"We can't simply show up at the school and traipse around the grounds, can we? Wouldn't that be trespassing?" Christina didn't have any desire to deal with the police again.

Jill thought for a moment. "I have seen children playing on the playground this summer, so they must allow that. The school is near the wharf, and people walk down to the water all the time. We should be able to take a little detour across the school property."

"Wouldn't people be suspicious if they saw three adults searching the schoolyard, especially if two are Plain?" Christina did not want their picture on the front page of the local newspaper. Nor did she want to get into trouble for doing something illegal. She was pretty sure Noah shared her sentiments.

Jill apparently never gave up easily. "Well, we could all mosey along as if we're enjoying the summer evening and sort of scout around for anything that might pertain to Blake. If someone tells us to leave the property, we'll apologize profusely and beat feet. How does that sound?"

Christina shrugged. She wished Noah would chime in with his opinion. "Isn't that school for young *kinner*? Your *bruder* wouldn't have been counseling any of them, would he?"

"The school goes up to eighth grade, so some of the students would be twelve or thirteen. Blake said he often spoke to younger kids to try to keep them from getting involved in any kind of substance abuse."

"Oh." Christina turned to face Noah. "What do you think? I'd like to help Jill, but how would we explain an outing on a weekday evening when we both need to get up early tomorrow for work?"

Noah exhaled hard enough to ruffle the dark hair hanging on his forehead. "Maybe we could think of something we need at the store."

"Our *mudders* would have picked up any needed groceries during the daytime, ain't so?"

"How about the hardware store or the drugstore?"

So he wants to go check this out too. I can see it in his eyes. "Daed would say he had whatever I might need from the hardware store. I'd better say I needed tissues or pencils and paper from the drugstore."

Jill looked from one to the other. "You will both come with me?"

Would Christina later regret this decision? "We can't let you go alone. But we won't have a lot of time to spend there."

"Anything is better than nothing. Thank you both so much."

Christina's mind spun in a thousand directions. She had to hurry home to help with supper, clean up, hitch the horse to the buggy, and head into town all before darkness fell. Was Noah plotting his adventure as well? Fellows had a bit more liberty than young women, so he might have an easier time getting away.

"Do you want me to pick you up at your house or at the end of your driveway or here at the store?"

"*Nee.* If I tell my parents that I need to go to the store, that's exactly what I will do. I'll have to bring the horse and buggy. Do you know where we tie up our horses on the far side of the shopping center?"

"Sure. I've seen buggies over there before."

"I'll meet you there." Christina mentally calculated how long it should take her to accomplish all her chores and drive into town before establishing a meeting time.

"Do you want me to pick you up?" Jill asked Noah.

"I'll meet you at the store too."

"Good. I really appreciate this, guys."

Guys? Christina supposed *Englischers* used the word as a generic term to include everyone. She glanced at the clock. "I'd better close up shop and hurry home." She hustled to the door to flip the sign and lock up, all the while considering various ways to inform her family of her plans. She hoped *Mamm* didn't insist that one of her siblings accompany her.

~

Getting out of the house had proven easier than Christina expected. She fanned herself with one hand as she sat in the buggy waiting for Noah and Jill to arrive. To her complete amazement, she even managed to get to the store a few minutes ahead of time. The clip-clop of a horse's hooves on the blacktop parking lot pulled her attention away from the evening's mission. *Please let it be Noah and not someone else to witness me climbing into Jill's car.* She did not want to be the topic of conversation on the grapevine.

Noah nodded as he stopped his black buggy beside her. Christina breathed a sigh of relief. If Jill would hurry up, they could get this whole business over with without being observed. She watched for Jill's car to enter the parking lot but was taken by surprise when the dark-haired young woman appeared at the opposite window of her buggy.

"Hi, Christina. I didn't mean to startle you. I parked out front."

"Okay." She never used to startle so easily. Now she jumped at the least little thing. Christina glance around before jumping out of the buggy and noticed that Noah did likewise. Most members of their community were probably finishing up evening chores and thinking about retiring, but occasionally someone would go out for a ride on nice evenings or make a trip to the store for some necessary item.

Noah made sure both horses were secure. "We don't want to leave them here for too long."

"I understand." Jill looked at one horse and then the other. "They sure are big."

Christina took in the young woman's fearful expression. "Have you been around horses much?"

"Not at all. I've always thought they were rather majestic animals, but I admired them from a distance. I've never ridden a horse, unless you count the pony ride at the fair when I was five." She backed up a few steps while keeping her eyes on the horses.

"Don't be afraid. This horse is one of the gentlest creatures I've ever seen."

"My horse is a *gut* sport too." Noah patted his horse's nose.

"If you say so." Jill's tone didn't sound too confident. "Are we ready?"

~

"*Ach!* What a *dumchen!*" Noah smacked his forehead.

"Who are you calling a *dumchen*, Noah Zimmerman?" Christina fixed him with a glare, her fists balled on her hips.

She was cute when she got riled, though he suspected she was teasing at the moment. If he wanted to be completely truthful, she was much more than cute all the time. "Me. I'm calling myself that. Wait a minute." He hustled to his buggy, reached inside, and pulled out a crinkly plastic bag. He carried it to Christina's buggy and tossed it in on the floor.

"What was that?"

"Your drugstore items."

"My what?"

"You know, tissues, pencils, and a writing tablet. I didn't see you here when I arrived, so I drove to the other end of the parking lot to go into the drugstore to pick up the things you said you needed. That way, you won't have to take time to do that when we get back."

Christina's lips formed an "O," but no sound passed through them. Had he overstepped his bounds? He only wanted to be helpful, but maybe she considered his action pushy or out of place. Heat crept up his neck probably a red glow as well, which would certainly spread across his cheeks in a matter of seconds making him look as foolish as he felt.

"Why, Noah, that's so thoughtful. *Danki.* I'll get the receipt out of the bag so I can repay you."

The breath he'd been holding whooshed out, causing additional embarrassment. "That isn't necessary."

"I certainly don't expect you to pay for my business supplies."

"I know, but I don't want to be repaid. Consider it a gift from one *freind* to another."

Freind? His feelings went deeper than that. The smile that lit her face warmed his heart. His knees wobbled ever so slightly in relief that he hadn't upset or angered her. He couldn't pinpoint exactly when his feelings had crossed that line from *freindship* to... what? He didn't know for sure.

Noah had admired Christina from afar for some time. He'd been mesmerized by her silvery eyes, but he had always kept his distance. That evening that Annie raced into the Quick Stop and blurted out the details of Christina's gruesome discovery made something trip in his mind. He suddenly couldn't bear to think that Christina could be in trouble or could be hurt. A protectiveness that Noah could only liken to a female bear hovering over her cubs completely enveloped him, and he knew he would do anything to protect or help the tiny, young woman who had taken up residence in his heart and mind.

When he summoned the courage to look into her sweet face, Noah's heart somersaulted across his chest. Her smile warmed his soul. Time halted. He couldn't remember why he stood outside of the store on a hot, July evening. He probably wouldn't even be able to

recall his own name at the moment if anyone asked. Christina seemed equally as transfixed.

"Well, I hate to break this spell, but do you two think we can leave now?"

Chapter Thirty-Three

Christina knew her face must be as red as the grape tomatoes she sold in little straw baskets at The Green Thumb. If she could have scurried beneath Jill's car, she surely would have. How embarrassing to have someone catch her staring at a man! How had she even permitted herself to do that? She caught Noah's wink from the corner of her eye. Now her cheeks grew hot enough to burst into flame. Christina raced to the car, jerked open the back door, and slid across the seat to hug the opposite window.

She stared out at a woman loading bags into her trunk as if that was the most interesting sight in the whole world. Jill's little car dipped slightly as Noah climbed in and folded his large frame to fit on the back seat. He jostled her arm as he settled himself, sending her heart into that crazy little flutter that it only did around Noah Zimmerman. She hoped all the traffic lights would be green so the trip would be short. Her heart couldn't stand this abnormal rhythm for too long.

Silence reigned inside the car for half of the drive. That suited Christina just fine. She needed to collect her wits and simply enjoy the blessed coolness of the air-conditioned car.

"Is it okay if I park in the public lot and we walk?" Jill glanced at her passengers in the rearview mirror. "I know it's hot, but..."

"That's fine." Christina and Noah spoke the same words at the exact same time. She peeked at him and returned his smile. She chided herself for her response. She was supposed to be keeping her distance from him for Annie's sake. Christina had not been doing so well with that resolution. She and Noah had been thrown together time and time again, and there had been little she could do about that.

All three leaped from the car as soon as Jill parked. People milled about the town square despite the heat. A band busily set up chairs and music stands in the pavilion, so the area would likely be much more active very soon. They set off toward the wharf and St. Mary's Academy.

Children shrieked and laughed in a backyard a few streets over. A girl in short shorts jogged on the sidewalk across the street while hanging onto the leash of a huge German shepherd that trotted along with his tongue hanging out. The whir of bicycle wheels directly behind them made them crunch together to allow the cyclist on the fancy, multi-speed bike to pass. Christina marveled at such a bike. What did a person do with all those gears? Her old bike had one speed. It made it up the hills by her power, not by some magic gizmo that made pedaling easier. And she had to backpedal to brake. She could just imagine herself flying over the handlebars on one of those elite bicycles when she forgot to brake with her hands. *Nee*, she would stick with her simple bike.

So far, she hadn't seen any other Plain folks ambling along the sidewalks surrounding the town square. To tell the truth, Christina would be very surprised to spot a member of her community here this evening, but one could never be certain. They certainly weren't forbidden to visit the town in the evenings, but they were usually too busy or too anxious to complete chores and crawl into bed to undertake a big outing.

The threesome shuffled along the sidewalk and pretended to window shop as they made their way toward the school. The old, red brick building, complete with a bell tower, presided over the hill that gradually sloped off to the bay. Christina had passed the school occasionally but not very often. It was a wonder that she remembered the big bell. Her family and *freinden* usually traveled to the river, not the bay, if they wanted a fishing trip. The spot on the Wicomico River that they usually visited was quieter and far less populated than the town wharf where people rented boats or fished and played on the beach.

Foot traffic dwindled once they reached the school. Most people either shopped or waited for the band to strike up a tune. At least folks seemed to be too preoccupied to notice Christina, Noah, and Jill ambling away from the activity instead of toward it.

"I'm sorry. I didn't realize it would be so crowded here tonight. I hope that doesn't upset you." Jill spoke softly despite the fact that Christina and Noah were the only people within earshot.

"That's okay. We aren't upset." Christina hurried to reassure the *Englisch* girl. Jill certainly did not need another concern on her mind.

"Maybe it's a *gut* thing there are so many people here. They will probably be preoccupied and not take much notice of us," Noah added.

They picked up their pace once they reached the school property and were out of view of most of the townspeople. To Christina's relief, the front yard was empty. "It looks deserted."

"Maybe. Let's check around back." Jill glanced in each direction before nodding for the others to follow her.

Christina's nerves tingled. Were they committing any offenses by milling about on school property? Surely various law officers patrolled the area tonight. Some probably weren't even wearing their uniforms. If they crossed any, she hoped they would only be told to move on and would not be fined.

The playground behind the school was strangely silent as well. Christina envisioned laughing *kinner* swinging high in the air, trying to touch clouds with their feet as she used to do, but the swings were still. No giggles came from the sliding board that looked like a giant tube. The place had been abandoned. Jill wandered off to explore but soon returned with an expression of utter defeat etched across her face.

"What is it, Jill?" Christina grasped the young woman's thin wrist.

"I don't see anything unusual here. I don't know what Blake expected me to find. Maybe this is the wrong place after all." Her lips trembled.

"Don't give up yet. We just got here. Let me think for a minute." Christina considered the playground as a hiding place but discarded the idea. Surely Blake wouldn't have hidden anything here that could so easily be discovered by curious little ones. Even something buried in the pea gravel would have been unearthed with a quickness. *Kinner* were *kinner*, whether Plain or *Englisch*. All dug in the dirt. All explored their world.

Christina glanced in a different direction. She spotted a brown sign fastened to a stake closer to the school. She trotted over to investigate the gold, sparkly letters painted on the sign.

"Is it anything of interest?" Jill called.

Christina waved her companions over. "Look." She pointed at the words. "It says, 'Please visit the children's garden near the wharf.' Maybe this is the part of Blake's riddle about a garden. What do you think?"

Jill's eyes lit up. "I think you might be right. Let's see if we can find that garden. I know you need to get back soon, so we can walk fast." She trotted off, leaving Noah and Christina to hurry behind her.

The road dropped sharply once they left the school property. The bay came into view almost immediately. Christina would have liked a moment to absorb the breathtaking view but knew they were pressed for time. Their pace quickened even more on the descent toward the wharf. Christina shaded her eyes to search for a garden.

"I don't know whether to look for stalks of corn or bushy tomato plants or what." Frustration edged into Jill's voice.

"I'm thinking it's a flower garden." Christina pointed in the opposite direction. "See those gladiolas? They're the tall flowers. There are smaller plants in front of them."

"I see them. I hope you're right."

Christina hoped the very same thing. She hoped even more that they would find the answers they needed to clear Blake's name and thereby, put this whole mess behind them.

They practically ran to the flower garden.

"It... is... the... children's... garden." Jill gasped between each word and fanned herself with one hand as if that would encourage more oxygen to flow into her lungs.

Sure enough, the neatly weeded and mulched rectangular plot sported a sign very much like the one at the school. Now what? At first glance, Christina couldn't spot any place where Blake could have hidden something. Had he buried the information? If so, they couldn't very well dig up the whole plot to look for such treasure. Had he hidden another clue here as he had at The Green Thumb?

Before they could determine their next course of action, a young man burst from the boathouse hollering, "Hey!" and flapping his arms like a giant hawk's wings. He raced toward them. Fear paralyzed Christina. How could they possibly be in trouble for looking at the garden? Isn't that what the sign at the school invited them to do? They hadn't touched a single thing. Their feet were still well away from the plants. They hadn't caused any harm whatsoever. So what was the problem? Beads of sweat rolled down Christina's back. Her brain screamed, "Run!" but her feet remained planted. Noah looked as shocked as she was.

"What in the world..." Jill broke off and stared at the man drawing closer to them.

If she hadn't been so frightened that they would be hauled away in the back of a police cruiser, Christina would have laughed at the comical sight of a grown man flapping as if he tried to take flight. She picked at her fingernails until Noah squeezed her hand. That simple gesture calmed her immediately.

"Hey!" the man shouted again.

"It isn't like we're trying to escape," Christina muttered. Noah chuckled softly.

The man stopped a foot away from them and gasped for breath. His black tee shirt bearing the town's logo clung to his body. His auburn hair curled around his slightly protruding ears. Scars along his inner arms caught Christina's attention. She tried not to stare, but how did someone manage to cut his arms so much? Several scattered tattoos must have been an attempt to hide some of the marks.

He coughed and wheezed like a much older man with a lung condition. He cleared his throat twice before attempting to speak. "Are you Jill?"

"Who wants to know?"

Though the *Englisch* girl tried to act tough, Christina saw through the ruse. Jill must be alarmed, to say the least, that this fellow knew her name.

"I'm Jackie Thompson." He thrust out a hand in Jill's direction, looked down at it, and wiped it on his jeans before sticking it out again.

Jill did not offer her hand. "Am I supposed to know you? Because I don't recall that we've ever met."

"Yes. I mean, no. I mean, I knew your brother. I'm really sorry about his, uh, passing. Blake was a good guy."

"Yes, he was."

Christina started to step a little closer to offer Jill support but realized her hand was still tucked inside Noah's much larger one. She freed her hand and scooted closer to Jill, who was on the verge of tears. The poor girl's emotions had to have been swirling around like the ice cubes in a vigorously stirred tea pitcher.

Jill sniffed. "H-how did you know my brother?"

"Blake helped me. He saved me, actually. If it wasn't for him, I'd still be doing drugs or pushing up daisies."

Jill flinched.

"Oh, sorry. Poor choice of words. Anyway, I've been watching for you."

"What are you talking about? How would you know I would come here when I only decided that myself a short time ago?"

"Blake said you were smart. He said you would figure it out."

"How do you even know I'm Blake's sister?"

"I've seen pictures of you. Blake was so proud of his baby sis. He talked about you all the time."

Jill gasped.

"What is it?" Christina whispered. She wasn't sure if she trusted this fellow. Did he really know Blake Sheridan?

"B-Blake called me 'baby sis.'"

Maybe this Jackie fellow told the truth after all. It couldn't be coincidence that he referred to Jill that way, could it?

"How do I know you even saw a picture of me?"

"You and Blake were sitting on the steps of your parents' house with the biggest Easter baskets I've ever seen on the ground in front of you."

Jill laughed. "I was six. Blake was ten. He thought he was too old for Easter baskets until he saw that one. I thought his eyes would pop out of his head." She ran a finger under each eye.

"I also saw a picture of you in a dark cap and gown. Blake was smiling down at you. He sure was proud of you."

"He was a wonderful big brother." Jill's voice caught.

For a moment, no one spoke. The foursome faced each other in complete silence until Christina's curiosity got the best of her. "How could you possibly know that Jill would be here today?"

"You must be the lady who owns the shop where Blake was found."

How did he know that? Was it simply a logical assumption, or did this fellow know more than he was telling?

Chapter Thirty-Four

Christina hesitated, not sure if she should reveal anything about herself. This man certainly seemed believable, but was he? Blake must have shown him pictures, though, unless he had been snooping around the deceased man's home at some point. Apparently, he didn't notice her quandary since he proceeded to answer her question.

"I didn't know Jill would be here *today*, but I've been watching for her every day that I've worked. And I do tend to work a lot. It does me good to keep busy."

"Why were you watching for her?" How had she become the interrogator? Christina peeked at her companions, who still stood mute as if transfixed by the whole situation.

"Her brother asked me to watch for her."

"Why would he do that? Maybe you should start from the beginning." Christina caught Jill's nod from the corner of her eye.

Jackie took a deep breath and blew it out in a long sigh. "Blake Sheridan and I became friends. He was my counselor first, but we got to be friends. Look!" He held out both arms practically under their noses. "These aren't scars from chicken pox. I was into drugs. Bad. Blake helped me turn my life around. He even got me going to church and every-thing. I probably wouldn't even be alive if it wasn't for him."

"I'm glad he helped you," Jill whispered and sniffed.

"Me too. Like I said before, Blake is—was—a great guy. I can't believe he's gone. But one thing I am absolutely sure of is that Blake Sheridan did not willingly take any drugs. I want to see that his name is cleared of any wrongdoing."

"So do we, Mr. Thompson," Christina agreed.

"Mr. Thompson is my dad. I'm Jackie."

"Okay. I understand your loyalty to Blake, Mr., uh, Jackie, but why did you expect Jill to show up here?" Christina's foot tapped on its own accord. They really needed to return to their horses and get home, but she had to hear this man out.

"Blake had been acting kind of nervous for a few weeks and always seemed to be looking behind him. I finally asked him what was wrong, and he said he thought someone was out to get him."

"Out to get him?" Christina tried to decipher the *Englisch* expression.

"Yeah. You know, after him, wanted to hurt him or get even with him for something."

"Why?" Jill asked.

Christina took Jill's question as an encouraging sign that the poor girl was finally pulling out of her shock.

"I believe he knew something about a drug deal and who was involved."

"Why wouldn't he go to the police?" Christina wondered aloud. That's what *Englischers* usually did, ain't so? Her peo-ple rarely involved the police in their lives, but she thought *Englischers* didn't have any qualms about doing so.

"He wasn't one hundred percent certain and didn't want to finger the wrong thugs, uh, people." Jackie chuckled. "I guess I can call them thugs since I used to be one. Anyway, that's the kind of guy Blake was. He didn't want to get an innocent person in trouble, and he paid a huge price for that.

I'd like to get my hands on whoever..." He broke off and closed his eyes as if in prayer. "No, my getting even days are over, but I wouldn't hesitate to go to the police with my suspicions."

"You might not want to say that too loud." Christina kept her own voice low. Just because she didn't see any lurkers, that didn't mean someone wasn't hiding or spying somewhere. Annie would be so amazed at the knowledge Christina had gained from listening to all her book reviews.

"She's right," Jill agreed. "You don't want to end up like my brother."

"Back to the issue. Why did Blake want you to watch for Jill's visit here?" Christina surprised herself at her boldness.

"He left something here with me for his sister. For safekeeping. In case something happened to him."

"He must have had an idea that someone might harm him." Christina shook her head. How sad. How frightening!

"If only he'd gone to the police, he might still be here." Jill's voice broke. She reached into her pocket for a tissue.

"He did what he thought was right," Jackie replied.

"H-he always did." Jill sniffed. "What did he leave with you?"

"It's at the boathouse. You got an ID on you?"

"I have my driver's license."

"I thought you recognized her from her pictures." Christina's suspicions about Jackie Thompson returned. Had he been lying to them, or did he simply want to make sure of Jill's identity before giving her whatever he had?

"I do recognize her, but Blake specifically said for me to see proof before I gave her anything."

"That makes sense." Noah spoke up for the first time since their initial greeting when Jackie approached them.

Jill fumbled in her purse and produced a wallet. She flipped it open so that her license showed through a little, plastic window. "See? We need to hurry so my friends can get back."

And so we aren't observed. Christina almost spoke aloud but thought better of it.

The foursome practically ran to the boathouse, but Christina was a bit leery about going inside with this stranger who might or might not be trustworthy. But she couldn't let Jill enter alone. She took comfort in Noah's presence right behind her. If Blake trusted this fellow, he must be reliable.

At the boathouse entrance, Jackie stopped and glanced over his shoulder at them. "My co-worker is back from a break. I'll bring it out to you."

Jill shrugged and then nodded.

Seconds later, Jackie bounded outside carrying a large yellow envelope. Waning sunlight reflected off the tape covering every edge. He passed it to Jill almost reverently. "I don't know what Blake put in here, but it must be pretty important. And he must have been worried it would fall into the wrong hands. I've kept it locked in the safe in the boathouse. Only the manager and I know the combination, so I know nobody has messed with it. Someone might be anxious to get whatever information is inside, so be careful."

Christina shivered. Were his words an omen? A threat? Surely not a threat. If Jackie had wanted the information in the envelope, he would have kept it and not rushed out of the boathouse the minute he spied them.

Jill clutched the envelope to her chest. "I won't open it out here. We'd better go. Thank you, Jackie."

"Anytime. I'd do anything for Blake—or his sister."

Even though the route back to the parking lot was completely uphill, Noah, Christine, and Jill set out at a brisk pace in silence. Talking would have slowed them and robbed them of the oxygen they needed to make the climb. Christina longed for the relative safety of the car and believed her companions did too. Plenty of people roamed the town square, but Christina still felt as if they had targets on their backs. She couldn't shake the creepy notion that they were being watched.

Christina surveyed the shops lining the square, not quite sure what she was looking for. Right as her gaze reached the ice cream shop, the door flew open for a family to exit. She blinked and stared. Her mouth dropped open, but she couldn't speak. Amelia Stauffer herded her three little ones outside followed by a man carrying a *boppli* in one arm and clutching the hand of a small girl with his free hand. The two women's eyes locked only briefly. Amelia barely nodded in acknowledgment before nudging her *kinner* in the opposite direction.

Whatever could that have been about? Even from where she stood, Christina could sense Amelia's discomfort, and she could see the crimson dots on the young *mudder's* usually pale face. Her haste to leave the area could only mean that Amelia had been embarrassed to have been discovered out on the town with an *Englischer. Nee*, Ryan wasn't *Englisch*, but he wasn't Old Order Mennonite either.

"Are you all right?" Noah leaned down to whisper in Christina's ear.

Her pulse jumped at the tickle of his breath on her neck. She nodded toward the ice cream shop. "Did you see them?"

"See who?"

"I guess you didn't."

"Who was it?" Noah's eyes shifted right and left, as if looking for some source of trouble, before settling again on Christina's face. "Did you see something we should be concerned about?"

"Well, I'm concerned about what I saw, but it isn't related to Jill or her *bruder.*"

"What is it, then?"

"Amelia Stauffer and her girls just came out of the ice cream shop with Ryan Miller."

"Maybe she needed something from town and he drove her. She does babysit his *kinner*, ain't so?"

"She does. You're probably right." Christina stowed that concern in the back of her mind. Right now, her worry centered on getting back to the shopping center where they had left their horses without mishap.

As soon as they slid into the car, Jill pressed the button to click all the locks. She still clutched the envelope as if afraid it would vanish into thin air if she loosened her grip. Christina reached forward to tap her shoulder. "If you want to open that, go ahead. The horses can wait another minute or two."

"I-I'm not sure. I want to know what's inside, but I don't want to know. I suppose that sounds ridiculous."

"It sounds pretty normal to me." Christina patted the girl's shoulder again. "You want to know whatever information your *bruder* gleaned, but you are afraid of what that information might be."

"Exactly." Jill sighed and leaned her head against the headrest. "Part of me says I should look inside the envelope while I have people with me. Another part of me says I should run home, lock all the doors, and close the curtains before peeking inside." She gave a nervous, little laugh. "And then there's that bitty part of me that wants to chuck the whole thing in the nearest dumpster and pretend I never saw it."

"I understand." Christina sat back and fastened her seatbelt. "But then you won't have any information to clear your *bruder's* name."

"True." Jill sighed again She lowered the envelope and picked at the tape. "Ugh! It's so taped up that I'm afraid I'll tear whatever is inside if I rip the envelope."

"Would you like me to try?" Noah leaned forward and held out a hand.

Jill sniffed. "Would you please?"

"I think I would feel better opening it away from here, though. For some reason, I feel very uncomfortable, like I'm on public display."

Christina shuddered. So she wasn't the only one experiencing the heebie-jeebies.

"I can work on the tape while you drive if you want," Noah offered.

"Okay." Jill relinquished the envelope. "Let's head back."

Nobody said a word during the drive to the shopping center. The scratching of Noah's fingernails as he picked at the tape was the only sound in the car. Christina's mind spun. What would be so important that Blake went to such extraordinary measures to protect it? What should Jill do with the information and where would be a safe place to store the contents of the envelope in the meantime?

"I got the last piece of tape loosened." Noah raised his head and peered out the window. "Just in time too."

Jill clicked on the signal light and turned into the shopping center's main parking lot. She drove around to the far side where Noah and Christina had left their buggies. The horses still contentedly chomped at the grass where they had been tethered in the shade of a few nearby trees.

Noah passed the envelope to the front. Jill didn't immediately grasp it. "Do you want to open it now while we're with you?" he asked.

Jill pulled the envelope from his grasp and traced her index finger over the scrawl on the outside. "This might be the last thing Blake ever wrote." She chuckled softly. "His handwriting always was atrocious. I used to badger him about writing neater." She swiped at a tear and drew in a shaky breath. "Would you two mind waiting another minute or two?"

"We'll wait." Christina glanced at Noah.

He nodded. "We will wait."

"Okay. Here goes." Jill reached inside the big envelope and tugged at the papers inside.

Christina turned to look out the side and back windows, not quite sure who or what she searched for. She and Noah unclicked their seatbelts and slid forward. When their knees bumped, fire shot from Christina's leg straight to her heart. She jerked her knee over and fought the temptation to check for a burn on her leg. Did Noah notice anything unusual? She couldn't risk glancing in his direction. Surely, her cheeks glowed as red as a stoplight on a dark night.

Jill gasped when the contents of the envelope spilled out onto her lap and the floor. "Oh my!"

"What is it?" Christina slid closer to the front seat. Another fraction of an inch and she would hit the floor.

"Look!"

Chapter Thirty-Five

Jill bent to pluck items off the floor and held three pictures up for Noah and Christina to see.

"Who are they?" Christina recovered her voice first after being startled by Jill's outburst. Her people did not believe in photographing themselves or others. Memories had to be stored in the mind rather than on paper.

Jill shrugged. "I'm not sure."

"Wait! Is that the man from the boathouse? Jackie Thompson, ain't so?" Christina pointed to a figure in one of the photos. "And is that your *bruder* with him?"

"Let me see." Jill pulled the picture closer to her face and squinted. "You're right. It is Blake and Jackie."

"Did he write anything on the back?" Even though she didn't have any photographs of her own, Christina knew from her dealings with *Englisch* neighbors that people often wrote dates or descriptions on the backs of their pictures.

"No names. Just a date. This picture was taken a week before Blake died." Jill studied the other two pictures. "I don't know who these people are. See if you recognize them."

Christina almost laughed. If Jill didn't know the *Englischers* in the photos, why on earth would she think Christina or Noah would know them? She took the pictures from Jill's hand anyway and held them over so Noah could view them too.

"I've never seen them." Noah shook his head and started to pass the pictures back.

Christina opened her mouth to agree but then snapped it shut. A little flicker of recognition flitted across her brain. "Just a minute." She grabbed Noah's hand and pulled the photos closer for a better look. "These are the fellows that came into The Green Thumb the other day." She flipped the picture over. Again, only a date had been scribbled on the back.

"I wonder who they are. What about that one?" Jill pointed to the third picture.

"I don't recognize them," Christina replied. "Aren't there any messages in that envelope? Surely Blake must have given some explanation." It seemed like an awfully mean trick to play if he only gave his *schweschder* obscure photographs and expected her to figure out his intentions.

Jill shook the envelope. "I don't see—no, wait. There's a paper stuck inside." She tugged just hard enough to loosen it.

Christina strained to see but couldn't make out all the words on the page. Once Jill unfolded the paper, words filled nearly every inch of space. It didn't help matters that the handwriting looked more like chicken scratch. "Is that Blake's writing?"

"Yes. Pretty awful, isn't it?"

"Can you decipher any of that?"

Jill laughed. "Fortunately, I became good at decoding his hieroglyphics years ago."

"Does he explain the pictures?"

"Let me see. I certainly hope he does." She remained silent a moment as she read before holding up the picture of the two young men Christina recognized. "These two are Blake's former clients."

"Do you mean he counseled them?"

"Yes, they used to do drugs but turned themselves around. Blake believed they were on the straight and narrow and said they could be trusted. In fact, they often looked out for Blake and escorted him to some of the less than favorable places he had to go to meet clients."

"I wonder why they acted so suspiciously in my shop? They wandered around as if they were looking for something, and they certainly didn't make me feel comfortable."

Noah patted her arm. "I'm sorry you were alone and frightened."

Christina's heart flip-flopped at the concern in his blue eyes. "I wasn't really afraid, just leery. I thought they were up to something fishy. Do you think they were looking for clues to solve the case too?"

"That's possible." Jill held up the photo of the two unknown men. "Blake said these two were the ones to watch out for. I don't know how he managed to get a picture of them, but I suppose he could have used his cell phone. Blake believed these two were responsible for getting a lot of the teenagers and young adults involved in drugs. He was trying to gather more evidence before going to the authorities." Jill sighed. "That was his mistake. He didn't want to falsely accuse anyone, and look where that got him."

Christina squeezed Jill's shoulder. "You can at least take some comfort in knowing he was a caring, fair man who truly wanted to help people."

Jill flicked tears off her cheeks and sniffed. "He was." She pressed the picture of Blake to her heart. "This is the last photo I'll ever have of him."

"But you will always have his memory in your heart and mind."

"Memories fade in time, though."

"They might dim a bit, but they don't disappear. I remember my *grossmammi's* big smile and her warm hugs as if I saw her yesterday. You remember your parents, don't you?"

"I do, but the images aren't as distinct as they once were."

"But they are still there inside of you. You will always carry your *bruder* in your heart too."

Jill pulled the picture away from her chest and studied it again. "He looks happy, doesn't he? I guess anyone could fake a smile for a picture, but Blake's smile looks genuine." She glanced at the handwritten paper again. "How interesting!"

"What's that?" Christina peered at the pictures over Jill's shoulder.

"Blake wrote that Jackie Thompson is pursuing counselor training."

"So he can help others too?"

"I suppose. Well, I'm sure some people might heed the warning of a person who had traveled the road they are on."

"That makes sense." Noah slid back on the seat. "We'd better get home before darkness falls."

Christina grabbed her handbag off the floor. "And before my *daed* sends out a team of searchers. What will you do with the pictures and note?"

"I'm not sure."

"Don't you think you should take them to the police? Maybe then they would investigate further." Christina didn't know why, but she had a sudden fear for Jill's safety. If this bit of evidence was turned over to the police, maybe whomever was responsible for any wrongdoing wouldn't bother Jill. Better yet, maybe they would be arrested and sent away.

"The detectives would probably say there wasn't enough proof here for them to make an arrest."

"Jackie could verify what your *bruder* wrote, ain't so?" Noah's fingers drummed on the door handle. He was obviously more than ready to head home but still anxious to solve the puzzle.

Christina picked up his thread. "Why wouldn't Jackie have already gone to the police if he wanted to see Blake's name cleared? If they were *freinden,* wouldn't he want to do whatever he could?" She almost choked on the word *"freinden."* Sometimes a person couldn't count on people they thought they were close to. A week or so ago she would have thought Annie would do anything in the world for her. Now she had the distinct impression that Annie would throw her to the wolves, brush the dirt off her hands, turn her back, and stomp away.

"He probably feared for his own life. Those guys would most likely turn on him in a heartbeat. I'm sure Jackie didn't want to end up the next victim."

An icy finger of fear traced up and down Christina's spine. Would Jill be the next victim now? If those guys got wind that she had pictures, anything could happen. She couldn't let another innocent person be harmed if she could possibly do something to prevent it.

"Oh! There's more in this envelope." Jill slid her fingers inside again to yank free several smaller sheets of paper. "Now I see why Blake asked Jackie to guard this packet."

Christina let her bag drop to the floor and scooted forward again. "What are those papers?"

Jill scanned each one. "It looks like lists of incidents involving those two guys: dates, times, and descriptions."

Noah gave a low, soft whistle. "They must have been very busy fellows."

"Apparently. And it looks like none of their deeds were good."

"Blake had a lot of evidence." Christina stopped herself before adding, "So why didn't he go to the authorities?" They had already established that he had his reasons for keeping the information to himself. "Maybe you should put all the papers and pictures in a security box or something and not keep it at your house. That is, if you aren't going to give it to the police."

Jill jerked around to make eye contact. "You're absolutely right. I have a security box at the bank, but they aren't open now. Do you think everything will be safe at my place tonight? Will I be safe?"

"I didn't notice anyone following us anywhere, but I am certainly not an expert at investigating or anything like that."

Jill slumped in the seat. "People can track so much with their cell phones."

There was another reason Christina could be grateful her people did not use the fancy phones that the *Englischers* carried with them everywhere. They could use basic phones for business purposes, but they certainly did not carry them around. Poor Jill looked so scared and sad. Christina spoke before she thought her idea through. "Would you like me to take that packet home with me? You can pick it up at the shop in the morning."

"Oh, would you?" Jill sighed and patted her chest as if calming her racing heart. "I won't be able to pick them up tomorrow. I have back-to-back appointments all day."

"That's all right. You can get it whenever it's convenient for you. I'll guard it with my life." Christina exaggerated her solemn expression, hoping to coax a smile from Jill.

The sad-faced young woman did manage a small smile. "Are you sure? I don't want to cause you any problems. Or maybe I should say any *more* problems."

"It won't be a problem. I'll tuck the envelope inside my store bag when I get inside my buggy. Not a soul will know."

"Okay. I suppose that's the best solution for now. I'll pick it up as soon as I can. I haven't even really read it all. I sure hope there are concrete facts I can take to the police, but I want to study it first to make sure nothing could further incriminate Blake."

"I hope you do take all this to the authorities."

"Feel free to read through the papers, if you can read Blake's scrawl. I promise it is English even though it might look like a foreign language."

"Maybe." Christina would only attempt to read the papers if she could find a few moments when she could be completely alone without any possibility of being interrupted."

Jill stuffed the papers and pictures inside the big envelope and passed it over her shoulder. Christina rolled it to a size that would allow it to fit in her bag, careful to avoid creasing it. She glanced at Noah. "Are you ready?" At his nod, she reached for the door handle.

"Thank you both for coming with me tonight. I hope it doesn't put you in an awkward position at home."

Christina patted Jill's shoulder. "We chose to *kumm* with you. You certainly did not force us."

"Thanks." Tears shimmered in the other girl's eyes before she tried to blink them away.

Noah hovered over Christina as they strode toward their waiting black buggies. He helped her climb in even though she had hopped in and out of buggies unassisted her whole life. She reached beneath the seat to extract the store bag and slid the envelope in among the shop supplies.

"Here." Noah pulled a smaller bag from a pocket and thrust it through the open door.

"What's this?"

"Treats for your *bruders* and *schweschders*. It isn't chocolate, so it shouldn't have melted."

Christina peeked inside the bag. "Lifesavers and peppermints. They will be thrilled. You didn't have to do that."

"I know. I thought it would be a nice treat. But I also thought if they were busy eating candy, they wouldn't ask you questions."

"*Gut* thinking. I need to pay you for everything." Christina laid the bag beside her and began to prowl through her handbag until a large hand stopped her.

"I don't want to be repaid."

"But..." Logical thought fled. Noah's hand on her arm sent little electric currents through her body that must have destroyed her thought processes.

"I *wanted* to purchase these things for you. Can't a person do something nice for a *freind* without being repaid?"

Freind? Right. Nothing more. Christina needed to keep reminding herself of that and ignore the tingling from his touch. She managed a smile and nodded. "*Danki.* I'm not used to people buying things for me, except for Daed."

Noah's smile lit his whole face. "I'm happy to do this for you. You do so much for others."

"I don't do much for others."

"You do every single day. You greet people with a smile. You help them with their garden needs. You deal honestly and fairly with your customers. You bend over backward to help a *freind*, even an *Englisch* one that you don't know very well."

"I only do what *kumms* natural to me. I don't set out to do *gut* deeds."

"You hit the nail on the head. It is natural for you to be thoughtful and kind."

Christina's cheeks burned. It was not natural for someone to pay her such compliments. She couldn't bring herself to look into Noah's eyes. Instead, she watched Jill drive from the parking lot. "Do you think she will be all right? I hate to think some bad person might be waiting for her."

"I know. We'll have to pray for her safety."

"I should have asked her to spend the night at my house. There are so many people around that someone would be bound to notice if a stranger approached."

"How would you have explained that to your parents?"

Christina shrugged. "I don't have any idea. My feeble brain hadn't thought that far ahead."

Noah chuckled. "There is nothing feeble about your brain. You are one of the smartest people I know."

Her cheeks grew even hotter. "You must not know too many people."

He laughed harder and patted her arm. "I'll follow you until you turn off on your road."

"Please don't feel that you need to go out of your way."

"It isn't much out of my way. I wouldn't be able to sleep tonight if I didn't know for sure that you got home all right."

A twinge of fear gripped her. She raised her eyes to search Noah's face. "You don't think there will be any problem, do you?"

"I hope not. I don't see anyone waiting around or watching us, but I'd rather err on the side of caution."

Christina coughed when she swallowed the lump of fear clogging her throat. She would trust *Gott*. He was always with her. That thought bolstered her courage. She would not give in to fear. "Let's go."

Chapter Thirty-Six

Noah had been right. Her siblings were so excited over their candy that they didn't hound her one bit about her trip to town. Sallie and Grace didn't even whine or pout about being left home since they were used to accompanying her on errands. Even her parents only asked a few general questions before letting the subject drop. Christina could breathe easier. The fact that she hadn't observed any cars on the road on her way home provided an even bigger reason for her to let her guard down. As soon as she got ready for bed, she would take a peek at the contents of that envelope.

After everyone had crawled into their beds and the house had grown quiet, Christina tiptoed across the wood floor to softly close her door. She clicked on a battery-operated lamp and settled herself on the bed with the big envelope. She hesitated. This could be the last thing Blake Sheridan ever wrote. She shivered. It would be like peeking into a grave.

Stop it, Christina! You've never been a fraidy cat. Besides, Jill told you to read the papers that had been so important to her bruder. Perhaps Christina, an objective outsider, could piece clues together faster and easier than someone who was closer to the situation. She gulped in a big breath, steeled her nerves, and extracted all the papers and pictures from the envelope. She planned to arrange them chronologically and see if that helped her make sense of the information.

A while later, Christian straightened her aching back and rubbed the bleariness from her eyes. She'd sorted everything and read all except the last scribbling. The going had been slow since she had to work hard to decipher Blake's handwriting. Her teacher would have kept him inside at recess to practice writing legibly.

She nearly laughed aloud at the image of Jill and Blake in an Old Order Mennonite school. They most likely had had a top-notch education. Both were college graduates. She, on the other hand, had only attended school until she turned fourteen and completed the eighth grade. She might not have all the book learning that her *Englisch* acquaintances had, but she always considered herself smart enough to handle most situations that came her way. Not brilliant, by any means, but not lacking in intelligence either. She smiled at the memory of Noah's words that she was the smartest person he knew. Such a sweet fellow! *Ach!* She needed to focus on these papers.

From what Christina had read so far, Blake suspected the two fellows in that one picture of selling drugs to other people. They sounded like real bullies who threatened people. She hadn't any idea what the penalty was for selling drugs or using them, but she knew these men were clearly in the wrong and would be punished somehow. Blackmailing people had to be a crime too.

She picked up the last paper dated the day before she found Blake in her shed. The handwriting on this page was even worse, as though the words were written in haste or in the dark. She squinted and held the paper closer to the lamp, hoping additional light would help. A translator would be a bigger help.

Christina struggled word-by-word and gasped at the revelation. Even though her brain knew she sat alone in her bedroom on the second floor of the house, her nerves prodded her to glance around in every direction. She half expected to find evil eyes staring inside her uncovered window. *You're crazy! There couldn't be anyone looking in the window unless they had wings and flew up to it or stood on a very tall ladder.* Words on a piece of paper should not frighten her.

Yet, they did. She reread them to make sure she hadn't decoded them incorrectly, but they told the exact same story. Those two fellows had raised Blake's suspicions for *gut* reason. Apparently, they had done other terrible deeds besides distributing illegal drugs. If they knew Blake had figured things out about them, which Christina believed they did, murder might very well be among their list of crimes.

Did anyone know about all the incidences detailed in these papers or was it only Blake, who was no longer here to tell the authorities? *Nee*, Blake was not the only one. Now she knew. Christina rubbed her hands up and down her arms, but her chill did not stem from the temperature of the room, and rubbing would not thaw the ice flowing through her veins.

Before she succumbed to an all-out panic that she would be the next target, she bowed her head in prayer. The Lord *Gott* would take care of her. She hushed the little voice that whispered Blake probably trusted the Lord too.

Christina gathered all the slips of paper and the photographs and thrust them back inside the envelope. She glanced at the bedside clock and groaned. She would never have guessed that so much time had elapsed since she started trying to piece together clues to this macabre puzzle. Now she would only be able to sleep for a couple of hours—if at all.

Barely two hours later, after a grand total of fifteen minutes of sleep, Christina crawled from her bed. The rooster hadn't yet roused himself, but waiting for him would not serve any useful purpose. She dragged herself through her morning routine and stuffed the envelope deep inside her bag where it should be safe. Christina considered leaving the thing at home since Jill had said she would be unable to fetch it today, but there was always a chance that the girl's plans would change. Besides, Christina wouldn't want anyone here to stumble upon it and read the information. Ignorance on their part could only be bliss. Could she keep Jill and Noah in the dark to protect them too? Probably not.

Christina shuffled into the kitchen and took a moment to gather her wits. Thankfully, *Mamm*'s back was toward her, so she would have an extra minute to plaster a pleasant expression on her face. "*Gut mariye, Mamm*. What would you like me to do?"

Ida whirled around, holding aloft the spatula she'd been using to flip pancakes. "*Ach*, Christina! Are you sick?"

"I'm fine." She tried to smile. Fooling *Mamm* had always been next to impossible.

"You look far from fine." She turned back to the big, black, iron skillet.

Christina took advantage of the opportunity to relax her hunched shoulders, smooth her tense brow, and clear her throat. She would have to divert *Mamm*'s attention from her appearance. "Would you like me to scramble some eggs?"

"Sure. I've already fried the bacon."

Christina was well aware of that. For some reason, whenever she'd had a rough night, her stomach heaved at the odor of bacon. If she could sneak a cracker from the package on the shelf, she might be able to calm her queasy stomach. Maybe a sip of juice would help, and that would not require any stealth. She normally awoke with a parched throat.

～

Somehow, Christina made it through breakfast and even responded appropriately when addressed by one of her siblings. Now if she could only get to work with encountering Annie, the day might get off to a passable start.

Christina pedaled her old bike as hard and as fast as her legs would pump. Once she had tucked the envelope away in a safe place, she would feel better. Out here in the open on a sparsely traveled road, she felt like fair game for anyone who might want the information she harbored.

She huffed and puffed in rhythm with the squeaky pedals. She made a mental note to find an oil can. Christina eased up only long enough to catch her breath after passing the spot where she usually ran into Annie and whispered a prayer of thanks that the red-haired girl was not in sight. Once she caught a second wind, she again pumped the pedals with all her might.

Her rubbery legs barely held her up by the time Christina hopped off her bike behind The Green Thumb. She had surveyed the entire area as she rode through the parking lot and was satisfied that everything appeared normal. Still, she approached the back door cautiously with the bag clutched to her chest. She didn't observe any sign that someone had attempted to enter the building, so she should be perfectly safe.

Christina unlocked the door, pushed it open far enough to squeeze through, and quickly locked it behind her. She sighed. She'd made it safely without encountering a single person, and her business was just as she had left it. She prepared to stow the envelope on a shelf but then thought better of that idea. The information might very well be safer in her bag beneath all the junk it held. She sure wished Jill found time to retrieve the envelope today. Christina tucked her bag in the most obscure place possible and stored the items from last night's shopping venture beneath the counter. She hustled to unlock the front door and to flip the Open sign. She yawned and rubbed her eyes. If she kept moving, she could stay awake. She hoped.

"*Gut*, you're here!"

Christina stifled a scream before whirling around. "Noah! You took me by surprise."

"I'm sorry. I didn't meet up with you on the road. You must have gotten an early start this morning."

"I did. I didn't have a particularly restful night."

"I know what you mean. Are you all right?"

He was always so concerned, so thoughtful. "I'm fine. My brain wouldn't shut down last night and allow me to sleep."

"Mine either. So where is the envelope?"

"Here, in case Jill decides to stop in after all."

"You didn't bring anyone in to help you today?"

"*Nee,* I don't want any of my *bruders* or *schewschders* to get mixed up in this crazy mess."

"I suppose you're right." Noah didn't appear to be in any hurry to leave.

"Don't you have to get to work?" It wasn't that she wanted him to leave. Not at all. She actually enjoyed his company too much, but she didn't want him to get into trouble with his boss.

"I wanted to make sure you were all right first."

"That's very nice of you, but as you can see, I'm fine." Christina donned her brightest smile.

"I want you to stay that way."

The words had been mumbled, but Christina heard them as if they had been shouted. "I will."

They chatted for a few more minutes until Noah absolutely had to be on his way. As soon as he stepped outside, Christina's smile vanished, and her forehead puckered in a frown. She had to believe that she would be fine. Customers would soon bustle in to keep her busy, and no one knew she had that telltale information except for Noah and Jill. Neither of them would advertise that fact to the world.

As expected, customers flowed in and out of the shop all morning, Christina rarely had a moment alone to collect her thoughts. Whenever she had to help a customer with something or retrieve a plant or pot, she would cast a wary eye toward the counter, where her bag resided underneath.

She nibbled at a peanut-butter-and-strawberry-jam sandwich at noon but poked it back into her bag when a disturbance outside the front door sent her heart racing. Numerous footsteps approached the entrance. Of all times for the place to be empty of customers.

Christina immediately relaxed at the sound of little girls' chatter. A devious person plotting harm would not bring *kinner* with him. "Amelia! It's so *gut* to see you. Only three girls today?"

"*Jah*, the others are with their *daed*. He had the day off."

Christina squatted and held out her arms. Three giggling youngsters ran forward at the same instant and threw themselves at her, nearly bowling her over. Her laughter mingled with their squeals.

"Don't encourage them, Christina. They are rambunctious enough on their own."

"They are normal, healthy *kinner*. They remind me of my little *schewschders*." She gave each girl a hug. "I'm so glad to see you today." When all three had received several hugs, Christina grunted and struggled to stand. "You'd better help me, girls. My legs went to sleep."

Amelia's six-year-old, Rhonda, grabbed one hand. Four-year-old Judith snatched the other. With no more hands to grasp, two-year-old Joanna tugged at Christina's dress. She made an elaborate show of getting to her feet.

"*Danki*, girls, I couldn't have done it without your help." She winked at Amelia over three little blonde heads.

"Have you been busy this morning?"

For some reason, Amelia seemed jittery. Did her nervousness have anything to do with the previous evening? Christina would try to put her at ease. She would wait for Amelia to broach that subject. After all, she really didn't want to explain her visit to town, either. "I've been very busy. In fact, this is my first lull."

"That's *gut*." Amelia's gaze traveled the perimeter of the room before settling at her feet.

Christina began to grow nervous at the other woman's discomfiture. It took all her willpower not to fidget. "Did you—"

"I brought—" Amelia began at the same instant. She laughed. "What were you going to say?"

"You first."

"I was going to tell you that I brought some fudge brownies, oatmeal raisin cookies, snickerdoodles, and slices of spice cake. I'm sorry I missed the morning crowd."

"That's okay. A lot of people stop in on the way home from work and always look for a sweet snack. *Danki*." Christina peeked inside the bag Amelia handed her and whistled. "I thought you were kidding. You really have all that stuff in here. You must have been baking all night."

"I had trouble sleeping, so I did get an early start."

"Early? You must have started baking right after you got home."

Even the tiny trace of color in Amelia's usually pale face vanished.

Christina clapped a hand over her mouth. What had she done?

Chapter Thirty-Seven

She wished a hole would open up in the floor of The Green Thumb and suck her down into it. Christina hadn't intended to say those words at all. Now she'd hurt and embarrassed the young woman standing mute before her. She reached out to squeeze Amelia's arm. "Forgive me, I didn't mean any harm. I didn't sleep much either, and my tongue apparently isn't waiting for any cues from my foggy brain today." She offered a tremulous smile and prayed her *freind* wouldn't spin around and dash out the door.

Amelia smiled. "It's okay. I wanted to talk to you about last night anyway and wasn't sure how to begin."

"I guess my big mouth opened up the topic, whether you were ready or not." Since Amelia's laugh sounded genuine, Christina relaxed a little. "You really don't have to tell me anything. It's none of my business."

"I want to tell you. I don't want you or anyone else to get the wrong idea or to think ill of me."

"I would never think anything bad about you. You are a *gut* person and an excellent *mudder*."

"I try." She glanced at her girls, who sat on the floor rolling a small rubber ball back and forth among them. She stole a quick peek at the door and lowered her already quiet voice even though there weren't any customers in sight. "When Ryan Miller came to pick up his little ones, I had been wiping down all of the toys. He heard me mumble that I had used my last antibacterial wipe. I sent Rhonda to fetch the spray bottle and a cloth so I could finish the job. I wipe everything down at the end of the day, you know."

Christina nodded. "That's a *gut* practice, I'm sure."

"Anyway, the bottle Rhonda brought was empty. Ryan, uh, Mr. Miller said he would take me to purchase more cleaning supplies. I told him I would make do and pick them up on my next shopping trip. But he said I deserved an outing and a break from cooking. When he said the *kinner* would enjoy a short trip too... that's all it took. Those little ears perked up, and four girls danced and squealed. I think the *boppli* would have celebrated too if she knew what was going on."

"I'm sure they were all excited." Christina wanted to be supportive and reassuring. "There wasn't any harm in going out for your supplies and even for a bite to eat. We all call drivers when we need one."

"True, but I'm a widow and he's a widower."

"It certainly isn't like you were alone together. You had five rambunctious little girls with you."

"I tried to refuse. I could have waited to pick up my supplies."

"But if you had the time and you needed those things to keep everything clean for the *kinner*, I don't see any harm in accepting his offer."

"It isn't like we were stepping out or anything. You don't think people would see it that way, do you?"

"Of course not." Christina laughed. "Besides you had five chaperones who probably clung to your arms and legs the whole time."

"That's certainly true."

"I'm probably the only one in the community who saw you, and I won't say a word to a living soul." Christina pretended to seal her lips.

"You and Noah."

Now it was Christina's turn to be embarrassed. Her cheeks burned. A snappy response evaded her. She, too, had hoped her little jaunt to town would have gone undetected. "I guess."

"If you saw me, I'm sure he did as well."

Was that a teasing gleam in Amelia's blue eyes? Her tone did not sound accusatory. "We weren't together. I mean, we were there together, but we weren't together. I mean... Oh, I don't know what I mean." Christina waved her hands about as if she could grasp the correct words from the air. She couldn't remember ever feeling so flustered.

Amelia laughed. She squeezed Christina's arm. "It's okay. I'm teasing you. If you and Noah wanted to go to town together, there certainly would not be any harm in doing so. You're young and single."

Christina held up a hand in stop sign fashion. "Whoa! Don't get carried away. Noah and I were in town at the same time. We shared a ride, but we aren't seeing one another. We're *freinden* who happened to go to town together." She rubbed a hand across her eyes. Could she possibly dig herself any deeper hole?

"Your face belies your words, my *freind.*"

"What do you mean?" Christina resisted the urge to put her hands to her cheeks.

"Your eyes get all dreamy when you say his name."

"They do not. You're crazy!"

"I don't think so. I, for one, think it would be *wunderbaar* if you and Noah had been together intentionally and not because you happened to share a ride. You're a special girl, and he is such a nice fellow. You'd make a splendid couple."

Christina swatted at her *freind's* arm. "I'll be ever so grateful if you didn't mention that wild idea to anyone."

"Why is it such a wild idea?"

"Because Noah and I don't think of each other that way." Did they? Why did her heart thump extra hard when she so much as caught a glimpse of the tall, dark-haired man?

"That doesn't mean you couldn't change those thoughts. Often, couples start out as *freinden*."

"Don't get your hopes up." Christina wagged a finger in the other young woman's face. "And don't go planning a wedding unless it's your own."

"I did that a few years ago."

"Most widows remarry. And you're young. Why, you are only a few years older than I am."

"And I have three *dochders*."

"Who need a *daed*."

"You sound like the bishop." Amelia sighed.

"Has he been after you about remarrying?"

"Not 'after me' really, but he has definitely mentioned it more than once."

"Don't you want another chance for love?" Christina could hardly believe they were discussing such a thing. Relationships normally remained private.

"I have to admit that I've thought it would be nice to have someone to share the load. But even though I've been alone since right before Joanna was born, I'm not sure I'm ready to move on yet. You, on the other hand, need to consider such things. You aren't getting any younger."

"I'm twenty, not eighty. I'm not ready either."

"Hmmm. Maybe we should call a truce."

"Okay," Christina agreed.

"And let's make a pact not to reveal each other's secret town adventures."

Their laughter masked the sound of footsteps entering the shop. Christina gasped at the sound of someone coughing. At least they had been conversing in Pennsylvania Dutch so her *Englisch* customers would not understand their words.

"I'm so sorry to interrupt your little party."

"*Ach*, Annie! I never heard you open the door."

"Obviously."

How much of the conversation had she overheard? Did she arrive at the end or had she picked up on the talk about Noah? Annie's stormy countenance even made the little girls pause in their giggles and game. What should Christina say? She started to apologize, but she hadn't done anything requiring an apology. Annie's face would surely burst into flame any second. What should she do?

"It's so nice to see you, Annie." Amelia smiled. "It's been a while."

Bless you, Amelia. Surely Amelia's soft tone and gentle manner would soothe Annie.

"You saw me last church day," Annie snapped.

"But we haven't talked in a long while. You haven't been in The Green Thumb much lately."

"That's her fault." Annie jerked her head in Christina's direction.

Was she planning to involve Amelia in their problems? Sometimes Christina couldn't remember how or why Annie had become so belligerent. It didn't much matter what Christina said or did because Annie took offense at everything.

Amelia stepped closer to the fuming redhead and dared to touch her arm. Christina saw Annie tense. Would she yank her arm away and yell at Amelia too? To Christina's surprise, Annie relaxed. Maybe Amelia would be able to diffuse this situation if not the rift between herself and Annie.

"Annie, dear, you and Christina have always been close."

"Were. Past tense."

"Whatever little tiff you've had, surely you can put it behind you. It would be such a shame to give up a relationship that has existed since you girls were my Rhonda's age."

Annie still glared but held her tongue.

Christina held her breath. Would Annie relinquish her anger or spew more venom?

"Annie?" Amelia spoke as she probably did to Joanna when the little girl was upset about something.

Annie shrugged.

Christina held her breath, waiting for Annie's response. She looked from Amelia's hopeful face to Annie's frowning one.

"Annie?" Amelia practically whispered this time.

"It depends on why you two were talking about marriage," Annie blurted. "Which one of you is planning a wedding?" She glared at first one and then the other.

"Neither!" Christina and Amelia cried in unison.

"Hmpf! What's the saying about protesting too much?" Annie's foot tapped the floor. "Maybe you are both trying to hide something."

Amelia patted Annie's arm and smiled her patient, loving smile that should charm anyone. "I assure you that I am not planning to marry. And didn't you just hear Christina say she wasn't ready to think of marriage?"

"What people say and what they do can be two entirely different things. Right, Christina?"

Christina opened her mouth to speak, but nothing came out. She had never deceived Annie. She had never gone back on her word about anything. She thought she had been a *gut freind.*

"Don't try looking so innocent."

"I-I don't know what you're talking about, Annie. I never lied to you." *In fact, I've bared my soul to you, which I now regret doing.*

"Your little helpless act sure got you the fellow you wanted, ain't so?"

"Helpless? When have I been helpless?"

Amelia butted into the conversation. "I would never consider Christina helpless. Why, she runs this business like someone who has been in charge for years and years. When a problem or crisis arises, she handles it."

"That's right. She's so perfect."

Christina fought tears. "I am far from perfect, but I try to do my best."

"Well, that was certainly *gut* enough for Noah Zimmerman, wasn't it?"

Christina gasped. "We're *freinden*. Just like you and I are—"

"Were!"

Tears sprang into Christina's eyes. She would never be able to reason with the stubborn girl. The relationship would remain severed.

"Hold on, Annie." Amelia's voice rose slightly, but the woman probably had never yelled or spoken harshly in all her life. "Even if Noah and Christina were more than *freinden*—and I am certainly not suggesting that they are—why should that upset you so much? I'd think you would be happy for your best *freind*."

"I don't have a best *freind*." Annie had mumbled the words, but Christina didn't have any trouble understanding them.

"Were you and Noah stepping out?" Amelia persisted. She kept her eyes fixed on Annie's face.

"*N-nee*."

"Has he taken you home from singings or indicated that he planned to ask you to ride home with him?"

"*N-nee*."

"Then you didn't have a relationship with him."

"Not yet."

"Have you cared about Noah for a long time?"

Christina willed Annie to tell the truth, even if that meant divulging her own secret crush on Noah.

"I, uh... I, uh... not so very long."

"Since when?"

"Since I found the man in the shed and Noah rushed over here and showed concern for me." Christina spoke softly and wiped a tear that trickled down her cheek.

"Is that right, Annie?" Amelia resumed that tone that *mudders* used when settling a dispute between *kinner*.

"I don't know." Annie shifted from one foot to the other. She gripped the sides of her dress in her fists. Christina and Amelia both stared at her. Even Amelia's little girls seemed to be holding their breath. Annie stomped her foot and pointed an index finger in Christina's face. "*She* has everything—her own business, *gut* sewing skills, a pretty face, and Noah Zimmerman."

Jealousy? How long had Annie harbored those feelings? Christina had never picked up any cues. She thought they'd had a mutual concern and respect for each other.

"Annie Wenger, did you hear yourself?" Amelia balled her hands into fists and planted them on her slim hips.

Annie's expression indicated she hadn't a clue what Amelia was talking about. Her brief confusion gave way to annoyance. She grunted and turned her focus on some obscure point across the room.

"Don't you look away from me!"

Annie's attention snapped back. Christina almost smiled. For Amelia's petite stature and quiet, gentle demeanor, she certainly commanded respect and exuded authority. Christina imagined the woman's *dochders* would never ride roughshod over her.

"Christina has been your *freind* since you were young scholars, ain't so?"

Annie nodded.

"Has she ever deliberately done anything to hurt you?"

Annie stood motionless as if she had to consider the question. After a moment, she wagged her head.

"Then do you honestly believe she did something to make Noah turn his attention from you to her?"

Again, Annie deliberated.

"Annie?"

Annie remained silent.

Amelia didn't drop the matter. "Had Noah seemed interested in you before the incident in the shed?"

"I-it's not fair!" The words exploded from Annie's mouth. "I don't have any talent. I'm not pretty. I don't have a fellow interested in me. And I don't have a job!" She sniffed hard but couldn't stop the tears that coursed down her cheeks.

Chapter Thirty-Eight

"What happened to your job?" Christina couldn't believe that Annie would up and quit when jobs weren't that easy to come by. Though Annie hadn't truly enjoyed working for her *onkle*, she'd often said she was glad she could help out with some of her large family's expenses. Christina moved closer and laid a hand on the girl's arm.

Annie frowned and batted at tears. She jerked her arm away. "What do you care?"

"I've always cared about you, Annie. You've been my *freind* for almost as long as I can remember. You are important to me. You must know that."

Annie shrugged but didn't try to speak through her trembling lips.

Amelia threw a glance at her happily playing *dochders* before addressing Annie. "You believe Christina, don't you, dear?"

Annie shrugged again, but the scowl slipped from her face.

Christina feared rejection again if she asked another question so was glad that Amelia voiced it for her.

"Do you want to tell us what happened with your job? Christina and I only want to help."

"Maybe you want to help, Amelia, but she only cares about Noah and that *Englisch* girl." Annie jerked her head toward Christina.

Christina gasped. "Annie! You know that isn't so." If dirty looks could kill, Christina would be sprawled on the floor right now.

"Isn't it? I've seen you *and* Noah get in that girl's car."

"She drove us to the hospital to visit Eleanore."

"What a coincidence that was that you both happened to be going to the same place at the same time with the same driver. It's not like you were so close to Eleanore anyway."

"I don't have to be a close *freind* to visit someone in the hospital, but Eleanore and I are *freinden*, as we all are."

"Oh, is she Noah's *freind* too?"

"Noah was taking something to Eleanore for his *mudder*."

"Sounds awfully suspicious to me."

Christina smiled and hoped she could make Annie do the same. "That's because you read so many suspense novels and look for mystery everywhere. You're a great sleuth."

"Don't criticize me because I like to read!" Annie stomped a foot.

"I'm not criticizing. I've enjoyed hearing about your books. I've even learned things." Christina cut off that line of thought. She couldn't let any details of her own so-called investigation slip out. For their safety, it would be best if everyone else stayed ignorant of those facts.

"Hmpf!" Annie crossed her arms over her chest. "Just who were you going to visit last night?"

Christina cringed. She hadn't seen Annie anywhere last night. How had the girl seen them? "L-last night?"

"As in twelve-plus hours ago. Surely you remember that far back."

"Sarcasm isn't very becoming, dear." Amelia inserted the quiet reprimand into the conversation. "I thought we were talking about your job."

Bless you, Amelia. If Annie had seen her and Noah with Jill, she might very well have seen Amelia with Mr. Miller too. It would never do for that tidbit to twitter along the grapevine. Where in the world had Annie been? *Please take the bait, Annie.*

"There isn't much to tell," Annie muttered.

Christina's hopes soared. Maybe the forbidden topics would be forgotten. At least for now.

"Did you quit your job for some reason?" Amelia's tone softened.

"*Nee.* I was fired!"

"By your *onkle?*" Christina was horrified. "How could he do such a thing? I'm going to march right over there and have a word with that man!"

Annie burst out laughing. If nothing else, at least Christina had lightened the somber mood a bit.

"He must have given you some reason, ain't so?" Amelia dared to ask.

Annie stared at the floor. "He said I talk too much and that annoyed his customers." She looked up with blazing eyes. Defiance overtook sadness. "I only chatted with customers who wanted to talk. And most of them did. I didn't tell tales or get personal. Besides, I'm sure I increased his sales by being outgoing. I talked up the specials of the day and usually sold them. People who came searching for corn left with watermelons too. If they came for tomatoes, I tossed in a cucumber. Then they would buy lettuce so they could make a salad."

"It sounds like you were a *gut* salesman," Amelia said. "Perhaps your *onkle* will reconsider."

"He is a difficult man to work for. He was quick to criticize and slow to compliment, not that I was looking for compliments. But at least it was a job, and I could help my family out a bit."

"I'm sorry." Christina reached out to pat Annie's arm, half afraid the girl would fling it off again. "I'll talk to your *onkle* if you think that would help."

Annie sighed. "Nothing will help. I'm a hopeless mess." Her shoulders slumped as she hung her head.

"Don't be so hard on yourself." Amelia patted Annie's other arm. "Everything will work out."

"Not for me. Nothing ever goes my way. I can't have pretty, smooth, dark brown hair. Instead, I've got this frizzy carrot-colored mop. I don't have silvery eyes with long, dark lashes. I have green cat eyes with invisible lashes. I don't have a handsome, nice fellow like Noah Zimmerman pursuing me. There isn't a man in the whole community who gives me a second look."

Christina was at a loss as to what she should say. Once Annie got on a roll, she couldn't stop. How long had she been harboring this self-pity or jealousy or whatever these emotions were that spilled out? Amelia's open-mouthed stare told Christina she didn't know how they should proceed either, but they didn't get a chance to utter a single word.

"All I ever heard from my *onkle* was, 'Why can't you be like Christina? She's pleasant but doesn't talk her customers' ears off. She runs a successful business by herself.' Then when I get home, *Mamm* starts in on me. 'I need your help, Annie. You need to *kumm* right in and get started with the cooking and chores. Christina probably doesn't dawdle. I'm sure she doesn't have to be told to do things. She's so responsible.'" Annie paused for a gulp of air. "Christina this and Christina that. I never measure up."

Christina gasped. She hadn't any idea Annie's family criticized her so much. *Please, Lord Gott, let me say the right thing and not add to the fire already blazing inside Annie.* "I'm so sorry, Annie. It isn't right to compare you with anyone, least of all me. Everybody is different. We all have our own strengths and talents, ain't so?"

"Hmpf!"

"You know you have them if you just think about it."

"Name one."

"Talking," Christina replied.

"Ha! That's a curse. I can't seem to keep my mouth shut even if I try."

"Your talking puts people at ease. Look at how you've made extra sales simply by chatting and being sociable. And you are smart from all the reading you do. Why, you could probably write a book of your own. Best of all, you can make people laugh. It is a true gift to be able to bring a smile to someone's face."

"Do you think so?" Annie poked at strands of unruly hair that had escaped from her bun.

"And your hair is fine, dear." Amelia picked up the conversation. "It's different. Not many folks have your red hair, so that makes you unique."

"We aren't supposed to be unique. We're all supposed to be alike."

"We can dress alike and believe alike, but we can't actually look alike or be alike. Your hair and lovely green eyes make you Annie Wenger."

Christina patted Annie's arm again. "You wouldn't be Annie any other way. And we like you exactly as you are." Well, maybe as she used to be before the whole obsession with Noah. Christina would take the chatterbox any day over the sarcastic, snippy girl she'd seen lately.

Amelia shook a finger. "And don't you worry about finding a special young man. There is a fellow who is exactly right for you. The Lord *Gott* will bring you together in His own time."

"Do you really think so?"

"Absolutely."

"*Mamm*, we're hungry." Rhonda tugged on Amelia's dress.

Christina hadn't even noticed that the girls had stopped playing. "Perhaps we can find you all a snack since you've been playing so nicely. Your *mudder* brought a ton of treats."

"To sell."

"A few less to sell can't hurt. In fact, I'll pay you for the cookies the girls eat too."

"You will do nothing of the kind. Like you said, I brought a lot of food. I probably would have saved something out for the girls to snack on during the drive home anyway."

Annie had been observing the banter but had remained silent. Christina could almost see the wheels spinning in the girl's head. She hoped her *freind* would give serious thought to the encouragement she and Amelia had offered. They hadn't simply been uttering pretty words to make Annie feel better. Annie, until recently, had always been a nice person and fun to be around.

"I should go." Annie stomped toward the door. "But then *Mamm* will want to know why I'm home early. I don't know how to tell her I've been relieved of my job."

"Why don't you wait and have a cookie or brownie," Christina called out. "That will give you a little time to collect your thoughts."

"I'll have to collect them while I dash home. I'm sure my *onkle* will head straight to my house as soon as he closes so he can report on my misbehavior."

"Misbehavior?" Christina and Amelia asked simultaneously.

"Don't look at me like I've grown a second head. Though if it's prettier, I'll keep it."

"What happened with your *onkle*?"

"I didn't blow up and yell at him or anything like that. I'm not that crazy. I do have a little self-control. He would really make my life miserable if I had said the words that wanted to fly out of my mouth."

"Did you say anything?" Amelia reached down to lift Joanna into her arms. Her other two girls clung to either side of her long, blue dress.

"I told him that I thought he was being unfair. But it was his business, so he was entitled to hire and fire whomever he wanted. Then I ran out the door."

Thank goodness she hadn't been rude, as long as what she just said was true. Sometimes when people were upset, they didn't remember conversations accurately. "That doesn't sound so bad. Your *onkle* shouldn't consider that out of line."

"But it wasn't a nice, sweet comment like you would make."

"Who knows what I would say or do in such circumstances?" Would Annie harbor her jealousy forever?

"I wish I could tell *Mamm* that the things she said were unfair."

"That might be a little trickier," Christina conceded.

"*Jah*, that might earn me a trip to the woodshed even though I'm grown." Annie laughed, but her eyes registered her concern.

"Don't you think your *mudder* would be the least bit understanding? Surely she wouldn't resort to such a drastic response." Putting herself in Annie's situation was not easy. Her life had apparently been different. Christina had always had a *gut* relationship with her *mamm*. As the oldest girl of six children, Christina had assumed many household and childcare responsibilities at a young age. Annie's words had been true that she had always been reliable and trustworthy. *Mamm* had depended on her. And Christina had started working with Grossmammi at The Green Thumb while she was still a scholar, so a *gut* work ethic had been instilled in her early.

"My *mudder* isn't like yours at all, Christina. She expects perfection. Unfortunately, I've never achieved that."

"None of us has. And we never will."

"You're as close as it gets, so you are always held up as an example for me to follow."

"Annie Wenger, you get that silly notion out of your head right away. I am nowhere near perfect. I have tons of faults and shortcomings like everyone else. I'm sorry your *mudder* compares us. I've never thought of myself as a pattern for someone else to follow."

"You don't have to. My *mamm* and *onkle* already hold you in that regard."

"Well then, maybe I should talk with both of them as soon as I close today."

"That would probably make matters worse. They would think that, once again, I couldn't keep my mouth shut and tattled to you."

Amelia jostled the little girl in her arms. "I have a feeling your *onkle* will realize what an asset you were to his business and will ask you to return."

"Hmpf! I might just tell him to find himself a quiet girl if he does." Annie blew out a sigh that set her *kapp* strings fluttering. "Who am I kidding? I'd slink back into his shop with my tail between my legs and try to be a model employee."

"You only need to be yourself." Amelia glanced down at four-year-old Judith, who tugged on her dress.

"I wish that I was *gut* enough." Annie shook her head.

"Ach! We forgot to get these girls a snack." Christina bent down to Judith's level. "I'm sure you're pretty hungry, ain't so?"

The little girl nodded.

"Well, ladies, let's find these three hungry girls a snack."

"We'd like a treat too."

All three women jumped at the booming voice at the front door. Christina's heart leaped to her throat. She would recognize those two fellows anywhere.

Chapter Thirty-Nine

Christina slipped her hand into the bag and withdrew two packages of homemade cookies and thrust them into Amelia's free hand. She tried to keep her voice light but failed miserably. "Why don't you take the girls out back for their snack? You can help, Annie."

"She doesn't—"

Christina cut off Annie's protest with a stern look and a barely perceptible nod toward the back door.

"Hey! We don't have all day. You need to wait on us now!"

"I'll be right there." Christina urged her leaden feet to propel her forward. She glanced over her shoulder and mouthed, "Go!"

"Everybody can stay put," the deep voice bellowed.

"Now!" Christina whispered with all the force she could put into the single word. She hurried to the door while praying that Amelia and Annie picked up on her unspoken message to flee. She willed her eyes not to stray to the counter where she'd stashed her bag. Thank goodness she had pushed it to the deepest corner of the lowest shelf.

She cut her eyes to the window in time to see Annie practically throw Rhonda and Judith into the buggy with Amelia and Joanna. She gave the horse a slap on the rump, and he took off before the girls were even settled. Why didn't Annie get into the buggy and leave with Amelia's family? She could return later for her bicycle.

Christina forced a calmness into her voice that she definitely did not feel. Her insides churned and threatened to embarrass her. Her heart thundered loud enough to rattle the windows. She tried to smile but abandoned the effort. "Can I help you with something? Or perhaps you would like to browse. I just got in some homemade treats but haven't had time

to—"

"We don't have time for any of that, but I'm sure you can help us."

Christina gulped. *Be calm. Play dumb.* "Were you looking for plants or supplies or homemade items?"

"Cut the crap! You know what we want!"

She jumped at the volume and vehemence of those words. *Think, Christina. There's not a soul around to help you. It's up to you.*

~

Glad to be off work a few minutes early, Noah pedaled hard toward The Green Thumb. He hadn't been able to talk to Christina that morning and wanted to make sure everything was all right with her. An uneasiness nagged at him all day.

A buggy had just pulled onto the road from the parking lot, but Noah hadn't been close enough to identify the occupants. He did recognize the redhead who crept around the side of the building. Instinctively, he braked and prepared to turn around. He didn't relish a run-in with Annie Wenger. Before he could get his bike headed in the opposite direction, she flew at him, waving her arms. "Wait, Noah!"

Annie didn't yell the words. In fact, she whispered, but Noah picked up on the urgency anyway. Something must be wrong. His heart skipped a beat. Was Christina okay? He waited for Annie to catch her breath and tell him what was going on.

"Christina... is... in... trouble."

Noah swung off the bike and prepared to drop it and sprint for the building. Annie's grasp on his forearm stopped him.

"You can't go charging in there." She explained about the two gruff-looking men and told him how Christina had made them all leave the shop.

"She's alone in there with them?" He got ready to make a mad dash.

Annie nodded. "But wait. Here's my idea."

Noah listened. His own brain couldn't even produce a logical thought. By the time he had heard her out, the fog swirling in his head had lifted and his thoughts had cleared. "*Nee*, Annie. You run for help. I'll go inside and pretend to be a customer."

"*Nee*, Noah. It's better for me to go in there. You're too close."

"Huh?"

"You're in love with her. You'll want to rush in to rescue the damsel in distress like the hero in a novel. I might end up finding you both slumped in the shed."

Noah's mouth dropped open. In love with her? Was he in love with Christina?

"Go, Noah. Hurry!" Annie gave him a swat on the arm and bounded off for the front door of The Green Thumb.

Annie's words rang true. He did love Christina. He abandoned the bike and ran at breakneck speed to the Quick Stop. Noah would never forgive himself if something happened to Christina. He should never have let her take that envelope. He should have snatched it out of her hands and brandished it like a sword so that anyone watching them from the bushes or parking lot in town should have seen that he possessed the information, not Christina. Why, oh why, didn't he think to do that? He dragged in a breath and forced his legs to race even faster.

~

"I'm not sure what you mean, sir, but if you tell me what you are looking for, I will try to help you." Christina stepped back two tiny steps. "Were you looking for plants for a garden? I have a variety of greens, peppers, and tomatoes." She could scarcely believe how calm she was. *Danki*, Lord.

"We aren't planting no garden, lady."

She took another bigger step backward as the more irate of the two men advanced. She grunted when she backed into a display shelf. Now what? She couldn't go any farther.

"*Ach*, Christina, I need to ask you something. It's of dire importance. Oh, excuse me, sirs. I won't take much time."

What in the world was Annie doing? Why didn't she flee when she had the chance? Christina frowned and shook her head ever so slightly. With her eyes, she tried to tell Annie to skedaddle. Would the girl understand?

"Look here, miss. We're in a bit of a hurry," the calmer man interjected.

"Make that a big hurry. Now, you just step aside." The bossier man attempted to nudge Annie out of the way.

The redhead would have none of that. She jerked her arm out of the way and butted right in front of the man, astonishing Christina with her bravery. She began speaking in Pennsylvania Dutch to let Christina know help was on the way.

"Hey, you talk in English so we can understand."

Annie fluttered her lashes and feigned embarrassment. "It's a personal matter, sir. I'd rather not have a man know my concerns."

Christina couldn't believe her ears or eyes. Annie brazenly stood her ground and exhibited complete confidence. Even more surprising, the two men actually blushed. Warmth crept up Christina's neck when she realized what the men must think Annie referred to.

"Later, lady." The meaner man recovered first. He grabbed Annie's arm.

"Excuse me!" Annie's voice rose in pitch and volume. She shook the big, grimy hand off her upper arm.

"*Gut*! You're still here, Christina. I need to get... Oh, excuse me. I didn't know you were busy." Noah rushed inside the shop and looked for all the world like a customer in desperate need of something.

Christina didn't know much about acting, but she'd say Noah and Annie did a mighty fine job of it.

"What is this, Grand Central? Hold up a minute, bub." The man's temper had obviously just about reached its limits.

"No, you hold on."

Everyone turned toward the door. Christina could have wilted in relief at the *wilkom* sight of Deputy Gaines and Deputy Wilson. Reinforcement came right in the nick of time. She pulled herself up to her full five-feet-nothing and squared her shoulders. She nodded at the officers who both had their hands near the guns at their hips. They glared at the two men who searched in vain for an escape route.

"What's going on here?" Deputy Gaines took the lead. His glare at each man could have nailed them to the wall.

"Can't a person shop in peace? Is it illegal to plant a garden, Officer?" The mouthier fellow did all the talking. "I'm trying to get this woman to cooperate and show me some suitable plants." He scowled at Christina.

"Is that so?" The deputy couldn't quite disguise a smirk.

"*Nee*, that's a bold-faced lie!" Christina slapped a hand across her mouth. That outburst escaped before she could consider any repercussions. Should she give the officers the envelope now? It wasn't hers to give, but these fellows would walk away free as birds without the incriminating evidence in her possession. Would the deputies believe the men came to The Green Thumb to purchase plants or would they believe the men came to harass Christina? She wished Jill would walk in and take charge of this situation. These legal matters were totally out of Christina's realm of knowledge.

"Ms. Brubacher, would you care to explain?" Deputy Gaines kept his eyes on the perpetrators even though he spoke to Christina.

Perpetrators? Annie would be thrilled that Christina had absorbed so many tidbits from her ramblings.

"Oh my gosh! Christina, are you all right?" Jill tripped over her own sandaled feet as she rushed through the door. The momentum carried her smack into the sneering, mouthy thug—another word Christina could attribute to Annie's book reviews. Jill jumped back from the man as if she'd touched burning coals. "You! You killed my brother!"

The man rolled his eyes. "Says who?"

"Me!"

"Prove it!"

"I intend to do exactly that." Jill's expression softened when she gazed at Christina. "He didn't hurt you, did he?"

At those words, Noah shot forward to stand so close to Christina that their arms nearly touched. He searched her face with such tender eyes that Christina almost reached for his hand to reassure him. Almost. "I'm fine."

"I should never have given you that envelope to keep for me. This is all my fault."

"You didn't twist my arm and force me to take it. I took the information for safekeeping of my own free will."

"Ms. Sheridan, do you have evidence to back up your claim?" Deputy Gaines asked.

"I certainly do."

The deputy nodded at his partner. "Lock that door. We don't need interruptions."

"You can't hold us here. You got nothin' on us."

Deputy Gaines narrowed his eyes. "That all depends, Mr. Grover, on what these folks have to tell me." The lawman smiled at the man's shocked expression. "Oh, I know who you are and your buddy here too. Right, Mr. Dale?"

Grover snapped his mouth shut. "We don't have nothin' to say. Came here for plants. Heard they had good ones."

Deputy Wilson grunted. "Right. So were you planning to can beans and tomatoes? You'd better get some jars too."

"Hey, why not? There's no law against it."

Grover. Dale. That's right. Christina had read the names on the information Blake provided but had forgotten them in all the confusion. She wouldn't forget them now that she had faces to go with them.

"Is the envelope here, Christina?" Jill's voice shook. Facing the men she believed responsible for her *bruder's* death had to be one of the most difficult things to ever experience.

"*Jah*, I'll get it." Christina only hoped the evidence was ample enough to prove Blake's innocence. She hated to move from Noah's side where she felt protected from all harm. Even more, she cringed at the idea of walking past Grover. She took a deep breath. Two lawmen with guns at their fingertips should make her feel safe, but for some reason, her nerves prickled. Christina truly did not want these fellows to see where she had stashed her bag on the off chance that they ever returned to her store.

Annie struck up an animated conversation with Jill. Did her *freind* pick up on her unease and hope to distract the man who paid entirely too much attention to Christina's movement? Her sigh of relief after maneuvering past Grover broke off abruptly when her arm was jerked nearly out of its socket. She fought to breathe as a strong, hairy arm wrapped around her throat. She heard guns sliding from holsters. *Please don't let them shoot me, Lord Gott!*

"Not a smart move, Grover. Let her go!" Deputy Gaines rushed forward with his gun drawn.

Christina heard Annie's gasp and Jill's shriek but couldn't turn her head to look at them. It took all her willpower to remain as still as possible so a trickle of oxygen could travel to her lungs.

"Don't come any closer, man, or I might have to tighten my grip on this pretty, little lady. You wouldn't want her death on your conscience, would you?" Grover chuckled.

"What do you know about a conscience?" Gaines snapped.

"I've heard of them, but I don't have one." His guffaw caused Grover to tighten his grip. Christina gagged. "Dale, relieve the gentlemen of their weapons."

Christina couldn't let that happen. If the officers were stripped of their guns, these evil men would have the upper hand, for sure and for certain. They might snuff out her life and hurt everyone else out of spite. They would take the evidence so that poor Blake's reputation would be forever tarnished. What could she do? Thinking became difficult when one's neck was being squeezed and oxygen supply was limited.

That's it! Limited oxygen. She could pretend to faint and hope she could drag Grover to the floor with her. He towered over her and outweighed her by about a ton, but she had to try. The others hesitated to make a move for fear the man would strangle her. Christina reached up as if to claw Grover's hands away, forced an exaggerated gasp, and went completely limp. She threw herself forward with all the strength she could muster. Her unexpected movement apparently accomplished her mission. Grover lost his balance and toppled to the floor on top of her.

Christina's breath whooshed out. The searing pain that ripped through her chest and side probably meant she had bruised ribs or collapsed lungs or some other dreadful injury. But she was alive. She heard a tremendous shuffling of feet and grunts but couldn't get herself twisted around to see what was happening. The pressure and pain only allowed her to take short, shallow breaths. Fog swirled through her head. She fought it, but unconsciousness threatened for real this time.

Chapter Forty

"Christina, are you all right?"

She cracked open an eye and blinked to clear her vision. The pressure was gone. She sucked in a deep breath which she instantly regretted. Pain shot through her ribs when her lungs expanded. She groaned and squeezed her eyes shut. Maybe she should just lie still.

"What is it? Where are you hurt?"

Christina couldn't ignore the concerned voice. She forced her eyes open to focus on the blue ones searching her face. Worry lines crossed his forehead. "Noah?" She tried to sit up.

"Wait. I'll help you." He slid an arm beneath her shoulders. "Can you sit or are you dizzy?"

"I'll sit. What happened?" She winced as Noah practically lifted her to a sitting position. The pain nearly sliced her in half, but she didn't cry out.

"You fainted."

"I couldn't breathe. Now it hurts to breathe." She tried to clear her throat to rid its raspiness, but that effort caused additional pain.

"I'll ask Jill to call for an ambulance."

"*Nee.* I don't want to go to the hospital. Where are those men?" She turned her head in time to see Deputy Wilson prodding a handcuffed Dale out the door none too gently.

"Deputy Gaines already took the other man out."

"You should have seen it, Stina. The officer jerked that man off of you like he was a sack of potatoes. He slapped the cuffs on him and practically dragged him out to the squad car."

Christina smiled. Annie sounded like she'd stepped right out of one of her beloved novels.

"You were amazing, Christina. Are you all right?" Jill hurried over and stooped down beside Noah.

"I didn't do anything."

"You sure did." Annie's eyes shone with excitement and something else. Admiration? "If you hadn't dropped and pulled that thug down with you, who knows what would have happened?"

"It was all I could think to do."

"Well, it was the right thing. I know we aren't supposed to be prideful, but I am definitely proud of you, my *freind.*"

Freind? Had the old Annie returned? Christina used the hand not trapped against Noah's side to rub her ribs.

"You're hurt, *lieb.* Where?"

Noah's whisper tickled her ear. *Lieb?* Is that what he called her? A weakness not connected with the drama of the day overtook her. Her heart fluttered like a lightning bug trapped in a jar. At a little nudge, she realized that she hadn't answered his question. "My ribs. I think I bruised my ribs when I fell."

"More likely, when that oaf landed right on top of you." Jill reached into her pocket and yanked out her cell phone. "I'll call for an ambulance."

"That's all right. I'm sure I'll be fine. Please give me a little time to get moving. You'll see."

Jill returned the phone to its assigned place. "If you say so, but I'm going to keep an eye on you."

"Amelia and the girls?" Talking and breathing at the same time had become difficult.

Noah gave her a gentle squeeze. "They are fine. They managed to get away from here before all the real trouble began."

"What a relief." Christina paused for the pain in her ribs to subside a bit. "The envelope?"

"I got it." Annie tapped her on the shoulder. "I know where you usually squirrel things away. I'm glad you didn't find a new hiding spot. Your bag was right where you left it."

"Who has the envelope now?"

"Deputy Gaines." Jill and Annie answered simultaneously, but Annie's enthusiasm and gift for gab quickly overruled anything Jill might have added. "He said he would present it as new evidence after Jill told him the gist of what was inside."

"*Gut.*"

"The best thing," Jill wormed her way back into the conversation, "is that they plan to reopen Blake's case."

"I'm so glad." Christina wiggled to sit straighter. She needed to get up from the floor. "They think there will be proof that those two men did something to your *bruder*?"

"I believe so. Deputy Gaines said he'd be back inside to get our statements as soon as he got his passengers settled."

Christina nodded. She hoped this would be the last time she ever had to answer an officer's questions. "I need to get up."

"Are you sure you feel like it? Are you dizzy or anything?" Noah tightened his arm around her.

"I'm okay. At least, I think I am." She wobbled a bit when her legs were forced to support her weight but leaned against Noah until her knees locked.

Jill reached out to squeeze Christina's hand. "I can't thank you enough for all you did to help me. And you too, Noah." She glanced at Annie. "And you, too. Without all your help, Blake's death would have been chalked up to another overdose. Now they will reconsider. Even if they don't change the ruling, we gave it our best shot. I'm so sorry that you got hurt, though. It should have been me."

"Don't even think that!" Christina squeezed back.

"It's true. I feel responsible. I should have kept that envelope with me. Then those creeps would never have bothered you."

"They would have shown up at your home, and you wouldn't have had anyone around to help you. You did the right thing by letting me hang onto the envelope."

Jill shook her head, sending her dark curls flying.

Before she could protest, Christina held up a hand to stop her. "All things work for *gut* for those that love the Lord *Gott*. I believe that."

"Maybe. But I still feel guilty."

"I'm glad you're all right too, Stina." Annie sidled closer. "I was so scared when that man grabbed you."

Christina patted her *freind*'s arm. "You didn't seem scared at all. You were very brave to return to help me when you could have gone safely on your way with Amelia."

"I wouldn't have left you here all alone." Annie winked. "Besides this was a real-life suspense story. I couldn't miss it."

Christina laughed. Leave it to Annie to focus on the excitement. "*Danki* for rescuing me."

"I didn't exactly accomplish that, but I tried."

"I appreciate that."

"And Stina, I'm really sorry for my behavior of late. I, uh. . ." She paused to look around as if unsure that she wanted anyone else to hear her confession.

Jill picked up on the hint. "I'm going to step outside and see if Deputy Gaines is ready to talk to me."

"I'm not leaving Christy, Annie, so you can either say your piece in front of me or wait until another time."

Christy. *His* name for her. And he didn't want to leave her! Christina's heart fluttered faster than a hummingbird's wings. Noah's strong arm still supported her. If she wasn't mistaken or wishfully thinking, he even tightened his hold just a bit.

Annie huffed. "Okay. I guess I'll make a fool of myself in front of both of you."

"You won't look foolish by saying what's on your mind and in your heart." Christina offered what she hoped was an encouraging smile.

"One thing I've always liked about you, Stina, is that you are always positive, even after nearly having the life choked out of you."

"I am thankful to still be here and that I have *freinden* who are willing to risk their lives to help me."

"You risked everything, even a reprimand from the bishop or worse to get involved with an *Englischer's* troubles."

"I only thought as Christians we should help anyone that we can."

"Now let me say my piece, in Noah's words, before I completely lose my nerve."

Christina nodded.

"I'm sorry I was so mean and hateful. We've been *freinden* practically our whole lives, and you've never given me a reason to behave so badly toward you. Your home has always been a haven for me. I guess I got a little envious of your relationship with your *mudder* and siblings."

A little? Christina gnawed her tongue to keep from speaking.

"I told you how critical my *mamm* and *onkle* have been. I never felt like I could do anything right. I looked at my life and then at yours." Annie raised a hand. "Before you say anything, I know I shouldn't compare or judge. I didn't judge you, but I judged myself and found myself lacking.

You had a *wunderbaar* family, a successful business, pretty hair and eyes,

and...," Annie dropped her gaze to the floor, "and Noah's attention. It wasn't that I was especially seeking Noah's affection." She raised her scarlet face to peek at the man still hovering over Christina. "No offense intended, Noah." Annie drew a deep breath. "But I did want some fellow to take an interest in me. When I realized Noah was interested in you, Stina—and I noticed that a long time ago, probably before the two of you did—my jealousy intensified. I am so ashamed of myself. I hurt you by my words and actions. Please forgive me."

Christina held out a hand to her tearful *freind*. "Of course, I forgive you."

"A-and I'm sorry for pushing your bike and making you fall. I hope you didn't get hurt."

"I'm sure that won't be the last spill I take on my bicycle. My feelings were hurt more than my body."

"I'm sorry."

"All is forgiven. Are we *freinden* again?"

"Do you still want to be?"

I've never *not* wanted to be your *freind*."

"*Danki*, Stina. I promise not to talk so much and not to go on and on about my books."

"Just be yourself, Annie. Do you know that I remembered a lot from your books? That information sure came in handy today. Please don't try to be someone that you aren't. I like you fine as you are."

"But other people don't." Annie's eyes misted. "I haven't met any fellows who would be willing to put up with me."

"You haven't met the right one, that's all," Noah interjected.

Annie's face brightened. "Do you think so?"

"I know so," Christina hurried to say.

Annie shrugged. She glanced at Christina and then at Noah and grinned. "I think I'll mosey outside."

Christina opened her mouth to ask why but snapped it closed when Noah gently turned her to face him. She looked up and fell into the depth of his blue eyes. Her breath caught.

"Do you have any idea how frightened I was when Annie told me you were in here with those two men? My heart nearly stopped beating. I was all set to race in here, but Annie convinced me to give her plan a try."

"Her plan?"

"To *kumm* back to ask you something important so I would have time to call for help."

Christina giggled. "If anyone could create a distraction by talking incessantly, it would have to be Annie."

"I'm glad her plan worked."

"I'm glad you came along when you did."

"I am so sorry you had to experience another nightmare."

"I halfway expected those men to show up at some point, but I didn't think it would be so soon. They must have been watching us in town." She couldn't suppress the shiver that shot through her body.

Noah tightened his hold. "Are you sure you don't want to see a doctor to make sure nothing is seriously injured?"

"*Nee*, I'm sure I'm only bruised."

"How about your neck?"

It might be a little difficult to swallow for a while, but I'll stick to soft foods."

Noah leaned down to rest his head against Christina's. Could that have been a kiss she felt on top of her *kapp*? The little currents running through her body registered it as such.

"When that man had you and threatened to... *Ach*, Christy, if I had lost you, I don't know what I would have done. I've never felt so helpless. I was afraid that any move the officers or I made would have caused that man to make *gut* his threat."

Tears sprang into her eyes. She hadn't cried when the whole ordeal was in progress. There hadn't been time. Now, she wanted to throw herself into Noah's arms and weep. She couldn't be sure if the strange emotions were due to the whole scary incident or to Noah's tender words. "I knew you wanted to help, but I'm glad you didn't try. Those men would have hurt you for sure."

"I wasn't concerned about myself. All I could think of was you—getting you free, keeping you safe. I would do anything for you. I want to take care of you and help you. That's the way it is when you love someone."

"Love?"

"I realized that life is much too short to keep my feelings to myself. Even if you don't feel the same way, I had to tell you how special you are and how much I love you."

"I do."

"You do what?"

Christina pulled away only enough to look into those mesmerizing eyes. "I do feel the same way. I have for a long time."

"You mean that you do love me?"

She nodded. Were those tears shimmering in his eyes too?

"Would you say it?"

"I love you too."

He hugged her close but immediately drew back. "Did I hurt you?"

Christina shook her head and smiled. She probably wouldn't have noticed if the ceiling fell in and debris rained down all around her. A single tear jumped from her eye and trickled down her cheek. Noah raised a thumb to halt it and then pressed his lips to the spot where it had been. Christina feared her heart would burst. This man who she had secretly loved for so long actually loved her too. "*Danki, Gott,*" she whispered.

"What's that?"

"I said *danki* to the Lord *Gott* for you."

"For you."

"For us." They spoke in unison and laughed.

"If you two lovebirds are ready, the deputies want to talk to you."

"*Ach*, Jill!" Christina attempted to pull away, but Noah didn't let her move too far. Her face burned and must be glowing brighter than the noonday sun.

Jill laughed. "Don't get all embarrassed, Christina. I think it's great that you two woke up to what all of us around you already knew. You're perfect for each other."

Christina peeked up at Noah's red face. Plain folks generally did not display their feelings, but apparently, she and Noah had given some sort of signal unbeknown to them.

Annie raced through the door and nearly collided with Jill. "Oops! Sorry."

Jill grabbed Annie's arm to steady herself. "Look, Annie. Don't they make an adorable couple?"

"For sure. Just think, Stina. The Green Thumb was the scene of a crime and the scene of its resolution."

Christina nodded. "And the setting for a new beginning for all of us."

Epilogue

"So, Christina, when are you getting married?" Jill fingered the pumpkin and scarecrow display near the entrance of The Green Thumb.

Heat raced to Christina's scalp like mercury rising in a thermometer on a July afternoon. She fussed with a display of homemade jams and jellies to keep her face averted. "We don't talk of those things."

"Like people don't know that you and Noah are crazy about each other."

"Jill!"

"I didn't mean to embarrass you. It's wonderful to see two people who are so devoted to each other. Maybe one day I'll find out what that's like." Jill sighed and flicked a dark curl off her face.

"I'm sure you will."

"You and Noah are getting married, aren't you?"

"We don't talk about that until we're published in a church service."

"Will you be published soon?"

"That's a secret."

"Right! Well, I want to be invited to your wedding."

Christina laughed. "You will be." How *gut* it was to see Jill relaxed and smiling. Blake's death had been ruled a homicide. His reputation had been restored. Grover and Dade would be punished for their crimes. Jill had become a close *freind* who visited The Green Thumb often. She had even been a guest in the Brubacher home on many occasions and drove members of the Old Order Mennonite community to destinations too far to travel by horse and buggy.

Thank goodness the bishop and ministers had agreed that helping Jill had been the right thing to do. They had not been too happy about involvement with the *Englisch* justice system, but assisting a person in need could not be deemed wrong. After all, the Samaritan in the Bible helped a stranger.

"Where is your helper today?"

"She is at her *onkle*'s place." Annie had been splitting her time between his produce business and The Green Thumb.

"I'm glad the man realized what an asset she was to his business."

"For sure. And she has been helpful here too." Their relationship had been a bit guarded for a while, but they had put the past behind them and were close again.

"It looks like you're keeping busy here even though the summer flowers are gone."

"I have fall items now—apples, pumpkins, and such—and lots of home-preserved jams, jellies, pickles, relishes, and vegetables. Poinsettias will be popular at Christmas. Then I'll have a little lull in the store, but I'm constantly growing new plants in the greenhouse. And I'll always have Amelia's and Marjorie's sweet treats, which folks seem to love."

"Speaking of sweet treats, here comes one strolling up to your door."

"What?"

"Hello!" a deep voice called out before the dark-haired man had even poked his head through the door.

"Hello, Noah!" Jill laughed. "I'm sorry, Christina. I embarrassed you again."

Christina clapped her cool hands over her burning cheeks and shook her head at the *Englisch* girl.

"How did you do that?" Noah looked from one to the other.

"Never mind." Christina playfully punched Jill's arm.

"I'm going to leave you two alone. I'll see you soon." Jill tugged up the zipper on her denim jacket.

"You don't have to leave," Christina protested.

"Yes, I do. Three's a crowd." Jill winked. "Besides, I need to stop for dog food on my way home. Adopting Sassy from the animal shelter was one of my best decisions." She waved over her shoulder on her way out.

Noah dropped his voice to whisper level. "Where is Annie?"

"She's at her *onkle*'s today."

"*Gut*." Noah covered the distance between them in two strides. He drew Christina into his arms and laid his head atop hers. "I've been waiting all day for this. Are you ready to talk to the bishop?"

Christina nodded against his broad chest. Noah's heart thumped in a staccato rhythm beneath her ear. She inhaled a mixture of wood smoke, spicy aftershave, and wintergreen mints. Noah's scent. "I am quite ready."

"*Gut*. If you are agreed, we will talk to Bishop Micah this evening, be published on Sunday, and take our vows a week from Thursday."

"I totally agree."

"That won't rush you too much?"

"Not at all. The days can't pass quickly enough for me."

"Me either. In two weeks, you will be my *fraa*—Christy Zimmerman."

"I like the sound of that."

"Me too." Noah brushed the briefest of kisses across her lips. "It has a nice ring to it."

At that moment, the little bell above the door jingled. Before Noah and Christina could jump apart, Jill peeked through the crack. "Caught ya! Don't forget my invitation!"

Christina snatched an apple from the display and tossed it at the door.

"Thanks!" Jill leaped to catch the apple and then ran out banging the door closed behind her.

Christina faced Noah. The love in his eyes stole her breath away. *Danki, Lord Gott, for setting my feet on the right path and for all your gifts, especially the one standing before me.*

Noah clasped her hands and tugged her toward the door. "Let's go talk to the bishop."

Acknowledgements

Thank you to my daughters, Rachel and Holly, for your encouragement and support, not to mention all the promotional and technical help. (Rachel, you've sent notices every time the library acquired one of my books! Holly, I wouldn't have a website or newsletter without you!)

Thank you to my fantastic, loyal readers, who eagerly read books, post reviews, and send me messages of encouragement. It's always wonderful to know that my stories have touched a heart or brought a smile.

Thank you to my mother, who read every poem, essay, and story I wrote while growing up. I wish you were here to read my books now, but I know you are celebrating my accomplishments in heaven.

Thank you to Dana Russell for all your support and for providing opportunities for book signings every time I release a new book.

Thank you to my Mennonite friends, Greta and Ida, for all the stories and information you have shared with me.

Thank you to my editor, Kimberly Steinke, for polishing my story.

Above all, thank you to God who blessed me with dreams, ideas, and stories. Without Him, I can do nothing. With Him, all things are possible.

About the Author

USA Today Bestselling Author Susan Lantz Simpson has been writing stories and poetry ever since she penned her first poem at the age of six. She has always loved the magic of words and how they can entertain and enlighten others.

Susan's love of words and books led her to earn a degree in English/Education. She has taught students from prekindergarten to high school and has also worked as an editor for the federal government. She also holds a degree in nursing and has worked in hospitals and in community health.

She writes inspirational stories of love and faith and has published a middle-grade novel (*Ginger and the Bully*) in addition to her inspirational romances (Plainly Maryland Series and Southern Maryland Amish Romances Series). Her novella, *The Christmas Fudge Miracle,* is included in the USA Today Bestseller Amish Christmas Miracles Collection. She was a finalist in the OCW Cascade fiction contest. She is a member of ACFW. She lives in Maryland and is the mother of two wonderful daughters. When she isn't writing, she enjoys reading, walking, and doing needlework.

Dear Reader

If you enjoyed reading Christina's Courage, I would appreciate it if you would help others enjoy this book, too. Here are some of the ways you can help spread the word:

Lend it. This book is lending enabled so please share it with a friend.

Recommend it. Help other readers find this book by recommending it to friends, readers' groups, book clubs, and discussion forums.

Share it. Let other readers know you've read the book by positing a note to your social media account and/or your Goodreads account.

Review it. Please tell others why you liked this book by reviewing it on your favorite ebook site.

Everything you do to help others learn about my book is greatly appreciated!

Susan Lantz Simpson

Other Titles by Susan Lantz Simpson

Plainly Maryland Series
Plain Haven
Plain Discovery
Plain Truth

Southern Maryland Amish Romance Series
The Promise
The Mending
The Reconciliation
Rosanna's Gift
Lizzie's Heart
Samuel's Return

Plain Paths Series
Christina's Courage
Amelia's Hope

The Christmas Fudge Miracle
in the Amish Christmas Miracles Collection

The Sweetest Gift
in the More Amish Christmas Miracles Collection

The Healing Season
in the Amish Across America Collection